About th

Geoffrey Gudgion served for over 10 years in the armed forces, and made his first attempts at writing fiction during quiet moments on deployment. He later stepped off the corporate ladder, in the midst of a career in marketing and general management, specifically to release time to write. Freelance consultancy paid the bills. His first novel, *Saxon's Bane*, reached #1 in Amazon Kindle's 'Ghost' category, and he now writes full time. When not crafting words he is an enthusiastic amateur equestrian and a very bad pianist.

Draca

Geoffrey Gudgion

unbound

This edition first published in 2020

Unbound
6th Floor Mutual House, 70 Conduit Street, London W1S 2GF
www.unbound.com

ISBN (eBook): 9781789651065
ISBN (Paperback): 9781789651058

Cover design by Mecob

Printed and bound in Great Britain by Clays Ltd, Elcograf S.p.A.

Draca is dedicated to the members of Her Majesty's Armed Forces who struggle with the aftermath of conflict, and to their families.

All author royalties will be shared equally with the veterans' mental health charity Combat Stress.

In support of

www.combatstress.org.uk

Ships came from east-way,
All eager for battle,
With grim gaping heads
And rich carved prows.
They carried a host of warriors,
With white shields
And spears from the Westlands
And Welsh wrought swords.
The berserks were roaring
(For this was their battle),
The wolf-coated warriors howling,
And the irons clattering

– Torbjørn Hornklove
Ninth century

Super Patrons

Ann Heath
Frances Hodson
Andrew Hounsell
D K Ivens
Brian Jackson
Ruth Jenner
Gareth John
Sylvia Johnstone
Andrew Jones
Janis and John Keast
Alison Lester
Michael Lischer
John MacFarlane
Rosalind Maclean
Adrian Martin
Nigel Masters
Tony Mattin
Ann Mayor
Bill Mayor
Sophie Mayor
Andrew McFarlane
Katy Miklausic
Rhiannon Mitchell
Richard Model
James Moorcroft
Bob Moyse
Barbara Northcote
John O'Brien
Håkan Olsson
Kate Orson
P.D. Pabst
Gill Pearce
in memoriam Jonathan Pearce
Jonathan Pinnock
Rhian Radice
Griet Randolph

Steven Ridlington-White
John Robinson
Clive Rogers
Tim Rogers
Diane Ruskell
Carol Rutherford
Richard Scothorne
Katy Senn
Sue Sexton
Christopher Sharp
Kerry Slade
Gary Smart
Stephen Snaith
Andrea Stephenson
Jonathan Sulenski
Christopher Swinhoe-Standen
Lisa Telford
Gill Thomas
Sally Thompson
Jonathon Tully
Bertrand Vivier
Alun Walters
Sandra Walters
William Walters
Jane Warland
Sandra Webb
Brian Wedge
Edward Weiss
Alison Wheelhouse
Suzie Wilde
Bernie Wilson
Helen Wilson
John Wilson
Simon Woolfries
James Wrigley

Figurehead Patron

Mike Cribb

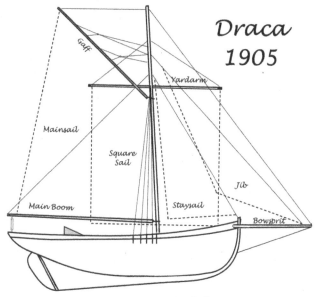

Draca
1905

Gaff

Yardarm

Mainsail

Square
Sail

Jib

Main Boom

Staysail

Bowsprit

Sail Plan

Cockpit

Engine

Head

Oilskins

Chart
Table

Table

Saloon

Stove

Bunk

Cabin

Bunk

Chain
(below)

Fo'c'stle
(storage)

Sails

Below decks

Chapter One: Arfræningr

(Old Norse: one stripped of his inheritance)

I: JACK

Jack's father didn't recognise him. Not at first.

Jack saw him coming, and waited at the hospice's entrance. Harry Ahlquist strode through the car park, tight-jawed, rolling his shoulders as he came as if bracing himself for a fight. The sun could have been in his eyes. It was warm on Jack's neck, warm enough for the sweat to stick his shirt to his back and to taint the porch with smells of tar and hot metal. And as Harry came closer he glared at his son in the what-are-you-looking-at way in which he might outstare a stranger.

He finally did a double take and stopped.

'Good grief, what brings *you* here?' Harry's eyebrows folded until vertical and parallel creases appeared in his forehead above the bridge of his nose. The eyebrows were thicker than Jack remembered, still sandy despite the silver over the temples, and they bristled in the old danger signal.

Jack swallowed, dry-mouthed, ridiculously nervous, like a boy caught playing truant. 'Hello, Dad. Same as you, I expect.'

They stared at each other. Neither tried to shake hands.

'How's Mum?' Jack had a twinge of guilt about staying away, even though he was staring at the reason.

'Well enough. She misses you. How long have you been back?'

'A while.' As he knew. That was Harry's way of reminding Jack of his failings. Jack turned away, refusing to take the bait, and walked into the building.

'You're limping.'

'Fell out of a truck and broke my leg. It's mending.' Jack kept it simple. At least he didn't need a stick any more. They stood at the door to a lounge room large enough to hold perhaps twenty ill-matched armchairs, some pushed back against the walls, others clustered around a blaring television. About half were occupied by sick, elderly people who looked as if they'd been waiting for something for so long that they'd forgotten what they were waiting for. French windows stood open to the garden, admitting hard sunlight and soft summer smells of cut grass and roses, a sweet layer over the undercurrents of floor polish and stale urine. A uniformed nurse near the door was putting a cup of tea beside a chair, her smile as shiny as the institutional china in her hand. Resilient. Caring but functional.

Jack caught her eye. 'Hi, Sandra.'

Sandra looked up and her smile broadened, probably because she'd recognised someone she didn't have to watch die. Jack wondered how anyone had the emotional strength to do Sandra's job: palliative care, with success measured by the gentleness of inevitable death.

'Hey, Jack.' She frowned past Jack at Harry, clearly wondering who he was.

'This is my father. How's Grandpa?'

Sandra winced, and spoke softly. 'Soon, now. Today's a good day, so far. We wheeled him into the garden.' She lifted her chin towards the French windows. 'He's talking OK.'

Jack nodded, relieved. In the early days, there had been

regular spaces in between doses of medication when they could talk; the calm between stupor and agony. Now his grandfather was on ad-lib morphine, you had to be lucky. Even when he was lucid, he could be confused. Jack stepped out into the garden, leaving Harry to fire questions at Sandra in brisk, sergeant-major tones.

Grandpa Eddie sat in a wheelchair on the lawn, face lifted to the sun, eyes shut, with an oxygen bottle for company. Lines trailed from his arm to a drip on a stand beside him. He'd lost so much weight that he'd shrunk within his clothes, and his neck stretched like a tortoise's through the gaping collar of his shirt. He had almost no hair left, just a few thin wisps of silver fluff, and no eyebrows either. Once he'd had great bushy things, thicker even than Harry's, as if a pair of rodents had crawled onto his face and nested. Like the hair, they hadn't come back after the chemo. Jack pulled a chair over to sit beside him, on the side away from the sun, and squeezed his arm.

'Jack, my boy!' Eddie's voice was surprisingly strong. Not quite at the level at which he used to bellow into a storm at sea, but still robust enough to belie the yellow skin. His eyes seemed to sparkle from deeper within their sockets, as if the man was shrinking inside himself. Broken veins on his face gave a bizarre parody of health, like an apple-cheeked skull.

'How are you, Grandpa?' Stupid bloody question. He was dying.

'There are good days, and there are bad days. The good days are when you come.'

Great. He was making sense. Sometimes he and Jack could have a decent chat; sometimes Eddie would rave as if another person was locked in the same body, someone altogether nastier.

'Are you comfortable?' How the hell do you ask an old

3

man if he can handle the pain? That's what the doctors had promised: *'We'll keep him comfortable for as long as we can.'*

Eddie didn't answer. For the first time Jack saw fear in his eyes.

'He's in the garden, now. He's coming for me, Jack.'

'Who's in the garden, Grandpa?' Sometimes Jack had to humour him. The hospice lawn held nothing more threatening than figures slumped on benches.

'No. My garden.' Eddie shook his head hard enough to shake the dangling tubes. 'Harald's waiting at the cottage.' Eddie pronounced the name in two, equally emphasised syllables in the Nordic way. *Har-Rald*. He groped at Jack's arm, staring at him again as if willing him to believe. Jack smiled in a way that he hoped was reassuring, and nodded past Eddie's shoulder to where his father was crossing the lawn. Sandra watched from the doorway.

'No, Grandpa, Harry's here.' Eddie had always referred to his son as 'Harry' rather than 'your father', so Jack used the old man's language. 'He's come to see you.'

Disbelief, then horror, tightened his grandfather's face into a rictus of fear as Harry's shadow fell across them.

'How did he find me?' Eddie kept his eyes locked on Jack, but shook his head from side to side, denying Jack's words. 'He's dead.' The grip on Jack's arm tightened as if Jack was a fixed point of safety in the middle of a nightmare. 'Harald's dead.' Beside them, Harry Ahlquist flinched as if he'd been struck on the face. Jack lifted Grandpa Eddie's hand and nodded towards his father.

'No, Grandpa. Look.'

Eddie turned, lifting one hand to shield his eyes as he squinted into the sun. Tubes snagged against the oxygen bottle.

'Not here.' Louder now, almost shouting. 'He's following

me.' Eddie tried to get up, lurching away from Harry so that the drip almost fell and Jack had to catch him. Sandra began to walk towards them, frowning.

'Harald died on the beach. He's DEAD.'

The shout turned heads all around the garden, and Sandra started to run. Harry squatted, dropping out of the sun's glare, and reached out a hand to touch the old man on the arm. 'Pa, please.' Eddie squirmed into Jack, whimpering, as Harry tried to turn him, and in a moment of sick pity Jack saw liquid dripping from his grandfather's seat. The tang of fresh urine cut the scent of flowers.

'Pa, it's your son, Harry.'

'Shot down like a dog.' The shout became a scream. By the time Sandra eased Harry away, Eddie was gripping Jack's shoulder hard enough to hurt. It was incredible that someone so sick could have such strength.

'Don't let him take me, Jack.' The scream disintegrated into a sob.

Sandra jerked her head towards the building. Time to go. Jack rose and slid his hand along his father's shoulders to turn him away. It was the nearest he'd ever come to giving him a hug.

'We'll try again tomorrow, Dad.'

Harry shrugged the arm away, his face working.

Jack rang Charlotte afterwards to say he'd stay in Grandpa Eddie's cottage for the night. It was two and a half hours' drive home, and the end was close. His wife didn't sound too fussed. She might even have been relieved. She had a girlie night out planned, it seemed. Pals from the gym. Harry didn't offer a bed, and it didn't occur to Jack to ask, so he bought a takeaway and a bottle of cheap wine and wandered through Eddie's cottage, wishing that his grandfather could drift away peacefully on a cloud of morphine. There was such fear in the old man's eyes these days. It didn't seem to be fear of death itself, but as the cancer ate into his brain he'd started raving as if the Grim Reaper lurked in the shadows. Today, it had been Harry, his own son. Two days earlier, it had been 'a Viking warrior in the trees'.

But then, Grandpa had always been obsessed with his Viking heritage. He was the kind of guy who taught himself Old Norse so that he could read the old sagas in their original form. The bookshelves in the cottage's front room were packed with volumes of Viking history. Some of them were antiques, printed in Old Norse with Danish translations. Some had paper bookmarks sticking upwards, each with some cryptic reference written in Grandpa's arthritic script.

Jack ran his finger along the books' spines, reading his grandfather's life in the shelves above the desk. A small photograph of his parents was wedged on a high shelf between almanacs and magazines, pushed almost end-on so the picture was partly obscured. A middle shelf held framed happy snaps of Jack's sister Tilly and her children. There was a larger one of Jack at his passing-out parade, his face tight with pride beneath the coveted Commando green beret with the globe-and-laurel badge of the Royal Marines. Dominating the bottom shelf, in between *Sagas of the Norse Kings* and the mighty *Old Norse Dictionary and Grammar*, was a big, framed photograph of Eddie's beloved sailing boat heeling under a press of sail, with a younger Grandpa at the tiller. The sails were traditional, red-ochre canvas; Grandpa refused to 'sully' a hundred-year-old boat with modern polyester. There was no other crew in sight, although *Draca* wasn't a boat to sail single-handed. They were probably hidden behind the sails, but the photo made it look as if Grandpa was on his own, grinning, one leg braced against the lee side of the cockpit, in his element.

A brassbound clock, a barometer and a compass ranged along the mantelpiece, beneath a framed Admiralty chart of local waters. In the recess on the other side of the fire, Eddie's magnificent, wooden model of a Viking longship sat on white-painted cupboards beneath more shelves of books. Grandpa had made that longship; he'd been quite a craftsman before his hands gave out. The smell of French cigarettes still lingered in the room, a year after he'd finally kicked the habit.

Jack couldn't stay in the room, not that evening, not on his own. He felt too much of an intruder. He took his wine into the garden, where Grandpa had made a seat by burying an old, wooden dinghy stern first in the ground so that the bows made a protective arch. It stood at the highest point of the garden, near the cottage, where there was a view through the treetops to the water. The bench he'd fixed to the thwart had been a perfect size, when Jack was younger, for an old man and a boy to sit side by side and tell stories. Since the previous winter, the boat seat had also been home to *Draca*'s figurehead, a piece of ancient, carved timber that Grandpa had found poking through the mud below the cottage one morning, on a day when extreme low tide and a northerly storm had combined to push the sea away from the land. Eddie had restored it, fitted it to *Draca* and brought it home after *Draca* was laid up. He'd cut a slot for it at the end of the bench so it would sit upright and stare at the sea beside him.

Ugly great beast. *'My pet dragon'*, Grandpa called it. *'A piece of Draca to keep me company.'* It was about four feet long, carved with a lattice of scales, and curved like a question mark or a bishop's crozier, except that the hook bending down over the shaft formed a snarling mouth that could have been any animal with a long neck and jaws. Once it had probably been much longer, but the neck ended in a scorched stump that Grandpa had trimmed, squared and fitted to *Draca*'s bow, like a figurehead. It had spoiled the lines of the boat, in Jack's view.

It had its own smell, that dragon. In still air it was strong enough to overlay the garden's pine resin and salt with something older: a charcoal and leather, old wood and male sweat kind of smell. Eddie had soaked it for months in the same stuff that they used to restore that Tudor ship, *The Mary Rose*: a polymer that drives out the salt water and hardens the timber. Somehow the carving still leaked scents trapped deep in its core. Jack had told Eddie it was probably an historical artefact, and that he should take it to a museum, but Eddie just laughed and said they were meant to be together: a Viking figurehead found by the descendant of Vikings.

Jack forced himself to remember the good times in this spot, not the ravings in the hospice: the stories, the shared confidences. He and Grandpa would come out here even in winter, light a fire in a cast-iron stove by the seat and talk, staring at the flames. This place, this panorama of the great natural harbour, had been part of Jack's childhood and youth. Freshwater Bay curving out to Witt Point; the island-dotted water stretching away until it met the hills rising beyond the sailing resort of Furzey; this vista had framed his times with Grandpa. Him and Grandpa. Always, in the good memories, just him and Grandpa. Jack wedged himself into the corner by the carving, put his phone within reach, cradled his wine and watched the long summer evening fade over the water. He and Grandpa's dragon would keep vigil together.

Jack woke with the kind of jolt that he'd have had if he'd let himself doze on patrol, resting up within an ambush position, and one of the sentries had woken him with a gentle touch and a wordless signal. *Contact!* For a moment he felt the adrenalin rush that comes before action, that familiar dry mouth in chill night air, but as his eyes probed the near-darkness he saw only the first stars over the harbour and the outline of Witt Point looming like a dark mass low against the water. His tension faded into mild loneliness as he remembered the names of the men he had thought were around him. 'Chalky' White, Donovan, Wolfe, 'Dusty' Miller...

But something had woken him, and he searched his memory for the sign. There'd been a noise, perhaps just the creak of the boat seat settling as the temperature dropped, and he stood, senses still tuned. Behind him, to the west, the sky was pale enough to outline the hills rising beyond the cottage. In front of him, the water shone faintly, showing the nearest islands dotting the harbour, patterns of darkness that merged into a black mass, like low cloud. A light mist forming over the water dissolved the shorelines in irregular patches. A stand of Scots pines covered the slope from the garden down to the water, and if Jack held his line of sight high in the trees he could let his peripheral vision scan the space beneath them.

He knew those trees. There was no reason why they should suddenly seem threatening. Their trunks stood clear against the mist below, their outlines and spacing irregular; the way a body of men might stand, watching, waiting. He began to understand why a deluded old man could think there was someone among them. A whole troop stood there, and any one of them could be a ghostly warrior. Two branches, lifting almost horizontally from a trunk, had been perfect for a childhood rope swing that had taken him far out and high where the land fell away. *Look at me, Grandpa!* Now they looked like two arms stretched in crucifixion.

But tonight there was movement between the trunks, a

shadow among shadows. And again, between different trees. The shape was indistinct, and always at the edge of his sight, disappearing into the background dark when he looked directly at it. If he'd have been on patrol, Jack would have snapped on his night-vision goggles and crouched into cover, weapon ready. As it was, he grabbed Grandpa's torch from the kitchen and threw a searchlight beam down the slope.

Nothing. The glare panned through the trees, making shadows dance, until the beam met the mist above the beach and was lost in a circle of opaque greyness. No people, no animals darting away, no eyes shining in the beam. Jack wondered whether to go down there. The torch was big enough to double as a club, if necessary, but he wasn't fully fit. Not yet. If he fell over a tree root he could set himself back weeks. He snapped off the torch and waited, listening to the whisper of branches in the wind. The tide must have been out. He could smell seaweed from the mudflats rather than the sharper salt of open water. He waited until his eyes readjusted to the dark, and when he still saw nothing, he turned to go inside. The day had been hot, but this early in the season the night was chill, and he was only wearing a light fleece and jeans. He'd sleep in his old bed, in the little room at the back of the cottage.

Getting to sleep was usually easy, with a little liquid help. It was staying asleep that was the problem.

One summer when Jack was a kid, the family stayed on a farm for their summer holidays, and the farmer set a magpie trap in his yard. In the centre, in a little cage within a cage, was a live one. The 'call bird,' the farmer said. He'd left it a dish of water and even a bit of dead pigeon to eat, but the thing flapped around making a lot of noise in that harsh, rattling way of magpies. As Jack and the farmer watched from inside his barn, three more magpies arrived and hopped down through the wire door to see what all the fuss was about. They went frantic when the farmer walked over and they couldn't get out, and he shot them, one by one, with a .22 rifle he kept for vermin.

The Taliban hadn't killed Jack outright because he was their call bird, but they'd used Dusty Miller for target practice. It was usually Dusty who woke Jack in the black hour before dawn, and always with the same pleading look, that way he'd stared at Jack as if he could do something. Dusty had come running back for him through the firefight in a mad, heroic, suicidal dash, and he was still coming back for him, pulling him out of the fug of sleep when the alcohol drained from Jack's system and all that was left was the sour taste of guilt. Sometimes, in those first moments of wakefulness, Jack could smell roasting meat. Then he'd have to walk outside and breathe clean air, whatever the hour, whatever the weather. He'd have run, if he could. Even in summer, the air just before dawn can be pure as snow.

There was a line of peach in the sky to the east as Jack laced his boots outside the door, enough to show the silhouettes of trees and the outline of the boat seat, hunched like a monk's cowl against the night. Grandpa's carved dragon would be in there, invisible, black within black. Jack reached in to touch its snout, and settled beside it until there was enough light to see his footing.

On calm, moonless nights the dawn starts in the sea, not the sky. Its flat surface reflects a light the human eye can't see. In time, the light softened to show tendrils of mist, still hanging between the trees and floating over the water. The outlines of the Scots pines began to form against it. Now the same two branches could be arms raised in surrender.

When the tide was just on the ebb it sucked at the beach below the cottage, a soft susurration at the limit of hearing. In the pre-dawn darkness it sounded like whispering, so human that he strained to distinguish the words. The break of each wave could be a soft consonant, an 'f' perhaps, followed by a longer vowel as the water spread over the shingle and left a softer, lisping retreat. F-aay-th, f-aay-th, endlessly repeated. It was as if a mass of men waited there, watching, murmuring among themselves and all of one, menacing mind.

Enough. Jack didn't want to start that line of thought again. Breathe the dawn. He stood, walking towards the threat, not running from it. Soon the sandy path beyond the garden gate was a faint paleness between black gorse, and its softness masked his footsteps through trees that were just trees. The track led along the coast and away from the beach until the dominant sound was not waves but the pre-dawn cacophony of seabirds. A stream flowed out into the harbour in Freshwater Bay, tumbling off the hills fast enough to stop the inlet silting, and sweet enough to allow banks of reeds to form at the water's edge. Their sound was a soft, silken rustle, as real a bridge onto the peace of Witt Point as the rough logs across the stream.

On Witt Point, Jack sat on a stone, sniper-still, at one with nature and its morning routine. Navigation lights winked out in the harbour, sending brief pulses of green and red over the water. Grandpa said he found them comforting, these signposts of the sea. Now there was enough light to see shapes moving, black within grey: the snuffling waddle of a badger, the dainty steps of a deer through the trees. He could inhale sea smells and pine resin and dew-damp grass. There used to be a Saxon chapel here, though there was nothing left of it but mounds in the grass and a few corners of dressed, mossy stones that had been brought up when some trees blew down in a storm. Even so, the place was cleansing, as if it had absorbed centuries of devotion and could give back a little of that peace. It was a spot where thoughts could be allowed to float to the surface of the mind.

And that morning, Jack could feel his grandfather slipping away with the tide.

II: JACK

Grandpa Eddie did not have a good end. He was drifting in and out of consciousness when Jack arrived, wired up to a morphine pump by his bed. Harry was already there and Jack hung back, feeling sorry for his father because he didn't seem to know what to do. Harry sat on a plastic chair, a little hunched but still with the sergeant-major's set to his shoulders, watching Eddie die. Harry's hands twisted in his lap and emotions crossed his face like cats' paws of wind across water.

'I called Tilly.' Harry spoke without taking his eyes off Eddie. 'She said she'd already been.'

'A few days ago.' Jack had given the hospice his sister's number. Tilly had clicked into the hospice in high heels, tight skirt and trout pout. She didn't bring her kids, and Grandpa had been sad about that. She'd seemed surprised that Jack was there. 'You never come to see *us*,' she'd moaned, and Jack had bottled his anger as Tilly wasted one of Grandpa's lucid moments, filling the silence with bright, brittle inanities until Grandpa closed his eyes, feigning sleep.

Now Grandpa was beyond conversation. There might have been things that Harry wanted to say, but he didn't have the chance. Jack left them alone for a while, but when he came back Harry hadn't moved so Jack stayed, waiting for his own turn to say goodbye. The windows were open, and a gentle breeze lifted and dropped the net curtains, letting in the sounds and smells of town. Traffic. Diesel fumes. The clatter and calls of workmen nearby.

The rip of machine-gun fire had Jack diving out of his chair, shoulder-rolling over the carpet, with his mind screaming at the impossibility and certainty of combat. Close range. Close enough to feel the vibrations of each round resonate in his body. Low cyclic rate, heavy calibre. He ended up crouched on the carpet, the fingers of one hand splayed, the other hand reaching for a weapon that wasn't there, and his father still sat in his chair, looking down at him with his eyebrows lifted in surprise. The burst finished with a scrape of metal over tarmac as a pneumatic drill was repositioned, and Jack's shoulders slumped in humiliation.

Idiot. Stupid, stupid, bloody idiot. He stood, brushing his hands down his trousers, too ashamed to meet Harry's eye, and turned away towards the door, muttering that he'd ask them to shut up. He stopped as Grandpa screamed from the bed.

'Don't let him take me!'

Grandpa was trying to get out of bed, but didn't have the strength. Harry held him by the shoulders, easing him back, and Grandpa looked up at him in a way that seemed to plead for something: mercy, forgiveness, understanding, who knew what?

'I tried to give it back. Honest. I tried...'

Jack lurched out of the door towards the main entrance, his shame hardening into anger, brushing past a nurse running in the other direction.

He'd lost it. Totally lost it. Thirty yards down the road they'd set up temporary traffic lights and plastic barriers, and two guys in hard hats and high-visibility jackets were digging a hole. They didn't hear him coming. One of them worked the drill, with vibrations rippling over his beer gut, while the other watched, leaning against a mechanical digger. He flipped the drill man on the arm to stop him when Jack stood beside them, shouting, and they swivelled their ear defenders up onto their hard hats. Jack had to repeat himself.

'There's a man dying in there!'

They both shrugged in a way that said *That's not our problem,* even though the words were, 'We didn't know about that.'

'Then for fuck's sake let him die in peace.'

The man against the digger pushed himself upright and squared his shoulders.

'You'll have to talk to the council if you want us to stop. We've got a job to do.'

Jack made a fool of himself again, and started shouting. All they needed to do was pull down their ear defenders and start the drill with studied insolence every time he opened his mouth and he was left raging at nothing like a kid in a tantrum. Someone behind him grabbed his arm as he started to swing at them, holding him while the two workmen dropped the drill and backed away, lifting their fists.

'Jack!' Sandra, the nurse, stared at him, forcing eye contact. Some buried logic in Jack's head told him she'd had training in restraint. 'It's too late, Jack. Come away, now.'

Grandpa lay across the bed, with his mouth open in a silent scream and his eyes staring upwards, but sunken so deep that they seemed to have fallen back into the skull. A look of absolute terror was frozen on his face.

Jack had never seen that before. He'd seen dead people, too many of them, and usually their faces were slack, as if they were asleep. Some looked slightly surprised until you closed their eyes. A few had faces still stretched in agony. But Grandpa looked petrified, and Jack wished he could have been there with him, even held him. Eddie's institutional pyjama jacket had fallen open so that his old man's body lay bare-chested in a tangle of sheets, a parchment husk of a man. Harry still sat on the same chair, staring at the body. Slowly, as uncomfortably as anyone breaking decades of distance, he reached out and touched Eddie's arm.

III: JACK

Jack picked Grandpa Eddie's raspberries that afternoon, a mindless task while his brain was numb with grief. The berries hanging in full sun were oven-warm, almost musty. Others hid under the leaves, cool and fat on a day when the heat had turned the shadows black and stunned the birds into silence. There was just the drone of insects wavering in the air. The hills rising inland, beyond the roof of Grandpa's cottage, were fading into a heat haze.

Jack's bad leg made him stumble on his way back to the house, and he laughed with black humour. Dropping the raspberries would have been too much irony.

Jack had a memory of early childhood. They'd all been here at Grandpa's on a rare, family visit, but he'd sneaked out alone to hide between the staked lines of fruit. He might have been escaping an argument in the cottage. He'd been very young, so small that the highest runners were out of reach, but loose canes arched over him, drooping down as if offering themselves for picking; succulent, pendulous fruit that burst on his tongue. The bowl that day had been porcelain, pretty enough for even a boy to wonder if it was quite the right thing for the garden and to hold it with solemn care on the way back. He'd been so pleased with himself that he didn't sense the tension in the kitchen.

Daddy Daddy look Daddy see what I got. He'd lifted the bowl in ruby-stained fingers into a thunderclap bark of anger. The shock jolted him so that the top layer of berries went upwards while the bowl fell, tumbling, spilling, to shatter across the flagstones in a blood splash of pulp.

Sorry Daddy sorry Daddy I didn't mean to do it.

Tears at the heart of rage, and the little dance on the spot that kids do when they're frightened and can't run. He may even have wet himself.

Look what you've done you stupid boy that bowl was your grandmother's.

A frozen, photographic image of a moment. His mother in the hall doorway, silent fear on her face as she cradled a chubby Tilly on one arm. Tilly wide-eyed, sucking her thumb. His father standing by the kitchen table, shouting, with both hands clawed in anger.

And Grandpa, smelling of sweat and cigarettes as he knelt beside Jack, one arm across his back while the other reached for fragments of porcelain.

There, there, no harm done, I never liked that bowl anyways. Don't shout, son, he only dropped it 'cos you shouted.

Had it always been like that, him and Grandpa against the rest?

And on the day that his grandpa died, Jack carried raspberries to his father. He told himself he was honouring Grandpa rather than needling his father, who'd have forgotten the incident long ago. Harry sat in Grandpa's front room at the kneehole desk in the recess between the fireplace and the dining room wall, and Jack waved the bowl towards him, lifting his shoulders in a half-shrug that made light of the moment. Nearly fifteen years since he'd left home and he still had to resist that urge to placate, with an apology ready in his mouth like a bad berry that he might have to spit out.

Harry grimaced, irritated, and turned back to the papers spread in front of him. The drawer hanging open by his knee looked as if it held bank statements and savings passbooks. It didn't seem right, somehow, picking over Grandpa's life so soon. Jack would rather have pulled a bottle of Eddie's elderflower wine from the cupboard under the stairs, sat in the garden with the bowl of raspberries and drunk to him, wherever he'd gone.

In the silence, Harry threw one of Grandpa's diaries backhanded towards a plastic recycling crate near his feet. That didn't seem right, either. Nearly forty years of diaries were in those cupboards, all in cheap, hardback, half-page notebooks, all labelled with the year and a 'volume' number. Volume 35 hit the edge of the crate and fell onto the carpet, fanning pages covered in Grandpa's awkward script. Jack did a mental calculation. Four years ago. He'd taken a week's leave and they'd sailed round the Channel Islands together. The last long voyage together. Good times. Jack bent over, quietly, and pocketed it.

'You could check the loft.' Harry didn't look up. He was hunched over the desk, shoulders tense, and he didn't want Jack there.

Jack found a corkscrew instead.

The tide had turned. The mudbanks glistened blue–brown but the boats moored out in the harbour were pointing seawards. *Draca* used to swing with the tide at a buoy in Freshwater Bay, between the cottage and Witt Point, but the mooring had been empty since arthritis kept Grandpa ashore and *Draca* was laid up in the boatyard. Grandpa had changed, after that. He'd always been old, to Jack, but somehow vital, the sort of guy who'd laugh into the storm with spray running down his face and white hair plastered to his scalp. But it's hard to sail if you can't grip a rope, and without his boat he became just an old man with salty stories to tell, a man who cursed as his hands fumbled at woodworking tools or a corkscrew.

The pop of the cork sounded muffled, as if the heat had robbed the air of its resonance. Grandpa's elderflower wine was fragrant, floral and sweet enough to sharpen the raspberries. It seemed appropriate, somehow, to have a moment of reflection, to sit in the garden and toast him in his own, tepid wine, eating the first raspberries of the summer. Here's to you, old man. Thanks for the good times. He took another pull at the wine, forcing his mind onto good memories, away from Eddie's screaming end and his own humiliation. Rages weren't him. Hadn't been. He'd been trained to kill but he didn't take swings at people. Never before. These explosions of anger were getting worse.

Grandpa had understood. He'd been gentle, when Jack first came back. Not in the cloying, gosh-it-must-have-been-awful way most people have, but with a quiet tolerance as if he'd been there. He seemed to understand that sometimes people don't need sympathy; they need time to work out how to live with the shit inside them. Homemade wine, a boat seat and silence between friends, staring out over the inlet. Good therapy for both of them. On one of Jack's first visits back, Grandpa had broken the silence to tell Jack he had cancer. Aggressive. Terminal. Soon. After that, Jack had come over a lot, usually on his own. Charlotte was probably glad to have him out of the house.

Jack leafed through the diary, looking for entries about their voyage. Each entry started with a weather report, like a ship's log. He'd forgotten that that was also the year that Eddie found the carving.

20th April. Wind ESE Force 4. Fair.

I'm soaking the dragon in an old bath, in the shed. Had to trim the burnt end so it would fit. Kept it in seawater, first, then polyethylene glycol. Had the devil's own job to find that stuff. Six more months, I reckon, before it's safe to take it out. It looks up at me through the chemicals the way a sick patient looks at a doctor.

Maybe it's Danish, from one of Guthrum's ships. He raided this coast in the time of King Alfred, him and his army.

Guthrum the oath-breaker, the Saxons called him, but then the Saxons wrote the histories so they're bound to have made him out the bad guy. I'd like it to be Viking.

'I thought you were going to help. There's still the loft to do.'

Jack slipped the diary out of sight. His father frowned into the sun by the seat, holding up an envelope to shield his eyes. Jack remembered that tone. It hovered between disappointment and mild contempt, and it was the voice he'd used to express disapproval when Jack became too old to be ordered around. It still made him feel like a teenager who wouldn't tidy his room.

'Have some wine. Lighten up.'

Jack had brought a spare glass and slid it along the shelf inside the hull.

'Too early for me.' Harry sat down, anyway. The silence stretched. 'Bit jumpy, are we?'

'Just a touch. It'll pass.'

A different kind of silence grew between them, the kind when you wonder what to say.

'How much leave you got?'

Jack took a deep breath. His father had to know sometime.

'I've left the marines.'

Another silence. Maybe a slight nod, as if this was only to be expected.

'Your decision or theirs?'

Jack took another breath before he answered. 'Mutual.' Technically, a medical discharge, but Harry didn't need to know that. This time, there was a definite nod beside him.

'A step too far, was it?'

For a moment the rage surged back, hot and furious, but Jack took another breath and focused on a pine tree out on Witt Point. He couldn't see the traces of the old chapel from here, but it was still one of the most peaceful views he knew and he stared at it until he could pick up his glass, without shaking, and take a sip that tipped into a gulp. There, he was learning.

'That's right, I couldn't hack it.' Jack refilled his glass, hoping he'd put enough derision in his voice to make Harry wonder if he was lying. He wasn't going to try to explain. Harry had served twenty-two years in the Royal Engineers without being shot at, always managing to be somewhere else when things got nasty, like being in Germany during the Falklands War. A warrant officer second class when he retired, a parade-ground sergeant major. Sure, he'd been to trouble spots. Northern Ireland, even peacekeeping in the Balkans, but he'd never seen action. He wouldn't understand.

'So what are you going to do?'

'Odd jobs, while I work out the next steps.' And living off his resettlement grant.

Harry breathed deeply a few times, as if he was working up to something.

'Pass us that glass then.'

Great. They might even have a conversation. Harry held the glass, not drinking, sitting upright and square so his shoulders filled the space between Jack and the figurehead, crowding him into the corner.

'Here's to Grandpa, then,' Jack prompted, and drank. Harry made a token sip.

Another pause.

'You always was close,' Harry said after a while. It was a statement, not a question, and it hung in the air with an implied criticism. 'Closer than you was to us,' he might have added. Shit, did he really wonder why Jack had spent his boyhood weekends on the water with Grandpa rather than at home, enduring the salad-crunching silence of Sunday Tea?

'We got along OK. I wasn't frightened of him.' Jack let Harry digest that for a while, and then waved the bowl of raspberries at him. Peace offering. Harry shook his head. Another long pause.

'Will you sell this place, Dad?' Jack would miss it, if he did. His father had no siblings to share the inheritance, and the cottage must have been worth a bit. Ten or twelve miles away by road, two across the water, Furzey was a playground of the rich, all smart yachts and apartment blocks. The same distance the other way, over the ferry at the narrow harbour entrance, was some of the most expensive real estate in the country. You'd pay more for a sea view round there than the average person would earn in a hundred years. Grandpa's cottage was small, one half of a semi-detached pair, and too remote from the bright lights to command top prices, but it was the sort of place a City family would snap up as a holiday cottage, like the one next door. Plus there'd be a huge premium for a mooring in the only deep-water inlet on five miles of shoreline.

'Probably.' Harry sipped his wine, a larger pull this time, and rubbed his spare hand on his trousers like he was wiping sweat off his palm.

'Oh, there's a letter for you.' He handed over an envelope with *Lieutenant Jack Ahlquist, RM* in Grandpa's script. Not any more, old man. It was still sealed.

'Can I ask a favour?' Jack held the letter loosely in his hand, unwilling to open it beside his father.

'Depends what it is.'

'I'd like something to remember him by. That photo of him in *Draca*. Maybe the model of a longship that he made. Perhaps his diaries, if you're going to chuck them?'

'Yeah. S'pose. But let me think about the diaries.'

Harry spoke without enthusiasm. Jack stood and took the letter down the garden.

He felt the intensity of Harry's scrutiny as he came back, but his father was too proud to ask what was in it. Jack gave it to him anyway and watched his eyebrows fold as he read it.

'I don't understand.'

'Neither do I.' Jack took the letter back and read it again. It was dated three months previously, so he'd written it after he knew he was dying.

Jack, my boy. He always called Jack that.

I have a request, something they wouldn't let me put in the Will. That, by the way, is with Cartwright and Johnston in Furzey.

Draca is in the boatyard. George Fenton runs it now, and will show you where to find her. She don't look in great shape any more, but then she don't need to for what I have in mind.

See if you can find a way of putting me on board, will you? Then take the old girl out to sea and sink her. Best of all, burn her. Somewhere off Anfel Head. Draca will know where. It's where she wants to be, and I quite like the idea of going out like an old Viking chieftain.

There's a challenge, eh? See what you can do.

Thanks for being around, these past few months. It's helped a lot.

Be strong, Jack. You always were the best of us, and still are.

Love,

Grandpa

That last sentence raised a lump in Jack's throat.

'He's mad.' Harry still used the present tense.

The anger flared, and died as Jack realised his father wasn't talking about 'the best of us'. Mad? Yes, '*Draca* will know where' was a bit strange, but the cancer had spread to Grandpa's brain by the end. He could act strange, sometimes, but Jack didn't think he was mad. He'd loved that boat. He'd rebuilt it from a wreck, with his own hands, and it was a part of him. Some people want their ashes scattered in a place that's special. Grandpa wanted to go down with his boat. Jack could understand that.

'I'd better go and talk to that solicitor.' When Harry stood up, he needed to duck to fit under the bows of the boat shelter.

'I'm not driving anywhere.' Jack poured more wine. 'I'll sleep here, in my old room.' He'd done that a lot while Grandpa was sick. 'And the offices will be shut by the time you get there.'

Harry snorted as he left. Jack didn't blame his father for the lack of emotion. Not really. Harry and Eddie had never been close. They lived ten miles apart and hardly saw each other. Strange how life repeats itself. A couple of times Jack had been here when his father rang, maybe after Jack had taken the old man out for a birthday pint, and the half of the conversation he could hear always sounded stilted, a duty performed and received, technically connected but not connecting in any personal sense. Soon Grandpa would say 'Jack's here – want a word?' like he was keen to hand over the phone. Afterwards the cottage would be quieter, as if some sadness or regret had settled on the place, and Grandpa would go and sit on his dinghy seat, even in winter, and smoke.

29th April. Wind SW Force 3. Showers.

It must be Harald Guthrumsson's. The saga fits. This is the only deep water inlet in miles.

After I finished translating, I spent a long time looking at the dragon as it soaked in its bath of chemicals. I even took a bottle of elderflower wine with me to help me think. I wasn't sure whether I wanted to keep it. I know what it's done now, what it has seen.

Maybe I should do what Jack says and give it to a museum. I fell asleep sitting on the floor of the shed, thinking, and I dreamed of blood and killing. There was a moment as I woke when I understood, but the wisdom faded like a dream. It was something to do with all deaths being steps towards Ragnarök, when even the gods must die and the world will drown, but I can't explain why that seemed beautiful.

Afterwards I felt strong and young again. I split logs with the axe, sending the pieces spinning over the garden until the sweat ran and my hands ached and told me I was old.

Maybe I'll keep it. A dragonhead for Draca. We were meant to be.

Jack rested his hand on the top of the figurehead, wondering what his grandfather had discovered, and why the carving had become so important to him. Jack hadn't sailed in *Draca* many times since Grandpa fitted it. By the time he came back from his first, long deployment, to Afghanistan, *Draca* was laid up. But he remembered going out with Grandpa once, just before he deployed, and seeing the dragon's scaly head snarling down and out at the ocean for the first time. Grandpa's hands were already troubling him, and he let Jack do most of the sailing, but he took the helm for a while and sent Jack forward to watch that carved head soar over the sea. *'Look at it,'* Grandpa had said, eyes shining, *'it's happy. The dragon's happy!'* So Jack braced himself against the forestay, with the boat heeling over and the foresails swelling in the wind beside him, and looked down. As if to prove a point, the ship put her shoulder into a trough so that the sea came in green around his legs, and the dragon rose with water streaming from that gaping jaw as if it had just eaten the wave. Yes, he could persuade himself that the dragon was happy, in a brutal, in-your-face kind of way.

He'd heard that Grandpa's sailing style grew more aggressive after that. It cost him a few friends.

And on the day that Grandpa died Jack let his fingers trace the scales on the dragon's head while he stared at the view, drowsy with wine, remembering the loving sea dog rather than the mad old man of recent weeks. The garden was in shadow now the sun had dropped behind the hills, though it still turned the yachts and far shore into sharp and dazzling colours. When Jack was a boy, Grandpa had read him stories on this seat. Sea stories. Sagas. Once he'd read Jack a saga in Old Norse, just to let him hear the music of the ancient, Viking tongue. He'd read poems of the sea with the passion of an orator in his voice, and he'd given Jack his love of books. That evening the old hull ticked with minute contractions of the wood as it cooled. It was a friendly, whispering sound that eased Jack into sleep with the memory of companionable silences on this seat.

He's standing in *Draca*'s bows, and in the scrambled way of dreams there is no bowsprit, but the dragon rises high above the stem. Impossibly, though naturally, *Draca* is propelled by great sweeps of oars, a motion he feels through his cheek where it rests against the dragon. It's a slow surge–pause, surge–pause that has water bubbling under the forefoot with each stroke. On the port side, vague in the mist, Freshwater Bay stretches beneath the shelter of Witt Point, and he knows but does not know this harbour that he has sailed since childhood; he only senses that the inlet is a place where deep water comes close to the land. Ahead of him, unseen in the mist, must be Furzey. Furze Oy, in Anglo-Saxon, Fyrsig in the old tongue, the island of gorse.

Surge–pause, and the pause is marked by the sound of water raining from the blades as the oars swing back to bite again. There is a tension, an excitement in the ship as they approach the land; the same, creeping, hunter's bloodlust that he'd felt with the troop around him, awaiting his command in the moments before action.

The carving against his cheek jolts to a blow, a sound so loud that they must have struck a rock, and his first thought is of failure; he had not foreseen such dangers in this place of soft mud and winding channels.

Jack grabbed the dragon for support, his eyes flying open and blinking, disoriented. His father stood above him, framed by the arch of the boat seat, with fury tugging his jaw into angles that were sharp as broken porcelain.

IV: HARRY

Harry Ahlquist found it strange that Old Eddie had finally gone. It wasn't like they'd been bosom buddies, not like some blokes are with their fathers, but it was still, well, strange. It made Harry think of an apple tree that used to grow in his garden. It was there before the house was built, and it was old and twisted and a bit ugly. Nice blossom, though. Then a branch dropped off in a storm and it was even uglier, all lopsided, until one autumn there was a bit of a blow and the whole thing fell over. Harry hadn't even liked it very much, but then when he'd cleared up the mess the place was different. A bit emptier.

Old Eddie had dropped a branch or two over the years. That sounded kinder than saying he'd lost his marbles. The wife always called him Old Eddie, usually in a tight-lipped, I-could-say-more-but-won't tone of voice. Never 'Dad' or 'Pa', nothing so chummy, and over time Harry had fallen into the same habit. That note to Jack was typical, going on as if Eddie was some latter-day Viking. There was a whole shelf full of books about Nordic stuff over the desk. Harry pulled one down that was bristling with bookmarks: a great, fat, leather-bound thing called *'Heimskringla'*. It wasn't even in English, so he doubted that it was worth much.

It had been a shock to see Jack at the hospice. There was something about the boy that always put Harry on the back foot, so things came out wrong. Two years since he'd seen him, what with the latest deployment, and Jack had aged more than that. You could see it round his eyes. And he was hiding something, too, like he was hunched over a hurt. It reminded Harry of when Jack was a boy, when the other kids were bullying him but he wouldn't let on. He was bright, always had his nose in a book, like Old Eddie, and it wasn't the sort of school that tolerated a smart-arse. Jack didn't say anything, he just bottled it up inside him and asked for boxing lessons for Christmas and birthday, and worked a paper round to pay for more. Harry always thought it was unfair that Jack was the one who got expelled after he beat the crap out of the ringleader. When Harry saw him at the hospice he'd got that same, hunted look. That stupid dive across the carpet was worrying.

Jack should never have joined the marines. He always tried to act the hard man but there was a softness inside him, like he was still weak even if his body was fit. He always had to be different, did Jack. Always had to go one better. Harry had known it would end badly.

Maybe he should have gone down to see the boy after he got back. Would have done, if it weren't for that stuck-up bitch he married. Harry just wasn't welcome down there, and Jack obviously wasn't bothered to come and see them. At least he came back to the cottage after Old Eddie died. Not that he needed much persuading. Had a key, it seemed. And there was some of his stuff in the small bedroom, so he'd slept there before. That should have warned him.

Not that Jack was any help. He just sat in the garden, drinking, and it wasn't even six o'clock.

Tilly came. Said she had to wait for her Darren to get home and look after the kids before she came over. She started work on the dining room and Harry let her take the dinner service that had been her grandmother's. She'd brought boxes and bubble wrap, and thought she might as well fill up the space in the back of her car with saucepans and anything useful from the kitchen.

She didn't stay long. Kids to put to bed. Still, it helped. Harry went through the desk and the cupboards in the front room while she packed stuff, and talked to her through the wall. Seems Eddie never threw anything away. There were boxes upon boxes of bills and correspondence. Savings books and investments, too. Harry didn't know Eddie played the market. It was adding up to a tidy sum, with the cottage. Not enough to retire on, even if he wanted to, but then the money was a bonus because he was only planning on the cottage.

Jack was asleep when Harry took him a mug of tea a bit later. He thought the boy might want to go for a walk, and maybe have a chat. Harry used to enjoy their walks, when Jack was a lad. They could talk, back then. But Jack was curled around that carving in the shelter like it was a pet dog, and he was snoring, with one leg stretched out and the other hooked under him. He'd finished the bottle of wine, and he looked quite innocent, like he'd forgotten whatever was worrying him and was a kid again.

Daughters are easier than sons. You can hug daughters.

Harry hadn't realised that Old Eddie kept a diary. The early ones, as Harry leafed through them, were written neatly like he was writing out a report and thinking about every word. In Volume 39, the one in the desk, the writing was all awkward angles like his knuckles. The last two entries must have been just before he went into the hospice.

24th April. Wind Westerly, 3, showers.

He's coming for me. He wants it, but how can I give it back? I tried. Honest, I tried.

And the whispering. Half the night, it went on, until the tide turned and swallowed the beach.

They always stay on the beach, the whisperers. They strain up the hill towards him, calling him back, like he's their enemy and they want to drag him away. But he just stands there, under the trees, as if the whisperers are nothing to him.

He's getting more powerful, feeding off my weakness. When I'm dead he'll drag us both down, the dragon and me. Sail us off to serve Hel in Niflheim.

Or will it be Rán under the waves?

Jack's coming tomorrow. He'll keep the warrior away. And the whisperers. The life force is still strong in Jack.

Poor raving bastard. He'd shouted about giving something back in the hospice. But then, as Harry knew, Eddie had lost a branch or two by the end. But one day later his writing made perfect sense, as if sanity had flipped back in.

25ᵗʰ April. Wind WNW Variable 4-5, intermittent rain.

It's a heavy thing, this cancer. If you added up every revolting bit there'd be just a few ounces of alien meat, but I still can't sleep for the weight of it.

Last night in the cottage. Over 50 years I've been here.

Jack came to help, bless him, and stayed. He sleeps lightly as well. For once I could share the demon hour before dawn with another human, and blow steam off tea as if I could puff away the funk. We sat in the garden in waterproofs and felt rain on our faces and I knew I was still alive.

And it was just me and Jack, thank God.

Harry felt a bit guilty when he read that bit. Eddie used a lot of words, sometimes, like Jack. Maybe, Harry thought, he should have been closer to Old Eddie at the end, but then he'd got a business to run. Going well, too, but he needed to keep on top of it. Sometimes, in the security trade, success means making damn sure nothing goes wrong. And the only way to be sure is to be there.

There was a file of correspondence from solicitors in a cupboard. That's where Harry found a copy of the will. It was recent, dated about the same time as that crazy letter to Jack. It was very short, but Harry had to read it several times while it sunk in, because he couldn't believe it. Eddie had left enough to Tilly for her to buy a decent, small car. That was fair. Harry didn't mind that. There were larger bequests to her children, which surprised him a bit, to be held in trust until they were older. After that there was a single, bald sentence.

I give my remaining Residuary Estate after payment of debts funeral and testamentary expenses to my grandson Jack Ahlquist, who has given me the chance to be the father I always should have been.

No other explanation. No mention of Harry or anyone else. That boy had wormed his way in there and persuaded a mad old man to change his will. Robbing his own family, for God's sake. When Harry went out into the garden he was so angry that if Jack hadn't been protected by that shelter he might have hit him. As it was, Harry smashed his fist into the side of the upended boat and Jack jolted awake, panic in his eyes until he recognised Harry and then he just looked puzzled.

'You knew, didn't you!' Harry thrust the will into his face, all scrunched up in his hand.

'Knew what, Dad?' The boy started to look defiant, the way he always did when he'd done wrong and was going to be punished, but Harry wasn't going to spell it out.

'Of all the underhand, conniving tricks!'

Jack blinked, and swallowed in that lip-licking way that told Harry he was still drunk.

'What the hell are you talking about?'

Harry hated it when the boy answered back. 'You know damn well what I'm talking about.' He threw the will at him and Jack's eyes went hard like someone who was ready to fight.

'I'll challenge it. Undue influence, or whatever they call it. Exploiting a vulnerable old man.'

'Let's see what you're so upset about.' Jack spoke so softly that it was dangerous, unnatural, and he kept his eyes on Harry's as he bent forward to pick up the paper from the ground. He was still staring at Harry as he smoothed it against his leg.

Harry wasn't going to stay and watch Jack's little charade. He turned away because if he had to stare at that blazing innocence for one more second he might have done something he'd regret.

He was so bloody angry that he smashed his Jaguar on the way home. Turned out into the path of another car. No one hurt, but it would cost. Big time. Now that *was* his fault. Well, legally it was.

Chapter Two: Bálför

(Old Norse: funeral pyre)

From the Saga of King Guthrum, ca AD 875

That winter King Guthrum laid down a mighty dragonhead ship for his son Jarl Harald, whom he loved and honoured most of all. Of oak did he build it, cut finely that it might bend with the sea, with benches of pine for twenty oars on the one hand and twenty on the other. The fittings were splendid, as befits a great jarl, and a richly carved strake rose to a wondrous dragonhead at the prow. As was the custom, this could be taken down, like the helm of a warrior, lest it offend the landvættir.[1]

Then Guthrum and Harald made sacrifice in this wise: Harald took a stallion that he loved, and calmed the beast, covering its eyes that it might not see whence the blow would come. Then they took their axes and struck; Harald between the stallion's eyes, and Guthrum at its neck such that the sound of the blows was one, and none could tell who made the killing wound. So mightily did Guthrum wield his axe that the stallion's head was wholly struck

1. Land spirits.

off, and the wise ones said that the fall of the blood was good, for the dragonhead tasted blood before ever a bowl was brought to its mouth.

Then Harald knew that the gods would sail with them, and would find them even in the furthest reaches of the sea, for the dragonhead was truly consecrated to the Æsir.

I: GEORGE

George Fenton enjoyed early mornings at Furzey Marina. She'd take a start-of-the-day turn around the boatyard, seeing who was around, while she savoured the *plinkplinkplink* noise of halyards slapping against aluminium masts in the wind. The sound always made her smile inside and think *'Why the feck aren't I on the water?'* but she didn't sail at weekends. Weekends were for rich folk who could afford to keep a boat idle during the week while they made their dosh: the clients who expected her and Chippy Alan the shipwright to work their arses off looking after them. There was always something that needed fixing before they could put to sea, and there was usually someone she wanted to find, like when they hadn't paid their bill.

It was mainly couples at weekends. A friendly bunch, for the most part. The men would smile at her boobs and forget they had a tide to catch. The women in their wake would roll their eyes in a way that reminded George of a stained-glass window she'd seen in a church: some martyred saint with her eyes on heaven and a big, open 'O' of a mouth. She'd looked as if she was only pretending to be suffering, and really having way too much fun under her robes.

George didn't like strangers wandering around the boatyard. Stuff went missing, and she had to answer to the owners even though she was just the Office Manager. So when she saw some guy put a ladder against Mad Eddie's boat she swore to herself and wandered over. *Draca* had been beached for years, propped up on timber legs on an old, tidal hard at the edge of the boatyard. Mad Eddie Ahlquist had paid the yard to unstep her broken mast, take out her ballast and float her in at the top of a 'spring' tide. She'd been there ever since, with her ballast put back to hold her down. She wetted her keel every tide and looked sorrier whenever George strolled that way. Green, slimy stains ran down her cheeks from her hawsepipe at the bow and from the cockpit drains under her counter, so that she looked like she was crying at one end and shitting herself at the other.

By the time she reached *Draca*, the man was leaning over the gunwale like a bum on stilts. When she challenged him he came down the ladder slowly, one rubber-booted step at a time, as if he was unsure of his footing.

'Jack Ahlquist,' he introduced himself. That checked her. She'd been about to get all aggressive. Now he'd turned, she could see the likeness. Same shoulders, same Nordic cheekbones. And totally fit enough for a girl to put her shoulders back.

'George Fenton.'

He blinked at the 'George'.

'My mum called me Georgia. George seems to have stuck. I'm also known as Georgie Girl to my more sexist customers, and the Boatyard Bitch to the ones what don't pay their bills.' She was talking too much.

He had a nice smile. 'This is my grandfather's boat.' He touched the hull and frowned at the smear his fingers left in the dirt.

'Then tell him to let us do some work on her. It's a crying shame to leave her like this.' The dirt matting the hull would wash off. Other decay might be more fundamental.

'I would if I could. He's dead.' He turned, pretending to move away from the ladder, but probably hiding his face, like he was being brusque to mask his feelings.

George wasn't surprised about Eddie. She made sympathetic noises at Jack Ahlquist's back, but she'd known it was coming when she last saw him, around Christmas. They'd had a weird conversation about rigging a jury mast in *Draca* so that she could carry a square sail again and put to sea like a Viking longship. Just one trip, he said. He never did anything about it, though. That day he'd asked Chippy Alan to unstep the figurehead, and he'd taken it away with him. George thought about Eddie, afterwards, because he reminded her of her mum before she died. Masses older than her, of course, but when George shut her eyes there'd been a greyness about Eddie in her mind. Not the grey of age, which can be quite healthy, but a dark, sick grey turning black at the edges. George knew what that meant. She'd seen it in her mum. The black takes over and then they die.

Now here was his grandson. An outdoorsy type, maybe an Aries.

'Got the key?' she asked him. 'Want to look?'

He hung back, so she went up the ladder first and regretted it halfway up when her shorts and bare legs went past his face. She looked down from the top, half expecting Jack to be staring up at her bum, but he was touching the hull again with his fingers splayed to show his wedding ring. George got the message. Arrogant sod. More of a Taurus, perhaps. She turned away as he began to climb.

Draca was a fair size: at least twelve feet in the beam and perhaps forty in length, plus her bowsprit, and flush-decked, with just the cockpit, a 'doghouse' cabin hatch and a skylight to break the sweep of teak. When George had first come to the yard about four years before, *Draca*'s deck had stretched away like a dance floor. Now it was a lumberyard of spars, draped with ropes. Drifts of leaf pulp had blown into corners, rotted and grown seedlings. Then, she'd had a mast and rigging. Now, she was a hulk.

Jack moved aft unsteadily, at a crouch, keeping well away from the edge. True, it was about twelve feet down to the hard, and there was only a shin-height wooden rail, but he looked nervous, like he was unsure of his footing. When they reached the cockpit, they found it half-full with a dirty scum of water, deep enough to cover the gratings and lap over the top of Jack's boot as he stepped down into it. He didn't seem to notice. The drains must have been clogged with leaves or debris, and he had to wade around in a mess of sodden rigging that had probably been there since they took out the broken mast.

'Shall I lead on?' Jack fumbled for the key, his boots trailing water as he stepped over the companion ladder coaming. George slipped off her trainers.

'How old is she?' She'd never been below deck in *Draca*. Her mast had sprung the last time Eddie took her out, which was soon after George arrived, and she'd been laid up ever since.

At the bottom of the steps, Jack turned in a space that had a chart-table to starboard and was cramped by a large, cast-iron engine casing just off the centre-line to port. George had seen similar spaces in other, classic boats, a kind of working 'wet space' where the watch on deck could come in oilskins and boots to look at charts or make a brew.

'Nineteen oh-five. One of the last of the sailing pilot cutters.'

'What kind of engine is that?'

'That,' Jack said, 'is Scotty.' He made it sound like a pet dog.

'As in "Beam me up, Scotty"?'

'Nah. As in good, Glasgow engineering. Pre-war vintage.'

'And it still works?'

'It used to. Bit temperamental. Grandpa wanted to change the ship as little as possible, so he kept it.'

Jack tapped a narrow door, port side, forward of the engine. 'Heads in there. Bit cramped. Fold-down basin and no shower. Foul-weather gear on the other side.'

He swung open mahogany double doors and went forward into the saloon, leaving a trail of wet footprints. He seemed even taller, now she was barefoot, and broad enough to fill the doorway. She followed, and stepped into an atmosphere.

Classic boats are like old buildings; sometimes you can sense a mood. When George was little, her mum used to drag her round stately homes where she'd gawp at the silver and oil paintings and lawns, and once in a while George would pick up an atmosphere. Happy ones, sad ones, downright creepy ones, maybe all of those in different rooms, and usually stronger in places like the nursery or the servants' rooms in the attics. Hardly ever in the grand, gilded staterooms. Her mum said it was because she was psychic and born with a caul over her head, but then her mum had some pretty weird ideas. George just knew that people leave something of themselves when they go.

She shivered, and tried to persuade herself it was the damp. The saloon was musty. It looked and felt empty. Book racks with no books. An old, iron stove, black and cold like the coal scuttle beside it. Teak woodwork, dark with age, grey with dust.

'Sleeping cabin through here.' Jack had to stoop beneath the deckhead. He opened a narrower door in the forward bulkhead, to one side of the stove. George peered around him at a cramped space with a single berth port side, and a narrow double to starboard. Both had leeboards fitted to stop you falling out in rough weather, and they looked coffin-deep without their mattresses. A hole in the deckhead showed where the mast had been. A tarpaulin had been stretched over the gap, but damp had come in just the same, making a puddle of slime on the deck around the void where the mast had been stepped.

'This was my bunk, as a boy.' Jack put his hand inside the single berth and felt upwards, making a metallic rattle against a curtain rail. Leeboards and curtains, very cosy. The atmosphere was stronger here. Soon she'd be able to put a name to it.

'Can you imagine what it was like, for a boy?' Jack's smile

broadened into a grin, his guard slipping. 'Sailing off to adventure? Channel Islands? One summer we went round Brittany into Biscay.'

'Just the two of you?' She was a big boat for two people to go cruising in, especially if one of them was a kid.

'When I was older, in my teens perhaps. Day sailing only, and Grandpa was stronger, back then. We both knew what we were doing.'

'People say he was a pretty wild sailor. Took risks.'

'Not with me, he didn't.' Jack sounded defensive.

'It was before my time, anyway,' George shrugged. 'Chippy Alan would know, if you want some local stories.'

'Chippy Alan?'

'Shipwright. Works here…' She stopped when she saw loss in his eyes. 'You really loved him, didn't you?'

'Grandpa…' Jack's voice faded away then started again, more strongly. 'Grandpa opened up horizons. He gave me permission to be myself.' He turned away.

'Fo'c's'le through there?' George nodded at another door, leading further forward. Jack pushed it open.

'Stores. Sail lockers. There's another pull-down bunk in there, but it's not comfortable. It's where they put the paid hand when the owner employed a crew.'

The 'bunk' wasn't much more than five feet long, wedged in behind a thick metal pipe that must have run from the anchor on deck to the chain locker below.

'I suppose that's what they mean by sailing short-handed,' she quipped.

He had a smile that started small but broadened, lifting his face. George felt she'd been given a glimpse of a sweeter person hiding inside that dour exterior.

'So I'd have one hull of a problem.'

And he could come back at her. It wasn't great humour from

either of them, but it broke the ice. Then she remembered his wedding ring and led the way back into the saloon.

'Will your family restore her? She'd be worth a fortune, done up.'

'Grandpa wants to be cremated on board, at sea, and for *Draca* to be scuttled.'

'Feck, what a waste!'

'It's also illegal. I checked. The authorities aren't keen on half-burned bodies washing up on the beaches. Besides,' he ran a finger over the table, leaving a shiny trail through the dust, 'I don't think I could do it. This ship is Grandpa. He bought her as a wreck and spent years restoring her. It would be like killing him all over again.'

The atmosphere in the boat caught George for a moment, and she shivered again. It lurked in the background, just enough to make her uncomfortable. She sniffed, trying to make it out, but smelled only damp and rot and a hint of stale tobacco. It was as if she was in someone's house without permission, knowing that the owner would be back soon. She stood still for a moment, trying to decipher this mood, and lifted her fingers to touch a deckhead beam. Here, where the dust hadn't settled, the wood glowed a rich, dark honey. The impression was stronger through her fingers, and she closed her eyes, listening. She had the sense that if that absent owner came back, he wouldn't like her and she wouldn't like him, but the boat was waiting for him. And it was definitely a 'him'.

Weird. Jack Ahlquist was standing beside her as she opened her eyes and dropped her hand, watching her with grey, gentle eyes that looked tired in the shadows of the cabin. She turned and made for the companion ladder up to the deck, still not sure why the boat made her so uncomfortable. Anyway, she had a boatyard to run.

II: GEORGE

Eddie Ahlquist didn't get the fireship funeral Jack said he wanted, but a bog-standard cremation. George went, to represent the boatyard, but got there early because the buses weren't convenient. She had over an hour to kill sitting on a bench outside a crem that had as much soul as a drive-through McDonalds.

Her mum had it right, although George had been young enough to sneer at the time. When her mum knew she was dying, she asked for a woodland burial, and chose a wicker coffin that creaked like a picnic basket when they lifted her. Her new-age girlfriends wore bright, Indian-print dresses, and burned joss sticks and candles in jam jars at the graveside. They'd all grown up in the Flower Power hippie era, and somehow never left it. One of them even brought finger cymbals. They wove yellow celandine flowers into her mum's hair before they closed the coffin. Strange how colours stick with you, even though George always remembered her not in yellow but in shades of silver and violet. They glowed like a Mum-shaped photo frame around her memory.

That happened, with people she knew. Colours, that is. Her mum talked about auras, which made George laugh because she made it sound like people walked around all lit up like a Christmas tree. She wished her mum had lived long enough for them to have had a proper conversation about that stuff. It was just that some colours seemed to fit when she thought of people. They told her about them, the way they told her that Eddie was going to die. On her bench outside the crem, George watched Jack Ahlquist arrive, and when she thought about him he had strong reds, moody blues and sad greys. Interesting but dangerous.

Then an older man came who could only be Jack's father and Eddie's son. All of them sandy haired, big boned and strong jawed. Jack's dad shepherded people outside the crematorium, shaking hands, the man in charge. He had the thick neck of someone who pumped iron, and a mouth that was a thin, straight line. When he smiled, the line got wider but didn't curve upwards, it just got bracketed by folds in his cheeks, sharp as the triangles on a navigation buoy.

George stayed on her bench because she didn't know anyone there apart from Jack, and he was busy with family. No one else came from the boatyard, not even Eddie's old sailing cronies. He'd lost a lot of friends in recent years, but that was sad.

George could learn a lot from watching people. At first, everyone looked the same. All in black, all with that funeral look as if they wore a passport photograph where their faces should be. She could make out the Ahlquist crowd, all hugs and kisses except Jack, and then there was an older man and two women who stood a bit apart, both more smartly dressed than the rest, and the only women in hats. A husband, wife and daughter, at a guess. The man was a short, lean, military type who stood very square. When people came up to the older woman, she offered her hand palm-down, fingers drooping, as if she expected them to go down on one knee and kiss it. No one stayed with them, and the three kept to themselves as if they knew it was pointless to try to talk.

Jack moved between them and the rest, half belonging to both groups, neither oil nor water, looking stressed. Like all the men he was sweating in his dark suit, with spots of damp staining his shirt across his chest. The younger woman must be his wife, so the military man and the duchess were the in-laws, and the families didn't get on.

Jack waved when he saw George. Nothing too enthusiastic, but enough for her to wander over and say hello. She was ready for the mother-in-law's fingers. If you slide your hand under that kind of regal greeting, then grip and twist, you can turn it into a proper handshake. The duchess didn't like that. She didn't like George's looks, either. The duchess was tall enough for her eyes to be at the level of George's hair, and George saw her wince. So what? George liked orange. It's a strong colour, and it was only a streak. While Jack fumbled the introductions the woman's eyes dropped so she was looking down her nose at George's skirt, and her mouth pursed into a tight, wrinkly, cat's–arse circle of disapproval. Maybe yellow was a bit bright for a funeral, but there wasn't much call for dark, smart stuff in a boatyard. At least George had put a decent jacket over it, and she bet the duchess couldn't tell that the jacket came from a charity shop.

Jack's wife introduced herself as Charlotte. Very upmarket, with the sort of accent you hear in posh shops. Her handshake was straight, if a bit cool. She was tall, like her mother, and slender and attractive, unlike her mother. Her black straw hat was broad-brimmed so she had to tilt her head to one side to whisper in George's ear.

'Thank God for some colour. I think Old Eddie would have loved it.'

George decided she was going to like Charlotte. She stayed near her as they were ushered inside.

Twenty minutes later George was like, 'was that it?' A whole life, nearly eighty years, reduced to one reading, two hymns, a three-minute drone from Rent-a-Priest and a poem?

Jack's father gave the reading, bellowing it out like a fire-and-brimstone preacher. Isaiah 61, the order of service said.

'The Spirit of the Lord God is upon me, because the Lord has anointed me to bring good tidings to the poor.' He stared at a young

woman in the front row, with two young children beside her. Another Ahlquist by the look of her, and the kind of blonde who's gone way too plump with motherhood. '*He has sent me to bind up the broken hearted…*' She didn't look very broken hearted. She had big, dark eyes, a snub nose and puffy cheeks, like a seal pup with tits. Jack's father didn't strike George as a preacher, either, but he turned that stare towards Jack as he finished, and thundered, '*To proclaim the year of the Lord's favour, and the day of vengeance of our God; to comfort all who mourn.*'

Rent-a-Priest did his job. He'd probably never met the man he was about to incinerate, even though he'd been fed the key facts and wrapped them up in lofty, churchy tones. Edvard Ahlquist, born into hardship as the son of a Danish sailor. Forty years a shipwright. Had his share of tragedy. Liked sailing and Nordic folklore. Let us pray.

Jack read a poem that was George's favourite. She didn't know many poems, but this one about the lonely sea and the sky had stuck, ever since she was a kid. Something in those words about steering a tall ship by a star had struck a chord. Other kids escaped into video games or petty crime but she was the loner who dreamed of sailing away. She couldn't even remember which school she had been in when she had learned it, but it had told her about a world beyond a dirty playground and the waiting gangs. She'd been in her late teens before she felt a tiller's kick for the first time, or heard Masefield's wind song, and then it had been like coming home. She still knew it well enough to shut her eyes and mouth the words with Jack.

Jack spoke with passion, as if he'd chosen that bit of the service. It was the only time some feeling for Mad Eddie came over. His voice caught, just a little, as he spoke those final words about a quiet sleep and a sweet dream when the long trick's over, and George opened her eyes.

He was watching her. Again. She blushed and looked away, angry with herself, but not before she'd seen that he was a bit full. He paused like he was collecting himself, then said, 'Sweet dreams, Grandpa,' as if he really meant it, but Rent–a–Priest was already standing to announce the final hymn. The next lot were waiting.

'*...Oh hear us when we cry to Thee*
For those in peril on the sea.'

The priest looked bored as he pressed the button.

III: GEORGE

Charlotte persuaded George to go to the reception afterwards. George had followed her out of the crem, wishing she had a dress like Charlotte's and the body to wear it. Charlotte's parents were in front of her, shaking hands with the line of Ahlquists. Charlotte's father was a lot shorter than Harry Ahlquist, and he was a stiff little man who tilted his whole torso to look Harry in the eye, leaning back rather than looking up. They shook hands the way boxers touch gloves.

'Will you come back to the house? The wife's laid on a bit of a spread…' Harry Ahlquist pushed out an invitation the way George would fend off a boat.

'Awfully decent of you.' Charlotte's father spoke in clipped, plummy tones, recoiling from the invitation so much that George thought he might overbalance backwards. 'But it's a long drive home…'

'Sure.' Harry looked relieved. His shoulders opened, bonhomie restored.

'You'll come though, won't you, George?' Charlotte turned, making big, pleading eyes. She must have been dreading being stuck with Jack's lot on her own.

'I need to get the bus back to Furzey…' George was like, *'Feck, no way'*.

'We'll run you back, won't we, darling?' Charlotte turned to Jack, who was last in the line of Ahlquists. He started and said 'sure' warmly enough, but his mind seemed elsewhere. Charlotte settled it by slipping her arm inside George's and leading them towards her car. George was too flattered to argue.

Harry Ahlquist's house was modern and a bit flash, the kind of place a man might build for himself if he'd made a shedload of money and wanted to show it by having the biggest house in the neighbourhood. There was a bar-and-games room where Jack's mum had laid out sandwiches and nibbles. She was a dumpy, homey sort in a black dress who fussed around everyone, but wouldn't stand still long enough to talk. Charlotte disappeared, leaving George clutching a sausage roll, looking at a lawn that was filling with people she didn't know. Beyond the lawn was a hedge with a gap and more steps down, and there must have been a swimming pool on the far side because shifting sunlight was shining upwards through the hedge.

George didn't fit with that kind of money. She'd find a taxi. The boatyard could pay. Eddie had been a customer, after all. She turned to go.

Charlotte had the kind of smile that made George think they shared some private joke, and she was holding two glasses of wine with a God-I-need-this look on her face. She'd taken off her jacket and hat, and had thick, brown hair pulled back into a ponytail in a way that emphasised her face. As she pushed a glass at George, she looked like a model who'd just walked off a photo shoot.

'Sorry. Queue for the loo. Cheers.' She winced at the taste but swallowed. 'Today's a day I'm really glad Jack's driving.'

'Where is he?'

'Probably being told what a naughty boy he is.' She swigged again and stared into her glass. 'This gets better. The first mouthful kills the taste buds.' She linked arms again as if they were old friends, and steered George onto the lawn. No one else tried to talk to them. All around, people were hugging each other and kissing children. *My, look at you, how you've grown.* Already it was more like a wedding than a funeral, but Charlotte and George stood alone, surrounded by enough grass to talk quietly without being heard.

'Looks like you don't get on.'

'Oh, they don't approve of me at all.' Charlotte panned a smile around the gathering, almost like she enjoyed their hostility.

'How come?'

At the end of the lawn a group of people gathered around Harry Ahlquist all looked at Charlotte over their shoulders at the same time, and turned away.

'Sergeant Major Ahlquist,' she lifted her glass towards him, 'didn't like Jack becoming an officer, and he especially didn't like him marrying me.'

'Why ever not?' She was friendly, she was lovely and, although her parents were a bit stuck up, George hadn't seen any pretensions. Charlotte lifted her glass towards Jack's mother, who was darting from group to group like a rather plump blackbird with a tea tray.

'That's the sort of woman they wanted for their boy. I bet she gets up early to dust the ceiling and iron the cat.'

'Meow.'

'Sorry, that *was* a bit bitchy.'

'I like her.' The only time George could remember her own mum baking savouries for her friends, they'd had cannabis in them. That was one weird party.

'And Harry Ahlquist treats her like a dishcloth.'

'He seemed relieved that your parents didn't come.'

'Mummy and Daddy have never forgiven him for boycotting our wedding.' She turned her head as Jack appeared beside her and said 'hey' like they were workmates; friends but not friends enough to touch.

'I'm just telling George some family history.'

Jack said 'Uh-huh?' in a tone that told George he wasn't too sure about that, but Charlotte carried on anyway. 'We wanted close family to wear morning dress, you see. Harry threw a wobbly and told Jack's people not to come.'

'But why?'

'Inverted snobbery.' Jack answered for her. He had a strange way of standing, with his weight on his right leg and his left leg flexed, on its toes. 'He said there was no way he was going to pretend to be a toff, so we could go to hell.'

I could see the pain behind his eyes. It must still hurt.

'So you had no one there from your side?'

'School friends. Marines friends. A guard of honour with an arch of swords outside.' He bent to touch his sister's children, who were playing catch around his legs, unaware of the social tides around them. A preschool boy chased a girl at the giggly-screamy stage of infancy. The seal pup with tits glared across the lawn like she could call them back with a look.

'That's Tilly,' Charlotte whispered, smiling sweet acid at Jack's sister. 'Daddy's little girl.'

'But no family?' George prompted Jack.

'Grandpa came. He defied the ban. That's why Charlotte's people came today.'

Jack watched the party with a let's-get-this-over-with look on his face. The children ran off around the corner of the house, the boy leading his younger sister, both laughing.

Charlotte smiled again, a bit more grimly this time. 'So we've gone our own way ever since. Now I'm the bad girl for taking…'

She stopped as a child screamed. It wasn't the grazed-knee scream of a tumble, but a high-pitched note of terror, and beyond the scream was a low thunder like a block being pulled along a wooden deck. The noise ended with an impact but the screaming continued for as long as it took the girl to run back across the lawn and bury her face in Tilly's skirts. The boy followed, also running, trying not to look frightened.

'There's a monster and it growled at her.' The boy was wide-eyed as Tilly knelt and hugged the girl, who snivelled into her chest. Jack disappeared around the corner of the house and came back cradling a black, wooden carving shaped like an arching horse's neck, about four feet long. It took George a moment to recognise *Draca*'s figurehead. Jack stopped at the edge of the lawn, keeping his distance as the girl's screams became frantic.

'Is this the monster?' Jack spoke gently, making light of the moment.

'It growled at her.' The boy was insistent.

'Like this, perhaps?' Jack dragged the carving against the boundary fence, wood on wood, so it made a low rumble. The girl still cried. 'Let's cover it up, shall we?'

Harry arrived to see what all the fuss was about, and Jack rounded on him, angry but whispering.

'That was supposed to be in the coffin with Grandpa.'

'Nasty thing. Shouldn't be part of a Christian burial.'

'Since when did you get religion?'

'You can take it back where it came from.'

'That would have meant a lot to him.'

'Well it's too late now. I'll find something to wrap it in.'

Harry strode off, shoulders stiff like he was biting back another comment. As Jack turned, holding the carving, it seemed the figurehead watched Harry go, not Jack. There was a darkness about it that wasn't just its colour, it was more like a shape that sucked in the light. If it hadn't already been in shadow when Jack propped it up against the fence, George would have checked to see if it threw one. It looked frigging evil and, if she had been a kid, it would have scared the shit out of her. She stared at it after the crowd drifted back to the lawn, and it stared back like it was aware. George swallowed, forcing back a weird sense that it knew her. More than that, she could believe it knew she was afraid. In all this crowd, was there only her and the little girl who could see that? It was unsettling in the way that thunder from an empty sky is unsettling. It makes you look around and shiver and wonder what the feck is going on. In the end, George turned away, the first one to blink, and gulped wine.

Behind her the funeral was turning into a party. There was no grieving, no tears, no retelling of happy memories. The children were the first into the pool. Tilly jumped in after them, wearing a bikini that bulged like her kids' flotation rings. One or two of the other parents changed into cozzies and joined them, and within a few minutes the focus had shifted to the poolside. Harry disappeared into a wooden changing hut, shouting at his wife to bring towels and spare costumes.

George wasn't tempted. She hadn't had a reaction like that about object, a thing, since she was a teenager and saw an ancient stone head in the British Museum. Aztec, or something. It was only carved stone, like the figurehead was only carved wood, but she knew something unspeakable had happened around it. She'd even thought that the horror was still inside it.

So she hung back, wishing she could go back to the yard. Soon only Jack, Charlotte and George were left on the lawn, looking over the hedge at the crowd around the pool, until Harry emerged from the changing hut. He strutted round the side of the pool, running his thumbs backwards and forwards inside the waistband of his swimming shorts and laughing with the people already in the water. He had a good body for a guy who must be late fifties, barrel chested and muscled like a man who worked out a lot, and he knew it. George could tell that by the way he called out to people. The words might have been 'having fun?' but the message was 'look at me'. And he didn't just jump into the water: he bombed, showering anyone still on the poolside. When he surfaced and stood, laughing, shaking the hair out of his eyes, the water had turned the hairs on his back from blond to a dark, streaky pelt. For a moment George closed her eyes, and the image of him silhouetted against the water stayed printed on her mind in shades of brown. She rarely liked people with browns. Too frigging opinionated.

'Come on, Jack, come and join us.' Harry had spotted the three of them still up on the lawn. He crouched in the water, his arms lying on the surface, shoulders glistening. There was an edge to the words that made them a command, not an invitation.

Jack shook his head, pulling back. Charlotte's hand came up and touched his shoulder in the first act of intimacy George had seen between them.

'Some other day, perhaps.'

His mother hurried down the steps to the pool deck, clasping an armload of towels. 'You've still got your old swimming shorts upstairs, love.'

'No thanks, Mum.'

Harry's hand smacked the surface, making a small splash of irritation. 'Get in here, both of you. Let's be a family, for once.' His smile hardened. Harry Ahlquist didn't like to be refused.

'I'd rather not.'

Tilly turned, standing belly-deep with a child in the crook of her arm, squashing it against a struggling bikini. Her eyes were on Charlotte, even though she spoke to her father.

'Leave them, Dad, if they think they're too good for us.'

Charlotte tugged at Jack's sleeve while Jack and Harry glared at each other.

'Time to go, darling. We need to run George home.'

Harry's jaw tightened so that small cords of muscle appeared in his cheeks. 'Bit stuck up for us, are you?'

'Bye, Dad.' Jack turned away.

'Too snooty, eh? So what's different about you?'

'Yeah, Jack, what's different?' The sunlight turned the glare around Tilly into an acid green.

Jack froze, and took one deep breath with his nostrils flaring before spinning round and lurching down the steps to the poolside. Charlotte rushed after him, reaching out a hand to restrain him. '*No, Jack!*' But the shirt she tried to grab was already being pulled over his head.

'What's different, eh?' The shirt landed in the hedge. The tension across Jack's shoulders twisted into wires up his neck, tight as a boat's backstay. He bent over, and a shoe spun through the air to clatter against a table.

'Don't, Jack.' Charlotte put her arm across his back, but he shrugged her off and almost fell over as he slipped off the other shoe. 'Jack, not like this!'

She was shouting, but Jack ignored her.

'What's different, you ask?' He pushed his trousers down below his knees and George tensed, wondering what the feck was happening. She gasped when he kicked out of them to stand in his boxer shorts, hands gripped into fists at his side. 'That's what's different. Now *back off.*'

On the far side of the pool, Jack's mother screamed and raised both hands to her mouth, dropping her armload. A blue-striped beach towel slipped off the tumbled mass and unrolled itself into the water. The party noise faded. Even the children shut up, and looked at the adults, but the adults were all looking at Jack.

His right leg was normal. Muscular. Hairy. Toned. So was his left, down to the knee. The knee itself and the top of the calf was a mess of white scar tissue, like melted candle wax, and the calf ended in a stump and the thin, shiny, metal shaft of an artificial limb. The foot still wore its sock and looked the proper shape, but was too big for the spindly stick above it. Jack's mother sank onto a plastic seat, hands still at her mouth, weeping noisily with her eyes locked on the leg. Harry just stared, his mouth slack.

'Badly done, Jack.' Charlotte retrieved a shoe from under a table, and pulled Jack's shirt out of the hedge. She pushed it into his chest and grabbed his arm to turn him towards the steps. 'Badly done.'

IV: HARRY

Harry Ahlquist went to Eddie's cottage straight after breakfast. The wife insisted. Said he had to talk before they lost their son for ever. He'd tried Jack's mobile all evening, after the funeral, but Jack hadn't answered. 'They'll be staying at Eddie's cottage', the wife said. 'Forget the office. Get down there and talk to him. And take that ugly bit of wood with you while you're about it.'

She had every right to be upset. So was Harry. Upset and angry. What the hell had been going through Jack's head, to lose a foot and not tell them? It was humiliating to find out that way, in front of everyone.

The Slut opened the door and they stared at each other without speaking. He'd hoped she'd have gone back to their apartment. Then her eyes dropped to the bundle in his arms. It must have looked a bit strange, still wrapped in a rug.

'Is that a weapon or a peace offering?'

'Old Eddie's carving. Jack left it behind.'

'You'd better come in.' She stood aside, inviting him into his own father's house, where she was slumming around in a loose shirt and no bra. 'Jack's upstairs. I'll call him.'

For a moment he stood in the front room, staring at used glasses and a nearly empty bottle of whisky, but there was no way she was going to make him feel like a guest in that house, so he walked through the kitchen into the garden, sniffing at the sight of dirty dishes piled in the sink, and at the litter of takeaway wrappers on the counter. Just like he thought: she was a slut.

He parked Old Eddie's dragon on the outside table and sat there until she came out with a pot of filter coffee and two mugs.

'He's coming. I'll leave you two to talk.' She sounded like a stuck-up receptionist.

Jack looked a mess: bloodshot eyes that blinked at the sunshine, unshaven, pasty skin, shirt hanging open. He was wearing chinos and high-ankle, soft boots, and Harry really couldn't tell, apart from the limp. They stared at each other across the table.

'If you've come to shout, I'm feeling a bit fragile this morning.'

That hurt. 'I've come to talk, not shout. I'd like,' Harry swallowed. '*We'd* like to understand.'

'I need coffee.' Jack swung his leg over the bench, and the sock on his false foot was loose and floppy above the ankle, too big for the shaft. For a moment, Harry was too choked to speak.

'Look, I'm sorry I did that with Mum there.' The boy gabbled out an apology, talking too fast in a voice that was gravelly and hung-over. 'I just lost it. Far too bloody theatrical. I made a fool of myself and I feel really bad about Mum.' He poured coffee and held one mug close to his face with both hands, blinking across it.

'Why hadn't you told us, man?'

Jack blew steam off his coffee and said nothing.

'We'd have helped, we'd have been there for you...'

'Would you?' Jack's eyes snapped up as he cut Harry off. 'Like you were "there for me" at my wedding?'

'That's different.'

'Is it? If you won't be there for the good times, I'm hardly likely to go running to you in the bad times.'

'She's wrong for you, Jack.' Harry regretted saying that as soon as he spoke. He always seemed to say the wrong thing with Jack, and this wasn't going how he'd planned.

'Don't you think that's for me to decide?'

Harry swallowed, wondering how to dig his way out. He'd come to mend things, not make them worse.

'I wanted to ask about your leg. See how we can help, you know?'

'Nah. Finish what you started, Dad. Tell me what gives you the right to say my wife is wrong for me.' He spoke real quiet, but hard at the same time, like the safety catch on a rifle.

'No. I don't want to make things worse.'

'Too upmarket for you, is she?'

Harry winced. The truth was painful. But that wasn't all of it, not by a long shot. He paused, wondering if he should say more. Hell, if not then, when they were putting their cards on the table, he might never do it.

'We saw her, once, before you married. That time we came over to your place.'

'Go on.'

'You was still on duty, so your mum and me went to the beach. *She* was there, though she didn't see us.'

'And?'

'With a girlfriend.' Two lovely women holding hands on an empty stretch of beach. Too far away to recognise them, without the binoculars. Harry often took binoculars to the beach, for seabirds and the like.

'So?'

'They were kissing.'

'Girls do.'

'Not like that.' Not with tongues, like lovers. Not with their hands on each other's backsides. 'She'd pushed her knee between the other girl's legs! For God's sake, you was engaged!'

The boy didn't show any surprise. He just blinked and sipped coffee.

'You didn't think to talk it through with me?'

'Every time we saw you after that, you was with her. Never

on your own.' Jack looked at him, waiting for more. 'Maybe one day you'll find out that the hardest part of being a parent is when you see your kid making a mistake, and you can't do nothing about it. Then the edict came about fancy dress for the wedding.' Harry swallowed. He never thought he'd grovel to his own son. 'Maybe I over-reacted.'

'And remind me, thinking about being there, what was your excuse for not coming to my passing-out parade?'

'I did. Came to watch you get your green beret. So proud, I was.' Now the boy was getting picky. Trying to make him squirm.

'You came when I passed the Commando Course, yes. You missed my commissioning parade.'

'Something came up at work.'

'Bullshit.'

Harry wasn't going to respond to that. One more smart-arse swipe and he'd walk out.

'Was that because you decided I was making another mistake?'

Harry flinched again at the bitterness in Jack's voice. Jack kept going, driving his point deep.

'You've no idea what that meant to me. Commissioned from the ranks. Chosen to lead the best troops in the world.'

'You weren't meant to be an officer. All that lah-di-dah poncing around. It's not us. I didn't want you to be hurt.'

'And Harry Ahlquist always knows best.'

'Like I said, something came up.' Harry stopped when he saw the look in Jack's eyes. There was such hurt and anger there. They glared at each other, cradling coffee, with the sun warm on Harry's head. He took a deep breath, forcing himself to stay calm, and nodded down towards Jack's leg.

'Are you going to tell me what happened?'

'IED. Underneath a truck.'

That figured. More casualties in the Middle East were caused by improvised explosive devices than by bullets.

'Since when did we have troops on the ground again?'

'There are a few small teams still working with local forces. Trainers, mostly. Some Special Forces. I had to go and see one of the local elders, and made a bad call. They were waiting for us.'

'Anyone else hurt?'

'Two of my men died.' Jack was holding himself together, Harry could tell. His voice was tight with emotion.

'Do you want to talk about it?' Harry tried to sound as understanding as he could.

'No!' Then, more quietly, 'not particularly.'

The kitchen window behind him reflected a shiny, picture-postcard view of pine trees and blue water, making it hard to see inside, but the fanlight was open and Harry heard a slight sound from within. *She* was listening. Bitch.

'I brought the figurehead back.' Harry nodded at the rug roll lying on the table.

'It should have been in the coffin. You said you'd put it in the coffin.'

'It don't feel right. It feels, well, nasty.' Harry couldn't explain. It was the wife who had put her foot down. Went all churchy on him and said they couldn't have a pagan idol in a Christian ceremony. She wouldn't even have it in the house. It was unlike her to come on so strong. Anyway, Old Eddie wouldn't know.

'But we could do better.' Harry squeezed jollity into his voice. 'Why don't we scatter his ashes at sea? From *Draca*?'

A pause. 'OK. I think he'd like that.'

'You and me? Together?'

It was the first time Harry had seen the boy smile in a long time. It wasn't a warm smile, not the great beaming grin he had as a kid, but it was a beginning.

'I brought the ashes with me as well. They're in the car.' Now it was Harry's turn to talk too fast. He almost tripped over the bench as he went to fetch them.

Jack looked shocked when Harry put the container on the table. Stared at it like it might bite. It was a cardboard cube inside a smart carrier bag with a string handle, more like something from an upmarket store than someone's remains, and it was heavy enough to land on the table with a bit of a thump. Jack swallowed before he spoke.

'*Draca* needs a lot of work. It'll be a few months before we can take Grandpa to sea.'

'Old Eddie ain't going anywhere.'

'I thought I might do her up myself. I've no job to go back to.'

'How will you fund that?' Jack wouldn't be able to use Eddie's money until they were granted probate on the will. Harry knew. He'd checked.

'The bank said they'll lend me money, based on the will and the probate valuations from the solicitor.'

'I still think Eddie was wrong to give you everything. Tilly's awful cut up about it.' Maybe he shouldn't have said that, but he'd dropped his guard after Jack smiled.

'It's what Grandpa wanted.' Now Jack was tense again.

'He wasn't himself, at the end. You didn't, er, say anything to him? To persuade him?'

'No.' Harry wasn't sure whether that tightening of Jack's hands around his coffee mug showed he was angry or defensive.

'Tell you what.' Harry had been thinking about this. 'You share it with Tilly and we'll say no more about it. Nothing for me. Just you and Tilly. Can't say fairer than that.'

Jack put his mug down and poured coffee into it as if it was a job that took all his concentration.

'Restoring *Draca* will take money. Quite a lot of money.'

'Yeah, but…'

'And I need somewhere to sleep near the boatyard. I can't commute from our flat. Not every day.'

'It ain't fair on Tilly…' The boy could be so bloody stubborn, sometimes.

'It's what Grandpa wanted.'

'You already said. He wasn't right in the head.'

They were like a pair of dogs, circling around the same pile of vomit. And just when they'd started to talk reasonably. Harry stood to go before he lost his temper.

'We'll talk about it some other time.'

'Deep joy.'

Jack didn't get up as he left.

The Slut was waiting for him with her backside against the driver's door of his Jaguar, and her arms folded across her chest. Harry walked up to her, and waited for her to speak.

'Harry, a word of advice. If you love him, back off.'

'Don't tell me how to handle my son.' Harry was already pretty riled.

'Someone needs to.'

'Get out of my way, woman.'

'You have no idea what he's been like since he got back, do you?'

Of course he didn't. They'd hardly spoken.

'He's had four jobs in three months. He's drinking too much, he's not sleeping and he's a pain in the arse to live with.'

'So why are you telling me?'

'I don't give a shit what you think of me, Harry, but restoring *Draca* would be good for Jack. For the first time since he was wounded, he's got a project. He's motivated, and he won't have a boss breathing down his neck. So back off and let him sort himself out doing something he enjoys.'

As she finished that little speech she pushed herself away from the car.

Harry didn't answer. Just got in and drove off.

Of course she wouldn't want him to give back the money.

Chapter Three: Drekahōfuō

(Old Norse: the dragon head on a ship's bow)

From the saga of King Guthrum

King Guthrum gathered a great army and harried in the Westlands, the folk fleeing before him wherever he went, for it was known that he had all men killed that stood before him. Then King Alfred came against him with an army of the West Saxons and there was straightaway a great strife both hard and long, but the end of it was that neither side had the victory.

After the battle King Guthrum withdrew to Jarvic[1] and gave his son Jarl Harald charge over a mighty force of longships. He commanded Harald to sail straightway to the South and to fall upon the great harbour of the West Saxons at Fyrsig, where all the longships of his fleet might safely lie. Furthermore Jarl Harald was not to harry the lands in between, lest the news of his army fly to Alfred like fire in dry grass, but was to fall upon Alfred by surprise from the South while Jarl Guthrum came against him from the North.

1. York.

Now Harald Guthrumsson was a great warrior and had good opportunity of choosing himself the foremost in strength or boldness, and many mighty men followed him and offered their sons to be his bodyguard and berserks. In Harald's dragonhead ship, the stem men were the best chosen, for they bore the jarl's standard, and the berserks took their place in the part which went from the stem back to the bailing place. Fearless were these men, strong as bears and mad like wolves. They bit their shields, and filled their foes with terror, and neither fire nor steel would deal with them.

Thus sailed Harald Guthrumsson with one hundred and twenty ships and half the army of King Guthrum.

I: JACK

As the sounds of his father's car receded, Jack stared at the carrier bag that his father had dumped beside the carving, dropping it with as little respect as a bag of shopping. Grandpa wasn't the first person Jack had known who'd died, but he was the first one that he'd loved. He'd never before had that jolt at the sight of a cardboard brick that was all that was left of a person. In Afghanistan he'd had to go through the personal effects of a dead marine, sending home treasures and tokens of endearment that, despite his efforts, would spill a fine, red, desert dust when the box was opened. It was desperately sad, but it didn't touch him personally in the same way. There was even a guilty sense of relief that he was still alive and it wasn't his effects that were being sent home. It had been close, though. The day that marine died, Jack had dug a bullet out of his own body armour.

And when marines died, they were blown away from unreality. They did not belong to the place that had destroyed them.

But Grandpa had belonged to this place. This place had belonged to him. The familiar scene of boats on the water should be different without him. Jack half expected to find a razor cut across the view like a slice across a sail; some rip that had opened, pulled Grandpa through and sealed itself behind him. There was just an ugly purple cube inside a bag as a sign that he'd gone, the way a suicide might leave a pile of folded clothes on a beach. Two bricks' weight of granules instead of a note.

Charlotte, coming through the kitchen behind him, didn't belong here. Jack decided he partly belonged; upstairs the small bedroom with the single bed still displayed Grandpa's cherished fragments of his childhood.

Charlotte's hand touched his shoulder, balancing herself as she swung her leg over the bench. Even in his hung-over state, the flash of her thigh was distracting.

'Hey, chum.' She put a fresh mug on the table.

'Hey, Lottie.' 'Charlotte' had always seemed too formal a name, unless he was ticked off with her.

'Thanks. For sticking up for me, I mean.'

'I didn't want to give him the satisfaction of being right.'

The flow of her movement checked and she settled more cautiously onto the bench, staying silent while she emptied the last of the coffee into her mug. As she replaced the pot, she stretched to squeeze his hand. 'Poor Jack. I really thought it could work. You and me.'

'So did I.' He paused. In front of them, the trees on Witt Point appeared motionless in the heat, but their reflections in the water were hazed by wavelets, and ripples ran through the reeds in the shallows. There would be enough wind to sail, out in the harbour.

'Why *did* you marry me, Lottie?'

She thought for perhaps two breaths before answering. 'Do you remember how we were always laughing together, before you were wounded? Those golden months between Afghanistan and the last, bloody deployment? You were the best male friend I'd ever had. The closest I'd been to loving a man.'

'Were?'

'Are. Even after all the crappy times since you came back.'

'We did have a lot of fun, didn't we?' He smiled, until he realised he'd used the past tense. Talking was easy in this place, side by side, staring at the view rather than each other.

'I think I was a bit in awe, as well, even before the honours list came out. We all were. And we were so perfect, the handsome hero and the general's daughter, the must-have couple for any gathering. Maybe I got lost in our own mystique.'

Jack formed a question in his head, testing the words, wanting to keep the tone light.

'I remember your father spouting off at dinner, once.' Jack dropped his voice in imitation of the general's gruff pomposity, punctuating each phrase with bulldog puffs of air through his lips. 'Good God! When I joined the service, there were three absolute no-nos: druggery, buggery and treason.' He slapped the table in pretend anger. 'Now druggery earns a slap on the wrist and buggery is positively encouraged! Next thing we know, treason will be a matter of conscience.'

Charlotte laughed. Jack could do a pretty good imitation of her father.

'Daddy thinks the world of you. They both do. And they know things have been difficult.'

'You've never told them you're gay, have you?' Jack remembered the hurt on Charlotte's face at that dinner.

'I'm not gay, I'm bi.'

Jack shrugged. 'Bi, then.' He didn't challenge her. 'But have you?'

She shook her head. 'I think they were starting to suspect, though.'

'And marrying me gave you 'air cover'.'

'I hope I was never so cynical.'

'You should have told me though. Before we married. That's the only thing that still rankles.' His words tasted of strong coffee and stale alcohol.

'We've had this argument. I thought that part of me would go away.'

Jack opened his mouth and shut it again, realising they were being drawn back into a well-worn channel. They were quiet for a while, watching the view, until she touched his hand again.

'We're best like this, Jack, almost like brother and sister.'

'But it's not enough, is it? For either of us.'

'We make love, sometimes.'

'So when was the last time?'

Charlotte let go of his hand, and began fiddling with the frilly edging to the carpet around the carving.

'You've changed, Jack, since you were wounded. It was easier to love the laughing hero. You've been pretty hard to live with lately, chum.'

It was a morning for long pauses.

'That thing's looking at me.' Charlotte stared at the rug, where one corner had fallen open, exposing the carved head like a monster in a baby's blanket. The way the light caught its carved eye gave it life. From this angle, the gaping jaw was a lascivious grin rather than a snarl. Charlotte pulled her shirt closed across her chest and held her hand there, beneath her throat, as if she'd spotted a peeping Tom.

'It's got good taste.'

Charlotte stretched to spin the wrapping so that the head was pointing away from them, towards the water. 'I don't like that thing. It's creepy.' Her breasts slipped within her shirt as she moved, pushing free. Jack swallowed, and shuffled a little closer on the bench.

'It's growing on me. Grandpa used to talk to it, like a pet.'

'Bloody ugly pet.'

A mile away over the water, the triangular sail of a yacht ghosted seawards. Jack put his arm around Charlotte's back and let his hand rest on her hip.

'I wondered, you know, Lottie. Even before we married. The way you look at beautiful women, it's the way I look at them. The way I look at you.' There was something about this place that inspired calm. It made for honesty.

'But you still married me.'

'Being with you was always so easy, so natural. And when I walked into the officers' mess with you on my arm, I was king of the world.'

'Nothing to do with me being a general's daughter then?'

Ouch. 'I hope I was never so ambitious.'

'Do you want us to separate?' She said that so lightly that she might have been offering him a cup of tea. Jack thought long enough about his reply for her to turn and peer at his face.

'We're still friends, Lottie. Does that have to change?'

'No. Our trouble is that we don't love each other enough to make a go of it, even if I could, and we like each other too much to end it.'

'But I think I'll live here for a while. Restore the boat. Try and make sense of my life. Think things through.'

'I'm cool with that. Don't spend too much time on your own, though. It makes you moody, these days.'

'Then come and see me. Come for weekends.' The thought of not seeing her, of drifting apart, was suddenly frightening.

'I could.'

'How about you, Lottie? Do you want to separate?'

'Nah. I think playing 'happy families' suits us both.'

Jack sipped coffee. They hadn't spoken so calmly since he was repatriated. Perhaps being in the cottage, away from their normal lives, was letting them look back on themselves from the outside. Charlotte pushed a curl of dirt from a whorl in the wood with a fingernail, grey spiralling over rose.

'What are you thinking about, Lottie?'

'George.'

Jack's shoulders slumped as he remembered the funeral.

'Someone else who deserves an apology.'

'Precisely. Let's go down there later, after I've checked in with the office.'

Jack groaned. He didn't want to see George Fenton, not until he was feeling stronger. He'd grovelled enough for one day.

Two hours later they sat together in the cottage's front room, Charlotte in an armchair with an iPad in her lap, bare legs stretching forever from beneath the modesty square of plastic. Jack sat at the desk, flicking through Eddie's diary of four years before, reading the entries for the Channel Islands voyage, and then on into Eddie's last excursions of the season, after Jack had returned to his unit:

23rd September. Wind WSW Force 5, falling. Fair.

Had an overnight sail with the usual reprobates from the yard. Rode the Westerly flow and put into Dartmouth for the night. Had a bit of a run ashore and were late starting back. Tide turning against off Anfel Head. Wind picked up. Seas short & ugly.

The lads said I carried too much sail. Dangerous, they said, and not the first time.

But Draca loved it. You could feel her come alive. That dragon on the bow is like the chrome Jaguar badge on Harry's car bonnet; makes you feel strong & want to go faster. It was like she was playing with the waves, dancing, and I was dancing with her.

I gave Chippy Alan the helm, and let him feel the ship at her best, but he was frightened. Not like him. We sort of fell out.

Wimps.

Charlotte's phone rang, and she answered it in the clipped, high-energy voice she kept for business.

'No problem... yah... I'm on the case...' She sat straighter in the chair as if her body was part of the voice, making her shirt gape. From time to time she'd lean forward for something in her briefcase, then sit back, not meeting Jack's eye. She seemed even more feminine in this most masculine of rooms. Ceiling-high shelves filled with books, model boats, charts and nautical instruments. No softness anywhere, except for the leggy woman with the tantalising shirt draped into a leather armchair. She made the Viking longship model on the shelf beside her look like a virility symbol.

10th October. Wind ESE, 5, gusting 7. Rain.

The dragon wanted the sea. So did I. Neither of us liked Draca being cooped up at the mooring.

I called them all. Again. Everyone who sailed with me, the men who used to badger me to come along. Now every last one of them said no. Couldn't they feel the joy of a strong ship in a storm?

I took her out anyway. One last trip before winter. Jack should have been there, just to see me. Seventy-five years old and still sailing single-handed.

Wind was light in the morning. Managed to hoist the mainsail on my own, too. Ran the halyard to the windlass. Bit slack but I did it. She holds her course at almost any point of the compass, if you lash the tiller. And I set the square sail, but that's easy after the main. Running before the wind with the square sail set, off Anfel Head, we were invincible.

But Draca didn't want to come home. Anfel Head again. Threw a fit when I turned, and fought me, all the way back. I think the dragon knows his friends are down there. The oath-breakers in the realm of Rán.

And that blow wasn't forecast. Wind 4, they said, rising 5. We had Force 7 and I couldn't reef. No strength in my hands.

Now Draca's hurt. We came back on the engine, trailing rigging. It was all I could do to keep the lines inboard and clear of the prop. If that had fouled we'd have been in real trouble.

Feel bad. Feel a fool as well. Don't want to see the cowards at the yard. If I'd have had help, we could have reefed.

But, now I'm back, I don't think it would have been such a bad way to go. I think if I went out again, and there was a big wave, I'd die happy. Especially in The Race, fighting a storm, like the oath-breakers. I think Draca would like that, too. End it together.

Jack frowned. 'The dragon wanted the sea...' Grandpa had imbued the carving with life and will. And what did he mean by 'the dragon knows his friends are down there...'? Rán, Jack knew, was the Nordic sea goddess, who harvested the souls of drowned sailors. Perhaps the cancer had been in Grandpa's brain earlier than they thought. Outside, the sun was on the water and a sailing breeze stirred the leaves; the wind was picking up. Inside, a fly beat itself against the window behind the net curtains: hum–smack, hum–smack, hum–smack. It evaded Jack's efforts to brush it through an open pane, and found another square of glass to assault. No matter. Chasing the fly had only been an excuse to stand behind Charlotte's chair and slide his hand into her shirt, but she pushed him away, tutting her irritation.

'Lottie, living with you is like being a kid in a sweet shop who's told he can't taste the goodies.'

'I'm 'working from home'.'

'Neither am I.'

'Maybe later.' Her fingers danced over the iPad, and Jack gave up. Above the desk, tufts of bookmarks waved from a mighty tome of Nordic sagas. He pulled it down, opened it at random and grunted in frustration when he saw it was written in Old Norse, with margin and footnotes in Danish. A yellow, sticky note pointed at a single word, *haugbúi*, with a caption written in Eddie's awkward scrawl: *lit. 'cairn-dweller'. Ghost, undead man.*

Jack put the book back, uncomfortable. Beside him, Charlotte stretched in her armchair, pulling her arms high and wide, and arching her back in a way that made him want to throw her bloody iPad out of the window.

'Let's go and see George.'

'I thought you were working.'

'M'bored. Done enough to show willing.'

'I can think of more exciting things to do.'

'Let's get it over with.'

They couldn't even flirt any more.

II: JACK

Charlotte dressed up for the boatyard, enough to make Jack wonder who she was trying to impress. Wide-brimmed straw hat, supercool shades, crisp cotton and a lot of leg. Shoulder bag with phone, iPad and suncream. Charlotte stepped through the boatyard like an exotic wading bird, tottering on heels that did wonders for her calves and nothing for her balance.

Jack's mood lifted at the sight of *Draca*. *His* ship. Or would be, soon. She'd been beautiful, once. Still was, until you came close, even without her mast, even with the tide so far out that only the aft end of her keel and the tip of her rudder were in water. She lay on blocks, tied to pilings and with 'legs' of timber supporting the hull, like a grand old lady on crutches. The bowsprit was still rigged, stabbing inland from beside the stem post and adding a fencer's elegance to a bluff bow, but her stern gave her grace. It swept up from the keel into a slender counter that would stretch out over the water when she was afloat, lovely enough to take your breath away.

'Is that it?' Charlotte's expression was unreadable behind the shades.

'I said she needed work.'

Jack walked on. He'd seen George out on one of the pontoons, and wanted to meet her in the open, not in her office like a schoolboy in the headmaster's study. He braced himself as they converged on *Draca*.

It was easier to apologise than he expected. Maybe the warmth of Charlotte's greeting helped. George brushed away his fumbled words, once she'd disengaged from Charlotte's hug, saying it was 'all cool'. She stood in an assertive, shoulders-back slouch with her fingertips pushed into the pockets of her shorts, a pose that went more with an old gaffer in a flat cap and dirty overalls, not a young woman in baggy shorts and a tight, hooped T-shirt. She reminded Jack of young marines, just out of training, who can scowl because they're trying to look hard.

'Have you decided what you're going to do with *Draca*?' George lifted her chin towards the hull.

'I'm going to restore her. Bring her back to her former glory. She's mine now, or will be when we're granted probate on Grandpa's will.' And George's hairstyle was strange, too. Close-cropped at the back, like an old-fashioned schoolboy's, and an orange streak through the front.

'Good. I'll send Chippy Alan over, our shipwright. He'll have a look at her with you and you can agree what's needed.' George turned, tilting her head to look Charlotte in the eye. 'Do you sail, Charl?'

'Charl?' Jack didn't think anyone had ever called her that before.

'No, but I'd love to learn.' Charlotte's smile broadened.

'I'll take you out, if you like. Are you staying long?'

Charlotte made a knees-together, bum-out squirm of delight.

'Leaving early in the morning.' The shades came off so that George could have the full, big-brown-eyes treatment. 'But I could come back at the weekend?'

George shook her head. 'Weekends are busy. Plus I need to keep the charter boats for clients.' She paused again, sniffing the wind, eyes on the sky. 'It's quiet today. All the kids are still at school. Take you out now, if you like, while Jack and Chippy talk about ropes and planking.'

Jack was on *Draca*'s deck when they walked out onto one of the pontoons. They were laughing together like schoolgirls playing 'dressing-up' games. Charlotte was in borrowed clothes, too loose on the top and too short in the leg. Her hair flowed in a ponytail behind a baseball cap, and her feet were pushed into canvas slip-ons so that she moved flat-heeled, like an athlete rather than a model. He watched them, bemused by their instant friendship, until the rattle of the ladder against the ship's side told him someone was coming aboard.

A tanned, lined face appeared, framed by tufts of grey hair under a dark, Breton cap. The man beneath the cap climbed with the steady pace of someone who has learned to take life as it comes. He paused at the top to catch his breath, holding on to the projecting length of ladder, and nodded at Jack.

'Chippy Alan.' He didn't smile. 'Sorry to hear about your grandfather.' Chippy spoke as he moved, steadily, the speech of a man who worked with his hands, who thought much and said little. 'Bit of a wild one, but I liked him. I'd have come to the funeral, but one of us had to stay here.' He followed the line of Jack's eyes to where George and Charlotte were pulling the sail cover off a small keelboat.

'Glad she's getting out. She works too hard.'

Chippy looked around him. They stood in the debris of the cockpit, which was sunk perhaps two feet below the level of the deck, shallow enough to drain into the sea, and protected by a high, teak coaming. The last time Jack had stood there, with George, he'd rocked on his feet in water, illogically surprised only to feel cold, soaking socks on one foot. Now the water had drained or dried to leave smeared dirt.

'Bit of a mess, isn't it?' Chippy bent to pick up a tangle of rigging, and rubbed his thumb over the ropes. 'I wouldn't trust my life to that no more. Chuck it?' At Jack's nod he heaved it over the side, where it splatted onto the blocks beneath. 'Best get started then.'

Two hours later they again sat together in the cockpit. The cabin below held a jumbled stack of deck panels and fittings that they'd lifted to examine the massive, oak hull frames beneath. Some of the two-inch-thick elm planking between the frames would have been Eddie's work of forty years before. Jack had managed to shift enough of the remaining ballast beneath the sleeping cabin to get to the mast footings, a heavy job moving iron bricks in a cramped space. 'Got a bad back,' Chippy said, excusing himself, but Jack didn't mind. There was only space down there for one person.

'Biggest damage is in the mast footings, but we was expecting that.' Chippy sat, very upright, on the helmsman's bench aft, with one hand resting on the tiller like an old man of the sea. 'At least the hull seems sound. Bit o' rot in some of the oak frames, but not so bad that we can't cut it out and scarf in new. Might be worth strengthening the scarf joints with extra timbers.'

Scarf joints. Timbers. Even, once, the richly evocative 'futtocks'. Chippy spoke the language of shipwrights. It might have been a younger Grandpa sitting there.

'More rot in the deck, but we may be able to patch that. Depends how deep it goes.'

Over Chippy's shoulder, the harbour shone in the afternoon light. Boats were heading back towards the marina like white-winged birds coming home to roost.

'New mast, of course, but then you knew about that. Your gaff and boom are fine.' These were the spars that ran above and below the mainsail, stretching it into its irregular, rectangular shape.

'Your standing rigging, stays and the like, is sound. Probably needs a new dressing of linseed oil.' Eddie had chosen traditional hemp rope rather than modern steel rigging. 'But a lot of your running rigging is worn.' Running rigging hoists and trims the sails, the sinews and tendons to the sails' muscle.

Jack looked away, wondering how to ask about his grandpa's last sailing trips. One sail moved erratically across the harbour, making sudden corrections like a learner driver. Jack wished he'd brought binoculars.

'Personally, I'd replace your sails.'

Jack switched his attention back to the old man at the tiller. Grandpa had fitted *Draca* out with canvas sails for authenticity, refusing to fit modern polyester fabric. They were still useable but were growing old and perhaps a little thin, like a shirt that has been worn too many times.

'That would cost a fortune.' And the old sails' faded russet colours were as much a part of *Draca* as Grandpa himself.

'Then treat 'em gently. She deserves some love and care.'

Chippy was quiet long enough for Jack's attention to wander back to the boats spread out across the water. It was curious to look at the hills and islands near Grandpa's cottage from this new perspective. The erratic boat was closer now, close enough to see that Charlotte was steering.

'Your grandpa was a shipwright, wasn't he? Like me?' Chippy stroked the woodwork by his hand, almost caressing it.

'That's right.'

'If you don't mind me asking, how does a shipwright afford a boat like this?'

Jack didn't mind. Chippy was growing on him, even if he had fallen out with Grandpa. 'My grandmother inherited money, and died young. Grandpa bought *Draca* as a wreck and restored her himself.' George and Charlotte's sail swayed from side to side as they changed position. George would bring her in.

'You sailed with him, didn't you?'

Chippy nodded. 'We was good friends for a while. I heard a lot about you. Dead proud of you, he was.'

'What went wrong, Chippy?'

'He went a bit wild.' Chippy bent to pick up a small brass tackle from the gratings. Jack recognised it as part of the system that lashed the tiller in place.

'In what way?'

Chippy spoke downwards, towards the tackle in his hand. 'Things changed, all in the space of a year. There was a group of us, see, who went out with him. Mostly retired folk, like him. A few of us still working. All men who liked to sail but couldn't afford a boat of their own. First sign we had that something was wrong was when he put that ugly great carving on the bow.'

'Grandpa was proud of his Viking ancestry.'

'Yeah, but it's a bit strange to spoil the lines of a lovely ship like this.'

'It became a kind of talisman for him.'

'But before that, he'd always taken care. Looked after the boat. Then he started taking risks. Chasing storms, carrying too much sail. We fell out.' Chippy shrugged, as if lifting regret from his shoulders.

'I found his diary. His mood seemed to change that year.'

'It reached the point where no one would sail with him no more. One of the group said he was like a man possessed, as if the boat had taken him over.'

'I wondered if the cancer was there long before we knew.'

'Maybe. But we'd been friends, see? Like a little club. He said things, hurtful things, like he wasn't himself. Then he took the ship out on his own in a bit of a blow. Crazy. An old man in a boat this size, in a gale. Sprung the mast. He was lucky to come back at all. Did he say anything to you?'

'At the time, only that he was giving up the sea. He said it was arthritis. "If you can't reef," he said, "you can't sail." He was pretty cut up about it.' Beyond his shoulder, George brought her boat alongside, very neatly.

Chippy stroked the timber by his hand again. 'Classic boats like this get under your skin, you know. Don't let her get too close.'

Beyond his shoulder, Charlotte and George had climbed onto the jetty and Charlotte was hugging George, life jacket crushed against life jacket. It seemed she'd enjoyed herself.

Chippy twisted to follow Jack's gaze. On the jetty, Charlotte pulled off her baseball cap and waved it at them, spilling a mane of brown hair that tumbled over her shoulder.

Chippy waved back. 'Shall we join the women?'

III: JACK

Jack took Eddie's last diary to bed that night. He had a niggling unease about that entry in the earlier volume about *the dragon knows his friends are down there. The oath-breakers in the realm of Rán...* It was too much like Grandpa's ravings about Vikings before he died. He had to push back a sense of intruding, almost of guilt, both at reading a private diary and at being in his grandfather's bedroom, even with Charlotte around to justify their taking the double bed. Perhaps especially with Charlotte around, performing her nightly grooming rituals in the bathroom next door.

1ˢᵗ January. Wind ENE, light airs, cold.

We like the fire by the boat seat. The dragon watches it with me now, in the darkness, and I can feel him come awake. The boat's wood clicks around us as the heat spreads, and the dragon shifts on the seat. I think it sees things in the flames. What would it tell me, if it could speak? This was more than a figurehead. They worshipped it like a god. Now we're just two old men staring into the fire and remembering the good times.

It saw movement, under the trees, before I did. I felt it tense. It knows whoever's there. Too dark to make anything out; just a shape moving in the darkness. It frightened me.

Jack looked up, frowning, remembering the movement he thought he'd seen under the trees, the night before Grandpa died. He'd visited Grandpa early in the New Year, probably within a day or two of that entry, and he'd seemed perfectly rational. Nothing to suggest that, in his eyes, the carving had life and personality. Jack was still staring at the wall, distracted, when Charlotte came back from the bathroom, wearing nothing but a towel turbaned round her hair.

Charlotte wore her nakedness lightly, as if it was her natural state. There was no display in the way she moved around the bedroom, no conscious allure, as if either Jack wasn't there or, at least, wasn't male. The sun on the water had bronzed her skin, leaving a pale shadow of the life jacket, a boundary between peaches and cream across her chest. She tugged on a thick, cotton nightdress that might have been designed by a Victorian penal establishment, and Jack's hopes sank. This was Charlotte-speak for 'not tonight'.

He lay on his side, watching her as she climbed into bed. He'd hoped that the morning's honesty might lead to intimacy, but she pulled the duvet up to her chin and made no move to come closer.

'You seemed to get on well with George, Lottie.'

'Mm. She's so wonderfully competent.' The sunlight had put the same kind of blush on Charlotte's face that she could wear after they'd made love. God, how long ago had that been?

'It looks like she's a good sailor.'

'She's going to give me some sailing lessons.' Charlotte turned to snap off the light.

'Oh?'

'Mm. You said to come back when I wanted.'

'Sure.' Jack paused, not sure if he could ask the question outright. 'She's an attractive woman, isn't she?'

'Sweet face. And a strong girl. Very *physical*. Must be all that hauling on ropes.'

Jack wished he could see Charlotte's face when she said that, but his eyes hadn't adjusted to the darkness.

'You fancy her, don't you, Lottie?' This was another 'first'.

Before the morning's conversation he could never have asked that question. Charlotte's tastes would have been the elephant in the room, known but never discussed.

Charlotte pretended to consider. 'Big shoulders for a short woman, but a very good body. Shame about the hair.'

This was bizarre. Jack reached out to touch her, sliding his palm up her leg, feeling the skin slip under the cotton.

'Lottie...'

'I've got an early start, Jack.' She turned away from him, mumbling her goodnight.

He was woken by a gentle vibration in the bed, a delicate shaking from Charlotte's side. A soft line of natural light, starlight perhaps, filtered over the top of the curtains, enough to show Charlotte's profile. She was on her back, mouth open, and Jack didn't understand what was happening until he made out the movement over her crotch and smelled her arousal.

'Let me do that, Lottie.' She froze, but he touched her face and let his fingertips trace downwards over her neck, her breast and the plain of her belly, where the nightdress was already bunched into folds.

Charlotte pushed his hand aside, spun onto her knees and sat astride him, coupling wordlessly, urgently. She rode him hard, eyes closed, until she reached a single, shuddering climax in which his own was incidental. Jack reached for her to pull her down, into his arms, but she slipped away from him and lay with her back bowed and her knees pulled up above her waist. He lay awake for a long time, staring at the ceiling, spent but somehow soiled.

He woke to grey, dawn light and a room filled with Charlotte's scent. She stood in front of the mirror, brushing her hair, wearing the same dark business suit that she'd worn to the funeral. Black seams ran down the back of her stockings into black shoes. Jack stood behind her and kissed her neck, his hands shaping her waist, and she turned to plant a farewell kiss on his cheek.

'I gotta go. Long drive. Early meeting.'

'Of course.'

'Bye, chum.' A touch on the face, a fleeting smile. The previous night wasn't mentioned.

The cries of the seagulls reminded him that *Draca* was waiting.

Chapter Four: Haugbúi

(Old Norse: ghost, undead man)

From the Saga of King Guthrum

Harald Guthrumsson's dragonhead ship flew so fast across the water that he entered the great harbour of the Saxons with just five of his ships. That night they stayed hidden behind an island, and his men lay in their ships without tjald[1] or any covering, that they might be ready for battle. There were those that counselled waiting, for they were yet few, but Harald believed in his strength and was bold, saying the fewer the warriors, the greater the honour. At daybreak while the folk yet slept he fell upon the fort called Fyrsig, charging out of the mist with ladders and axes.

And the joy of battle was with them, for it was a fight of which the skalds would sing; Harald Guthrumsson and his berserks-gang running shoulder to shoulder through the fort, killing as the Saxons dashed sleep from their eyes, before a shield-wall could be made. It was a sword-time, a blood-time, and Odin was with them.

After their victory Harald and his warriors made blood sacrifice

---

1. Awning.

to honour the Æsir. They brought with them bowls from the sacred places, some of copper, some of stone, and with them the holy arm-rings on which oaths were sworn, so that all the array of the temple was with them.

Then they slew captives and captured their blood in the bowls. With some they sprinkled their ships, and the rest they gave their dragonheads to drink, that the dragonheads might taste victory and know that they honoured the gods.

When he had given thanks thus, Harald feasted with his warriors.

I: GEORGE

George liked Charlotte coming over on weekdays for sailing lessons. 'Working from home,' Charl called it. It was good to have company, especially girl company, and there wasn't much of that round the yard. Some people like sailing on their own. George liked someone to talk to, and Charl was fun to be with. George would take her down the pub any time. Friendly, too. Most women with posh accents tended to get all superior with George, like Charl's mum, but Charl looked her in the eye and laughed a lot, like they were two naughty kids having a dare.

She reminded George of someone she knew at school just before her mum died. This girl was about a year older so she seemed all grown up, and like Charl she was tall and classy and beautiful, the sort of girl who's so popular she has friends dancing round her. George had known girls like that in other schools, but this one was different because she was kind and let George join her group. Those few months were George's happiest days at school. Any school. She may even have had a bit of a teenage crush on her. It went wrong, of course. George got too confident. Let her get close.

George's mum always said George had a healing touch, and George believed it because she'd massage her mum's shoulders and the sides of her head when she was sick, and it made her feel masses better. Sometimes George could make her sleep just by stroking her head. Her mum taught her some words to help her concentrate, like a little song, and showed her how to use her fingers, but the power, she said, was inside. The trick is to empty yourself, a bit like a trance. Healing can be unlocked but it can't be taught.

George never tried it at school. She didn't want to stand out. Not until there was snow that January and her friend took her toboggan out onto the hillside, but too many girls tried to sit on it. The friend came off with her hand wrapped in the tow rope but the toboggan kept going with the other girls, and next thing they knew there was a lot of screaming and her friend was holding up her hand with her fingers sticking out in all the wrong directions.

What George did was just instinct, and this girl was the best friend she'd ever had, so she stroked that mangled hand and muttered the words and let her mind find that special nothingness. As she pulled the fingers back into place she felt the heat flow through her hands into her friend and knew she'd be OK.

It must have looked more spectacular than it was. The fingers were probably only dislocated, although George didn't know that, so they just slipped back into place with a sound like rolling dice and George stroked her hand some more, just to make sure, feeling all warm and happy. Her friend stared at her hand and closed the fingers, ever so gently, and they worked. George smiled at her, pleased, but her friend pushed herself away with her good hand, sliding on the snow on her bum, staring at George, frightened. The next day no one wanted to be with her. They said she was a freak, a witch like in the films, but real. After that George didn't try healing any more, even when her mum fell really sick.

So when someone like Charl wanted to be friends, George was a bit wary. People like Charl lived at the centre of the crowd, while George lived on the edge, knowing that friendships can hurt. One step at a time. George thought about her a lot, wondering what she saw in her. But George's memory of Charl seemed to fit with yellow, and yellow is a happy, friendly colour. There were pinks in that mental image as well. Pinks go with love and friendship, but George wasn't sure if that was real or if it crept in because she really wanted the friendship to work. The mind can fool you like that, if you aren't careful.

But by the third lesson, George was starting to relax. It was a day of leaden cloud, low enough to brush the hilltops. Showery, summer rain made little plastic 'puk' noises against their foul-weather gear, but there was a good sailing wind so they went anyway. They were coming up to the harbour entrance, close-hauled into a south-westerly, when Charl interrupted a monologue about navigation buoys and rules of the road.

'Have you always sailed, George?'

'Nah.' George paused. Maybe it was time to release a little truth. It was no use pretending to have had a fairy-tale childhood. 'Me mum died when I was fourteen. Then I had three foster homes in two years, between that and leaving school, and the last one was here, on the coast. I got a job in a boatyard, weekends and holidays, and learned. It was the first time I'd found something I was good at.'

'What about your father?'

'Never knew him. I think he'd moved on before I was born.' Enough. George looked around her, and waved an arm at the harbour behind them. 'Did you know this is one of the largest natural harbours in Europe?'

Charl frowned as if she'd recognised the blocker. One day, George would tell her a bit more, but not yet. It'd be too embarrassing. George had met Charl's parents. She had two of them, and they looked rich. Charl hadn't been dragged around the markets in a camper van, selling hand-made charms and bracelets, astrology charts and magical pixies. All cash in hand, nothing to spoil the benefits. Charl's parents would have driven her to school in a flash car. George's mum waited at the school gates in baggy, Turkish trousers like an escapee from a harem. And there'd been lots of schools. Always moving on, always leaving debts behind them. When George was really young, she thought all families did this, but as she got older, kids noticed her mum was different, and kids are cruel.

After a pause, Charl reached over and squeezed George's hand where it rested on the tiller.

'George, you're awesome.' She sounded all soft and tender so George didn't know what to say.

'Here, you take her. Just keep her heading out to sea.' George handed over the tiller and settled back against the cockpit, just as a wave burst against the bow, spraying over Charl before she could duck.

'You beast! You did that deliberately.' Charl shook her head like a dog, with water running down her face and her hair turned to rats' tails. She blew a wet strand away from her mouth and began laughing, and George had an urge to give her a hug. They ended up huddled together in the corner of the cockpit where the cabin gave them some shelter from the spray, with Charl steering one-handed. Behind them stretched a meandering, novice's wake.

'How's Jack getting on, George?'

'With *Draca*? Much faster than I expected. He's there all hours.' He'd be at the yard before George, though she was an early starter, and still be there late into the evening. 'Chippy Alan will finish the structural stuff on the hull next week. Then we can step the new mast and rig her.'

'What's he like, around the yard?'

'He's a bit quiet. Withdrawn, like. Him and Chippy Alan get on all right.' Jack was friendly enough when they did speak, but they didn't talk much. She was a bit hurt by that.

'He wasn't always quiet. When we married, he was...' Charl lifted one hand and flapped it, like she was struggling for words. 'He was a god, a hero, and we were the golden couple.'

'What, a real hero?'

'They gave him a medal. Then he went off a second time, when he was wounded, and he came back changed. He'd have these brooding silences when I couldn't reach him. He'd start shouting if I tried too hard. Such rages. You saw one after the funeral.'

'It must be a bit harder than getting over man flu, having your foot blown off.'

'I stayed in the cottage, last night. It's getting worse. Like something's taking him over.'

George reached out and corrected the course herself rather than interrupt.

'We've had our ups and downs, Jack and me, but we're still good friends. More friends than anything else, these days.'

Charl's honesty surprised George. Her thigh pushed against George's, even through their foul-weather gear, but then it was a small cockpit.

'If you and Chippy could lift him out of himself from time to time, I think it would help.'

'Sure. I'll try.' George was well flattered.

Charl gave her an awkward hug through the bulk of their foul-weather gear.

'Thanks, George.'

'Aren't you afraid I'll make a play for your lovely husband?' George returned the pressure on Charl's leg, just so that she'd know that George was teasing.

'He is gorgeous, isn't he? When he's in a mood though, you could have him, with pleasure.' Charl didn't sound as if she was joking. 'But when we first married, before he was wounded, he was like a Great Dane, all bounce and bark. Sometimes I had this urge to throw him a stick.'

Laughing together was fun. Bonding.

'And you know what they say about men with big hands?' Charl nudged with her leg and opened one hand in her lap, suggestively. Her smiling eyes stayed on George's, as if she was testing her reaction.

George stood, uncomfortable, and scanned the horizon. Ahead of them a line of whitecaps, clear and sharp as a weather front on a forecast map, showed where the tidal flow sweeping round the bay clashed with the main stream flowing down the channel.

'Let me show you how to change tack.'

'What's happening over there?' Charl had seen it too.

'It's called The Race. Two streams merging. It comes and goes with the tides. The wind is pushing against the tide at the moment, so it would be a bit lumpy. It gets a lot worse under Anfel Head.' George pointed at the line of cliffs that swept away to the south.

'I don't mind living dangerously.' And that from a woman who'd squealed and grabbed George for support on her first outing.

'Nah. Maybe when you've a bit more experience.' George took the tiller and altered course. Charl had the confidence of someone who's never seen a bad sea up close and personal. Soon the wind was on the quarter, filling both sails in great, swelling curves.

'So how did Jack win his medal?' George asked as they settled on the new course.

'I heard more about it around the barracks than from Jack. I gather he ran up a hillside under fire to bring a machine-gun back into action after it was knocked out by an RPG.'

'RPG?'

'Sorry. Rocket-propelled grenade. I was a barracks brat, you see? I grew up knowing the lingo.'

'Watch your steering.' Charlotte had let them turn away from the wind, and the boat heeled as it caught them square on the beam.

'Sorry. Jack actually got knocked over when a bullet hit his body armour, but he just stood up and kept going. They say he shot two Taliban off the gun as they were turning it against his troop.'

'Wow.'

'Pretty awesome, huh? His men idolised him. His sergeant got quite emotional when he described that run. Imagine that, a hulking great marine sergeant going dewy-eyed. He said the hillside around Jack was boiling with bullet strikes.'

'Were many killed?'

'Marines? Amazingly, only one of the machine-gun team. Wolfe. I hardly knew him. The other one in that post was only knocked out by the grenade. What was his name? Miller, that was it, the one they all called 'Dusty'. He told me he came round, all groggy, just as the position was overrun. He saw them finish off Wolfe and turn on him, and then Jack came charging in and blew them away. One of the Taliban actually fell on top of Miller, they were that close. Miller made it sound like a spectacular goal at football.' Charl wiped her fingers over her eyes. Her voice caught a little as she continued. 'His Military Cross wasn't announced for a few months. He's very quiet about it, though. Never told his family.'

'Why not? I'd be dead proud, me.'

Charl thought for a moment. 'I'll let him tell you that, if the subject ever comes up. Anyway, by the time the honours list came out, he'd volunteered for another assignment. "Training job," he called it, though I think that may have been a cover story. Three men went with him: Dusty Miller, Chalky White, one other I can't remember. Miller and White came back in body bags, and Jack came home without a foot. And he's never forgiven himself.'

They were both silent, absorbed in their thoughts. The rain had stopped, lifting back into a sky of dirty cotton wool. Charl turned to George with the wind blowing her hair away from her face in raggedy streamers and emotion shining in her eyes.

'It's wonderful to be able to talk like this, George. It's good to be friends.' She put her arm around George's shoulders again, and squeezed. Charl was a woman who touched a lot. She hugged her again when they came ashore, squeezing George's body against hers as if that was the only way she could show how much fun she'd had.

'Come to the cottage on Sunday, George. Let's prise Jack away from the boat and have a barbecue.'

As George accepted, she wondered if Charl would have kissed her on the lips if she hadn't turned her cheek.

II: JACK

Jack was seeing things.

Two days before, he'd grabbed breakfast at the outside table, toast in one hand and a pen in the other, while he made a 'to do' list for *Draca*. The early sun had been low and dazzling across the water of the harbour, making him squint at his notebook, and out of the corner of his eye, Grandpa's legs had stretched out of the shell of the boat shelter. It had been such a natural, friendly sight that Jack didn't even look up. They moved, uncrossing and recrossing at the ankle, before that pulse of *wrongness* had Jack's skin prickling. The image had been so clear that he had walked down the lawn, swallowing in dry-mouthed disbelief, until he could see into the shelter as far as the seat. The dragon watched him back, alone, its mouth gaping in silent laughter. The shadow of a branch played across the bald patch of earth where Grandpa's feet had scuffed the grass bare.

And, more tangibly, when the girls came back from their sail, he'd just found his grandfather's flameproof Zippo lighter in one of the cockpit lockers. He was sure that locker had been empty. Jack picked it up, caressed the polished steel and flipped the lid. It needed refilling, but it still worked. It was such a personal, tangible relic that for a moment Eddie seemed supernaturally close. His hands had cut the timbers at Jack's feet, and had shaped the carpentry of the chart-table.

Jack held the lighter pinched between his fingers and rolled it along the top of the hatch, like a square wheel, listening to the crying of seagulls and the slap of halyards against aluminium masts. Wafting out of the hatch came the smell of newly cut wood and, still, the faint scent of French cigarettes. And on a far jetty, beyond the rotating corner of the lighter, *clunk*, Charlotte and George were embracing. *Clunk.* Still hugging. *Clunk.* With a kiss that was not quite a lover's kiss. They turned and walked down the jetty towards the office, looking at each other and laughing together like a pair of teenagers whose body language says *'I wanna be like you'.* They both carried a bag in their left hands with their life jackets hooked over their right shoulders in a way that pulled their open foul-weather jackets back from their curves. Synchronised allure. But who was displaying to whom?

Maybe it had been a mistake to bring it out into the open. In the past, Charlotte had been so discreet that he hadn't even had to look the other way. Jack lost sight of them among the boats.

Clunk, clunk. What would Grandpa say to him now? Would he be engaged in the restoration project, or would he think Jack had let him down by not scuttling the ship with him inside it? Would he understand Jack's horror of burning bodies? How he'd allowed a clinical cremation rather than risk the same stink that Chalky White and his own, roasting foot had made? Jack hadn't even held his father to his promise to cremate the figurehead with him.

'Sorry, Grandpa.' Eddie felt so close that it wasn't strange to speak out loud.

'*Draca* ahoy!'

Jack lifted his head over the rail. George stood below, looking up at him from beneath a baseball cap with 'Boss Bitch' embroidered above its peak. She'd discarded her foul-weather jacket and he had an echo of that first day when she'd challenged him from the bottom of the ladder. It might even have been the same tight, hooped T-shirt.

'We must stop meeting like this. People will talk.' Jack hadn't meant to flirt. It just came out.

George didn't smile enough. It transformed her face. A

broad, heart-shaped face, he realised, that tapered into a delicate chin. She had a way of standing with her tummy slightly out that made her look less lean than she was.

George lifted the cap and finger-combed a strand of orange hair out of her eyes. What was it that Charlotte had said? *Nice body, shame about the hair.*

'Me and Charlotte are going to the pub. Do you want to come?'

And she was his wife's girlfriend. Despite himself, he felt a stir of prurient interest. Just for a moment.

'Thanks, but I'll crack on here.' He hefted a sander lying by his elbow.

George looked disappointed. He could bet Charlotte wouldn't be.

That night in the cottage, he waited up for Charlotte.

And heard Grandpa.

He'd read somewhere that many people 'see' dead relatives after a bereavement. They say that the subconscious throws an image or a memory onto a place, so perhaps that was why he sometimes felt he had company.

The evening that he left Charlotte with George, it was a cough. Jack had pulled Grandpa's last diary out of the desk to kill time while he waited.

2nd January Wind NE, light airs, cold.

Jack's here. The change is shocking. Limping badly, using a stick. He's driving a little automatic with plenty of miles on the clock that he's bought with a 'resettlement grant'. Can't use a clutch pedal, he said, then bent down and rolled up his trouser leg. The poor kid. I had to sit down. I couldn't speak so I just hugged him. First time I'd cried in nearly forty years.

He hasn't told Harry and Mary. They've got a right to know, I told him, but he wants to find his own way and his own time. I didn't really understand why, until he told me what Harry had said when Jack was selected for officer training. So bloody proud, Jack was, until Harry crushed him. As good as told him he couldn't hack it.

Then Jack said he made a bad call on his last trip. Men died. 'I failed,' he said. 'I feel bad enough without Dad saying I told you so.'

So I'm sworn to secrecy. It shouldn't be too hard. It's not as if I see Harry much, and he already made his token appearance at Christmas.

Jack threw the dragon on the grass to make room for us both in the boat seat. Maybe I should tell him about the dragon. He ought to respect it a bit more.

I didn't have the heart to tell him my news. He could tell I was sick but I brushed his questions aside. Tomorrow.

Jack smiled to himself at the sound of Grandpa's rumbling, smoker's cough in the garden, that way he had of clearing his chest with lungfuls of salt air. Jack even started to put the diary away, guiltily, until he saw the ugly cube of ashes on the shelf and had another 'can't be' jolt. He walked out into the garden, feeling a fool but half expecting to see Eddie. It was still twilight, the impossibly late light of the longest days, and as he stared at inevitable emptiness he reassured himself with the thought that it must have been an evening walker on the coastal path.

No matter. Even if it wasn't a trick of the mind, having Grandpa around the cottage didn't frighten him.

He preferred Grandpa's company to Dusty Miller's. He didn't feel so bad about Grandpa.

3rd January. Light airs, variable, cold.

Hard to believe Jack's leaving the Royal Marines. They were his life. I remember when he first passed his Commando course he carried his green beret everywhere with him, even when he was in civvies. He'd take it out and brush it, smooth it down a bit, as if he couldn't quite believe he'd passed the course. Royal Marines Commando. The elite.

We lit the stove by the boat seat, opened a bottle of wine, and stared at the flames, and it seemed the right moment to tell Jack I had cancer. The smokes had done for me at last. I told him I'd rather go this way than as a senile wreck in an old people's home. At least I'll die while I'm still alive. Sometimes I believe that. It's a great idea until a doctor looks you in the eye and says you won't see another Christmas.

It was his turn to hug me, and that let out a lot of stuff that I'd bottled up inside me since the diagnosis. Twice in two days. After that we opened more wine, chucked another log on the fire, and got drunk together.

Afterwards, I put the dragon back, respectfully. I know all its dark secrets, now. We've spent a lot of time together these last few weeks, out in the boat seat, and I can guess what it's thinking. It wants open water. It wants a storm, and salt in its teeth. Well, it won't get that from me any more.

One last journey, perhaps, but not yet.

I haven't told Jack about the shadow in the trees. He might not believe me. Might think I'm mad.

I think he's a warrior. And if the dragon knows him he's a Viking. What does he want?

The old man had been a lot more delusional, a lot earlier, than Jack realised. He remembered that stay. Quite emotional. Understandably emotional.

But also rational. No hint of spooks in the trees. Jack dropped the diary on the desk, reluctant to read evidence of his grandpa's mental decline. It would be intrusive. Disrespectful.

He stared at a pile of his stuff that Charlotte had brought from their apartment ('if you're moving in here') and dumped in the middle of the room: a suitcase of clothes, his officer's ceremonial sword in its hard, leather scabbard and a framed photograph of his troop in Afghanistan. Thirty dusty men cradled weapons with the easy familiarity of veterans, as if they were extensions of their bodies. Raw recruits hold their rifles self-consciously, and untried soldiers proudly, as symbols of their warrior status. Only when they've been in a few firefights do they hold them with that casual, tools-of-the-trade manner. On the back of the frame Jack had written the troop's names: White, Donovan, Wolfe, Miller... All good men. A brotherhood. Dusty Miller stood grinning at the camera behind his shoulder. Wolfe was killed by an RPG on an Afghan hillside swept by bullets, exposed because Jack had stretched the perimeter too thinly. Dusty died on the last trip, died because Jack had taught him that he could run through fire and survive. Why couldn't he remember more about Chalky White? He was just a face in a photograph and the lingering smell of burning.

Charlotte didn't return to the cottage that night. Perhaps she had driven back to their apartment in the light. Perhaps she had stayed with George.

Strange how gently, how harmoniously, two lives can slip apart.

III: JACK

That night Jack dreamed about Dusty Miller. Again.

Dusty wears an issue khaki vest, camouflage trousers and desert boots, the kit they'd wear off duty in the base. Chalky White sits on the ground behind him because Chalky doesn't have any legs, but his trousers are folded neatly over his stumps as if he's going on parade. Chalky wears gloves and Jack knows that's to save his hands as he swings himself along the ground, but for now he is still. They both are, and they both stare at him with dark, sunken eyes within faces that are pale as paper. Their lips are dark too, neither black nor brown but an unnatural, dull, blood-and-earth colour.

'How are you?' Jack asks, and it seems the most reasonable of questions.

Dusty Miller makes a slight movement that might be a shrug. 'We're all right.' His lips may or may not have moved with the words. He shows neither pleasure nor anger at Jack's presence. Chalky White just watches.

'What's it like?' Being dead, he means.

Another shrug. 'It's OK.' No enthusiasm, but no horror either.

There are things Jack wants to say, but his tongue will only ask platitudes. He thinks he is whole again, and he could walk towards them, but his two legs are locked to the ground and a cloud drifts between them. He stares at them as they fade, hoping they understand, but the cloud smells of smoke and he knows that soon it will stink of burning plastic and rubber and charcoaled meat. He leans into it and bellows the way a charging marine will bellow away his fear as he runs into dust clouds through the smack of passing bullets, bellow as if the sound alone will keep the flames away until he is woken by his own screaming and lies panting in the darkness in a room filled with the tang of smoke.

The wardrobe mirror reflected a faint, flickering line of light above the curtains, the red light of fire.

Jack could dress quickly. He kept his prosthetic foot within reach of the bed, often still wearing its sock and trainer, and with his jeans crumpled around its ankle. It was almost as easy to strap on his leg as it was to hop to the window, and he didn't want to ruin his night sight by putting on the light.

It took a while for his mind to adjust. Down through the trees, possibly on the beach, was a fire. He could see the light reflected off the branches, even though the flames themselves were masked. His breathing began to slow. The wind was in the east, and the smoke smelled of damp wood, not burning meat. There was enough moonlight to show it drifting in thinning trails between the trunks of the Scots pines, coming up the hill towards the cottage. Enough light to read his watch and see that it was barely midnight. Miller and White faded into the shadows as his heart rate dropped from thumping panic to just-run-a-mile speed. The nightmare was real but unreal, the product of his own mind.

But there shouldn't be a fire on the beach. Jack laced on his other trainer and let himself out into the garden, moving silently across the grass to the back gate, where he'd be able to see downhill between the trunks of the pines. He could see movement down there, indistinct shapes between the trees, and hear distant laughter. Kids, probably, getting away from parents with illicit booze and a few bags of crisps, and they were trying to burn enough driftwood to choke the hillside. There'd be a pile of bikes on the path somewhere.

Then he froze, pulse pumping in the same skin-prickling fear as the nightmare. If he hadn't had his hand on the gatepost he might have fallen. A slight change in the wind sent the smoke in a different direction, across the hill rather than towards the cottage, and it was enough for the starlight to silhouette a figure against the smoke, a figure that had been invisible among the trunks of the trees but which stood motionless about fifteen yards away. The faint greyness rolling beyond showed first the outline of a helmet. Some part of Jack's brain was still thinking logically, and told him that the eggshell shine about the helmet's dome was *wrong*; helmets mustn't reflect light. They're matt Kevlar, not polished steel.

The smoke shifted a little more, enough to reveal broad shoulders and a torso whose minimal waist suggested body armour. Jack tried to swallow but had to suck his tongue to force moisture into the desert of his mouth. He could not speak. Now he could make out an arm that trailed a weapon with casual familiarity. This too was wrong. It wasn't the stubby barrel of a SA80 assault rifle. A curved wedge of shadow might be the magazine of an AK–47, but the 'magazine' was more like the head of an axe. Jack swallowed again.

'Dusty?' His voice sounded tight and high with fear.

The figure moved, a subtle shift of angle towards Jack as if its focus had been beyond him, towards the boat seat, and for a moment Jack thought he was staring at a skull. The smooth, bone-like dome dropped to dark hollows where eyes should have been, but the still-functioning logic told Jack that skulls don't have noses, and this figure's face bore a hard, vertical line that divided the eye sockets. Nor do they have a plume of long hair, like a horse's tail, growing from high on the crown and lifting gently in the breeze.

'Dusty?' Stronger, that time. Somewhere nearby, glass clinked against rock and smashed in a cackle of juvenile laughter.

The smoke rolled, shifting, and hung pearlescent beneath the trees, an empty screen as the figure faded from reality the way Miller and White had faded from his nightmare.

Jack wasn't sure how long he stayed there. Long enough for his bare torso to chill and for his shivering to be constant.

Back in the cottage he poured himself a whisky. A large one. His hands were shaking so that the bottle rattled against the glass, but perhaps that was just the cold.

Jack went down to the beach at sunrise, carrying a Thermos of coffee. Normally, it would be a good time to be out, those midsummer hours between sunrise and the first stirrings of the human world. The seagulls have finished their dawn screaming and flown to their feeding grounds, so the sounds are foreshore sounds of lapping water. That morning the place seemed fresh and chill, the water a steely grey that became white and then golds and blues while he sat on a rock, sipped coffee, blinked at the numbness in his head and stared at the charred remains of a bonfire. A light debris of beer bottles, cans and the white-plastic circles of empty six-packs littered the beach. Kids. Real.

Jack didn't often go to the beach below the cottage. It was a shingle-and-seaweed, slime-and-bladderwrack place, and it was edgy in the way that bleached driftwood, contorted like old bones, can be edgy and slightly threatening. He'd always felt that, always preferred the peace of Witt Point and its mossy stones. Grandpa had liked it though. This was where he'd found the carving. He'd tried to throw it back before he went into the hospice. Jack had come to look after him one night, and searched the empty cottage and garden before he found him down here, covered in mud, carrying the dragon, shouting incomprehensibly. Something about how it wouldn't sink, or wouldn't leave him. Jack still felt sadness at the thought of the raving old man his grandfather had become.

Jack captured an empty plastic bag rolling over the shingle

and filled it with the night's rubbish, his mind grating at what the figure under the pines might mean. Dusty Miller was a feature, asleep and awake, a product of nightmare or waking flashback. Jack couldn't control his dreams but he could control the flashbacks, force them away with hard work or exercise or whisky. Especially whisky. And it was usually Miller; Chalky White didn't come very often, but then Jack hadn't had to watch White die.

But Miller in the woods, when he was awake, was a Miller he couldn't control. This was madness, the thing Jack feared most of all; the loss of self, of self-respect and the respect of others.

Jack trudged up the hill, his mind sifting information the way he might shuffle a pack of cards.

Like Grandpa saying he saw a Viking in the pines, words Jack had dismissed at the time as the delusions of a dying man.

The diary entry about the dragon having a friend in the trees.

Him thinking he saw Miller.

Maybe they shared the same delusions. Either they were both mad, or neither was mad.

There were only a few tracks down to the beach from the coastal path, weaving through a tangled undergrowth of bracken and bramble. Damp, early-morning air had dewed the foliage and put enough of a crust on the sand of the paths to show prints: a badger's tracks and the faint, powder-puff marks of a grazing rabbit.

And a foot, pressed into the sand at the edge of the trees, next to the sign of his own trainers tramping downwards. A man of about Jack's size, barefoot and facing uphill with the toes pointing towards the cottage. Jack knelt to examine the fragile imprint, his unease growing at the way the toes and heel showed clearly, but not the pad behind the toes, nor the sweep of the arch. There were only the beginnings of lines from the toes back towards the heel, as if the foot had been more bone than flesh.

As Jack watched, the drying crust began to crumble, sending miniature landslides from its edges to fill the skeletal valleys beneath.

IV: DIARY OF EDVARD AHLQUIST, VOLUME 39

10th January. Flat calm. Heavy frost.

The cancer's spreading. Secondaries, the doctor called them, in my head now, and my liver. No point in operating. He asked if there's anyone to look after me, since I'll need care all the time soon. Cheerful sod. Live-in care or a hospice. I can have as much liquid morphine as I want.

I don't want to go into a hospice. There I'd be just waiting to die. At least here I have a life of sorts.

There was a herd of deer on Witt Point this morning, grazing down near the waterline. If I'm dying, how come I'm seeing everything so clearly? They were the same brown as the salt marsh, but I could see so sharp it was like I had binoculars in my brain. Then when they turned and ran up the slope their white backsides were bouncing away like tufts of cotton wool. Beautiful. It's worth a bit of pain to have moments like that, but then it gets too bad and I swig the Oramorph and next thing I know I've lost a couple of hours. Hours are too precious to lose.

Hard to think that all this will still go on without me. Those deer will still be there in the early mornings. Where will I be?

I called Harry. He ought to know. He said he'd come over. It doesn't feel good having to ask him, and he sounded like it didn't feel good to be asked.

The warrior comes closer when I'm not in the garden. Edge of the lawn, last night. I watched him from the bedroom. No moon, but enough starlight to see some kind of helmet with a horsehair plume that blew away from him even though there was no wind. The panic had me gasping for breath until I could suck oxygen.

Chapter Five: Fǣgþ

(Pron. 'f-ay-th'. Anglo-Saxon: vengeance through
generations; a blood feud waged against the kin of a
murderer)

From the Saga of King Guthrum

*Now in Fyrsig there were two halls where folk worshipped the
crucified god, one for men and one for women, and Jarl Harald slew
not the women.*

*There was among them one of great beauty called Witta, that is to
say the white. Harald Guthrumsson took her hand, and straightway
it was as though fire passed through his body, and at once he would
lie with her. The woman Witta fought against him and he saw
that it would not be except by force, yet Witta fought so valiantly
that Harald honoured her for her courage, and she alone was spared.
Harald claimed Witta for his own, keeping her by him and saying he
would win her willingly.*

*Jarl Harald dallied in Fyrsig, for the ships of his fleet had been
scattered. He harried in the lands about, doing great scathe[1] and*

---

1. Damage, harm.

taking much plunder. King Guthrum came by land with the rest of his army and was wroth with Harald, for they had not brought Alfred to battle. Guthrum swore that Harald loved the woman so witlessly that he neglected all that was seeming for his honour.

Draca

I: HARRY

Harry found a way of helping Jack with the boat. Three evenings that week, after work. Being with Jack was much easier when The Slut wasn't around.

It started by accident. Helping, that is. Harry called Jack, just to see how he was getting on, and could hear lots of bashing in the background, like someone was struggling with something metal. *'Do you know anything about engines?'* Jack asked. Of course he knew about engines. Royal Engineer, wasn't he, for twenty-two years?

Not that Harry wasn't challenged by that museum piece in *Draca*. Scotty, Jack called it, like it was a person, and Scotty had probably been a great little engine in 1935. Designed to start on petrol and then run on paraffin once it was going. It needed a thorough overhaul, and the chance of getting spare parts would be zilch. At least it was air-cooled rather than water-cooled, so they could run it even with the boat out of the water.

Run it. That was a laugh. Harry turned it over a few times with the crank lever you needed to start it, and got nothing but a few wheezes and one sodding great bang that blew a cloud of smoke out the exhaust. Best he could offer the boy was to take it all apart, clean everything with petrol, and put it back together again with a new fan belt and plugs. No promises.

But it was good to be involved. They couldn't talk much, at first, because Jack was making lots of noise. Caulking, he said. Seemed to involve a lot of hammering. But then they had a break and a cup of tea. He'd run a cable from the shore so they could use power tools and have a brew.

Jack perched on the steps up to the cockpit, and Harry sat on the floor of the chart-room, with his legs stretched out over the deck and his back against the wall. Or bulkhead, as the boy insisted on calling it. Jack didn't seem to want to talk much, like he had something on his mind, but Harry felt good to be there. They hadn't spent this much time together since before Jack's wedding.

'He did you proud, didn't he?' Harry looked over his shoulder into the main cabin. He hadn't realised how big the boat was. It'd be worth a bit, done up.

The boy didn't answer.

'I still wonder what he was thinking.'

Jack sipped his tea and watched Harry.

'Did he say anything to you?'

Jack shook his head.

'Only, you spent a lot of time with him, didn't you, before he died?'

'He was a lonely old man. He was dying. I was here when I could, when he needed me.'

'All right, all right, keep your shirt on.' This was going to be hard if the boy was going to be all antsy, but they had to have it out. 'Only, my lawyer says I could challenge the will.'

He stiffened, which was what Harry had expected. Actually, Harry was flying a kite. His lawyer had said he hadn't got a hope in hell without evidence. Undue influence is bloody hard to prove, especially within families.

'And will you?' Jack's hands around his mug seemed big, all of a sudden, like they were grabbing a weapon.

'Nah. Wouldn't do that to you, would I?' And Harry couldn't prove anything anyway.

'Do you promise? Only, I'm borrowing shedloads of money against the will...'

Harry didn't like the look on Jack's face. Too bloody hard by far. 'Nah. Promise.'

'Do you mean that, Dad?'

God, Harry wouldn't want to get on the wrong side of Jack

these days. 'I swear.' Harry laughed, nervously. 'Cross me heart and hope to die.' Anyways, if the boy wasn't going to admit it, Harry might as well make the best of it.

Jack relaxed a bit, but he still watched Harry like he didn't trust him.

It was the next day before Jack began to open up. They sat in the same places, except this time Harry had bits of engine scattered all over the floor around him. It was getting dark early that night. The sky behind Jack was thick with black clouds, and he'd stretched a tarpaulin tent over the cockpit, so they needed the hand lamps. He started talking about his deployment, but in a way that told Harry he was circling round something he really wanted to talk about. And then, in the middle of a decent conversation, he blurted out a weird question.

'Do you believe in ghosts, Dad?'

Harry thought the boy was having him on. The light from the hand lamps shone upwards from below, so Jack's eyes seemed all sunken and dark, like when kids shine a torch under their chins to make themselves look scary. If Harry had been an impressionable sort, there'd been a couple of moments crawling round the boat that could have seemed spooky, like when the bare bulb of the hand lamp made the boat's ribs stand out, and the shadows danced as if there was something hiding in there. That sort of thing. But what kind of a question was that? Harry laughed.

'Don't be bloody daft.'

It was only when Jack threw his tea over the side and went back to work that Harry realised he might have been serious.

He always seemed to get it wrong with Jack.

II: DIARY OF EDVARD AHLQUIST, VOLUME 39

17ᵗʰ January. Light airs, variable, cold.

Harry came. It was awkward. He was all stiff and brisk as if death was nothing more than packing to go away on holiday. He brought Tilly as well, so we couldn't really talk. Pity.

Harry asked me what they could do, but they blinked when I told them. If they can't offer companionship, then at least they could be useful. Shopping. Cleaning. Gardening. Washing. All the stuff I can't do no more. Harry don't do housework, but he did a bit of digging, clearing the weeds in the raspberry patch.

Now there's a challenge for me. Live to eat this year's raspberries. They always fruit early, down there in the dampest corner, where they get the sun nearly all day.

When Harry thought I wasn't looking he eyed the cottage in a calculating sort of way, like he was guessing its value. Tilly went through the cupboards. Said she was cleaning.

They didn't stay long. Tilly had to get home for her kids. I hope she brings them here while I can still talk to them.

Harry shook hands when they left. Backed away when he thought I was going to hug him.

I should have gone quietly with a heart attack or a stroke. Out like a light. This slow dying is inconvenient for him. It might mean we have to talk. Maybe that's why he brought Tilly.

When they'd gone I sat in the boat seat with my three pals for company. Oxygen, morphine, and the dragon. I wished Jack lived nearer.

I came inside when the whispering started. The Viking always comes when there's whispering.

III: GEORGE

George cycled out to Eddie Ahlquist's cottage for the barbecue. Jack's cottage now, Charl said. The bike was the only way to get there, since the buses were crap on Sundays and George couldn't afford a car. It meant that Jack and Charl didn't hear her coming, though she could hear them fifty yards away, yelling at each other in the back garden. George climbed off her bike by the front gate, wondering whether to go in, so the shout from Jack was loud and clear.

'Play your girlie games in the city, but don't shit in my backyard.'

George stood there, thinking *'Woah, too heavy'* and wondering what to do.

'Live and let live. Happy fucking families, right?'

That must've been Charl but it didn't sound like her. Much too shrill. If George walked away, Charl would think she'd stood them up, so George rang the bell of her bike, made as much noise as she could pushing it over the gravel of the drive and dumped it by the house. The silence felt dangerous, like when the wind drops before a squall. Charl appeared around the corner of the cottage, mangling her hands on a tea towel. Her upper body was all angles, with high, sharp shoulders as if she'd put too much starch in her cotton shirt, but then all curves around the bum. Those tennis shorts were way too tight.

'Hi George.' Charl's voice was tinny-bright, the way people speak when they're trying to pretend that everything's OK. She gave George an arms-length hug that was still close enough for George to feel the tension across her back.

'You all right, Charl?'

'Fine. Fine. We're in the garden.' She led the way before George could ask more.

Jack was raking coals in a portable barbecue on a stand. He turned to give George a small kiss on the cheek but his smile was a bit thin, even when she gave him her token bottle of wine. George remembered Charl's wince at the funeral, so she'd bought the best she could afford, a supermarket special-offer red. There was a bottle already open on the outside table, next to the barbecue.

'Lovely view.' It was, too. She wasn't making conversation. A long, overgrown garden sloped down to a hedge that separated it from the coastal footpath, and beyond the path there was scrubland of gorse and Scots pine and bracken curving around Freshwater Bay towards Witt Point. The harbour stretched away to the right, with the islands overlapping across the channels, and cloud shadows moving over the water under a light south-westerly.

'Thanks. Grandpa loved it.'

Another silence. There was too much unsaid between these two, and George was stopping them saying it.

'George, come and help me with the salad, will you, while Jack gets the barbecue ready?' That, George guessed, was Charl's way of saying 'let him stew on his own'.

Their kitchen was small, just big enough for an old, stand-alone cooker and a two-seater table that must double as a work surface. Charl stretched to close the fanlight, very quietly, and turned to George, her mouth pulled into a hard, angry line.

'What's the matter, Charl?'

This time the hug was closer, much closer, but Charl probably needed to hold someone and to have her back rubbed.

'I swear I am *that* close to walking out.'

George eased her away and held her shoulders. It felt a bit strange to hug a woman when she wasn't wearing a bra. She supposed that if you've got a model's figure like Charl, you can get away with it.

'Should I go?'

'No! No, please stay. Sorry, you walked into a bit of a spat.'

'Do you want to talk about it?'

Charl let her go, and reached for a chopping board.

'I've cut that guy some slack of late, God knows I have...' She brought a knife down on the globe of a lettuce, slicing it in two, and then hacked the pieces into shreds, massacring them.

'Let me do that.' George took the knife before they had one of Charl's fingers in the salad. Out on the terrace, Jack had his back to them as he poked at the coals, and his shoulders were tight so the muscles inside were bunching under his shirt. A Great Dane, Charlotte had called him. Right now, he looked more like a wounded bear. George wished she didn't feel like one of the dogs yapping at his heels.

'We used to have a social life together. At least, we did when he wasn't on deployment. The officers' mess. Parties. Friends. Life used to be fun. Now...'

'Now?'

Jack held his hand over the coals and stared into the flames as if he was looking through them to something far away.

'I tell you, George,' she touched George's arm so that she'd look at her. Her eyes were softer now, almost tender. 'The main reason I come now is to see you.'

'Aw, Charl.' George put the knife down and hugged her. 'That's one of the nicest things anyone has ever said to me.'

'I mean it, George. You're fun.' She broke away, and passed her some tomatoes for slicing. Outside, Jack still held his hand over the flames, and George frowned until he jerked it away. It looked like he'd been testing himself, and reached the limit. He flexed his fingers around the coolness of a bottle, held them there, and tipped wine into glasses.

'Come and have another sail. I'd be sad if you stopped coming.'

'God, I'd love to. Fun time. *Me* time.'

'Well, do it soon, before the schools break up for the summer. It's chaos after that, and there might not be a spare boat.'

Jack appeared at the kitchen door, a glass in each hand. Charl glared at him and there was an awkward silence, but George smiled, embarrassed at the way he was being made to feel an outsider in his own house.

'Wine?'

Charl and George said 'yes' together so exactly that Charl managed to grin as Jack bent to open the fridge, the kind of look that left Jack as the outsider. He pulled out a bowl of marinating meat. 'The barbecue's ready. I'm going to start cooking.'

George followed him outside, wanting to be friends with both of them, and stood beside him without speaking as a great slab of beef sizzled and dripped. Jack took a gulp of wine, which dissolved some of the tightness across his back.

'I cycle to Witt Point quite a lot on my days off.' George nodded down his garden. 'It's one of my favourite places.'

He relaxed a little more. She'd said the right thing.

'Me too. I go there most mornings, now, and watch the world come awake. It's peaceful.'

'It's a thin place.' George spoke without thinking, and bit her lip. Now he'd laugh at her.

'What do you mean?'

'Oh, I dunno. Spiritual, maybe.' Jack looked at her like he expected more, so she swallowed and kept going. 'Have you ever been to Lindisfarne?'

He shook his head.

'I went there years ago. Coach holiday with my foster

parents. They were very Christian, see? Took me to the Holy Isle. There's been a monastery there since the seventh century.'

'What's that got to do with Witt Point?'

'Lindisfarne's a place where God and man are close. You can feel it, even if you don't believe. God and man, gods and people, whatever. You feel that the veil between this world and the next is thin, almost like it's not there. Witt Point is like Lindisfarne, a thin place.'

Jack looked at her quite hard, almost staring at her, long enough for George to remember that he had grey eyes. At least he wasn't laughing. The stare broke into a smile that was gentle and soft and made her go a bit melty inside.

'I'd turn that steak, if I were you.'

He swore under his breath and flipped the meat in a flare of blazing fat.

'I hope you like it chargrilled, George.'

He'd relaxed.

'It'll still be pink and runny in the middle.'

Jack winced, and his eyes went distant. Somehow she'd spoiled the mood.

'You all right?'

He snapped back into focus and pointed towards Witt Point with his tongs.

'There used to be a chapel there too, I'm told.'

'Yeah. Saxon. Have I done something wrong, Jack?'

'You? Nah, George. If it wasn't you it would be someone else. It's just that…'

Behind them, the kitchen door opened.

'I don't understand…'

Charlotte put bowls of salad and bread on the table beside them, and slid her arm inside George's.

'You like history, George?'

'Local stuff, yes.' George kept her eyes on Jack's back. He'd gone tense again. These two needed to make up. They were both all right with her on her own but spiky when they were together.

Charlotte's arm tugged at George's. 'Let's walk around the garden.'

George let herself be led away, hoping she wasn't going to spend the day bouncing between them like a tennis ball. Charl held her close, so close that one boob was pushed against George's arm.

'So why local history?'

George liked the way Charl was interested in her.

'Like I told you when we went sailing, I drifted around in my childhood. No roots, see?'

Charl smiled at her in a way that was warm and not at all patronising.

'This is the first place I've felt settled.'

Charl picked a raspberry and offered it to her.

'Try that. They're full of flavour. We could have some for pudding.'

George held it in her fingers while she worked out how to put her thoughts into words.

'I guess if you feel you don't come from nowhere, you want to belong *some*where. Here's the best place I know.' George hadn't opened up this much for years.

'So you researched local history.'

'Just the stuff that interests me.'

'Like Saxon chapels.' Charl braced her arms back against the boundary fence in a way that tightened her shirt across her breasts.

'It was dedicated to Saint Witta. Hence Witt Point.'

George pointed past Charlotte's shoulder towards the point, and realised she was still holding the raspberry. It tasted good.

'Never heard of her.'

'Local saint. She's supposed to have been a virgin who walked on water to escape the Vikings. People used to make pilgrimages to her chapel in the Middle Ages.'

Charl's smile hardened a little as Jack came down the garden towards them.

'The meat's cooked.'

George paused as they turned back towards the cottage and for the first time she saw the inside of a seat made out of an old boat. Perched on the bench was Mad Eddie's figurehead, arched over, like it was staring down at them. It must have been hidden from view by the boat when they were nearer the house.

'That thing gives me the creeps.' George stared back at it.

'What?' Jack seemed bemused.

'Eddie's figurehead. It makes me uneasy.'

'It's creepy, but it's only an old carving.' Charl looked amused.

'More like an idol. And I'm frigging sure it's watching us.'

'Ooh, shall we dance around it?' Charl skipped up the garden towards it. Jack stayed near George, his eyes following the way Charl's tits jiggled inside her shirt. Charl stopped when she slopped wine on her arm.

'Seriously, Charl.' George didn't know how to describe that sense of menace. It felt even stronger here than at the funeral.

'Oh, don't be so po-faced.' Charl licked her wrist, giggling at George.

'What's the matter, George?' At least Jack wasn't laughing at her.

George took a deep breath. 'Me mum said I was psychic. I sense things.' She glanced at him, nervously. 'And I don't like Eddie's carving.'

Jack still wasn't laughing. He looked at her a bit too long to be comfortable, like he was thinking.

125

'Do you mind if we try something, George?'

She let him lead her out onto the coastal path. It was away from the carving, anyway. Jack stopped her on one of the little tracks that wove through the undergrowth down towards the shoreline.

'Stand there. Can you sense anything?'

Jack was taking her seriously, and this seemed to be important to him, so George shut her eyes, faced down the hill and stood there palms out, listening at a deep, intuitive level.

Nothing. Nothing there, not on that spot, not that could be felt through her awareness of that carving. That was so strong that she began to arch her back as if someone held an icy knife between her shoulder blades. She turned, opening her eyes, and all three of them – Jack, Charlotte and the dragon – were looking at her in a way that made her hunch her shoulders and fold her arms across her chest. Jack lifted one eyebrow in silent enquiry. She pushed past him, shaking her head.

'Your meat will spoil.'

IV: GEORGE

Charl was back again during the following week, pretending to work while she took business calls on her smartphone in the cockpit of a charter boat.

'I like 'working from home'.' She ended the call, grinning at George like a naughty schoolgirl.

'You must have a dead understanding boss.'

'It's all about results, hon. If I bring home the business, they don't ask too many questions.' Charlotte stretched like a cat, still clutching her phone.

'Well I hope today's worth it for you. There's not much wind.'

There hadn't been enough of a breeze to sail in the harbour, and it wasn't much better out in the bay. Without the motor they just about had steerage way, making one and a half knots out of a light southerly.

'It's already worth it.' Charl smiled at George in a way that made her feel warm and liked.

'Did you ever find out what all that was about with Jack on the path?' For a moment, George regretted changing the subject. She always seemed to do that when someone started to be nice to her.

'He did clam up, didn't he? I got it out of him later, though. He thinks he saw a ghost there.' Charlotte began putting suncream on her legs. The way she bent forward stopped George seeing her face.

'And do you believe him?'

'I wouldn't have done. He's had problems, you see, since he came back. Sometimes, he hasn't seemed himself...'

'But?'

'I've been reading Eddie's diaries. He saw it too.' Charlotte lifted her head. She looked nervous and worried at the same time. 'I'm not sure what to do about this, George.'

'Tell him to get rid of that carving. It's frigging evil.'

'You think they're linked?'

George shrugged. 'Dunno. But it's worth trying.'

They were quiet for a while. Charlotte unfolded a few more yards of leg onto the seat and resumed her creaming, moving her hands in slow, sensuous strokes. A gentle sea moved in towards the land, making the boom swing over their heads as they rolled then sway back until it was brought up by the main sheet with a snap and a jar. It wasn't a comfortable motion.

'Do you want to go back, Charl?'

'Why?'

'Well, you ain't learning much and we're going nowhere.'

'We could always go for a swim.' Charl looked over the side. The sun lanced into the water, making shifting patterns below them like shards of green glass.

'I haven't brought a cozzie.' Swimming hadn't occurred to George.

'Neither have I.' Charl grinned at her with that look that made her part of a private joke.

'I don't know...' George had never been skinny-dipping before, and she wasn't used to getting her kit off in company, even girl company.

'Come on, George, live a little!' That was a dare.

'Not out here.' George was still thinking about it. That water did look good. 'We could anchor in the bay, if you want to swim.' George kept her options open. She'd think about this on the way in.

They dropped the sails and anchored in about three fathoms, far enough off the beach to be away from prying eyes unless they had powerful binoculars. It was a weekday, and they were at least a mile from the nearest beach car park, so there weren't many people. When George turned around from slotting the swimming ladder in place over the stern, Charl was taking her shirt off as if it was the most natural thing in the world. George looked away and picked up a fender, concentrating on tying a long length of line to it.

'What are you doing?'

'Safety line.' George secured the other end of the line to a cleat and threw the fender overboard. 'There's a light tide running. Less than half a knot, but it would be hard to swim against if you're tired. The fender acts as a float, and keeps the line on the surface, downstream. Swim for the line if you have problems, and pull yourself back.'

'Aye, aye, captain.' Charl threw a saucy, bare-chested salute. Now she was laughing at George, but not in a nasty way. She turned away a little as she dropped her shorts and kicked off her canvas shoes, and George thought she'd kill for a body like that.

'You coming?' Again, that grin, like they were partners in crime. Charl made no attempt to cover herself as she swung out onto the ladder. She slowed as her foot met the water, and yelped as it reached her calves. She stayed there, hands on the rail, eyes wide, with her skin tightening. George giggled. She should have warned her. The sea's frigging cold early in the season, even on a hot day.

'Do you still want to do this?'

Charl nodded and made one more step downwards, taking short, gasping breaths with her mouth wide open, and it was George's turn to laugh because Charl looked like a stranded fish. George relaxed. This was something she knew how to do. She turned away and pulled her own kit off before she changed her mind.

'That's the wimp's way in.' George kept her back to Charl

and climbed over the rail on the seaward side, holding on to a stay, feeling Charl's eyes on her. 'Just take the hit.'

She jumped, tucked her knees into her chest and bombed.

If it had been August or September she could have let herself sink downwards with her body rotating in a cool silence that is no silence because by the time she'd have begun to float upwards there'd be the sea's background noise of tiny clicks, and maybe the whine of a propeller somewhere. But in early July the cold squeezed her, forcing her to unfold and swim hard to generate some warmth. It was her only thought: fast, urgent movement until her skin numbed. She stayed below the surface, pulling hard away from the boat, and surfaced for air about thirty feet off.

Charlotte was still on the ladder, about one step lower so her bum was just above the water. She'd probably stopped again when the cold touched her girlie bits. Sod that. George swum back, just as hard, and trod water off the stern to keep her limbs moving. If you can get through the first two minutes, the rest is easy.

'You're a frigging wimp, Charl.'

'It's freezing!'

George splashed her, making Charl squeal and tense so that a vertical line appeared in the skin between her shoulders.

'Get your arse in here, girl. This was your idea.'

Charl stayed there, so George grabbed Charl's hips, braced her feet against the stern and pulled her, shrieking, off the ladder.

'You're cruel. I hate you.' No, she didn't. She'd have been laughing if she hadn't been so busy spitting seawater. George splashed her again, pushing water at her face.

Charl was a surface swimmer, the kind that paddles around with their nose well above the water, like a dog. George liked to go deep, to duck-dive down until the bottom looms in patches of weed and sand. Down there she could spread her arms wide and still, and look up towards patterns of light on the surface. That time with Charl was best of all. The water felt different when she was naked. She hung there weightless, limbs starred out, enjoying the touch of the water in new places, and the sensation of her chest floating upwards. Above her, Charl was a fuzzy paleness in dazzling green light, and George couldn't remember when she had last been that happy.

By the time the cold drove them back on board George didn't feel embarrassed. Even though you couldn't see much in the water, it seemed a bit pointless to try and cover up after they'd splashed each other and had play fights that became slippery tangles of limbs and softness. They took it in turns to kneel in the cockpit beside a bowl of fresh water from the boat's tanks while they helped each other rinse the salt out of their hair. The boat had one small towel in the heads and that had to do for both of them, so they needed to let the sun dry them.

George lashed the boom to a stay to keep it off the cabin roof while they sunbathed. With the mainsail folded on to it, it gave them privacy from the beach at eye level, but Charl didn't seem that bothered anyway. She knelt there so she could see over the boom and sail to the beach while she brushed her hair.

'You look like a mermaid, Charl.'

'The looks of a mermaid, the voice of a frog.' She put her hands down, made a short, shuffling hop on her knees towards George and croaked. 'Niddip.'

'We'd better top up the suncream.' George tended to burn, and she was showing bits of herself that had never been tanned.

'Shall I do your back?'

George decided that girls did backs much better than blokes. She'd had a boyfriend once who rubbed it in like he was sanding the deck. Charl's touch was gentle, even sensuous, working outwards across her shoulders as she lay face down on the cabin roof, until Charl's fingertips brushed the edges of George's breasts in a way that was pleasant and strange at the same time, almost a caress.

'How are things with Jack, Charl?'

'Up and down. He's obsessive about restoring that precious boat of his. 'The Other Woman', I call it.'

'She's going back into the water soon. It'll be different when you can go sailing together.'

'Actually, I rather like this sort of sailing. I think Jack's style might be a bit macho.'

Charl's fingers worked their way down George's spine and smoothed the curve of her waist.

'Do you have a boyfriend, George?'

'Nah. Not at the moment.'

'Really? I'd have thought someone as lovely as you would have men queuing at your door.'

George looked over her shoulder, searching Charl's face in case she was making fun. She wasn't.

'I can reach there, thanks.' Charl had begun spreading the latest dollop of cream over George's bum. George turned over, took the bottle from her and started on her legs. Charlotte sat watching, hugging her knees.

'And they're not queuing. I'm too short, and I have a habit of frightening men off.'

'You're not fat at all. And I'd love to have some of your curves.'

'Seriously?' George stared at her, not really believing.

'At school I was called The Stick Insect.'

'And I was called The Witch.' That slipped out without thinking. George's guard must have been way down.

'Why on earth…?'

'I'll tell you about it some day. Not today. I'm having fun.'

George turned over onto her tummy, pillowing her face on her arms. They were quiet for a while; George had broken the flow. The fibreglass roof of the cabin was hot against her chest.

'Don't you miss having a boyfriend, George?'

'Not really. Most of them just want to grab my tits and get inside my knickers. I haven't found one yet who'd treat me as an equal.'

'Have you ever made out with a woman?'

George turned her head, sharply. Charlotte was lying beside her, with the towel rolled under her cheek. They made eye contact.

'Nah.' George swallowed. *Oh, feck.* 'Have you?'

Charl's grin said it all.

'What was it like?'

'Hot.' Charl said the word like she was licking her lips. All sultry and smoky. Something told George this wasn't ancient history.

'What, while Jack's away?'

Another cat-with-cream grin.

'George, darling, have you ever had 'Surf 'n' Turf' in a restaurant? Steak and lobster?'

'It's a bit out of my price league, Charl.'

'Well, Jack is all the beef I could ever want. It's just that sometimes I like to taste a little fish.'

George lifted up on her elbows, staring at Charlotte. Her mouth was dry.

'Charl, are you hitting on me?'

'Would you be terribly upset if I was?'

Upset? George was, just a bit. And flattered. More upset than flattered because until then they'd been like children, playing together. It had felt natural, after the first few minutes. George had been able to tell herself it was innocent. Now she felt like a sphinx with her boobs on display, and she caught herself pushing her body backwards to hide them between her arms.

'Nah. Not upset. Bit surprised, though.'

Charlotte rolled on her back, giggling.

'Oh, the look on your face, George!' She lifted one hand to touch George's cheek with the back of her fingers. 'Lighten up, girl!'

'Charl, I think you're beautiful and I love spending time with you, but you...' George swallowed again, picking her words. She didn't want to lose her. 'But women don't turn me on in that way. Can't we just be friends?'

Charl made a little pout. 'Of course we can, darling. Who knows? One day you may wonder what you're missing!' She reached over and gave George's bum a friendly slap.

George settled her cheek on her forearms, watching Charlotte and wondering if she would be like the men who disappeared when she wouldn't jump into bed with them. For a moment, George even wondered if it was worthwhile giving in, just to keep her.

So yes, she was sad, though she thought she hid it. Not so much that Charlotte had come on to her, but more for the new ground rules it brought. And the first of these was that they wouldn't be skinny-dipping together again.

But then there had been moments when they were playing in the water when she'd felt the beginnings of a different kind of excitement; something daring and exotic. On the deck, she'd pushed Charlotte back instinctively, absolutely, but then she realised she was just a bit curious. George turned her face away, flushing with embarrassment.

V: DIARY OF EDVARD AHLQUIST, VOLUME 39

25th January. Wind ESE, 3, Fair, Cold

It's just me and the dragon, now. Plus a bloody great oxygen cylinder that I keep in the front room because it's too heavy to drag around with me. There's a smaller bottle that's a bit more portable. I take it for the headaches, even when the breathing is ok.

The whispering follows the warrior, like they hate him, but he's much stronger than they are. He was there while we were on the boat seat, I'm sure. We were looking at the flames in the stove and I didn't look up. Daren't. But the dragon knew and moved.

I had this urge to end it all in one great ball of flame. Wait until the warrior is close, and push this little oxygen bottle into the fire. It's small enough to fit in the stove. For a moment that felt beautiful, and it was like the dragon was encouraging me, making me think I'd be doing them a favour.

How big a bang would this bottle make? Would it be enough? Would it be too much? Don't want to wreck the house. Things to do, first. I need to decide what happens to the house, after.

God, I need some human company, particularly when it hurts bad. The dragon's all right but he don't talk much. Jack comes whenever he can. Every weekend, now, and at least once during the week, bless him.

VI: HARRY

Harry Ahlquist was pleased when Jack invited them to *Draca*'s launch. The wife wasn't too sure about rubbing shoulders with all those smart yachtie people, but it was a sign that things were getting better with their son. Jack probably wanted to thank him for all the work he'd done on the engine as well. Plus it was on a Saturday, so Harry could take time off work, no problem. Tilly and the kids went too. Tilly wasn't so keen, but Harry insisted. It was important they let Jack know that, as far as the family was concerned, the door was still open.

It wasn't what Harry expected. He'd had this idea that they'd be sliding *Draca* down a slipway. Get his mum to smash a bottle of bubbly over the bow and say 'I name this ship', all that sort of stuff. But they just floated her off on the tide. Bit disappointing, that.

Jack was standing on deck when they got there, looking down at the level of the water. A couple of people stood ready to pull the props away from her side, and a rope ran from her back end out to a powerboat lying offshore with its engine ticking over, ready to pull her off. There was water all around her, so there was no way Jack could come to them. The boy looked worried when he saw them. Maybe he thought they'd say the wrong thing and embarrass him in front of his yachtie friends.

About a dozen people were already there, gathered around a table where they'd laid out a bit of a spread. Of course, The Slut was there, turning some kebab things on a portable barbecue, and the boatyard girl who'd come to Eddie's funeral was serving wine in plastic glasses. She came over and spoke to them, real friendly, and they were chatting away all natural like when The Slut came over with a plate of things on skewers.

Harry forced a smile when the wife poked him in the back. 'Be nice.'

Of course he'd be nice. They were all on their best behaviour. He said hello as sweet as you like, even though she replied in a way that made him wonder if she knew something they didn't. She passed that plate of food under their noses like they were all pally. There was only the look in her eyes to show she was acting.

'Fancy a nibble? Mrs Ahlquist? Tilly? George? Harry? Fresh off the grill. How about the children, Tilly? Shall we take the meat off the skewers for them?'

George. A funny name for a girl.

'What's that?' The wife sounded suspicious. She don't like exotic stuff.

'Special treat. My contribution to the day. Steak and lobster.'

George the boatyard girl snorted and turned her head away, which made Tilly suspicious so she sniffed at her skewer. The wife just put her nose over the plate.

'I don't know. Smells a bit spicy, to me.'

'Go on, Mrs A. Surf 'n' turf. Your tongue won't have had so much excitement for years.'

Now Harry was sure she was making fun of them. George spluttered and pretended to choke, but Harry could see she was trying not to laugh. Why was he missing the point? Even Tilly looked puzzled. The wife put her skewer back on the plate like she'd changed her mind.

'I'll have you know I cook very well, thank you very much.' The wife was in a huff now. 'Good, plain, English cooking. And no, thank you. I've just had lunch.'

They hadn't, but both their backs were up. They'd come prepared to be nice. Now they felt like they'd picked up the wrong fork at a fancy occasion and everyone was laughing at them.

They were saved by a cheer. Jack had untied the ropes holding *Draca* to the pilings, and waved them over his head. Out on the water the powerboat put its engine into reverse and the line tightened. Slowly, ever so slowly, *Draca* eased backwards to the sound of more cheering and the popping of champagne corks. George backed away from Harry's group, saying she'd go and help with the lines.

'I'll come too.' The Slut went with her. As they walked away, George thumped The Slut on the arm, all playful, like she was cross and laughing at the same time.

Harry took Tilly's kids along the jetty where they wouldn't get in the way, thinking that children are easy at that age. You can hold their hands so they don't fall in the water, and you can never say the wrong thing because even if you do, they don't know it. So he stood on the fringes with a kid in each hand, listening to them babbling away, and watching the crowd as *Draca* was hauled alongside. The Slut sprayed Jack with champagne, whooping as *Draca*'s side squeezed the fenders against the jetty. George heaved at ropes, pulling *Draca* in, and you could see the effort it took by the way she had to lean into it. Harry wished Jack had found a girl like that. No airs and graces, and not afraid of hard work.

It was strange to see a woman doing that sort of thing though. Boy's haircut, workmen's gloves and enough strength to haul a big boat to shore, but a lumpy sweatshirt and a woman's arse as she bent to wind the rope around one of those bent metal things on the jetty. And all the time Jack stood on deck with his weight on one leg and the other bent at the knee, waving to the cheers. When he ducked to dodge a cork, Harry saw the boy as a child again, all tousled hair and laughter and happiness. Made him feel quite full.

It hurt though, to see the way he climbed down to the jetty.

The boy used to be so fit. Had to be, in the marines. The boat was riding high in the water and it was quite a step down. Jack moved like an old man, holding onto the rigging with both hands and reaching out with his good foot until his toes touched. The way he did that stretched his trousers high on his bad leg, and Harry tried not to stare. The shaft made it look like there was just a stick of bone above his boot.

Harry hung back with the grandkids, keeping them out of the way until things calmed down on the jetty, and watched Jack kiss his mother. At least those two were talking. The wife must have raised her voice over the hubbub because when the sound of the powerboat faded away she forgot to lower it and Harry could hear half their conversation.

'Wish you'd come and see us,' she was saying.

Jack had his back to Harry so he didn't hear his reply.

'Then come midweek, on your own.'

His shoulders lifted.

'You're both so stubborn. He's here. He's trying.'

It was time for Harry to say hello. He let Tilly take the kids and shook Jack's hand so hard the boy was a bit taken aback.

'She's looking good, Jack.' He'd give praise where praise is due. The boy looked cautious, like he was waiting for a 'but'. Harry meant it though. She looked smart. Nicely sanded decks, fresh varnish on the woodwork and new, shiny fittings. Jack had buffed the brass compass and instruments in front of the cockpit until they gleamed. He'd done himself proud. Now why couldn't he take a compliment? And what was it about the boy that always put Harry on edge? He got all knotted inside.

'Will you sail her today?' Harry asked.

'There's a bit of work to do yet, Dad. Get her ballast back in her and then fit her out.' He looked at the sky, which was a flat, windless grey like the sea beneath. 'And I don't think anyone's going to sail much today. That's why everyone's here drinking my champagne.'

'So it will be a while before we scatter the ashes, then?'

'A few weeks.'

'Well, show us around then. Let's see what you've done since I fixed the engine.'

Jack put a plank against the boat's side so the women could get on board, walked up it and turned to Harry from the deck.

'Come on, Dad.' Jack held his hand out to him, before anyone else. Harry felt quite choked as he climbed on board.

Maybe Tilly shouldn't have worn shoes with high, pointy heels. She nearly fell over when they stuck between the planks on the jetty, so the kids got away and ran ahead of her, running up the gangplank until Jack put his hands under Wayne's arms and swung him aboard, laughing. It was a wonderful, happy moment, when Harry thought everything might be on the mend. Little Wayne danced with excitement as he landed on the deck, shrieking out questions in his high, piping voice.

'Uncle Jack, is this the boat you stole from Granddad?'

Harry groaned inside as the moment crumbled and the laughter in Jack's eyes turned to pain. He let the kid go, very gently, and glared at Harry. That old, defiant look was in his eyes again.

'Jack, I...'

Jack turned his back.

'Tilly, you'll have to take those shoes off.' His voice was flat, like he'd lost interest in the day.

'What, and spoil a decent pair of tights?'

'Those heels will wreck the deck, Tilly.'

'But we've come over here special to see the boat.'

'Then take your shoes off.'

Like his mum said, the boy could be so stubborn. He wouldn't give in, even when Tilly had a huff and said she wanted to take the children home. The wife said she was too old to go swinging on ropes and wouldn't feel safe to climb on board anyway, so they all left.

Harry looked back as they crossed the yard, wondering if they'd been too hasty. On the boat, The Slut was giving Jack a hug and George was watching them from the end of the jetty where she was tidying up ropes, still in her workmen's gloves. It had all started out with the best of intentions. But for The Slut, it might have worked.

VII: DIARY OF EDVARD AHLQUIST, VOLUME 39

30th January. Wind SE, 4, rain.

Jack came again. He doesn't talk about Charlotte much. I think they're having a rocky time. She rang him, this morning, and gave him a lot of verbal. Not sure what that was all about.

Bring her over, I said, take my room with the big bed, but I think he likes having time out.

He'd find it easier to get a job now if he'd gone to university. Should have done, he was bright enough. Always reading. When he came over here as a kid, he only wanted to do two things – sail and read. Sailing was fun, but words were a hunger for him. If he'd have been my son I'd have encouraged him to stay on at school, but Harry didn't want to know, and Jack was always trying to please his father, back then.

Learn a trade, Harry told him, and you'll never starve. Carpentry, perhaps, because Jack was good with his hands. But Jack wanted to prove himself, and followed his father into the armed forces.

Maybe that's why he went into the Marines, to impress Harry. I think that's what he's always needed – his Dad's approval. Harry would never praise him, though. He'd think it would make Jack soft or big headed. Harry's hold over Jack is never to be pleased, whatever Jack does.

Poor kid. Fancy spending your life needing something you'll never get.

VIII: JACK

Chippy Alan fished a spark plug out of a cleansing bath of petrol, wiped it dry and screwed it back into *Draca*'s engine casing.

'Now try it.' He climbed back up the steps into the cockpit to give Jack space to work the crank handle.

Jack prayed to whatever gods ruled boat machinery, and heaved. And again. On the third pull the engine coughed, rattled, coughed some more and settled into a noisy, irregular clatter.

'Good man, Scotty.' Jack patted the casing and adjusted the petrol/paraffin mix until the noise subsided into a steadier hum.

'Looks like you're burning old rags,' George called from beside the tiller. Jack poked his head out of the hatch. George had twisted to watch a cloud of dark, oily smoke drifting on the wind astern of them.

'More like engine oil.' Chippy wiped his hands on a rag. Behind Jack, Scotty made a single, explosive sound, somewhere between a backfire and a dropped hammer, and died. The line of smoke stopped as if someone had lifted a dirty paintbrush from a sheet of paper. Chippy shrugged. He didn't look surprised.

'What did your dad do to it?'

Jack told him, as best he knew.

Chippy pursed his lips. 'You don't feel like asking him back to do it again?'

'Not if I can help it.'

'I'll do my best, but I'm a shipwright, not a mechanic. You might need a new engine.'

Jack groaned. 'I can't afford a new engine.' The bank loan

was nearly gone. There'd be nothing more until the lawyer was granted probate on Grandpa's will.

'It belongs in a museum, not a working boat.' Chippy sat on a cockpit bench, still wiping fuel off his fingers.

'It's always been a bit temperamental.' Scotty was part of the ship. He needed to be coaxed into helping, that's all.

'And it's petrol.' Chippy sounded disapproving. Petrol engines are more of a fire risk in a boat. 'Don't put sentiment before safety.'

'Petrol/paraffin. Grandpa wanted to keep her in her original state.'

George sat with one elbow hooked over the coaming and the other arm lying on the tiller, almost shapeless in a loose sweatshirt. She squinted upwards at the new mast, where they'd set the standing rigging that braced the mast and bowsprit but not yet the running rigging that worked the sails.

'Hence no radar.'

'Nor satnav, but you can do that on a tablet computer these days.'

George pushed the tiller. 'No auto-steer, neither.'

Jack lifted a light line and block out of a locker. 'But she'll hold her course in almost any wind if you lash the tiller.' He was beginning to feel defensive about his ship.

George touched one of the belaying posts beside the cockpit, a thick, upright block of timber with a horizontal metal rod through the top that was used for securing the running rigging. The square post had been worn almost to a circle and polished a rich honey brown by over a century of use.

'And no winches.' Modern boats had drum winches that could tighten rigging with relative ease. George had a teasing look in her eye.

'Nah. You need muscles in this ship. Real sailing.'

'I love mussels. Especially steamed with a nice plate of fries.'

Jack pretended to ignore her. 'You can't be shellfish in this ship. Everyone has to pull their own weight.'

They exchanged a flicker of eye contact. Jack enjoyed her company, even if she was Charlotte's new best friend.

'All the more reason to have an engine you can depend on,' Chippy Alan sniffed.

'She sailed without an engine at all for her first thirty years.' Maybe he'd move back on board when *Draca* was fitted out and operational.

'Not in this harbour she didn't.' Chippy was right. *Draca*'s keel dropped nearly seven feet below the surface, and there were too many twists in the channels and too much tide for a big boat to rely on sail alone. She had to have a working engine.

'I need to get a job. Earn some money.'

'Welcome back to the labouring classes.' George stretched out her legs, bare and shapely beneath her shorts but not long enough to reach across the cockpit. She squinted into the sun as a weak splash of sunlight made its way through the cloud and turned the orange streak through her hair into a Day–Glo yellow.

'There's plenty of work around, this time of year.' Chippy threw his rag into a bucket. 'Tourist stuff, mainly.'

'In olden times,' George opened one eye, 'once we'd bent on the sails, she'd be considered seaworthy.'

Jack wanted to sail her even more than George. He'd spent half an hour that morning on the boatyard's pontoons, admiring *Draca* from all angles. She now had all her ballast aboard, eleven tons of iron he'd heaved and stowed by hand, and she floated like an ocean thoroughbred, beautiful, begging to be unleashed. It was like having a new sports car and not being allowed to drive it.

'In olden times,' Chippy's tone was more cautious, 'they

didn't have no echo sounders, nor electric lights, nor any of the stuff that needs batteries to work. Which means a motor to charge the batteries.'

'The batteries would last us for a day sail, though, if they're topped up with shore power when we go. And Grandpa kept all the old oil lamps working.'

'But even your iPad needs charging, else you're back to charts and sextants.'

'We wouldn't need it out in the bay though. That's our back yard.' Jack only noticed the 'We' after he'd said it.

'Unless you get fog.' The wash from a passing boat lifted the bow as it passed under *Draca* and the pontoon. Beyond Chippy's grizzled head, the bowsprit rose, dipped and rose again against the expanse of water beyond, as if to say *'What are you waiting for?'*

'We could choose a clear day with steady winds. Wait for this storm to pass.' The watery sun was a sign of a forecast blow. 'We need another few days to finish fitting out, anyway. Say a week including sails and running rigging.'

'And you really need a shakedown sail to make sure everything else works.' The look in George's eye dared him to go.

'I'd need an experienced crew though.' He kept his eyes on George, returning the challenge.

'You mean I don't qualify?'

Chippy stared at both of them and snorted in a way that said they were fools. 'Looks like I'd better strip down that engine then.'

Jack's ghost foot, the one that he could feel but that wasn't there, woke him that night. The pain was like a bad cramp that he couldn't fix by stretching; he just had to lie there and take it until it faded. It always went, eventually, though it could leave him panting on the bed with the covers pushed off his sweating body, far from sleep.

And in the dark, on his own, the memories would come.

Of shock as the IED detonated and the ground itself swung a fist into his belly.

Of weightlessness as the truck dropped back through boiling clouds of dirt to hit unseen, solid earth.

Of anger at being suckered into a trap. Anger at the betrayal that would have made it possible.

Of shoulder-barging the truck door as they landed, unbelievably upright, and training kicked in. Deploy. Spread out. Take cover. Assess.

Except his legs wouldn't work. Nothing fucking worked. He just dangled there useless with his head on the ground and his foot trapped inside, with his leg buckled at this obscene angle that hurt like hell with his weight hanging off the fractures.

And of Dusty Miller running towards him through thinning dust, while Jack shook his head from side to side, making a keening noise that was more in his skull than his ears, because by then the fuel had caught and the truck was burning. And each time he threw his head to the left, Dusty was two paces closer until he was no closer at all but sinking to the ground as if he was suddenly very tired. But Jack had his foot in the fire and all he could think was *'What the fuck are you doing? Get the hell over here and get me out of this'.*

Worst of all, of Dusty lying there staring at him with his mouth working but no sound. Every now and then as Jack thrashed around there'd be the dust splash of a bullet around Dusty and a pop as if Jack's ears were under water. Such a harmless little pop, like a kid's cap gun.

And of smells, because Chalky White was still inside,

slumped against the wheel, and Jack had glimpsed the mess where his legs had been. Pray God he was dead before he burned.

The noise in the garden made him lift his head off the pillow, ears straining. It had sounded like the creak that the boat seat made when someone sat in it and the wood shifted with the weight. Moonlight shone around the curtains as if the garden was full of hot snow, and then faded to blackness in a heartbeat as a cloud passed over. That wooden groan was enough for Jack to swing out of bed, pull on his leg and stand at the window with a curtain lifted. The landscape outside was monochrome under a thin, glassy sky that shone like old men's tears.

Jack couldn't see the whole garden from his old room, just a tapering strip of lawn fading towards the trees and the harbour. The corner by the boat seat was out of sight, hidden by the bulk of the main bedroom. What he could see were patterns of silver grass between black shadows of trees, shadows that moved as the wind pushed ahead of the storm.

Then a hint of another kind of movement. Just a glimpse of a leg or a body that appeared and disappeared beyond the hard edge of the building. Jack lurched out onto the landing, kicking his prosthetic foot free of the trailing jeans, and into Grandpa's room, where he could see the whole garden.

Nothing, at first. But then a shadow moved within a shadow, near the boat seat. Enough to show him shoulders, a waist and an arm that gripped a long, thin shape that could have been a weapon. A head-high movement that might have been long hair or the plume of a helmet, moving in the wind. Jack backed away, keeping his face well back from the window, in the steady, slow way he'd moved when the Taliban were close but unaware.

At the bottom of the stairs, his ceremonial sword lay propped against the wall, waiting for him to find it a home. The blade made almost no sound against the leather scabbard as he drew it.

The kitchen also offered no view of the boat seat, only the table outside. The moon shadow of the house lay in a hard line across the grass.

His mistake was the bolt on the kitchen door, which stuck then snapped back against its mounting, a sound as soft but as certain as a detonator. Knowing that surprise was lost, Jack threw the door open and rushed into the moonlight, sword raised. He hadn't thought about whether he was going to challenge whoever was there or hit them with the sword and ask questions afterwards.

He had the fleeting impression of dissolving images, the way birds will scatter from bread at the appearance of a dog, and the garden was his, empty, while he stood on the grass bellowing a challenge, waving his sword.

The crisp tickle of grass against his good foot brought him back to his senses, and he lowered his point, sinking onto his knees on the grass. The sword's tip speared the lawn so that his cheek rested against the cold metal of the basket around the grip.

He began to laugh. Even he knew it was a strange, manic kind of laugh. He'd just realised he was stark bollock naked and chasing Grandpa's ghosts around the garden with a ceremonial sword.

As his laughter quietened he heard waves against the shingle on the beach, the tumble, spread and fade once again sounding like the soft whisper of many men.

Fa–ey–th… Fa–ey–th…

IX: DIARY OF EDVARD AHLQUIST, VOLUME 39

10th March Wind SW, 4-5. Showers.

I made a will. Did it proper, with a lawyer.

Harry don't need the money, he's done well for himself. Besides, did he really expect to ignore me, then scoop the lot? He's spent 40 years punishing me, wrapped around his anger until it's become part of him. Encysted. That's a word I learned from a doctor.

I never should have married his mother. We were just kids, fooling around. She was a rebel; I was her bit of rough to be flaunted at her parents. Accidents like babies weren't supposed to happen to spoilt brats like her. At least I stood by her and did the right thing. Her family helped, but God, did I pay for it, year after shrieking year. Always shouting about the smart people she could have married, the doctors or the lawyers.

Ok, so I strayed. Any man would if he had to put up with all that verbal.

Tilly would waste it. No matter how much you give her, she's always got her hand out for more. She'd be like the lottery winners you see on the telly who have a few years of flash cars and holidays before they're back on benefits. I've left something for each of her kids, though, in trust so she can't blow it.

But Jack would make use of it. We've always been close, him and me. I got my second chance at being a father, and maybe I did it better second time round. Encouraged him. Deep down, Harry was always threatened by Jack. He always had to knock him back.

Right now Jack's drifting. With this he could start a business, or go to university like he always should have done. And I like to think of him here, in the cottage. It makes the leaving easier.

If the dragon went down with me and Draca, would the warrior leave Jack alone?

X: JACK

On the day before the 'shakedown' sail, Jack carried the carving into the boatyard. It wouldn't seem as if the ship was truly ready for sea until Grandpa's dragon was once again on her bow.

There had been three days of mounting excitement as the storm blew over.

On the first day, Chippy Alan put the engine back together, crouching on the chart-room's deck while the rain lashed the skylight and the wind howled in the bare rigging above. Scotty fired on the third heave, and settled into a sweet, steady tick.

On the second day, the barometer rose, and George climbed the ratlines to the crosstrees to help with the halyards and running rigging. Scotty still sang.

On the third day, they bent on the mainsail, the one sail that 'lived out', secured to the boom and gaff. They stowed the jibs and foresails in the fo'c's'le sail lockers. For a while Jack considered abandoning the old square sail, an antiquated rig whose yard meant extra weight, high on the mast, but it really drove the ship forward when the wind was steady on the stern or quarter. In the end he took it. It was how Grandpa had sailed.

The forecast for the following day was a steady westerly, force four, with a moderate sea on the tail of the storm. If the engine still worked, they'd sail. And with a slightly self-conscious air of ceremony, Jack installed the dragon.

It was lighter than its bulk suggested. The arched head in his arms was like a ghost of its former self, encased in an invisible sheath of polymer. Grandpa had treated it like a living thing. He'd wanted it to be with him when the ship was scuttled. Well, maybe Jack would drop it back in the ocean with Grandpa's ashes. Either that, or give it to a museum afterwards. Sometimes Jack could understand why Grandpa spoke of it like that; the way the light caught its carved eyes could make them seem to follow you if you moved near it, the way the eyes of some oil paintings follow you. It was just a thing, a carved lump of wood, but as Jack carried it to the ship and smelled a sailing wind, he felt an excitement that was more than his own. When he sat in the dinghy under the bowsprit and lifted it into position, its gaping jaws seemed so hungry that they might have bitten a lump out of his shoulder in their impatience to be away.

Jack grinned at Chippy and George, who watched him from the jetty. George frowned back at him with her lips pursed into a narrow, tight line, but he wasn't going to let her dislike of the carving spoil the moment.

'Roll of drums!' Jack held the dragon against the bow, poised over its metal holder. There should be more ceremony to this.

The rumble of distant thunder came so much on cue that Jack laughed, jolting the dragon so that it slipped home of its own volition, mashing the edge of Jack's hand between the carving's base and the metal socket. His laughter became a grunt as he freed his hand and cradled it. Blood welled into his palm and trickled between his fingers.

'You OK?' Chippy asked. George scanned a sky almost empty of cloud, still frowning.

Jack swore under his breath, pushing a triangular flap of skin back into place. 'No problem. Looks messy but nothing serious.'

'That's weird.' George still stared at the sky. 'There ain't no thunderclouds.'

Jack held the carving in place with his injured hand in its mouth, and tightened the fittings with his good hand.

'It's in a hurry. Like me.' He felt slightly foolish and tried to make light of the moment.

'Don't say stuff like that, Jack.'

Jack looked at George. It wasn't like her to have a sense–of–humour failure. The carved tongue felt slick and sticky against his palm, and he smeared the blood on the dragon's face before he reached for the next nut.

'Hey, lighten up. It slipped.'

'It looks frigging evil.'

Jack looked up, and the dragon seemed to look back at him, a mess of bright red blood sliding down the trough between its tongue and its lips.

'Hail to the dragon!' He made it a mock obeisance, folding awkwardly on the dinghy's seat.

'I'm not joking, Jack.' George stormed off towards her office. Jack looked at Chippy, lifting his arms as if to say, *'What was all that about?'*

Chippy didn't react. 'You'd better get that cleaned up. Might need a stitch.' He steadied the dinghy so Jack could climb out one-handed.

Jack paused on the jetty, his mood only slightly dented. He and Chippy stood together, admiring a ship that was finally ready for the sea. The dragon's head rose above the level of the deck, as high as Grandpa Eddie could have fitted it without interfering with the rigging, as like a Viking figurehead as possible in a ship with foresails. As they watched, a single gob of blood oozed from the dragon's lip, and hung there as if on a fine, stretching thread until it fell into the water.

Chapter Six: Gjálfrmarr

(Old Norse: steed of the sea)

From the Saga of King Guthrum

King Alfred and his army pursued King Guthrum to Fyrsig, and there made siege. Now Fyrsig stands on good ground within marshes, hence King Alfred could not come against Guthrum, nor Guthrum against Alfred, for the marshes lay between them and a few men could hold the causeway against many. Nor could Alfred attack by sea, for Guthrum's fleet was the greater, but Alfred had piles set across the harbour mouth and men to guard them so that no Viking ships could escape.

Yet Guthrum and his army suffered not greatly from the siege, for they lay in the halls at Fyrsig while the army of the Saxons must needs endure the winter in the fields about. There were fish to be caught within the great harbour, and fresh water from the river. Furthermore Guthrum sent raiding ships across the harbour, now to the East, now to the West, landing each time a half day's march from the army of the Saxons and doing scathe in the lands about.

At the Spring festival when night and day are balanced, Guthrum feasted and held sacrifice for the success of the raiding season. Now there was among the Saxon women one who was troll-wise[1] and had been a völva,[2] but was now Christian like all Saxons, by the command of King Alfred. This woman they made to say the poems of seidr,[3] and they gave her the sacred bowls filled with the blood of sacrifice, that in the sprinkling of the hlaut[4] she might see their destiny. The woman spoke the poems and read the pattern of the blood, and proclaimed that the Norns had woven the fates of Guthrum's people, and their destiny was set; one woman would cause the deaths of half the army, and their deaths would be without honour so their shades would not be chosen for the einherjar.[5] But these warriors who were denied the ranks of Odin would cry out to the gods, and the one that set their fate would be haugbūi,[6] undead, denied even Niflheim, for as many generations as Guthrum had years.

Guthrum liked these words very ill, and said that the woman spoke them as a Saxon who wished to put fear into the hearts of the Vikings so their weapons would be as sticks. Guthrum spared the woman, lest she curse him, but he feasted no more in Fyrsig.

1. Fey; knowing the ways of the spirits.
2. Prophetess, seeress, wise woman.
3. Pagan magic or sorcery, including the shaping or foretelling of future events.
4. Sacrificial blood.
5. Warriors who have died valiantly in battle and are chosen for Valhalla.
6. Literally 'cairn-dweller'; undead spirit, ghost.

I: JACK

Chippy helped them cast off, throwing the head rope to George on the foredeck. He was smiling to himself at Scotty's steady purr. George and Jack waved back as if they were heading off to cross the Atlantic rather than for a single-day shakedown sail.

Jack kept *Draca* on the engine in the harbour. She drew a lot of water, and he wanted sea room around them when they hoisted the sails. He waited until they were far enough beyond the harbour mouth to have a mile of deep water downwind before he turned her into the wind, throttled back and lashed the tiller to hold her there.

Hoisting *Draca*'s mainsail was a job for two people, especially if one of them had a cut hand. From the beginning, they had to haul the weight of the gaff, the boom that stretched the sail out into its four-cornered shape, and the sail itself was of a canvas thick enough to weather a heavy storm. *Draca* didn't have winches, so they had to swig it, heaving the halyard away from the mast to take up the last of the slack while the sail flogged loose, crackling like rifle fire.

Back in the cockpit, George gestured towards the tiller, letting Jack, as *Draca*'s skipper, feel that moment when they killed the engine, let her fall away from the wind and with the mainsheet hauled home felt that first pull of the sail. *Draca* curtsied to a swell, sluggish at first until she gathered way, heeled a little and the rudder bit the water. George and Jack grinned at each other, sharing the moment: a living ship under a storm-washed sky, and a silence broken only by the bubbling of water flowing past the hull.

'Shall we see what she can do?' Jack lifted his chin towards the foresails, still furled around their roller-reefing gear.

George didn't answer, but unwrapped a foresheet from a belaying post and heaved at the jib. As the foresails filled, *Draca* put her shoulder down and charged.

Jack whooped with the joy of that moment. After ten weeks he knew every plank in that boat, every crevice, every stinking corner of her bilges. He'd shaped her, sanded her and cursed her. He'd scraped away her flaws and made them good, and kicked her faltering engine. He'd dressed her in newly mended sails, furnished her with shiny new fittings, and he loved her. *Draca* was a thoroughbred of the sea, and she showed her breeding in the way she took the wind.

Jack set a course off the line of cliffs that stretched south-west from Anfel Head, meeting a long, heavy swell on the tails of the storm and a breeze strong enough to send wave tops tumbling over themselves and rustling down their lee slopes. For *Draca*, who'd been built to ride out far more extreme weather, this was a wind to play with. She climbed the side of each wave and soared over into the trough, shoulder-barging the swell the way a porpoise might leap and dive for the sheer exuberance of living. The old lady was back and loving it.

Jack handed George the helm and made his way forward, resting his hand on each rope and stay, feeling the boat's mood through his fingertips. He used to go forward without thinking, rolling with the boat, scarcely needing to hold on, even in a strong sea. Now he needed to go hand over hand on the grab bars on the skylight roof until he could lurch from them to the stays. When he reached the foredeck, he crawled. His balance was wrecked, but it was worth the effort. He lay flat beside the bowsprit and peered over the gunwale to watch the stem slice the waves. Beside his head the dragon rose and fell, rose and fell like a carved horse on a fairground roundabout. Jack remembered that sail with Grandpa just after he had fitted his new figurehead, and now he understood. The dragon, too, was happy.

'Squall!' George's shout made him look up. She pointed at the darker line racing towards them over the water, and Jack knew he wouldn't make it back to the cockpit before it hit. He was only at the level of the mast when *Draca* fell into a trough and spray sluiced around his legs. At the crest of the following wave, the wind became a sudden, angry whine through the rigging and they were blown so far over that the tip of the mainsail's boom touched the water. Jack was condemned to witness George's skills as a solo yachtswoman while he was wedged into the angle between the skylight and the deck.

She was good, very good, but it almost seemed that *Draca* was fighting her. At first George laughed, a high, bubbling whoop as if the life inside her couldn't be contained, but the tiller kicked in her hand, and her look darkened. By the time Jack tumbled into the cockpit, George had a real battle on her hands, with both feet braced against the lee side of the cockpit, and both hands on the tiller while she heaved hard to hold her course.

Jack reached for the tiller to help her, and the wind dropped. Just like that. It was uncanny. One second they were battling to steer, the next the squall had passed and they were riding the waves as smoothly as ever, with the wind steady on the starboard bow. They looked at each other and George shrugged as if she didn't quite believe the sudden peace.

'If I didn't know better,' she laughed in a way that made fun of her own words, 'I'd say your boat has just thrown a hissy fit.'

That wasn't the only time. They made *Draca* work, testing her at every point of sailing. It was bonding, in a platonic, working-together way. George not only knew what to do without being told, she was a much better sailor than Jack, the difference, perhaps, between a weekend yachtsman and

someone whose life is on the water. She'd never sailed *Draca*
before, but she understood how to set the foresail in a way
that made the ship easier to steer, and how to coax the last
ounce of power out of her. When Jack had the helm, *Draca*
ran sweetly through the water and he and George would stand
braced in the vee between the cockpit's deck and the lee bench,
while the rigging hummed *Draca*'s happiness. When George
took her, the battle began, and *Draca*'s hum became a howl of
rage. It reminded Jack of a time he'd watched a woman tame
an unbroken horse. The beast had leaped around a sand school,
snorting, snatching at the rope that tethered them together.
As soon as the woman thought she'd calmed it, it would be
off again, bucking and kicking. Eventually, George gave *Draca*
back.

'You take her. She knows her master.'

It was a day for fanciful notions.

In the afternoon the wind eased, and they began to relax.
Something had changed between them, born out of that shared
working of the boat, and they were both putting off the
moment when they'd have to turn for the harbour. They
hadn't spoken much, other than about the boat and sailing,
but it didn't seem to matter. The clouds were clearing and
they sat in the cockpit in companionable silence, basking in
the sun. There was enough space to sit without touching, just,
and watch squadrons of gannets streak along the wave troughs,
close enough to see their creamy-yellow heads and bandit-
striped eyes. Beyond them, the massive chalk cliff of Anfel
Head alternately shone white and glowered grey as clouds
passed over.

'Anfilt Thuna,' George muttered, as if to herself.

'Sorry?'

'The Saxon name for Anfel Head. I found it in a local history book. It means the anvil of Thunor, or Thor.'

'An vil you tell me how it got the name?'

George groaned. 'You should be hammered for that. I suppose it does look a bit anvil-y.' She stood and peeled off her life jacket and fleece. A light perspiration had formed on her forehead. 'It's getting warm.'

Jack looked away and began to lash the tiller into position as George stuffed her shirt back into her shorts.

'Let's try the square sail.'

Jack went forward with her to set the sail, pleased to find that *Draca* held her course. When he returned to the cockpit George stayed near the cabin skylight, one hand resting on the boom with her eyes screwed shut against the sun, enjoying the rise and plunge as the waves passed under them, racing to the east and steepening as they neared the land. She'd found the point where the whole ship felt balanced. With such a long swell, *Draca* would lift her stern and surf down each wave, surging forward until the wave passed underneath and the stern dropped back into the trough. There the boat would wallow, for a moment, readying herself for the next charge forward. The sensation was even better with the square sail set. Most foresails tend to drive the bow downwards, even slightly, but the square sail was a lifting sail. It would scoop wind from the surface, letting the old lady pick up her skirts and run.

Jack should have looked away, and watched the sailing rather than George, but he found himself smiling at the sight of her standing there, her eyes closed, with the wind flapping her shirt against her and that orange-streaked hair whipping like a banner above her head. With each wave her body would rise, find a moment of exquisite weightlessness, then sink into the trough in a glorious, elliptical swoop. Yes, he knew she was his wife's girlfriend. That also meant she was probably gay, but he was just watching, and trying to unpick a complicated set of thoughts.

Jack was lost in guilty admiration when the wind veered without warning, sending the boom swinging across the deck in a vicious gybe that sent *Draca* rolling almost broadside to the wind. As they broached in the trough of a wave, Jack unbalanced and lost his grip on the tiller. He spun round, grabbing at the cockpit coaming for support, and glimpsed the boom sweep George off the deck like an enormous cricket bat, tumbling her towards the rail before the mainsail blocked his view. As he fought to bring *Draca* back under control he kept glancing back at the wake, fearing to see George's head passing astern and all too aware that her life jacket was at his feet.

When they righted, George was hanging overboard with one arm hooked around a stay, the other hand grasping the gunwale, and her legs trailing in the water. By the time Jack brought *Draca* back onto a safe course, she'd hauled herself back on board and was working her way aft, soaked to the waist, holding the skylight grab handles and swearing beneath her breath.

'George, I'm so sorry.' Jack felt really bad. That had been close.

She jumped into the cockpit, and slammed the edge of her fist into the cabin hatch.

'Bitch!'

'I didn't see it coming...'

She threw herself onto a cockpit bench, trailing rivulets of seawater, and shook her head.

'Out of the blue. Literally.' George's smile was weak, and Jack could see that she was shaken. 'She has a few tricks to play, doesn't she?'

'It was a gust. The wind veered.' And he should have seen it coming.

'Yeah, sure.'

'I think it's time to head back.' Jack felt a fool, and the mood was broken. Nobody likes a near miss, especially when they're in charge. George nodded, and put on her life jacket before reaching for the ropes. They were both quiet as they turned towards the harbour entrance.

Half an hour later they'd made little progress. Jack had forgotten how slow *Draca* could be into the wind, and the tide was taking them to the east, away from the harbour.

'Let's start Scotty.' Jack had switched from delaying their return to accelerating it.

Of course Scotty wasn't going to start. The bloody boat was playing with them. No matter how hard Jack heaved on the crank, the engine would only wheeze like a smoker's laugh before it died, coughing dirt. Jack gave up after fifteen sweaty minutes.

'We could anchor in the lee of the castle.' George lifted her chin towards a long sand spit on the horizon that ended with the squat, ugly shape of a Napoleonic fort. There was shelter and a safe anchorage beyond. 'Wait for the tide to turn in our favour.'

'Which will be the middle of the night.'

'Just after 4 a.m. It will be getting light by four-thirty.'

Like many people whose lives are framed by the tides, George had that kind of information in her head.

'Looks like we'd better get an early night then.'

Jack's mood lifted with the satisfaction of coming to anchor under sail, sailing as his grandfather would have liked, without a motor or any modern aids. Even the anchor light he hoisted up the mast was an old, kerosene hurricane lamp, to save on batteries. Back to basics.

After they'd secured the boat, George called Chippy Alan at the yard. He'd have raised the alarm if they hadn't shown.

She sounded stilted and at pains to emphasise that it wasn't a situation that either of them had sought. When she killed the connection they looked at each other, awkward at being thrust into each other's company in this way.

'I haven't much in the way of food, I'm afraid. Some tinned stuff. Soup, coffee, the remains of a packed lunch. Whisky.'

George smiled at him. She seemed more relaxed than he was. 'Whisky.'

II: GEORGE

George knew, like anyone who's done a lot of sailing, that boats have characters. She noticed it more with older, wooden boats. Modern, fibreglass boats might have characteristics, but classic boats had characters. They had moods, and they could be quirky. Someone who'd spent their life ashore might laugh, but no true sailor would scoff at the idea that a boat could have attitude and, by the time they anchored, George was sure that *Draca* was playing with her.

What was more, George was going off *Draca*. Sure, she was lovely, all vintage lines and polished teak. Pilot cutters like *Draca* were built to ride out the weather off a port, waiting for a ship that would hire the pilot. The cutter's crew would put him aboard, follow the ship into port, pick him up and do it again. Week after week. They were all-weather, working boats, without the lines of an ocean racer or the belly of a fisherman, but graceful enough to turn heads in a harbour. George had expected *Draca* to be a bit of a bruiser, but she hadn't expected that mean streak. Maybe that gybe had been a fluke wind, but it felt nasty. Malevolent, even. *Draca* was a bit like some men she'd met who were handsome on the outside but dangerous on the inside. In that way, *Draca* was the opposite of Jack. He was dangerous on the outside but probably dead gentle on the inside, like he was wearing a suit of armour, or a shell, like a crab.

George stood on the foredeck, ready to drop the anchor, as Jack sailed her into the anchorage, leaving just enough way on the ship to turn into the wind before he told her to let go. As George slipped the pick she could swear that figurehead was looking at her over its shoulder.

'I've got my eye on you too,' she muttered at it as the chain rattled through the pipe and dragged out as they drifted astern on wind and tide.

She knew Jack felt bad. She would have done as well. He'd almost put her overboard and now they were stuck there waiting for the tide, but George didn't really mind. If Jack hadn't been married she'd have been quite pleased, in a way. Jack was interesting: all that brooding, hunky silence and a smile like sunshine through cloud. As it was, they'd have an evening getting to know each other a bit better, and then she'd go into the forward cabin and shut the door.

She'd known Jack was watching her before the gybe, but she had stayed there and kept her eyes shut. There was a floating, almost weightless sensation as they fell off the top of a wave that was a bit like swimming under water. Just before the gust hit and they broached she'd been wondering whether to take her shirt off to top up her tan. After all, she had a bikini on underneath. She'd let her mind drift, and maybe she shouldn't have felt so safe. Jack seemed younger when he was sailing, like those little lines had been shaken out of his face. The way his hand gripped the tiller had bunched the muscles in his forearm. Big hands. Did Jack know that Charlotte fooled around?

That gust took them both by surprise.

People open up when they're watching a sunset from a boat, especially the kind that can only come after a storm, when the sky is washed clean but the clouds are still piled up on the horizon, greys on pinks. There was just the sound of the seabirds coming back to roost on the sand spit, all crying out to each other. Gull noises, and the steady slap of the halyards against the mast. Even that's a different sound, in an old boat. Rope on wood, not polyester on aluminium. Jack and George sat sipping whisky with their backs to the cabin, one on each side of the cockpit, with their legs stretched out on the benches. An eddy of the tide had turned the boat, conveniently, so they didn't have to crane their necks to watch the sun go down in glory, and the sight gave George the kind of feeling she had once had in a church, all full and happy and almost weepy. But then she was starting her third whisky.

'Your granddad would be pleased. With the way you've done up *Draca*, I mean.' They'd been quiet for a while, but the silences were comfortable.

'He liked you, you know. If he'd have been forty years younger he'd have been after you.'

George grunted, remembering Eddie's hand on her backside. 'Sometimes he forgot his age.'

Jack stared. 'Did he cause problems?'

'I can look after myself.' Jack waited, watching her, and she shrugged. 'Eddie was a 'patter'. He'd touch my bum like it was his way of saying hello. A bit sad, really. He was just a lonely old man. If he'd have been a bit younger I'd have kneed him in the balls.' Besides, she knew Eddie was going to die. She'd seen the darkness around him.

Jack laughed, a little nervously, and turned back to the view. The light across his jaw made his evening shadow look like the crust of seeded bread.

'Grandpa had his demons.'

'Don't we all.' That slipped out. *Frigging whisky*. George had been thinking about colours, that trick she had of closing her eyes and linking people with colours. They go black towards the end, like her mum's had, though she hadn't known what she was looking at then. It just frightened her. Mad Eddie had walked in his own shadow on that last visit, and she knew.

Jack looked at her sharply, but she kept her eyes on the seagulls massing over the sand spit and silhouetted against the sky. She wondered how to dig her way out of that remark. The sun had dropped below the horizon, and the undersides of the clouds were turning from pink to peach.

'And what are your demons, George?' He sounded surprised. She'd have understood if he'd said that in a way that asked what could possibly be as bad as having your foot blown off, but he didn't. He sounded kind. Interested.

It took George a while to answer while she gathered her thoughts. The whisky was warm in her gut and the sky swayed backwards and forwards with the motion of the boat, gentle here in the shelter of the anchorage.

'I'll trade you. One of yours for one of mine.'

In the time it took him to answer, a solitary gull side-slipped across the sky, hovered and soared back again without moving a feather.

'Go on.' Jack made the words sound heavy.

She took a deep breath. Whisky and the sunset made it easier to talk.

'Not belonging. Being the outsider, being different.'

'Different?' Jack looked at her, hard enough for her to shut her eyes. His outline stayed printed in her mind, now lighter than the sky beyond rather than silhouetted against it, echoing the sunset in pinks and blues: friendship and sensitivity. The colours encouraged her.

'Lots of schools. Several foster homes. I've always been the outsider, looking in.'

'But how "different"?'

Looking at the last touch of light in the sky is a bit like staring into a fire. Truths come out. Another deep breath.

'I told you in your garden. Me mum said I was psychic. I'm sensitive to things other people don't see.'

'What sort of things?'

'Atmospheres. Moods. Motivations. I can see quite a lot about someone's character. Not with everyone, though, and I have no idea why it's there with some people and not with others.'

'Does it work with me?'

George swallowed. 'Very well.'

Jack looked away. An eddy was turning the boat around its anchor, and distant street lights began to appear beyond his shoulder, hooped in tiny necklaces along the shore. Behind them the land still loomed between sea and sky, a featureless grey mass in the gathering dark. Jack spoke towards the lights rather than her.

'I'm not sure I'm comfortable with that.'

'Nor were the kids at school, if they found out. They called me The Witch. I learned not to talk about it.' The headlights of a solitary car made their way along the line of lights. 'Don't worry though. I like what I see. In you, I mean.' Was that a bit pushy?

'And what do you see?'

'Oh, you're trouble!' It was time to lighten the mood. 'As much to yourself as other people. All that energy, and it's all turned inwards.'

He snorted, but didn't say anything. Over on the sand bar the seagulls were calming down after their last squeal of the evening. Soon it would be too dark to see his face.

'It's almost...' The whisky let her blunder on.

'It's almost what, George?' Jack's eyes were shadowed. He didn't seem angry, just sad.

George took another sip, then pushed her glass away, realising she'd reached that dangerous stage where you think you can keep drinking.

'It's almost like you're folded round your own pain.'

Jack's shoulders lifted and dropped in a great sigh, and he turned his face away again. She needed to change the subject before she wrecked a friendship.

'Why did you make me stand on the path by your cottage?'

Another pause.

'I saw something there. Something I can't explain. You'd said you were psychic...' His voice trailed away, then picked up again. 'Actually, I was a bit disappointed when you didn't feel anything.'

'But I did. Not from that spot though, just from that frigging carving behind me, like it was about to stab me in the back.'

'I think I'll get rid of it once we've scattered Grandpa's ashes. Give it to a museum or something. Can you feel it now?'

George turned her senses inward, listening. 'No.' She was relieved. It would have spoiled the mood.

Jack sipped again and reached for the bottle. George had the impression of ropes knotted across his back. Not just ropes: cables, the thick, ugly ones they use to moor ships. She shook her head as Jack waved the bottle at her.

'There was something else my mum said about me.'

Only the slightest lift of his head showed that he was listening. He was just an outline now, with paler patches where the last of the light touched his cheek.

'She said I had a healing touch.' George thought that if she put her thumbs into those knots she could smooth them away, reach inside his protective shell and let the real Jack out. She was probably too pissed to think about what might happen afterwards.

Jack lifted his bad leg a little so the heel moved over the bench with a noise like a wooden block shifting on a deck.

'You'd need to be a miracle worker to fix that.'

'Not all wounds are physical.'

He rested his head back against the cabin roof. It was too dark to see his expression, but there was a shine where the last of the light caught his eye.

'True.'

'Your turn.'

Jack was quiet for a long time, but George didn't prompt

him, knowing that some truth was working its way to the surface. The first of the stars were appearing in the sky and when he spoke it was upwards, towards them, with the whisky cradled on his stomach.

'After this happened,' he shifted his injured leg without looking down, 'I was almost happy.'

George waited. He had to explain that.

'The first time you come under fire, and don't get hurt, you feel almost ecstatic. You learn that you can survive. Then there's the second time, and the third time, and people are wounded or killed, and you realise it's all a gamble. You roll the dice with each contact. You lose a free 'life' with every passing bullet or bomb. Eventually, statistically, you're going to get hurt. When they took off my foot, or what was left of it, part of me was happy because I wouldn't have to roll those dice again. Deep down, I'd wimped out.'

The shine in his eye was brighter. George looked away, and tipped the last of her whisky into her mouth. This guy needed a hug, but she didn't know him well enough for that. Besides, she felt too much chemistry of another kind.

'Come over here.' She scrambled out of the cockpit to kneel on the deck, facing him, and patted the timber coaming between her knees. 'Sit with your back to me.'

Jack's outline shifted, angling towards her, but he stayed where he was. She tapped the wood again.

'Sit! Don't worry, it's not a come-on.'

Jack was probably pleased she'd changed the subject. His silhouette moved, ducked under the boom and slumped onto the seat in front of her knees, his movements whisky-heavy. His back rose above the coaming from his shoulder blades upwards, and his presence was suddenly very physical, very close. He smelled of salt and sweat and damp wool.

'What are you planning, George?'

'Shush.'

He'd put on a fleece against the evening chill, and at first George worked through it, starting with the trapezius muscles between his neck and shoulders, squeezing them between her thumbs and fingers, smoothing away the tension. His shoulders dropped and he arched his neck, sighing, but George wasn't getting to the real knots. You can't do that with a frigging great lump of teak and a fleece in the way, but she dug deep until her knuckles and then her fingertips reached over his collar onto his neck. There was an area of soft skin with downy hair on his nape, and when she touched that she stopped, embarrassed and a bit confused. They'd reached a moment where things either happen or they don't.

Jack stood, holding on to the boom, still looking away from her.

'I'm sorry.' George meant it. She was spoiling two friendships: one because she was getting too close and one because she wouldn't let Charlotte get closer.

'No.' He said that as if he meant 'it's all right'.

'I didn't mean…'

'It's OK. Really.'

'I think I'll go to bed. We've an early start.'

'There's a fresh duvet in the sleeping cabin.' He spoke like he was reading from a script. 'You'll have more privacy there. No sheets, I'm afraid. I hadn't planned…'

'It's all right.'

'I'll stay up here until you've finished in the heads.'

'Sure.'

He didn't turn round as she climbed down into the chart-room.

It took George a while to settle. She splashed water on her face from the old, fold-down porcelain bowl in *Draca*'s cramped little head, and stood in the saloon afterwards, looking up through the chart–room at the outline of Jack's shoulder against the stars. George felt she was an intruder. All around her was old wood, dark and shiny, with every space filled with tightly fitted cupboards. The saloon smelled of books and old tobacco, new varnish and a paraffin pressure lamp that hissed on the table and made its own fug. A moth danced with death around its glow. This was a male space: the sort of cabin that should be filled with bearded explorer blokes in chunky sweaters, sitting on those leather benches, smoking pipes as they wrote their journals.

She wondered whether to apologise again. In the end she just called out 'goodnight' and went forward. *Feck, when you're in a hole, stop digging.*

The sleeping cabin was more cramped, even claustrophobic. The mast rose through the middle, and there was no skylight, so the deckhead pressed down on her, short as she was. Even with the electric light on it was a place of shadows, the sort of cabin that made her open the door to the fo'c's'le to make sure there was no one there.

With the light off, a faint glimmer of moonlight came in through two circular scuttles cut into the hull, one on each side above the bunks. They were the old–fashioned, brassbound ship's windows that hinged inwards or could be screwed tight to the hull with wing nuts, and she cracked them open to get some fresh air. She climbed into the single bunk, drew the curtain behind her and felt like a child in a tent in the dark, listening to the noises outside. For a while Jack moved in the saloon, and the wooden rumble must have been the cockpit hatch closing. After that there was just the slap of water against the hull and the rattle of the anchor chain as the boat moved with the tide, tugging against it.

George knew she was dreaming, and that sort of made it OK, at first. She sat on the deck with her legs dangling into the cockpit either side of Jack's shoulders as if there'd never been a coaming in the way, and the texture of his hair through her fingers was strong and wiry, long enough in her dream to flow over the backs of her hands, so sensuously that she wanted him. She wanted him so much she ached, and when his head began to turn in her hand she leaned back, closing her eyes, knowing he was going to kiss her there, over the ache. His lips were light and hardly touched, just a tease, enough to make her need him more, and she moaned and opened her legs a little further. But her knee brushed against the hull, chill and real, and she began to wake even though she fought to stay in the dream.

How could Jack fit into that narrow bunk? But then his breath was at her neck and she became fully awake, eyes snapping open, as a beard dragged across her throat. As the first scream rose in her chest she flailed upwards with her arm, expecting to hit flesh but instead sweeping through the curtain. Enough moonlight came through the scuttles to hint at unfamiliar outlines of mast and lockers, but the darkness was not empty. There was breathing near her face and the stink was vile, like rotting seaweed. George was still screaming as she snapped on the light, expecting to see someone crouching on the deck between her and the still-closed door.

The cabin's emptiness shut her up, but she swung her legs out of the bunk, gasping for air. Whoever it was must have got out of the room somehow when she had screamed. Jack? She couldn't believe it of him. George wrenched open the door, ready to fight, with some vague idea of grabbing a knife from the galley. Anything was better than being cooped up in that tiny cabin, wondering what was on the other side of the door.

Jack was half out of the bed he'd made up on a bench, blinking in the shaft of light from the cabin, and George knew immediately that it hadn't been him. He'd thrown back his duvet and had one foot on the floor. The other still stood beside his bench, still weirdly wearing its trainer and with his chinos crumpled around its goblet-shaped fitting. His hair was tousled and he was naked apart from boxer shorts, like a confusing echo of her dream, and she dragged her eyes away to stare into every shadow of the saloon. For a moment the only sound was her own breathing, fast and shallow.

'George, what's wrong?'

She couldn't understand how no one else was in the saloon. Even the hatch was still closed. Surely they'd have heard the rumble as it was opened? She spun back and opened the door to the fo'c's'le, where the shadowed blackness felt evil until she found another light switch and saw just lockers and racks of sails.

'George, tell me!' Jack grabbed his leg and was pulling it on as she ran past him through the saloon into the chart–room, groping for the hatch. George had to have air. Fresh air. Open space that didn't stink of rot. She took great gulps of it in the cockpit, waiting for her breathing to slow. She'd gone to sleep in just knickers and a sweatshirt, and the air was chill on her skin, but there was a sharper cold between her legs that she touched, exploring. She groaned, disgusted with herself at the dampness she found. When Jack appeared she was huddled on a bench in a corner, stretching her sweatshirt downwards to hide the humiliating stain. He stood on the companion ladder, head and shoulders out of the hatch.

'What's going on, George?'

He sounded gentle but she squirmed away from him, with her mind lurching between possibilities. Not Jack. No way anyone else could have come on board. Maybe a dream. Can you smell a dream? But she'd felt the breath, heard the breathing and smelled the rot after she was awake. George didn't know which was worse: the idea that she'd nearly been fucked by a ghost, or that she'd enjoyed it enough to get wet. She began to shiver, maybe with cold, maybe with shock.

'Could you bring my clothes, please?' The calmness of her voice surprised her. *It* was still down there. She had nowhere further to run. 'I don't want to go below any more. And a towel?' She either had to face this one out or jump overboard. George stared along the ribbon of moonlight that lay across the sea, watching how it fragmented and reformed out of the blackness. It was pure. She wanted to shower, or bathe. Wash her whole frigging body.

Jack put her bundle on the other bench without a word, and retreated into the cabin. He shut the hatch behind him completely, noisily, as if to emphasise that she had this space to herself, and she was grateful for that.

She lowered a bucket into the sea, and used one end of the towel to wash. Everywhere. Particularly the places where she'd dreamed she'd been touched. Jack was between her and it, which was some comfort, and if the night hadn't been so frigging cold she'd have stood there naked for longer, letting clean air brush over her skin. When she was dressed she threw the knickers overboard and slid back the hatch.

Jack arrived with mugs of hot, powdered chocolate, and settled himself back into 'his' corner of the cockpit. He'd dressed too. He waited for her to speak, and the silence was like waiting for thunder. George blew steam off her drink and sipped. The mug rattled against her teeth but the warmth slipping down her throat was almost as good as a hug.

'Jack, either I'm hallucinating or your boat is haunted.'

She told him. Not everything, not the sexy bits. Well, not all of them. She told him about the breathing and the smell and the touch on her throat. She didn't say she'd thought it was him. And she certainly didn't say that she'd wanted him. But talking about it made her relive it, and the shivers turned into shakes until she wanted him in a different way. She needed Jack to put his arms around her like her mum had held her when she was hurt and little, and for him to tell her everything was going to be OK. But he got up and went into the cabin, and she felt abandoned until he came back with the duvet from her bunk and a pillow, and tucked them round her in the cockpit. Then he fetched his own bedding and made a nest for himself on the other side, and she had to be content with that. At least she had someone with her, someone who listened and didn't tell her she was being stupid.

'You told me you were psychic,' Jack interrupted her when she started to repeat herself. 'Perhaps you're sensitive to things other people can't see.'

Which was a gentle way of telling her that no one else had had this problem. Not that he didn't believe her, just that he'd never heard of it before. At least he wasn't laughing at her.

'You said you saw something in your garden.'

'I may have done. It might have been... more like a memory.'

A memory he wasn't going to explain. The silence stretched and George cradled her mug, even though there was only a cooling sludge in the bottom. Up here, all was pure, but she felt as if she was sitting on the back of something nasty, and only Jack's presence was protecting her.

'George, how is it you can see things about people's characters?' The question came out of the darkness. His tone was neutral, like 'I'm interested but I don't want to say I believe it.'

George thought long and hard before she spoke. No good had ever come of telling people before.

'Some colours seem to fit people, when I think of them. Maybe colours are just my brain's way of painting intuition, and the intuition comes from the stuff I see. Body language. Faces. Eyes, especially eyes. I dunno.' Now that she'd started, it was easier to talk in the dark. 'I've learned to link the colours with the way people are. They hardly ever lie, but they can mean different things.'

She forced herself to talk. Sitting beside the hatch was like sitting at the entrance to a cave, knowing that some vile reptile lurked within.

'Like what?'

If she reached out her hand towards him, across the blackness, *it* might be there, on the steps, within touching distance...

'Well, if I think someone fits with green, it could mean they're a healer, or it could mean they're jealous.' She didn't sound calm any more. Brittle-bright. Trying so hard to be normal that she was like a bad actor.

'As in 'green with envy'.'

'Right.' Keep talking. Fill the night with words. Just don't start thinking about the sleeping cabin. 'Reds show strength or anger, but also sex. The colours are just a mental picture though, never for real.' Not since she was a kid, anyway. 'Once, years ago, I saw a holy man, and when I thought of him he was almost pure white.' The memory of that old man was suddenly very strong, and she clung to it. One set of foster parents, the Christian ones, had taken her to Lindisfarne, where this old monk had looked at her with eyes that were kind and wise and peaceful. Afterwards her image of him was white, like his hair, with just a hint of violet round the edges. Only time she'd ever seen that.

'And white's good?'

'I think you only get to white when you've conquered everything else. I dunno. No one's ever told me why I see them or what I'm seeing. I don't look for them, don't really want them, they're just there.'

'So what do you 'see' in me?'

'Tell you some other time.' When she hadn't just told him what reds meant. 'But at least you don't have as much brown as your father.'

'Brown?'

'Browns tend to be self-centred and have strong opinions.'

Jack laughed. 'That fits.'

'And your mum has a lot of pink. Pink means love. And greys. She's tired.'

He was silent at that.

'It was stronger when I was a kid. Got me into all sorts of trouble.' The talk was doing her good. Words fell out of her mouth without thinking. Anything to keep her mind away from what had happened below. Besides, it was friendly, wrapped up in a duvet, with the stars above them. It was frigging cold but she was sort of warm inside because he was giving up his sleep to stay with her. This was the gentler side of Jack, inside the shell.

'How come?'

'Well, for a start I could tell when grown-ups were lying. That really pissed off my teachers.' She hadn't opened up like this to anyone for years. And he sounded interested.

'Seriously, George, what do the colours tell you about me?'

She thought for a while, wondering how to answer.

'There's the kind of blue that means moods, but can also mean kindness. Right now, there's a lot of blue and it's a good, kind blue. There's grey, a darker grey than your mum's. Something beyond tiredness. Sadness, even depression.'

Jack grunted.

'And a lot of red.'

179

At that she shut up and turned away from him, hoping he hadn't thought she was flirting.

She didn't think she had slept. Now that she wasn't talking, the memories came back and she squirmed, feeling dirty. Small draughts of cold air would find their way under the duvet, no matter how much she tried to make a cocoon of it. If she lay facing the hatch, its darkness gaped like a mouth and she didn't want to close her eyes for fear of what might come through it. It was worse if she turned away. In the end she lay on her back, half sitting so she could look over the cockpit coaming at a world beyond. Above them, patches of stars showed where there were gaps in the clouds, and if she hadn't felt so wretched it would have been beautiful. Out in the channel a navigation buoy pulsed red, hypnotically, and she fixed her eyes on it, hoping it would send her to sleep. In time it began to drift across her vision, sliding away as the boat turned. Slack water.

A hint of paleness came into view where the buoy had been, just the faintest definition of a horizon, which slid aft as the boat swung, until it lay across the stern. On the other side of the cockpit, Jack stirred, turned over and settled back into sleep. George felt safe with him there, like she was anchored to him. She wished they knew each other well enough for him to hold her.

He woke when the seagulls began screaming at each other on the spit. It was just light enough to see him look round, fixing the boat's orientation.

'The tide's turned.' Jack's voice was an early-morning, too-much-whisky growl. George grunted, fidgeting under the duvet with the need to pee, but there was no way she was going below in the dark.

'I need coffee.' Jack stood and stretched, a darker outline filling the space beneath the boom. George winced as he snapped on a torch and the cockpit filled with a dancing beam of light.

'You OK?' She liked the way he asked that. Gentle. Concerned.

'Coffee sounds good.'

George slid the hatch shut behind him and used the bucket.

Putting to sea always lifted her mood. It even worked after a night like that. Feck, especially after a night like that. There's a sense of anticipation about cranking up an anchor, pumping the hand winch on the windlass and watching the chain come up glistening in the light of a torch that she held in her teeth. Already they had that thin, grey light of early dawn, but not enough light to work effectively and thankfully not enough to see the dragon against the sea. The ghost light, she used to call it. Maybe she'd have to find another label. They'd already hoisted the sails and they flapped and cracked behind her. A new day. Salt smells and seagulls, and a sense that they could go anywhere the wind took them, as if there was somewhere calling from beyond the horizon. Leave the crap behind. George had insisted on doing the heavy work on the foredeck, wanting to purge herself with exercise. Besides, she wasn't sure about Jack's balance in the dark, and he had the trickier task of navigating them out of the anchorage under sail alone.

'Up and down!' She called over her shoulder to let Jack know that the anchor was almost aweigh. Any moment now her bow would come off the wind and she'd start sailing, and George would have to crank like crazy to bring the anchor up before it grounded again.

'Hold on, George. I want to try something.'

She heard the metallic clank of the starting lever.

The frigging engine fired at the first turn.

III: JACK

It took Jack some time to feel at ease with *Draca* as they sailed back. He'd checked out the sleeping cabin right after George had freaked, and again while he was making coffee. Nothing, of course. Just the faint smell of seaweed and salt as he secured the scuttles for sea. But George had clearly believed there was something there, and it rattled him a little, especially after the previous day's incidents. There had been times when it felt as if *Draca* was alive and showing a mean streak. So he sat with his hand on the tiller, half expecting problems that never came. *Draca* behaved herself all the way, taking them to the harbour channel in a single beat into the wind. By the time the edge of the sun gilded the haze on the horizon, he knew that the life he felt through the tiller was natural, the dance of wood and sail with sea and wind, and the night's fears seemed absurd.

George caught him looking at her, once. She was huddled in the corner where she'd slept, clasping a mug of coffee, with her face puffy and smudgy-eyed with too little sleep. She stared aft down the wake to where white cliffs marked the eastern end of the great bay, rising nearly twenty miles across the water from Anfel Head as the gull flies. The line of chalk slabs shone like a gap-toothed smile in the dawn light. They were still shadowed at their base, so they seemed not to be connected to the sea but floating above it. George was shapeless inside her foul-weather jacket and life vest, and her hair was tangled with salt, but something inside him turned a small but troublesome cartwheel. What was it about him and gay women? At that moment she looked at him and smiled in a way that lit up her face, then blushed and turned away as if she'd read his mind.

Jack didn't like this idea that she could see things about him. He believed her, or at least he was sure that she believed that she could. But he wasn't comfortable enough with himself to want to be known too well, and he certainly didn't like the idea that she might be able to see what was going on in his head. If she'd been able to do that the day before, when she had her back to the mast, they'd both be embarrassed.

Some women wear their sensuality consciously, like a designer dress. Jack saw it in the way they held themselves, always thinking of how they might appear. Charlotte was like that, aware of herself, living the pose, even wearing make–up to the gym. George was short and a little broad-shouldered, but she had a natural allure that shone from deep within her. Jack shifted on the bench. A married man shouldn't feel like that. And no way did he want to fall for another gay woman.

'Charl said you won a medal.' George broke an easy silence that stretched far back along the wake.

Jack shrugged. 'I did something stupid and got away with it.'

'Something about running up a hill under fire,' she prompted.

A day before, Jack would have closed down the conversation. Now, he didn't mind her asking.

'Tell me about it.'

Refuse, evade or dilute?

'Please? Take my mind off last night?'

Jack swallowed. He'd give her the short version.

'My troop were searching a compound. I'd sited a machine–gun on the hill above us to give us cover, but the Taliban crept in and knocked it out with a rocket-propelled grenade.' Jack paused, assembling his words. *Draca* danced under his fingertips on a morning to lift the spirits. 'What I did wasn't brave, in the truest sense of the word. Brave people consciously put themselves into danger. I just got angry. Bloody angry. I also knew that if the Taliban reached that gun position before I did, they would turn the gun on us and we'd be in deep shit.'

'So you ran up the hill.'

'And was halfway up it before I realised how many of them there were. That was scary.' More than scary. He'd put his head down and screamed one, long, twenty-yard 'fuuuuck' until a bullet knocked him over. 'By then I could only go forwards because the safest place would be behind the gun.' He'd fallen into that sangar almost gibbering with fear, rolling over, shitshitshitshit, and squeezing off wild bursts at anything that moved.

If George could really read his mind she'd know he didn't deserve that wide-eyed look. He decided to balance the facts with a little honesty.

'I learned things about myself that day. Uncomfortable things.'

George waited, watching him. She was a good listener.

'We so rarely saw the enemy, you see. There'd be an IED by the road, or a suicide bomber in a truck or a burka or an RPG from behind a wall. For once, I saw men with AK–47s who were trying to kill my men. Clear, legitimate targets, in the open.' Jack paused on the brink of a deep truth. 'One second I was in a funk, the next I'd grabbed the machine–gun and I felt invincible.' Rabbit to Rambo in two bursts from a Minimi.

'So what was the uncomfortable thing you learned?'

'I hosed them away, and it felt *good*. It was payback time for every sniper round, every IED, every dead marine. I watched them drop, one after another, and it was exhilarating. Bloody marvellous. So if you like what you see in me, George, you aren't seeing everything.'

'And afterwards?'

Oh, she was sharp. Afterwards he'd wished he could hide from the respect, even awe, that followed. He'd walked that slope, later, and stared at the bodies lying humped in the killing ground. One of them was so young that he had just a downy moustache and fine hairs where his beard would have grown. Blue Afghan eyes had stared at the sky, and stayed staring at the sky as flies crawled across them, sucking at the whites.

'Afterwards I felt like a psychopath.' And a failure, as he sorted through the effects of his dead marine.

George lifted one foot off the bench and pushed it gently against his knee. 'I'd say you did your job. Frigging well, by the sounds of it.'

Chippy took their lines as they came alongside in the marina, his face tight and disapproving. That irritated Jack. Who did Chippy think he was, her father? And besides, George was a grown woman and nothing had happened, had it? Perhaps that made him a bit cool as George left. She and Chippy moved off towards the marina office together, a gangly old man and a pint-sized woman in tight jeans, and Jack decided he needed to talk to Charlotte again, soon. This marital limbo couldn't go on.

He grabbed a couple of hours of sleep, crashing in the sleeping cabin where George had started the night. Part of him wanted to prove to himself that there wasn't a problem there, but there was also a practical reason. The scuttles were easily shaded, so it could be a dark space even in daylight.

He slept deeply, wonderfully, and dreamed of *Draca* riding the slow, long swell of the open sea. She climbed the side of each wave under the square sail alone, pushed by a following wind, and at the crest she hung there with her bow clear of the water as the wave passed underneath. Then the bow would drop until she smacked the downward slope and sent a flat sheet of foam hissing away over the surface. The dragon stood proud at the bow, rising high above where the bowsprit should have been, and a man that could have been Miller rode the dragon as if it was a horse, with a leg dangling over the sea on each side. One of his arms was wrapped around the dragon's neck, and the other waved above and behind him for balance, rodeo style. He whooped as they fell off each crest, his long hair lifting from his shoulders, and he laughed at the crash and spray that followed. The laughter rose with them from the trough to the crest until it became another shout of joy.

IV: DIARY OF EDVARD AHLQUIST, VOLUME 39

18th March. Wind SSE, 3, fair.

A day to lift the spirits. There's a high pressure system bringing a fool's summer, and it's warm enough for shirtsleeves. There's even a skylark singing over the grassland behind the cottage, so high that he's just a dot in the sky but making a sound so loud he might be in the garden. It's all too beautiful to leave.

There may be other evenings, but I taste each one with the thought that this might be the last like this. The last time I see the gorse on Witt Point looking that gaudy yellow, so bright in the sunlight it almost hurts. The last time I see the shine spread across the harbour as the tide turns the salt marsh from flat browns and greens into ribbons of water.

I think the warrior wants the dragon. Maybe the dragon wants the warrior. He was under the trees again last night, aware of us, and we were aware of him. As I get weaker he gets closer. Soon he'll be in the garden.

I don't want him to take me. Will he go away if I give him the dragon?

V: GEORGE

George didn't sleep much that night, which was crazy, when she hadn't slept the night before in Jack's cockpit. She crashed out early, then woke when the day was just showing in the east, and it was all Jack-frigging-Ahlquist's fault.

She knew all the problems. All the reasons why it was a bad idea to let him get close. He was moody. He drank too much. Far too much. And there was the little problem of him being married, to a woman who wanted to be her friend.

Charl was sweet, and she hadn't tried it on again. It had taken George a while to get her head around the skinny-dip. So much for her ability to read people. She hadn't seen it. Charl rang the yard soon after George got back from the sail with Jack and, instead of being happy, she thought, '*Oh feck, what do I say about spending the night in Jack's boat?*' But all Charl wanted was to see if George was free for a sail that weekend. She even booked a dinghy for a lesson when George told her there were no charter boats available. George didn't mention the night at anchor. Now it felt like she was hiding stuff.

Which she was.

An hour after Charl, Jack called, just to make sure she was OK. That made her feel all warm inside. Jack said he was worried about her, then lingered on the phone like he didn't know what to say. Most of the time Jack was hard and cool on the outside, but when he let his guard down he was all vulnerable. When they were sailing his face came alive and George saw the real Jack Ahlquist, someone who laughed and was at one with his boat. Plus he'd stayed up with her when she was freaked out by a ghost, and he hadn't made fun of her. In the cockpit, in the darkness, his voice had been soft as a pillow and she'd so wanted him to hold her. Just hold her, nothing else, so that his strength was all around her, making her safe.

Most of all, she'd seen the gentleness inside him. On the sail home, George had shut her eyes and the shades of tenderness made her all full and happy and a bit achy where girls didn't oughta ache. Shit. It was all a frigging nightmare.

It was so early when George let herself into the marina that she could still see the riding lights on boats out in the mooring lines. She knew Jack wouldn't be there. He'd moved *Draca* round to his own mooring off the cottage the day before. If he and Chippy weren't working on the boat any more, it was pointless him paying fees to the marina. Still, the place seemed a bit empty.

She thought she'd cycle along the coastal path before work. Clear her mind. If she set a good pace, she could reach Witt Point in half an hour. George didn't really think they'd meet, but Jack had said he went there most mornings, very early. And if they did meet, it would be good to know if he was as screwed up by this as she was.

Whatever 'this' was. After all, Jack hadn't said anything. But she could ask him if he thought she was an idiot for reacting the way she had in his boat.

She knew the place to sit: in the ruins of the old chapel. The foundations were just humps in the grass, with a few stones poking through, but the stones would save her from getting her bum wet. *Draca* lay at her buoy in Freshwater Bay, stern-on to Witt Point where there was deep water close under the hill. *Draca's* dinghy was tied to the little jetty so Jack couldn't have been on board.

She sat there, watching, for maybe half an hour. The cottage, over the pine trees, showed no sign of life. She could have walked up there to see if his car was outside, but that would have left footsteps in the dew across his lawn, and it would just be too frigging embarrassing to be found in his garden. Besides, what if he didn't feel the same way? What if the colours were lying, for once?

Below her, *Draca* began to swing around her buoy, the way boats do when the tide turns, but George had this uneasy feeling that *Draca* was aware of her. The boat moved with the slow, steady sweep of an outsized second hand on a clock, and George shivered when the figurehead came into view and it seemed to be looking at her over its shoulder. It stayed at the new angle, pointing towards the sea rather than the land, now swinging just enough to keep her in view.

Stupid idea. It was time to cycle back to work anyway.

She was halfway to the marina before she realised that the tide wouldn't turn for another half hour.

VI: DIARY OF EDVARD AHLQUIST, VOLUME 39

10th April. Wind NW force 4–5, rain.

Jack said he'd brought something to show me. He handed over this small, flat box, all coy like a kid with a school prize, and inside was a medal. Jack said he did something stupid and got away with it, but that was a throwaway line and I could see he treasured it, even more than he had that green beret.

I asked him if it was to do with his leg, and he said no, it was the trip before. Afghanistan. He's kept it quiet ever since, but wanted me to see it before I died. I hugged him and told him I was proud of him and always had been. Even a medal couldn't make me more proud.

He hasn't told his parents. I didn't need to ask why. He couldn't tell Mary without telling Harry, and Harry would probably make some throwaway comment about all gongs being a lottery, or say that they give them away with cereal packets these days. He's spent his life wanting his Dad's praise, and now he's won something so precious he daren't risk the pain of Harry trashing it.

Chapter Seven: Veizlu-fall

(Old Norse: the failure of a feast)

From the Saga of King Guthrum

King Alfred sent word to King Guthrum in this wise; that as the siege could not be resolved except with much blood, King Alfred would pay silver, and grant frith[1] and safe passage to King Guthrum if he gave his oath to sail with all his ships and men and to harry no more in the Westlands. King Alfred would swear this treaty upon the book of his crucified god, and demanded of Guthrum what he held sacred, since Guthrum believed in the old gods.

Now it had been the custom of the folk since the days of the Ynlings to swear oaths upon a sacred ring; such oaths were binding and any man who broke them was declared outlaw and killed. Guthrum held the sacred arm ring of his folk, a ring mightier than all other rings, that had been forged with spells and great sorcery by Yngvi, who ruled after Niord, successor to Odin himself. On this would he swear.

---

1. Pardon, absolution for acknowledged crimes.

192

For the giving of the oath Guthrum consecrated a vé,[2] a sacred place, by sacrificing a horse beneath an ash tree and sprinkling its blood on the tree and on the ground, that Alfred and all with him should know no man would do violence in that place. The vé was ringed with the dragonheads of their ships, that they might bear witness. Then Guthrum reddened the dragonheads and the ring of Yngvi with the blood of the sacrifice, and Alfred accepted this troth.

Afterwards Alfred and Guthrum feasted together, but Alfred would not eat the meat of the sacrificial horse, saying it was not the way of the followers of the crucified god. The folk of Guthrum liked this very ill, saying the oath was not yet made.

Guthrum passed the horn over the fire and drank to Odin, Njördthur, and Freyr, but Alfred would not drink until he had made the sign of the cross over it. At this the jarls were wroth, but Guthrum, in order that the siege be lifted, said that Alfred made the sign of the hammer of Thor, and they were quieted.

This treaty was then sealed with the exchange of high-born hostages, and the warriors made ready to depart the Westlands.

---

2. A sacred place for the taking of oaths, or judgement or ritual. No Viking would desecrate a vé with violence.

I: JACK

Charlotte breezed through the cottage's door that Friday evening, planted a sisterly kiss on Jack's cheek and called him 'chum'. Her weekend commuting was becoming a pattern. She was still in her business suit, the one that turned her backside into a charcoal tulip, and she groaned a little as she stretched away the journey.

'Bad week?' Jack realised he sounded a little cold, but Charlotte would only be here to see George, and he wasn't sure he wanted to go along with that any more.

'I need a shower. Then Friday wine.'

Here at least was a shared ritual, one of the few structures they'd created in their marriage. Charlotte rarely drank during the week, but she'd let rip on a Friday night. With the first glass, they dumped whatever was stressing them. The second opened up discussions. A third glass could make Charlotte playful, even frisky. If they ever made love, it was likely to be on a Friday. If she went to a fourth, she could be anywhere on a spectrum from belligerent to gloriously uninhibited.

They pulled the cork in the garden, sitting on the lawn in a pair of folding chairs to catch the last of the sunlight, with the wine in a bucket of ice between them. A holidaying family had arrived in the cottage next door, and they tried to ignore the noise of a man kicking a ball with two boys not much older than Tilly's kids. It was late enough in the day for the shadows to be stretching, but the sun still turned the fair-weather clouds into puffballs of shining white.

Charlotte was on her second glass before Jack told her about the engine failing on the shakedown sail with George.

'We had to anchor and wait for the tide to turn,' Jack finished, 'which meant the middle of the night.' If George told her, and Jack hadn't, it would look like he was hiding something.

'And?' Charlotte gave him a lowered-eyebrow, suspicious look.

'And nothing. But if I can't trust the engine I need to replace it, and I've spent the bank loan.' Jack made the engine the main point of the story.

'Oh.' She sounded relieved, as if she'd been fearing a confession. 'Then borrow some more.'

'The bank won't lend me any more. I've asked.'

'Why not ask your father? He helped you fix it before. He might want to be involved.'

'I don't know…'

The trainer-on-plastic thump of a hard kick of a football came from next door.

'We could invite them for Sunday lunch.'

The ball smashed into the dividing fence, loud enough to be an intrusion. Jack was too surprised by Charlotte's suggestion to be irritated.

'You must be joking. After the way they've treated you?'

'You should talk to them more.'

'Won't you be sailing with George on Sunday?'

'No boats available. She's giving me a lesson in a dinghy tomorrow instead. Late afternoon. And we might go for a drink, Sunday evening, after George finishes work. I doubt if your parents would stay late.'

'*Another* lesson?' Jack tipped the last of his wine into his mouth and reached for the bottle.

'Sailing lessons, I find, are rather like orgasms.' Charlotte's languorous, leg-trailing pose told Jack she was teasing, not flirting. The wine was having an effect.

'How come?' It was the best line he could think of on the spur of the moment.

Charlotte licked her lips. 'One is never enough.'

Laughter was good for them. They'd laughed a lot in the early days, before sex got in the way. Jack refilled her glass.

'How do you think Sunday lunch will go? If they come.'

'I hope they'd appreciate the olive branch. You might even get some help with a new engine.'

'It'll be a disaster, Lottie.'

'Just watch me. Charm offensive. I'll call them myself, later. Happy families, remember?'

Over the fence the cry of 'No, Freddie, like this…' preceded another kick. The ball sailed over the fence, bounced off the boat seat and rolled towards them over the lawn. Jack threw it back, waving away the apology.

'Once, I thought that we'd be like that.' Still on his feet, Jack watched the father and children next door. 'You know, the nuclear family, two kids and a mortgage, all that stuff.' He kept his voice low, for her ears only.

'Us? Yuppies with puppies? Nah. I don't fancy you with a muffin top,' she poked a finger into his stomach, 'and I could never see me wiping bottoms.'

'We never spoke much about homebuilding, did we?' Jack spoke in the past tense without thinking.

'You were always going away. Now you're here.'

'But you don't seem particularly keen to change that.'

Charlotte shrugged. 'I have my career, you have your boat.'

'So is this how we're going to be, weekend friends who have sex once a quarter?' Jack was a glass ahead of her, enough to be blunt.

'I told you once before; our problem, chum, is that we don't love each other enough to change it, and we like each other too much to end it.'

'But one day, one of us will meet someone.'

'And I'm sure we'll stay friends afterwards.'

The setting sun reached under the clouds, making an upside-down landscape of greys and peach. Jack looked down, swirling his wine, wondering if and how to ask an important question. The lightening of the mood encouraged him. 'Lottie, I'd like to be free to look for that someone.'

The garden was very still. Even the football game faded into insignificance. When she didn't speak Jack looked at her, and she was staring at him with eyes that seemed more calculating than angry. Slowly, carefully, she put her glass on the ground, stood and kissed him on the lips.

'Dear Jack. I haven't been very fair to you, have I?'

'And I haven't made it easy for you, since I came back.'

'It just seems a bit final, that's all.'

'I don't think I'm cut out to be celibate, Lottie.'

'Let's think about it for a few days.' She sat down and reached for her wine. 'I'll stay over. Work from here on Monday. You could take me out in *Draca* and show me the ropes.'

The tide was flooding. *Draca* pointed towards the sea.

'I need a crew. Someone with a bit of experience.'

'Then ask George. She has Mondays off.'

Jack was used to the idea of Charlotte and George, though it wasn't a comfortable one. Him and George, that had seemed to work, maybe too well from his perspective. But him, Charlotte and George, all in one boat? The idea was awkward.

'I don't know if she'll come. She thinks *Draca* is haunted.'

Draca swung to her mooring, her new, royal blue enamel moving like silk in the reflected ripples.

'Seriously?' Charlotte sounded incredulous.

'She had a bad experience when we were at anchor.'

Jack heard disbelief in his voice. *Draca* looked sleek and professional, an impossible location for spooks.

'What is it about this place? George thinks there are ghosts in the boat. You saw something under the trees. Old Eddie wrote about ghosts in the garden.'

Jack was still on his feet, and kept his back to her, staring down the lawn towards Freshwater Bay.

'Grandpa was a bit deranged, towards the end. And I've slept well in the boat.' And his 'sightings' had only been a couple of times, after all. He'd had nightmares but no other incidents, not even shadows since that night when he'd run into the garden waving his sword like a lunatic. In fact he was sleeping better than ever.

'How exciting, though. I must ask George all about it.' Charlotte sounded as if she'd just learned a delicious snippet of gossip.

'Tread carefully. She was pretty shaken up.' Jack hadn't spoken to George for a couple of days, but she had a way of being on his mind.

'The poor thing!'

Jack sat down beside her, angling his chair so he could watch Charlotte's face. 'You're fond of George, aren't you?'

'She's sweet. Wonderfully compact.' Charlotte gave him one of her teasing, provocative looks. 'And totally fit.'

Jack gulped wine.

'Are you two an item then?'

The football smacked into the fence again.

'Jack, you're not jealous, are you?'

'Because if you've found someone special…' Jack swallowed. 'I mean…'

'I like George a lot. I think she likes me too.'

Charlotte kept her eyes on Jack's and let the tip of her tongue show, a moment of feline pinkness.

'She's a natural blonde, too. Has the cutest little tuft of golden fluff.'

198

Jack stood up, fast enough to turn heads next door, and spun round, glaring at her. He was too shocked to shout. Charlotte grinned back at him, mischievously.

'Oh, it's so easy to wind you up. Like pressing a button.' She grinned at him as if it was all part of some big tease.

As Charlotte's admission sank in, Jack felt sadness growing inside him, not anger. A delicious, illicit abstract had been building in his mind, born in shared laughter and physical teamwork, in a moment of weightlessness at the top of a wave and in the image of George, tousled, blinking at the morning and cradling coffee, with distant cliffs shining astern. Now Charlotte had shown it to be an impossible fantasy. He took several deep breaths before he emptied the dregs of the first bottle into their glasses, and wrung the neck of another.

'Like you just said, Lottie. Don't you think you're being unfair?'

Charlotte held her glass ready, but spoke towards the view.

'She's very beautiful. You must be very fond of her.'

Jack froze, fresh bottle in hand, staring at Charlotte. She did a double take at his face and laughed.

'*Draca*, silly!' She pointed down the garden towards the water. Her laughter died as she watched him. 'Good God, you fancy her!'

'Have some more wine.'

'You do! God, you're blushing!'

'No I'm not.' Jack sat back in his chair and swigged.

'You'd like to fuck her!'

'Lottie, please!'

'Can I watch?'

The garden seemed suddenly very silent. Birdsong, children playing, footballs, everything became irrelevant and outside the bubble that was Charlotte and Jack.

'That's sick.' Jack swallowed.

'Go on, tell me you haven't thought about bedding her.' She leaned towards him over the arm of her chair, with a seductive, half-smiling look on her face.

'Lottie, please!' If Jack had tried to lie, she'd have known. He stood up again, turning his back on her. The father in the garden next door waved as he ran for the ball. Charlotte stood behind Jack and lifted her glass at the neighbour. She let the other hand cup one cheek of Jack's backside.

'I think it would be awesome to watch George being fucked.'

'That's not funny.' Jack was horribly aware that Charlotte wasn't joking.

'Sorry.' Charlotte sounded mischievous, not sorry. She rested her face against Jack's shoulder, watching the children next door tackle their father for the ball. Her hand stayed on Jack's backside with her thumb slowly stroking over his crack.

'Do you think she's a screamer?'

II: DIARY OF EDVARD AHLQUIST, VOLUME 39

20th April. NE, 4, Fair, cool.

The closer I get to death, the better I see him.

 The dragon saw him first, tonight. He sort of tensed up like he was alert and watching, and I peered to see what he was looking at. Couldn't see anything, at first. It was the middle of the night, a few stars but no moon. I'd only gone out there because I couldn't sleep. The warm snap is over but I couldn't be bothered to light the stove, just pulled on a sweater and an overcoat, and sat there in the dark. I didn't mind the cold. Cold is clean. You have to be alive to feel cold and smell salt.

So I was sitting there in the dark, shivering but alive, letting my eyes adjust. The sky was a bit paler than the land, like charcoal in the stove, and in a while I could just make out the hump of Witt Point. After a bit more I could see the trunks of the pines because the water beyond them reflected the sky.

Then the whispering started and the dragon shifted, just a creaking of the wood, but he was watching. He knew before I could see anything, and then there was movement that I could only see if I looked away, at first, but I kept very still and then there was this warrior in his war glory, chain mail and helmet and all.

I was so scared I had palpitations and sucked oxygen, thinking I was going to die of fright before the cancer got me.

Now I'm sure. The dragon and the warrior belong together. I'm keeping them apart.

I think they want to join their friends off Anfel Head.

III: JACK

Jack knew Sunday lunch was a bad idea as soon as he saw Harry climb out of his car.

When Harry was in control, he was all affability. He'd sound so bloody reasonable as he told Jack why he was in the wrong. When anyone went against Harry, and he still thought he was in control, the rages could be terrifying. And when he knew he wasn't in control, he had a way of radiating silent disapproval. At a distance, like when he was climbing out of that flash Jaguar of his, it showed in a rounding of the shoulders, so that he seemed shorter and more hunched. Close up, Harry's face was slack and his eyes were half lidded into a blank mask, a dumb refusal to engage.

Jack thought they were going to shake hands on the doorstep, but Harry turned away to snap at his wife while Jack's hand was still lifting from his side. Harry hadn't made eye contact.

'Get over here, woman.'

Jack's mother stood by the car, fussing away some imaginary imperfection in a bunch of roses. Harry stayed on the doorstep, his tweed-jacketed shoulder stiff in front of Jack's face. They'd both dressed up for the occasion, Harry in a jacket and tie, and even a waistcoat, and Jack's mum in the kind of outfit she could have worn to a wedding. Charlotte stood in the hallway in jeans and cashmere, squeezing Jack's arm in reassurance.

At Harry's command, his wife scuttled over the gravel, slightly bent over the blooms, talking in tight, bright, false-happy bursts as she came.

'Starting to rain. That's unkind. Hello, dear. And Charlotte. Bought these for you. They're going over a bit but they're all the garden centre had.' She pushed the blooms at Charlotte in a way that fended off a kiss, but Charlotte managed to plant one anyway as Jack's mother squeezed past her in the narrow hallway, still talking. 'Let me find a vase. I know where they are.'

'Let me do that, Mrs Ahlquist...'

Charlotte followed her towards the dining room, a bemused look on her face.

'Old Eddie had one in the sideboard.'

'Please let me do that later...'

Harry filled the space in the narrow hallway. Jack had to back against the wall to let him through, and another moment passed when they might have shaken hands. Harry walked into the front room without speaking, and enthroned himself in the armchair in the window. As Jack stood in the doorway, Harry looked around the room as if inspecting it for changes.

'Drink, Dad?'

The rattle of crockery came from the dining room next door. 'I'm sure he had one here...'

'Beer.'

'Maybe in this cupboard?'

'I believe Tilly took a lot of stuff.' Charlotte sounded so polite she was almost patronising. 'We haven't replaced it all yet.'

Charlotte met Jack in the kitchen, and swigged wine with a God-I-need-that look on her face. Jack whispered 'happy families' at her and sucked a mouthful of his own wine before taking Harry his beer.

The silence in the front room was a palpable, winter-chill entity centred on the chair in the window. Harry sat with his eyes fixed on a point in the middle of the carpet, his face hanging like an empty sack and his beer untouched at his elbow. Charlotte joined them, wearing her best sales executive smile, and took one of the remaining armchairs tentatively, as if she half expected a hidden whoopee cushion. The smile faded when Harry didn't look up. Chopping noises came from the kitchen and Jack raised an eyebrow at Charlotte.

'Your mum's arranging the roses.'

'Always best to bash the stems.' Jack's mum arrived, bearing the vase before her. 'There we are. Now where shall we put them?' She tried to reach past Harry to put them by the model longship, but almost tripped on his feet and earned herself a scowl.

'Sit *down*, woman.'

'Maybe on the mantelpiece? No, the vase is too big. Desk, then. 'Scuse me, dear.' Jack had taken the desk chair to leave the three armchairs free. He resisted the urge to take her bloody flowers and hurl them out of the window. He almost had to prise them out of her hands and lower her into the remaining chair. She sat on its edge, knees together, clasping a glass of sweet sherry in a genteel pinch grip, holding it as high and central as a fencer in the en garde posture.

'Well, this is nice.' Jack's mum sipped her sherry, a tight little smile nailed to her face.

'The roses are lovely, Mrs Ahlquist.' Charlotte sat interview-straight in her chair, panic starting to show in her eyes.

'Did you have a good journey over?' Jack made an effort.

'We know the way,' Harry growled.

The silence stretched. Jack's mum's eyes darted from side to side behind her sherry glass. Now she reminded Jack of a recruit hiding behind his rifle in a gun pit, wondering where the next attack is coming from.

Charlotte sighed and unfolded herself from her chair. 'I'll finish the vegetables.'

'Let me help, dear.' Jack's mother jumped up fast enough to spill sherry on her fingers. 'Oops. Silly me.' She licked her fingers and fumbled for a hankie. 'Messy puss.'

A look of pain flickered across Charlotte's face. Serve her bloody right.

It was only a question of which one of them would erupt first, but Jack hadn't expected it to be Charlotte. Afterwards he felt bad that he hadn't challenged Harry earlier.

Charlotte had been a trooper through the meal, exchanging inanities with his mum while Harry glowered his resentment towards the tablecloth. A gilt-framed mirror hanging over the sideboard reflected the thinning patch on the back of his head. The dining room still had traces of a woman's touch: floral wallpaper, framed landscape prints, a cut-glass bowl on the sideboard that Tilly couldn't fit in her car. All hints of the grandmother Jack had never known.

'Lovely casserole, dear. What's your recipe?'

'Ready-frozen I'm afraid, Mrs Ahlquist. Tilly took all the pots and pans, but she left us the oven. Still, it's better than I could make it, and it leaves more time to talk. Much better to chat, isn't it, Mr Ahlquist?'

Harry grunted and tapped his now-empty beer glass on the table. Jack would let him ask, if he wanted more. At least then they'd get some words out of him. Pointedly, he topped up his own wine, and Charlotte's.

His mum filled the silence, again. 'And were the peas frozen too?'

Charlotte looked at Jack in wide-eyed desperation.

Jack knew what was happening. Harry would be formulating words in his head, feeding off his own anger, so that when the explosion came he'd be quite articulate. When he was in one of these moods, Jack had learned to ignore him. Harry's victory would be in making everyone nervous, and then tongue-lashing them for their failings. The best defence was to ignore him, let him sulk, and not to provoke the outburst. Success would be sending him home with it still bottled up inside him. Charlotte didn't know that, but then she hadn't had to grow up with him. As she gathered the dirty main-course plates, she laid her hand on Jack's mother's arm.

'We do have a pudding, Mrs Ahlquist, but I think it's time for you to take Mr Ahlquist home.' Oh, clever. Talk about him as if he wasn't there. Now brace yourself. 'He's clearly not enjoying himself.'

Jack inhaled, touched Charlotte on the back in support and waited for the lit fuse to reach the charge. The fisted beer glass lifted off the table like the hammer of a revolver, and struck down, gunshot-loud.

'Two years, woman. Two years it has taken you to invite us.'

'And it might be a little longer before I try again, Mr Ahlquist.' Good girl, she was even smiling.

'Dad, don't call Charlotte "woman". It's not respectful.'

'Two years.' Harry almost spat the words at her.

'As I recall, Dad, you told us to "go to hell". Your words, not mine. Don't blame us for taking you at your word.' Jack swigged wine.

'Don't drink so much, dear. It's bad for your liver.'

Jack took another gulp.

'Mr Ahlquist, I thought it was about time we at least tried.' Charlotte was still calm. 'Perhaps I was wrong.'

'For God's sake, woman!'

'Dad, use that word again and you're out. Straight away.'

'Can you imagine what it's like to be invited into my own family home by, by…'

'Don't, dear.'

'By what, Dad?' Jack felt his own safety catch slip.

Harry breathed like a bull, nostrils flared. 'By someone who's driven a wedge through this family.'

'Actually, today was Charlotte's idea. She wanted to build bridges.'

'Maybe she wanted to gloat. Rub it in that you got the house.'

'Only you could have thought like that. Actually I wanted to spare her this kind of scene. Better the abstract than the insufferable reality.'

Jack's mother picked breadcrumbs off the table, one by one, and dropped them onto her side plate. She was blinking back tears. 'Please, Harry. Stop it.'

'She wouldn't even tell us when you had your leg blown off.'

'I wouldn't let her. I needed to be strong before I could listen to your put-downs.'

Harry stood, suddenly enough for his chair to overbalance and hit the sideboard on its clattering way to the floor. 'We're going.' He glared down at Charlotte, who swirled her glass on the table and watched it as if it held particular fascination. 'I hope you're satisfied, young woman. You've cost us our son.'

'I haven't taken your son, you fool. You've thrown him away.' She too stood up, dabbed her napkin to her lips with finishing-school poise and left the room. She squeezed Jack's mother on the shoulder in passing. That unexpected tenderness unlocked tears and Jack had to stand to take his mother's hug. She held him the way she'd held him before his deployment to Afghanistan: in a pray-God-this-isn't-for-ever kind of hug, and it went on long enough to irritate Harry even more.

'Get on with it, woman. We're not welcome here.'

Charlotte appeared in the doorway, clasping a volume of Eddie's diaries. She spoke to Harry with a steely coldness.

'Before you go, I have something for you. If you ever wonder why Old Eddie left everything to Jack, it's in here. If you want Eddie's views of your skills as a father, they're in here too. You may learn things about Jack that surprise you. You may even learn something about yourself.'

She held it out to him but Harry kept his hands by his side with his fingers clenching as if he wanted to hit her, so the diary hung between them like an unshaken hand. After a pause, Charlotte sighed and put it on the table.

'I didn't think you'd be man enough to read it. You're all mouth.'

Jack's mother reached across, picked up the slender book and slid it into her handbag. 'I'll take it.' She paused as she passed Charlotte, eyes down to where her hands fretted to close the clasp.

'I'm sorry, dear.'

For a moment, Jack thought Harry was going to hit his mother, but he stormed out of the room, his face working. Jack's mum winced as the front door crashed back on its hinges, and turned to follow.

Charlotte and Jack stood staring at the abandoned mess on the table in a silence broken only by the soft click of the front door closing behind Jack's mother. Jack slumped back into his chair and reached for the wine.

'Which diary did you give them?'

'Top of the pile. The last one.' Charlotte sat, sighing, and fiddled with the stack of dirty plates and cutlery. The sound of car tyres spinning on gravel came down the hall. 'He needed to learn a few home truths.'

'I haven't read much of that.'

'I have. All of it. And I hope he reads it.'

Charlotte began to draw patterns in congealing gravy with a knife. 'Are you going to say "I told you so"?'

'Actually, I was going to thank you for trying.'

She was quiet long enough for her knife's tip to make two, slow, mosquito-whine circles over the plate.

'Jack, I knew there were differences, but I never realised it would be that tough.'

'Actually, neither did I.'

She dropped the knife onto the stack of dishes, closed her eyes and let her head tilt backwards, so that her throat moved as she swallowed.

'He'd be so bloody pleased with himself if we broke up.'

'Now you understand, Lottie.'

'At least, when you were in the marines, the officers' mess gave us some kind of family.'

'I don't really miss that.' The officers' mess belonged with broken dreams, failure and guilt. It was a part of his life he'd rather forget.

'I do.' Charlotte stared at Jack across the table, and for a moment she seemed very far away.

IV: HARRY

Harry kept his temper long enough for the wife to get in the car. How dare she support The Slut in front of him? He couldn't believe she'd actually apologised. In all the years they'd been married she'd never been so disloyal.

Then she made it worse by telling Harry it was all his fault. How the hell did she expect him to react when The Slut treated him like that? Talking across him like he was a child. *'Time to take him home.'* Anyone would lose their rag, wouldn't they?

The wife didn't say much, just sat with her face against the car window, not looking at Harry, and sniffling.

'If I'd have been her,' she said after a bit, 'I'd have tipped the food over you.'

Harry braked so hard she was thrown against the seat belt and the driver behind held his hand on the horn. *Screw you, too.* They ended up half on the verge.

'What the hell do you mean by that?' Harry shouted.

'You showed her what you thought of her without opening your mouth. Before you even got through the door.'

Harry asked her how the hell did she think he was going to feel, watching that woman play Lady Gracious in his own father's house? That's where he lived when his mother was alive. He grew up there. Then he had to put up with the sight of The Slut swanning around like she owned the place with her nipples poking through her jumper.

The wife wouldn't back down. He'd never known her so stubborn. 'We had one chance,' she said, 'and you threw it away. You just sat there, glaring at the floor.'

'Better to say nothing than open my mouth and make it worse.'

'You couldn't have made it any worse than you already had.'

Harry had to remind her that The Slut hadn't even bothered to cook for them. What kind of welcome is that? They'd never give guests frozen stuff from the supermarket. They'd got standards.

'I think you should write and apologise.'

Harry hit the wheel. She just didn't get it. And no way would he ever crawl to The Slut. They stared at the rain until another car blared its horn as it manoeuvred around them.

'Oh, drive home before you cause an accident, you poor bloody fool.'

Harry had a drink and calmed down a bit at home. He felt bad about the day, but deep down he was bloody frustrated to have been kept at arm's length when Jack was hurting. When they're kids, you can tell them what's safe and what's dangerous. If they have a knock you can say 'there, there' and slap on a plaster. You can make them tougher so that the knocks don't hurt so much and the big kids leave them alone. Then when they grow up and leave you they make their own way and sometimes you know it's going to end in tears.

Jack was always so determined as a kid. Wouldn't give in, and he'd never admit he'd made a mistake. And when this sordid bloody marriage broke up, as it was bound to do, he'd be too proud to let his family get close even though he'd be hurting even more.

Maybe one day he'd realise all this was only because they cared for him.

And maybe when they'd all calmed down, him and Jack could go for a walk, just the two of them, like they used to do. Keep the door open. Let him know they were still there for him when things went wrong.

Harry was sitting in the lounge, looking at the view down the garden as the light faded, when the wife came in. They hadn't spoken since they'd got home. She hadn't even offered him a cup of tea. She'd stopped crying but she looked all worn and sad. She came straight up to Harry, dropped Old Eddie's diary in his lap and told him that if he didn't read it, she'd never forgive him. Then she turned to leave, without another word.

'Mary…' he called after her, half pleading, half protesting.

Mary just walked out of the room.

V: DIARY OF EDVARD AHLQUIST, VOLUME 39

23ʳᵈ April. Wind NW force 4, rain.

I tried to give the dragon back. I thought he might leave me alone then. It had to be soon, while I had some strength left, which meant it had to be today, on the tide, before Jack came in the evening.

I took a hip flask of morphine but I had to leave the oxygen behind. Couldn't carry the bottle. Dragging just the dragon down the hill exhausted me, but we made it through the trees to the jetty with a few long rests.

It was hard to let it go. I couldn't throw it, but I heaved it to the end of the jetty and stood it on end, looking at the water. All I could think of to say was 'ask them to leave me alone, old friend,' and then I let it topple so it did a nosedive into the water.

It wouldn't go. It floated, just, with water washing over it, but there wasn't enough current to take it away. I watched it for an hour until it grounded on the mud as the tide ebbed. It lay there looking at me like it was a dog that had been left behind, all hurt and betrayed, so I pulled it within reach with a boat hook and managed to bring it ashore.

Jack found us under the pine trees. I'd finished the morphine by then. Maybe I'd slept a little, but I knew I couldn't make it back to the house on my own. He brought me oxygen and more morphine before he tried to move me. There's a time after the pain goes and before sleep comes when I can think straight, and I realised how I must seem to him, filthy with mud, cradling the dragon. I tried to explain that this was the place of the massacre and Harald's balefire, and he just stared at me. So I told him about the warrior and how he wanted Harald's dragonhead back and might take me too, but I don't think I made much sense. Jack just looked sad and said it was time to talk about the hospice.

Dear Jack. He's the only one who cares.

Chapter Eight: Eiðabrigði

(Old Norse: the breaking of an oath)

From the Saga of King Guthrum

On the day appointed for King Guthrum to set sail from Fyrsig with all his army, Jarl Harald seized the woman Witta and placed her in his dragonhead ship. While they were still close to land Witta saw her people standing on the shore, and great was their lamentation for her. Straightways she climbed over the shields at the baling-place and made to leap into the water. There was a warrior with Harald named Ragnvald, a great berserk, who seeing this stretched out his sword to restrain her. But Witta jumped nonetheless and swam towards the shore, though she was sore wounded.

Harald Guthrumsson was wroth and turned his ship to pursue Witta. When there was no more water, but only mud, he shed his boots and all his armour save his shield, and leaped down to follow her. Witta threw herself flat upon the surface and crawled, bleeding, in the manner of an eel. Harald lay his shield flat upon the mud, that he might not sink, but he was a heavy man and came not nigh to her before the mud held him fast by the legs.

The Saxons, seeing a woman of the crucified god pursued by a Viking, gathered on the shore and loosed arrows to protect her. Harald, whose shield was beneath him, was struck.

Thus died Harald Guthrumsson, whom the skalds later called Harald Siltefótr, that is to say Harald Mudfoot.

I: GEORGE

George was glad that Charl asked her to crew for them, not Jack. It kept things straight, if that wasn't a frigging awful pun. Even so, she said no at first. She was still waking up in sweats and taking showers in the middle of the night at the memory of that touch in the bunk. But Charl was insistent during their sailing lesson and made it into a dare, so George accepted. Anyway, she wanted to prove to herself that she could sail in *Draca* again without freaking out. And it was a way to spend a day with Jack. She still couldn't get him out of her head.

And after all that, when they set out she wondered if Jack wanted her there at all. At first she thought that she'd walked in on one of their tiffs, the way she'd done at the barbecue, so it seemed safest to steer clear and help Charl load the dinghy. They were motoring *Draca* out through the harbour, with the engine running sweet as her mum's old sewing machine, before George sussed that Charl was needling Jack.

George was leaning against the hatch with Charl, leaving Jack to navigate the channels that run between the islands from Witt Point to the sea, and George was probably talking too much, filling the awkwardness with words and telling Charl about mudbanks and tides and how *Draca* drew a lot of water. Charl rested her cheek on her hands, grinned at George and interrupted her.

'So if we see the seagulls walking, it's time to change course.'

They laughed and George relaxed a bit. She'd been a bit cool with Charl on the last dinghy lesson because she didn't want Charl to think she was up for it, but with Jack there she felt safer. George might almost have given Charl a girlie hug, but she didn't want her to get the wrong idea. Plus George didn't want Jack to think she was only Charl's friend. That thought made her realise that both their bums were pointing at him as they leaned on the hatch, so she turned around and hooked her elbows behind her instead, grateful that her boobs were wrapped up in a life jacket.

'You all right, Jack?'

'Fine.'

He didn't sound it. Or look it. George closed her eyes against the sun and his outline was blazing red, which could mean either anger or passion; it's hard to tell the difference. At that moment George guessed anger.

Charl also turned and parked her elbows behind her like she and Charl were a double act. She'd left her life jacket unclipped so it hung open at the front. If George had to fit a colour to Charl right then, it would have been green, and a bit of red. Green's a complex colour that can mean several things, but George would have guessed deceit or jealousy, with an overtone of sex. Something was going on between them.

'Only Jack could be moody with two lovely ladies to play with.'

Jack didn't speak. Something had changed in him since the last time she'd seen him. On the way back after that night at anchor, he'd been relaxed and friendly, letting her see the sweet, gentle guy inside, even if he had been knackered. Now he was inward again, the crab in its shell.

'Oh, poo. You're no fun. I'm going to make some coffee.' Charlotte winked at George and went below. George moved to sit nearer to Jack, where Charl wouldn't hear them over the engine.

'Jack, have I done something wrong?'

'Of course not.' That was a shutdown. 'Charlotte and I have a few issues to resolve, that's all.'

'Only I wondered if you'd rather I hadn't come.'

Jack leaned against the tiller, spinning the boat around a

navigation beacon into the main channel. 'I'm glad you felt able to. Come, that is. After last time, I mean.'

'It's just a day sail. It's not as though you're asking me to stay overnight.' George shifted on the bench as she realised that sounded a bit sexual. Jack stared out across the water but he was using sailing as an excuse for not making eye contact. That hurt.

Charl was a lot better company than Jack, that morning. They laughed a lot, getting the sails up, even though George did most of the work. It was fun. Girls together, like it had been in the beginning, but it was safe now because Jack was there. And *Draca* behaved herself. She performed as well as anyone could wish, even when George took the tiller, on a day of patchy cloud with islands of sunlight racing over the sea. It was a good day to be on the water. In the late morning George sat beside Charl in the cockpit, trying not to let their legs touch in the cramped space.

'So tell me about this ghost, George.'

Charl had asked about that during their sailing lesson but George had brushed it away, embarrassed. Now, even sitting in *Draca*, that night didn't seem as bad as it had at the time. Ghost stories go with dark evenings and low lighting, not with fine sailing weather when the wind hums through the rigging and blows everyone's hair all over the place.

'My mum used to say there are three kinds of ghost.' George spoke to both of them, to make sure Jack was included. He was standing with one leg braced against the lee lockers, the other on the deck, and staring forwards like a helmsman should, but George could tell he was listening. Charl lay with her feet up on a bench and her back to the hatch.

'Most 'ghosts' we build for ourselves, in our minds…'

Jack looked at George sharply.

'...like people we've loved. I still think about my mum, f'rinstance.'

They fell into a trough so the hull made a small 'boom' against a wave, and spray hissed out over the water. They were clear of the shelter of Anfel Head, and picking up a bit of a sea from the easterly flow. Jack glanced up at his course and at the wind before staring at George again. He looked hunky enough to make her forget her train of thought.

'And?'

'Only a few are dead people, condemned to relive a great sadness. They're trapped. They can't let go. They're frightening but they can't hurt you. Not unless the fright gives you a heart attack.'

'That's two.' The way Jack was listening made George nervous. It was like she was answering an exam question, and George had never been good at those.

'Exceptionally, you hear about the really evil ones. The ones that have will. "Volition", Mum called it. They have the power to act. They can prey upon the living. They're either nasty spirits or the ghosts of bad people who can't find rest. She said they try to keep doing in death what they used to do in life.'

'Gosh. Awesome.' Charl's eyes were big as she stared at George. 'And have you seen any of those?'

'Only one. About fifteen feet behind you.'

Charl squealed and spun onto her feet, staring down into the chart-room. George hadn't meant to frighten her that much, but her reaction made George laugh. Even Jack smiled.

'Sorry. Not now. The night we anchored.'

George must have been well relaxed to have joked about that. Charlotte sank back onto the bench, breathing hard with her hand to her throat.

'How absolutely awful for you. Were you terribly frightened?'

So Jack hadn't mentioned the details. 'I freaked. Totally freaked.'

'George, can you help me go about?' Jack interrupted. 'We're going nowhere in this tide.'

George stood up, wondering if Jack was breaking the conversation to help her. Anfel Head was still on the quarter. They were close-hauled into a good westerly breeze, but had the tidal flow against them.

'Isn't this where we've seen rough water?' Charlotte asked. 'It looks calmer today.'

'The wind and tide are working together, so the sea's calmer,' Jack explained, 'but it's like swimming against the stream in a river. A lot of hard work to go nowhere.'

They turned to put the wind on their quarter, almost running before it, and they all felt the ship respond. Now they had a pushing wind with the sails bellied out and full, not a sliding wind with them sheeted close to the centre-line. The motion was easier: a bubbling, happy surge that blew away George's fears of going below.

She didn't make a big thing of it, just took a deep breath and backed down the steps into the chart-room, all nonchalant as if she was going to the head. Which she was. She even dumped her life jacket so she could use the cramped little head properly.

Afterwards she stood in the saloon, riding the movement of the boat, senses tuned. *Draca* was alive, in the sense that all classic boats are alive. They creak as they work, like their bones and sinews are moving, but the atmosphere wasn't threatening. On this course she was sailing just a bit faster than the waves, so there was a smooth climb then a gentle tilt into a wallow, over and over again. Sometimes the tilt was followed by a mild boom, like distant thunder, as the hull hit the next wave. It was as natural as a church in sunshine, not the dark, creepy-headstone horror she'd felt before.

George turned as Charl came down the steps behind her. Beyond her, Jack held the tiller and watched them. From this angle, he looked like the hero in a schoolboy's adventure yarn.

'Was it here?' Charl stood behind George in the saloon. There wasn't space to stand side by side.

'Nah.' George pointed towards the door into the sleeping cabin. 'In there.'

'Are you going to look?'

George shook her head.

'I think you should. It's like falling off a horse: you've got to get right back on.' Her hands touched George's hips and pushed her gently forwards. 'Go on, show it who's boss.'

George went. In the sleeping cabin, a spotlight of sunlight shone through a scuttle and made long, looping, orbit patterns over the starboard bunk as the ship rolled. That dazzling circle of white was enough to light up the whole cabin, and the place felt as wholesome as new bread, empty of any vibes but the natural sounds of the hull as it moved through the water. The noises were louder here, near where the bow was smacking the waves, one small fo'c's'le and two inches of elm away.

George began to laugh, her mind filled with the crazy idea that she'd got her body back. She could stand there, where it happened, with her arms stretched wide, feeling female and strong and unthreatened. She was still laughing when the ship hit a bigger wave than most, and this time the 'boom' was followed by the hiss of spray falling back onto the sea outside. The ship checked for a moment, which threw George forwards, then backwards as the bow lifted, and Charl was behind her, braced against the bulkhead. Charlotte's arms went around George to steady her, and it was the most natural thing in the world to be there and happy.

'I love it when you laugh.' Charl's face was in George's hair, and her arms stayed around her a bit too long, and a bit too high, until it wasn't natural any more and George broke away.

'Don't, Charl.'

'Oh, poo.' Charl made that pursed-lip pout that turned everything into a game. She lifted her hand to George's face and stroked her cheek with the back of her fingers.

'Seriously, Charl.' George brushed her hand away and pushed past her, kept going through the saloon and the chart-room and grabbed her life jacket on the way. Jack lifted an eyebrow and asked if she was OK, but George didn't answer and strode forwards until she could lean against the mast with her back towards the cockpit. She stood there, breathing hard, angry. She wanted to be friends with Charl but it was going to be hard if she kept hitting on her.

When the wind's on the quarter, sails can act like a whispering gallery. They pick up sounds from way aft, like from the cockpit, and funnel them round the curve of canvas, so as George stood by the mast, she couldn't help hearing raised voices, especially when the speaker was facing forwards, like Jack. At first he spoke softly, perhaps asking what had happened, which became a louder rant about Charl trying it on in his boat. He said something she only half understood, about giving Charlotte air cover with her parents being one thing, but her shitting in his boat was too much.

That really ticked George off. It sounded like it would be OK anywhere else, but not in *Draca*, like Jack didn't care about her. Then Jack almost shouted *'She's not one of your bloody sex toys,'* which sounded more protective, but George was losing her cool by then.

Charl must have turned away from him and faced forwards, because her next words were clear. 'You just want her all to yourself,' she said.

George lost her rag.

Charl was leaning against the doghouse hatch cover when George turned, and she straightened when she saw George's face. Jack seemed all clenched and angry but looked more worried as George came close. George stopped by the hatch, legs braced against the roll of the ship, and glared down at them. It was easier to show how angry she was when her head was higher. If she'd stepped down into the cockpit she'd have been in among them like a yapping dog.

'I am not a piece of meat,' George almost spat the words at them, 'and just for the record, I have no frigging intention of going to bed with either of you.'

'George, please…' Charl looked upset, but not half as upset as George felt.

'You two think that because you've got money you can mess around with people. Well I don't want to frigging play any more.'

Jack called after George as she ran forwards, but George waved her arm behind her as if she could brush him off, and after that they left her alone. George sat cross-legged on the deck, as far forward as she could go between the bowsprit and the rail, thinking that she made the same frigging mistake every time. If she let people get too close, they hurt her. She thumped the desk with her hand, sniffing, and was cross with herself for that as well.

Before long the boat began a long turn, a three-quarter circle through the wind until they were pointing back towards the harbour. Jack took it in stages, effectively sailing single-handed, but there was no way George was going to go back and help. Close-hauled into the wind, trim sails. Tack through the wind, trim sails. Ease off the wind to a beam reach, and the boat heeled until George was forced to stand. From time to time the noise of their argument reached her, rising and falling in gusts, like the wind, though the words weren't clear now the wind was on the beam. Jack sounded well angry.

Jack sailed *Draca* hard, like he was using the ship to hit the world. They punched through waves, scattering enough spray to soak the foredeck. And George. But no way was she going to move.

Too hard. Soon the lee rail was on the water and it was difficult to stand, so George sat on the deck with her feet braced against the bowsprit and glanced back towards the cockpit.

Jack had a fight on his hands. It reminded George of the squall on the first day they took *Draca* out, when it seemed like the boat had a mind of her own. Now *Draca* was trying to turn further into the wind, towards the line of surf under Anfel Head, and George muttered *'Ease the mainsail, you fool,'* as she watched Jack struggle.

He did, and he still had to fight. It was illogical. Jack had both foresails set, which should have helped him keep his line, but even when he'd spilled wind from the main, the ship was fighting to turn in, until the sound of the bows hitting the waves had a background chorus of breakers on rocks. It was like *Draca* had a death wish.

It ended as suddenly as before. One minute Jack was fighting her, and George was thinking she'd have to swallow her pride and help, the next *Draca* was docile as a puppy, letting the wind blow her head round, away from Anfel Head. George stood, mainly so she could turn her back on the cockpit, just as *Draca* fell into a trough hard enough to throw her off balance. George fell on her knees, pitching forward on her face, and as she reached for support she ended up grabbing the dragon's head.

It was the first time she'd touched it, and she felt it move.

It vibrated the way rigging can vibrate in a strong wind, but there was something else that made George recoil.

George could swear that frigging thing knew her. It knew her the way a man who'd groped her might know her.

And it was laughing.

II: JACK

A muffled thump resonated into Jack's sleep, the kind of thump the butt of a spear might make when it was struck against a deck, if the deck was covered by a fur. Enough of a beat to mark time for oarsmen, for there were also creaks that might have been oars, but not loud enough to carry far, even over water. The tempo was slow, so great oars could sweep backwards to bite again at the next impact, but the excitement was mounting. The intervals between beats were shorter each time, carrying them forwards towards release or violence.

Them? Jack stirred, flinging his arm out into the tangled emptiness of his bed in the cottage.

Now there were moans, a woman's moans that sounded just after each thump.

Oh fuck.

Jack flung back the duvet and sat up, cursing, as the moans rose into whimpers and the dividing wall with the next cottage shook to the impact of a bedstead. He pulled on his leg, lifted the bedroom curtain to spill light onto his wristwatch and glimpsed a garden painted in black shadows and silver moonlight. No other movement. Miller was back in his head, not in the trees. He'd slept for under three hours.

A weight hovered on the edge of memory like a forgotten nightmare. It went with the stale taste of whisky in his mouth and a tiredness that made his face feel as if it was hanging slack from his skull, with his jaw and cheeks suspended from his eye sockets. Outside, Witt Point was a dark mass but Freshwater Bay was totally black and *Draca* might not have existed.

Draca. The thought of the day was like a punch in the gut.

He'd had a parting of the ways with Charlotte. Fooling around under his nose was a step too far. They'd kept things under wraps for so long, almost pretending to themselves, but once they'd started talking, Pandora's box was open.

The couple next door reached their operatic finale, and Jack resisted the urge to give them a round of applause. He thought chasing kids all day was supposed to kill your energy for that. Maybe he'd sleep on board *Draca* until they went home.

Perhaps he should get away for a while. Sell the cottage, once probate was granted, and sail the world.

The itch in his foot brought him back to reality. How can a foot itch if it isn't there? Sometimes, in bed and half asleep, he'd reach beyond the stump, fumbling among bedclothes as he tried to scratch.

Reality told him he couldn't handle *Draca* solo. In good weather, maybe, if he was whole and fit, but not if he couldn't balance on a moving deck.

Jack groaned again at the thought of George. She'd been made to feel sordid, and in his boat. He was angry with Charlotte, and angry with himself that he felt so bloody protective over his wife's girlfriend. Jack lay in bed, staring at the ceiling, and with each digital flicker of the bedside clock he felt worse about her.

When there was a line of light in the east, he gave up trying to sleep.

By sunrise he was sitting on the stones at Witt Point, nursing a flask of coffee, pushing a bacon roll down onto the ball of guilt in his stomach, but savouring a chill in the air that was almost autumnal. Somewhere nearby, hidden in the trees, a robin sang its heart out, a cleansing touch of normality. Below him, *Draca* swung around her buoy, tempting him against all logic to risk a solo sail. The sea can't make you feel good about yourself, but sailing forces you to think of other things, and reminds you that there are fine things in life, even if you aren't one of them.

A heron launched itself from the shoreline, flapping away from its morning fishing ground with slow wing beats: a present-day, leg-trailing pterodactyl with its head sunk back between its wings to balance the sabre beak. Once, he'd have tensed at such a sign, and watched with thumb on safety catch for whatever had startled the bird. Now he was just curious. Perhaps the instincts of combat were fading, or maybe he was just too tired to bother.

The footsteps surprised him. It was too early for walkers. There was a patch of gravel on the coastal path where a spring washed down to the tideline near the heron's stand, and the crunch of stones carried enough to tell him that someone was approaching, walking slowly rather than with the purposeful stride of a hiker.

'George?' Surprise lifted his voice. 'What are you doing here?' God, he sounded like his father.

George shaded her eyes with her hand, squinting up the hill towards him. 'Couldn't sleep. Thought I'd have a cycle and walk before work.'

Something didn't add up. She'd told Jack where she lived, and it must have been at least ten miles away.

'I can offer you some lukewarm coffee if you don't mind sharing the cup.'

George sat cross-legged on a stone nearby, huddled into her fleece, holding the coffee two-handed and staring at the sunrise rather than Jack. Neither of them seemed to know what to say. Then they both spoke at the same time.

'Look, I'm sorry…'

'Has Charl…?'

A moment of awkwardness.

'You first.' An embarrassed flicker of a smile crossed George's face.

'George, I'm so sorry about yesterday. I feel awful about the way we treated you.'

She shrugged. 'You,' her emphasis made the 'you' singular, 'done nothing wrong.' She spoke the way Jack used to speak before officer training. *'Nuthink'.*

'Charlotte's gone, I'm afraid. Last night.' If George wanted to kiss and make up, it was too late.

'S'all right.' She hunched further into her fleece.

'We're breaking up.' So if the girls were still an item, Jack wasn't going to stop them. They'd just have to find another venue.

George made a slight snorting noise. 'I'm surprised you was together in the first place.'

'We got on well. We were easy together.'

'Must've been hard though. For you, I mean.'

'We've both had things to forgive.'

She looked at Jack. 'What, playing away?' The way she lifted one eyebrow lightened the question.

'God, you're direct.'

'Sorry.' George looked away. 'That was out of line.'

'But yes.' Maybe Witt Point was inspiring him to be open. Charlotte knew, anyway. 'There was an army physiotherapist when I was recovering.'

'You don't have to tell me, Jack.'

Strangely, he wanted to. There was something about George's broad, open face that inspired honesty.

'She'd done two tours in Afghanistan as what they call a 'battlefield physio'. She'd seen things. Horrible things. She understood.' Jack felt vulnerable for a moment, almost emotional. 'For some months it was her job to touch me. We became friends. I was weak.'

George shrugged. 'So you evened the score.'

'It wasn't like that. Retribution, I mean. I never thought I'd stray, but I was pretty screwed up for a while. Maybe I still am. Charlotte's had a lot to cope with.'

George stared into her coffee cup, swirling the dregs as if she had something on her mind.

'Why are you here, George?'

She threw the dregs on the grass and handed Jack the cup. 'I said things, yesterday, when I was angry…'

'You had every right to be.'

'But I hope we can still be friends.' Her eyes flickered upwards towards his face and away again, and for a moment she seemed childlike and vulnerable.

'I'd like that, George.' And he would. A straightforward, uncomplicated friendship. A meeting of equals with no hidden agendas, now he and Charlotte had split.

George tugged at tufts of grass near her feet.

'That physio: is that why you reacted when I tried to give you a shoulder massage?' She shredded seeds from the stalks with her thumbnail.

'I'd failed that way once before.' Plus he really didn't want to get involved with another gay woman.

'Did you love her?'

Jack shifted on his stone. George was pushing her luck with these questions. It was too personal.

'I don't think either of us would have called it love. But there's a common language between people who've known that kind of shit. A bond. And she saw me at my lowest. She knew what had happened, and she didn't despise me.'

That slipped out without thinking. Exhaustion, maybe, or a deep need to be understood.

'Why would anyone despise you?'

Deep breath. He'd talked himself into this. 'I told you some of it, in the boat. I led two men to their deaths. One of them died because I was screaming and he tried to get me out.'

'Was he a friend?'

'Friend? No, not a friend. But we'd worked together. We were a team. He ran into a killing zone to rescue me, and was shot before he reached me. And the thing I feel worst about, looking back, is that when he was killed I was so wrapped up in what was happening to me that his death was about as significant as that seagull, just a lot uglier.'

George unfolded her legs and wrapped her arms around them, her cheek resting on her knees, listening with her eyes on Jack's face.

'You know,' Jack continued, 'some part of me still saw myself as a hero in waiting, the kind of guy who staggers out of the fog of battle with a Hollywood wound and says *'It's only a scratch, sir!'*, before he charges back and clears out three machine-gun nests, single-handed.'

George laughed, a nervous, release-of-tension laugh. She was making eye contact now, but it was Jack's turn to drop his voice and mumble towards his hands.

'But when the pain got bad, I disintegrated. As my father would say, I couldn't hack it.'

'I think you beat yourself up too much.'

They were quiet for a while, but the silence was natural.

'Would you come out in *Draca* again?'

'Might do. If you got rid of that figurehead.'

Jack snorted. 'I probably will. After we scatter Grandpa's ashes.'

'It's evil, Jack. Like it's aware.'

'I don't see that.'

'Maybe it needs you.'

This time the silence was less comfortable.

'I'm glad you came,' Jack said eventually. 'What you said about staying friends...' He tried to find words with the right sensitivity. 'Charlotte and I were friends for a long time before…'

'Before you was lovers.'

'Yes.' How do you tell a girl you know how to be a friend, just a friend? 'I think, in a way, it was our best time.'

George stood up, a little abruptly.

'I gotta go. Time for work.'

As she walked down the hill, Jack wondered if he'd said the wrong thing.

III: HARRY

Harry found it hard to read Old Eddie's diary. Eddie used to have such neat writing, in the same curly copperplate that you see on fancy certificates. In his last diary it was all angles, and none of the angles the same, like the legs of a dead spider.

It was sad, too. Harry knew that his father went a bit weird, towards the end, but he hadn't realised he was deranged. It was quite a blow to realise his own father was crazy. All right, so they called him 'Mad Eddie', well, at least some people did, but that was like a nickname, a label they gave him because he could be so bloody exasperating. Finding out that the guy was really off his trolley was embarrassing, like when he wrote about that carving as if it were alive, and raved about Vikings in the trees. He could have been locked up in a loony bin for that.

It was obviously the cancer. It got to his brain, before he died. Thank God they didn't have to have him certified.

Then there was the stuff Eddie wrote about how Harry had a downer on Jack. So hurtful, that, even if Eddie was losing his marbles. The wife said Harry should go and talk to Jack about it, just the two of them, but Harry wasn't sure. How can anyone turn up and ask *'Was I a good father?'* It'd be too embarrassing for both of them. Besides, they hadn't exactly parted on good terms after that lunch. But Mary got upset and threw the diary at him so Harry gave in and drove over there, one afternoon after work, midweek when he knew The Slut wouldn't be there.

It was awkward. Jack just stared at him on the doorstep, blinking at him with bloodshot eyes. He hadn't shaved, either. Really was letting himself go. After a bit, Harry swallowed and found his voice.

'I thought we might go for a walk. Have a chat.'

Jack looked at him long and hard, but then he shrugged and turned back inside the cottage. He didn't invite Harry in, just left the door open, but Harry followed anyway while Jack fetched a jacket.

They didn't discuss where to walk, but Harry headed towards the hills that rise about six hundred feet behind the cottage, in a line that runs for miles, all the way down to the cliffs at Anfel Head. It would be good exercise and there were great views from the top. An old bridleway angles up the side of the hills, and they didn't talk much at first, just got used to each other's presence. It was easier that way, to let things come to the surface in their own time.

The boy was the first one to call a rest, when they'd hardly gone a couple of miles and climbed maybe halfway, up to the level where it gets really steep and the farmland becomes open grass hillside. Jack called after him, and when Harry turned the boy had thrown himself on a wooden seat by the track. That made Harry quite pleased, at first. Jack was nearly thirty years younger, and Harry wasn't even puffed. He'd been in front and hadn't seen that the boy was struggling. Harry went back and sat beside him so he could get his breath back.

'I used to enjoy our walks, when you was a kid.'

'You were always keen to prove how strong you were.' Jack closed his eyes, breathing hard. He looked pale.

'Got you fit though, didn't it? You can thank those walks for getting you into the marines.'

Jack bent down, rolled up his trouser leg and unstrapped his foot. God, the boy knew how to make Harry feel small. The limp was so slight now, and he'd been behind him…

Jack began to massage some cream into his stump, working his thumbs and fingers into the flesh and grunting with what might have been pain or relief. The skin was pink and blotchy, and seamed with scar tissue like a badly wrapped present.

'Are you going to tell me what happened?'

'Are you sure you want to know?'

Now what did he mean by that? 'Of course.'

'I already told you. IED. Underneath a truck.' Jack spoke in short, clipped sentences but flat, like he was a machine. 'The blast broke both my legs and killed my driver. My foot jammed in the door and the petrol tank blew up. I hung there until the fire burned my boot off. Another man died trying to get me out. End of story. Shall we walk?' His freshly creamed stump made a soft, sucking noise as he pushed it into the socket.

'Let's sit here a while.' Harry felt bad now about striding out, and that stump looked angry. 'Enjoy the view.'

They were high enough to see over the heathland and salt marsh to the harbour. The sky threatened rain and the clouds were moving away from them at quite a lick, out over the harbour and inland, but it was calmer in the shelter of the hill.

'Old Eddie wrote that you won a medal.' That was one of the entries that hurt most of all, suggesting that Harry would have rubbished it. It was hard to forgive Eddie that, even if he was mad.

Jack winced. 'Did he? I didn't read that far.'

'But did you? Win a medal?'

'Not for this I didn't.' Jack lifted his foot off the ground.

'But you were given one?'

Jack sighed. 'Operational Service Medal. Campaign medal. Standard issue.'

'Ah.' That made sense. The boy stretched out his leg and pushed his hands into his jacket. He wasn't making this easy for Harry. Maybe he was expecting an apology for that lunch that had gone wrong.

'Does it hurt?'

'Sometimes. It can chafe when I walk. The foot can be painful too, even though it's not there.'

Harry squirmed on the seat.

'How's the boat?'

'Sailing OK. Needs a new engine, but I can't afford that until the solicitor is granted probate and the estate pays out.'

'We must scatter Old Eddie's ashes together soon. Let's fix a date when we get back.'

'Sure.'

'Eddie said you should have gone to university.'

Jack slumped a little. 'Bit late for that now.'

'You still could though, especially with Old Eddie's money. Become a mature student or whatever they call them.'

'Might do.' The boy watched him as if he wondered where all this was leading.

'No one in our family has ever gone to university.' Harry tried to sound enthusiastic but Jack just looked surprised.

'Don't tell me you're getting ambitious for me?'

Harry closed his eyes, trying not to react. Jack reminded him of a youth he had had to sack once, all sullen and hostile no matter how much Harry had tried to motivate him, the sort of kid who hunches into his hoodie and says 'yeah, whatever' if you offer him the chance to do something different. Jack didn't wear a hoodie, and he used clever words, but the attitude was the same. Sullen. Unresponsive.

'Every father wants the best for his son.'

'Until they achieve it.'

'What do you mean by that?' Harry was getting pretty riled. Jack could only push him so far.

'Do you remember the day I came home and told you I'd been selected for officer training?'

'Sounds like you're going to remind me.' Maybe they should have kept walking.

'I was so bloody proud. Selected from the ranks to lead the finest troops in the world. I was walking on air. Do you remember what you said?'

'Nah.'

'You asked if I was afraid that they'd find me out, one day.'

Harry shifted on the seat. 'You're twisting it. Taking it out of context.'

'What context would you like me to put on it? That you didn't think your son should be an officer, or that you didn't think he could hack it if he did?'

'I was worried for you. Didn't want you to be hurt, if you got ahead of yourself. You can understand that.' The first rain began to fall, in large spots that soaked through to his scalp as soon as they hit his hair. Soon they'd have to move.

'Ahead of myself or above myself? Our family have never been officers either, have we?'

'What's happening to you, boy? You was never like this before.' Never this aggressive. Never so disrespectful. Harry stood up. Stump or no stump, he needed to walk.

'It was the proudest day of my life, and you took me off at the knees.'

'One chance remark, and you're letting it sour your life.' Harry was really angry now. He had to leave before he started shouting.

'But it wasn't one chance remark, was it, Dad? It was every bloody time that I achieved something!'

'If that's what you think of your father, after all I've done for you, then, then…' Harry turned away, striding up the hill.

'Grandpa's diary.' Jack shouted loudly enough to stop Harry. 'One of the last entries I read said something about never getting your approval. What else did he say, Dad?'

Harry put his head down into the rain and walked. God, he'd

tried, but Jack had finally, totally ticked him off. He bellowed his last remark over his shoulder.

'He was *mad*.'

IV: JACK

How was it that Jack and his father could never meet without fighting? Jack promised himself every time he saw Harry that he wouldn't lose his rag, and within ten minutes he could feel the tension rising. Jack never used to shout at him. Wouldn't have dared, but that hillside had been an echo of childhood. How many times had he watched Harry stride away while he struggled to keep up?

Why is Tilly allowed to stay home and play, Daddy?

If she was allowed her dolls, why couldn't he read a book?

Tilly's a girl.

Just before they stopped, when the leg was hurting like hell, Jack had this distant memory of sitting by a path, bawling his kiddy eyes out because he was too tired to go on.

Toughen up, little soldier, you won't get big and strong like that.

At least Jack hadn't told him about Charlotte. His father would have been so bloody smug.

Not that Jack would have had much to tell him. He hadn't spoken to Charlotte since the night of the row on board, although she'd sent him a text to say she'd come over at the weekend, 'to talk things through'.

Jack's fuse was definitely getting shorter. But then, he hadn't had time to prepare himself. He'd only just come ashore for a shower. He'd taken to living on board. Not because of Dusty Miller – Jack hadn't seen him under the trees for weeks – but just while the cottage next door was let. Jack had grown used to the isolation of Grandpa's cottage and had made the mistake of wearing shorts one hot morning, forgetting that he had neighbours. Within a minute the children next door were glued to the fence, open-mouthed, eyes wide and locked on Jack's leg. The older one nudged the younger one as if shooing him away, knowing that they shouldn't stare, but both stayed, watching him move around the garden. After that they found reasons to keep looking, even when Jack was wearing chinos.

He found he liked sleeping on board. The bed in the sleeping cabin was a little cramped at the foot, but there was a subtle movement to the boat, even when it was moored in Freshwater Bay, that was soothing. The sounds of the water against the hull were gentle enough to lull him to sleep, and he could mask the scuttles so that the early-morning light didn't wake him. It was cosier than the cottage, even if he did have to row ashore for a shower. What he couldn't understand was why, if he was sleeping more soundly, he was so perpetually tired.

And there'd not been a hint of anything like George's experiences, so he began to think the ghost had been in her mind. There were still dreams, but the dreams were of sailing and the slow breathing of the ocean, not of agony and death. He even wanted them.

Until the night after his row with Harry.

He'd had six solid hours' sleep before the oars woke him, but was still deeply under. Before that, in his dream, there'd been a sense of excitement, the dry-mouthed tension that comes before action. He crouched with Dusty Miller near a compound, watching, thumbs on safeties, senses on hyperdrive. No words, no radio, hand signals only. Dawn breaking, night-vision goggles off. A whole troop is with him, behind him. Why are they bunched together? The boat, of course. The engine won't work so they have to use oars, but the oars make too much noise. There's a growl of wood on wood like distant thunder, even though every oar is wrapped with wet sheepskin to muffle the sound, and with each rumble the boat surges forward and water bubbles under the forefoot. Dusty and Jack stand in the bow, one each side of the dragon, ready to jump as soon as the keel touches. They must get close, under the walls, kill the sentries silently and be in among the enemy when the real fighting begins. Then there would be the wild exhilaration of combat, a taste that is both fear and joy, sharp-focus adrenalin and dusty confusion. The motion jerked as the keel struck, and Jack leaped off the bow, expecting to splash into shallows and run, crouching, for cover.

His right foot hit the cabin's deck before he realised that it was just the boat snagging against its buoy, and he came fully awake as his left stump kept going and he crumpled sideways into a locker. Folded into the corner with his cheek against cold wood, Jack stared into the near-darkness of the cabin, disoriented. He expected to be unleashing the choreography of battle: the crouching rush of fire teams, the murderous double taps. Practised. Synchronised. Adrenalin was surging through his body. He lay there panting, with his weaponless fingers scrabbling at carpet fibres.

Oars. Jack could still hear them, even as his mind registered the loom of dawn through a shaded scuttle, and his hands reached for his prosthetic foot. In the main cabin, the skylight shone with weak, pearl-grey, featureless light. Fog. It clung dripping to the rigging, dewed the cockpit and thickened the air so that he could not even tell the direction of the shore. At the limit of vision a darker mass moved, a mere suggestion of a vessel, but the fading sounds were of many pairs of oars, and the wash that had the boat tugging at its buoy was of a larger vessel than *Draca*. A vessel too large to take easy avoiding action if it came across them in the dark, and Jack could see no lights.

He hailed into the fog, wondering what kind of idiots, and what kind of boat, went rowing through mooring lines in that kind of visibility, but when Jack strained to hear a reply there was silence, not even the rush of water past a hull.

But as the wash reached the shore, the wavelets on the shingle once again made the whispering of many men, a long, rippling sigh of 'f-aay–th… f-aay–th'.

V: GEORGE

George thought that summers flowed out of Furzey like the ebb tide. In peak season, the place was awash with families, a high water that she thought would never end. Then, a bit at a time, the big crowds faded away until the only ones left were the families with holiday homes or long summer lets, squeezing out their last days on the coast. Soon it would be the best time of the year, those weeks between the schools going back and the onset of the autumn storms. Then the visitors would be mainly old empty-nesters and young lovers, so the locals could kick back and enjoy the sun while it was still warm. Already the harbour was less crowded. There was space to sail without dodging dinghies.

George took the marina's workboat out by herself, just for fun, on a day when wind and rain kept all but the serious sailors off the water, and motored past Witt Point. *Draca* was at her buoy in Freshwater Bay, with her dinghy riding astern, so Jack must have been on board, even though she couldn't see him. She didn't go too close as he might have thought she was pushing, but George was worried about him. She guessed all his friends were in the marines, and she knew what it was like to be alone.

She made an excuse to call him, a simple admin question about his account, and found he was living on board. That worried her even more. George didn't like the thought of him cooped up with whatever nastiness lived in *Draca*, even if Jack couldn't see it.

Two days later, on a morning of glassy calm, *Draca* motored out from behind Witt Point. George would have known it was *Draca*, even a couple of miles away and with her sails down. There was no other boat on the water with an outline like hers: big, flush-decked, with a long bowsprit and a square sail yard, and a counter that pushed way out over the water to stretch the sail area. With the binoculars, George could make out the figurehead at the stem and see Jack's head and shoulders at the tiller. When he reached the main channel he turned left towards the boatyard rather than right towards the sea. Chippy Alan joined her as *Draca* angled in towards the fuelling pontoon.

'That engine's smoking a bit.'

Was it only the engine? There was a rain-cloud darkness about the boat that unsettled George. When Chippy took the bow line and Jack put the engine astern, George wasn't sure how much of the fog around the stern was real and how much was the shadow around Jack. Chippy and Jack called to each other as Jack killed the motor, but George watched, thinking *'Feck, if I can see it, I mean really see it with my eyes open, it's getting strong.'* She knew what that meant.

'You gotta get that engine fixed.' Chippy was cheerful, but then he could only see smoke, not the darkness.

'No money left, Chippy.' Jack sounded happy enough but it was all a sham, like he was an engine made of glass. Any minute he could come to a crumbling stop as it shattered. The darkness swam around him as he jumped ashore.

'Hey, George.' She got a hug, a good one like she was his sister, and a kiss on the cheek. 'Can you sell me some fuel and water?'

'Sure. It comes with free coffee. Special offer this week.'

Jack's face brightened, but he'd gone a long way down. You could see it in his eyes.

'Doing any sailing?' George didn't ask about Charlotte. She didn't know if Jack wanted Chippy to hear they'd split, and she wasn't going to let on, even to Chippy.

'Nah. Need a crew.' He tapped his hand against his bad leg,

but his eyes were on George. 'Can't trust my balance under sail.'

He didn't need a crew, he needed rescuing, maybe just from himself, but George was sure it was something more. She took a deep breath.

'I'll crew for you, if you like.' Something inside her said *'Feck, what are you doing, girl? In that boat? You forgotten what happened?'* George suppressed the inner voice and qualified her offer. 'Provided it's a day trip, and we're back before dark this time.'

She'd have risked another night talking in his cockpit, but no way was she going to sleep below deck.

Jack grinned and some of the care fell from his face. The old Jack was still in there, somewhere. He sniffed the air.

'Good. As soon as we have a wind.'

He was dead on his feet, as if all his energy had been sapped. He stumbled on his own deck as he pulled the water hose to the tank inlet. When their eyes met, he'd smile, but otherwise he stood, gripping the stay for support, and blinking at the morning while he waited for his tanks to fill. He reminded George of a boat that needed a tow, wallowing in the waves, drifting towards the rocks.

But Jack didn't know how close the rocks were, and George had no words to warn him. She wished she had a way of getting him off that boat, because every instinct in her body said it was dragging him down, but if she told him that, he'd just laugh. She'd seen that darkness before; that way someone's brightness fades and when she shuts her eyes all their colour becomes grey, and the grey grows heavier and blackens.

She'd seen it around Eddie Ahlquist, the last time he visited the yard, and George had known what it meant. It was sad, but he was an old man. It happens. Now she saw it growing around

Jack, even without closing her eyes, and she almost wished she was as blind as everyone else.

At the end, the last and only colour is black.

VI: JACK

'Power dressing', Charlotte used to call it, somewhere between 'business casual' and a cocktail party in the officers' mess. Hair pulled back to make her face more severe. Dark, outsized shades that totally obscured her eyes. A cream linen jacket that was all shoulders and waist, a plunging V over a loose chemise. It was the kind of outfit that revealed little but hinted at lots. Her greeting in front of the cottage was perfunctory; Jack's was cautious. She held back in a way that said *'Don't even try to kiss me.'*

'There are cases in the car.' She popped the boot of her BMW remotely and strode towards the cottage, carrying just her shoulder bag.

'It's a bit late for you to be moving in, Lottie.' There were two large cases, and they looked heavy.

'I'm not.' Charlotte turned on the doorstep. 'Since you insist on splitting up, you're moving out. That's the rest of your stuff from the apartment.'

She waited for him in the front room, still standing, still wearing her shades. Jack stared at her from the door, the cases dumped behind him in the hall.

'You didn't return my calls.' Her shades glared at him above a mouth set in an unsmiling, immaculately lipsticked line. This distant ice-woman persona set his mental alarm bells ringing.

'You were coming here anyway.' And he was still ticked off with her.

'I've appointed solicitors. You'll be hearing from them next week. I take it you're not going to contest the grounds of adultery?' Charlotte delivered the words like a prepared text, without any preamble.

'I'm going to make some coffee.'

Jack left her standing there, although he didn't think she'd finished her speech.

He took a tray outside and they sat opposite each other at the outside table, she with her back to the view. A summer ago he'd stared at his father in the same place, and defended her. Today she wiped the wood with a cloth before she put the pristine sleeves of her jacket anywhere near it.

'Won't you take those ridiculous shades off? At least do me the courtesy of looking me in the eye.'

She folded them onto the coffee tray. 'You look like shit, Jack.'

So it was 'Jack', today, not 'chum'.

'Thanks.'

They stared at each other. Charlotte took two, refined sips, as elegantly as an actress on a shoot.

'So you're making a pre-emptive strike. Put the blame on me, and save yourself embarrassment with your homophobic family.'

She shrugged.

'Adultery,' he prompted.

'That's right.'

'Don't you think you're being a bit hypocritical? Not so long ago you wanted to watch me fuck George.'

'That's different. I'd have been part of it. Have you?'

'Have I what?'

'Fucked George. She fancies you, you know.'

'Absolutely not!'

'So there's just your physiotherapist.'

'We had this out months ago. I strayed. I'm sorry and I'm ashamed, but I came back. You were simply the first of us to have evidence.'

'Meaning what?'

'Meaning your girlfriends don't count?'

For the first time, she was off her guard. A light sheen of perspiration formed across her forehead.

'Prove it.' The words were belligerent, but she wouldn't meet his eye. She examined her fingernails where they lay on the table top, perfect ovals of varnished pink on sun-bleached grey wood. 'Anyway, even if you could, my solicitor says that same-sex relationships don't count as adultery. Not in English law.'

'How very convenient for you. Interesting that you take legal advice in case I have evidence of something you've never admitted.'

'Can you?' Her thumbnail traced the whorl of a knot. 'Prove it, that is?' She kept her eyes lowered.

Jack let the silence hang. She wasn't telling him everything. Her left hand curved around her coffee cup, cradling the bowl with long, elegant fingers. There was a faint band of paler, slightly indented skin where her wedding ring had been.

'Lottie, why can't we put the legal posturing to one side for a moment and talk as friends?'

Charlotte tapped the table as if she'd grown bored with playing with the grain. Her eyes flickered upwards, and dropped again.

'Can you? Prove it, I mean?'

This was important to her. *Legally* important, whatever she said about the definition of adultery. Jack stared over her shoulder at Witt Point to calm himself. High, thin cloud robbed the sunlight of its shadows, though the trees seemed to droop in the heat. A late-summer storm was brewing, and by that criterion Charlotte had arrived about two days early. They should be having this argument to the crash of thunder, not in the clammy prelude.

'No.' What's more, he didn't have the will or energy to fight her.

'Then it's your adultery.' Charlotte visibly relaxed, though she still spoke towards the table, as if embarrassed.

Some wounds go so deep, so unexpectedly, that their significance can take a while to have its full effect. A marine with a severed artery may fight on, unaware that he's dying. The anger within Jack surfaced long seconds after the words were said, erupting in a fist into the table top that made Charlotte flinch and recoil, her eyes flaring. A bone-china cup danced, then rattled in quarter circles on its side in a saucer of spilled coffee. Jack flexed his shoulders, feeling a trickle of sweat on his backbone as they glared at each other across the wreckage of cups and spills. Slowly, the mood deflated as their marriage bled out into Grandpa's garden. Charlotte dipped a handkerchief in a glass of water and began to dab at a spot of coffee on her cuff.

'It was always George, wasn't it, Charlotte? The reason you came here? Not about being with me.'

'You're no fun any more, Jack. There's no social life, no mess life, no glamour.'

'Have you spoken to her?' Jack needed to know if Charlotte and George were still seeing each other. Accidental encounters would be raw for a while.

'A couple of times. She's been too busy to give me a lesson since we all went out.' Charlotte surprised Jack by reaching over the table and touching his hand. 'Jack, let's just accept that it isn't going to work, and part as friends. Sailing all day and getting pissed at night doesn't do it for me.'

'I thought you enjoyed sailing.' Jack was going through the motions.

'But not all the time. Not in a howling gale. Not in the wet.'

'I haven't taken you out in a gale.'

'Don't be obtuse. You'd like to. Maybe it's a man thing. Fight the elements, and all that. I wouldn't mind sipping a chilled glass off a tropical beach, in the sunshine, but not all that yo–ho hearty stuff getting there.' She half stood and leaned over the table to kiss him on the head. Her chemise hung clear of her body, and Jack registered her figure with as much emotion as he might a model's photo in a Sunday supplement. It caught the eye but for once provoked no response.

'You said you wanted to be free to find a 'significant other'.' Charlotte straightened until they could look each other in the eye. 'Think of this as giving you that freedom. Now I'm going to gather my stuff from upstairs. There's not much here.'

Jack heard her turn on her way to the kitchen door.

'I think you and George would make a good couple.'

Jack snorted. There was only one thing worse than getting together with a woman on the rebound, and that was getting together with a gay woman on the rebound. He felt surprisingly calm, now that flash of anger was spent. Perhaps a bit numb, but there was even a growing sense of release; Charlotte had taken the decision for them. After a while he pulled a bottle of white wine out of the fridge, wrung its neck and poured two glasses. He stared at the condensation frosting the glass below the level of the wine, and when Charlotte didn't return he swigged. Tiny tears of wine trickled down the inside of the glass, kissing and retreating from the surface, until there was movement behind him at the kitchen door.

'Join me? Toast our futures?'

'I've got to drive.' She stood beside Jack until he realised she was waiting to say goodbye. As he climbed to his feet she pointed at the bottle and glasses. 'Jack, you've got to cut that out. It'll kill you.'

'And today will really help me.' That was unfair, and he regretted the words as soon as they were spoken.

They hugged briefly, awkwardly, neither at arm's length nor close, and she was gone.

She was right about the booze though.

Tomorrow.

VII: GEORGE

On the day that Chippy Alan hurt his back, George took the workboat over to Witt Point, though it was evening before she could finally lock up the office. The workboat was a lot faster than cycling all the way round, and she told herself she was on boatyard business. Maybe she and Jack could do each other a favour. As George rounded the point, Jack was at his jetty, stacking shopping bags ready to load into *Draca*'s dinghy, and George had a stupid flutter at the sight of him, enough to wonder if this was a good idea after all, but it was too late to turn back. Jack had seen her, and waved. He stood waiting to take her line, and shouted across the water.

'Tide's on the ebb. What do you draw?' Jack pointed at the workboat's hull, and George understood that he was thinking about the risk of her grounding.

'Just over half a metre.' The workboat was shallow draught, designed for inshore chores like pulling a line of boats or carrying the judges for competitions in the harbour. 'But a metre under the screw.' She was so flat bottomed that as George throttled back the boat rocked in the wavelets of her own wake.

Jack grabbed the line, wrapped a turn about a cleat and stood with his weight on his good leg, the other slightly bent at the knee.

'Then your screw will be deep in mud at low tide. How long are you planning on staying?' He stared at the outboard, a beast powerful enough for the workboat to be used as a rescue boat for dinghies in trouble. It was a practical question that George didn't take personally. Jack's jetty was a ramshackle affair that went just far enough out into the channel to allow a small dinghy to tie up at most states of the tide. It wasn't designed for eight-metre powerboats.

'Maybe an hour, if you're free? I've an idea I'd like to float by you.'

God, he looked tired. Tired and bent over, like he was carrying too much weight. George could have reached out and touched the shadow around him.

'Let's talk on board *Draca*. You won't have to watch the tide, out there.'

It was still daylight. That suited George.

Storing a boat is five times faster with two people. One in the dinghy, passing up bags, one in the cockpit. One in the cockpit, passing down bags, one in the saloon. They worked in companionable silence until everything was below decks, when George sat on the top of the companion ladder and watched him stow. Any seagoing boat has a complex arrangement of small lockers, often in obscure places, and the task of stowing provisions is best left to the one who will have to find them.

'You planning a trip, Jack?' He was kneeling on the chart-room's deck, pushing tins into lockers. His shoulders would stretch as he reached into a bag, and then his bum would go a bit higher in the air as he crouched and found corners for food. The bags left on the bunks in the saloon bulged with fresh fruit and bottles.

'I thought I might go away for a while.'

George was glad his head was down when he said that. Her face would have given her feelings away. She swallowed.

'Single-handed?' She wouldn't want to sail *Draca* on her own, even with two good legs.

'I'll take it easy. Short hops between ports. Stay in harbour if there's a blow forecast.' Jack rocked back on his heels and glanced up at her with a look on his face that was so lost and hurt that George wanted to give him a hug.

'What about your engine?'

'It hasn't let me down since that night we anchored.' He was hunched, all defensive, like he knew it was a bad idea.

'What's happened, Jack?'

He grabbed another armload of provisions and bent forward again, hiding his face.

'Nothing that won't be sorted out by a good divorce.' He spoke into the deck, and pushed a bottle of wine into the locker with enough force to rattle the jars and tins inside. George didn't know what to say. Jack needed a hug, not platitudes. When she didn't speak he looked up to see if she'd heard.

'Do you want to talk about it?' she asked, as their eyes met.

'Not particularly.' Jack reached into the bag and pulled out the next bottle. For a moment he stared at it as if surprised to see it in his hand.

'Sod it. Let's open one.'

George followed him into the saloon cautiously, eyes probing the corners, ready to back away. Again, she that sense of trespass, just faintly at the edge of her senses, not yet enough to be threatening. They sat at the table, George nearest the door to the chart–room, sipping wine from shatterproof ship's glasses. Or rather, George sipped and Jack gulped. He'd slumped backwards into the bench so that his neck rested against the top of the cushion and his eyes stared upwards through the skylight.

'You know, I don't think I mind about Charlotte, not really.' Jack did need to talk. All George had to do was sit there and listen.

'Looking back, I don't think we were ever in love.'

He was fooling himself about not minding. George could see it in his face. When she shut her eyes his colours were mute, and around them was that swirling darkness that made her want to hold him and pull him back towards the living.

'And I've been a bastard since I came back.'

He tilted his head forward and took another gulp. Across the chart–room, the cockpit hatchway framed the top of a pine tree on Witt Point, moving slowly with the boat against a flat grey, early-evening sky. Already the nights were drawing in. Autumn was coming.

'People who feel bad about themselves do shitty things, and that makes it worse. It's a downward spiral.'

Shadows were forming in the corners of the saloon. Not yet dark enough to hide anything, but enough for George to wonder how long she could stay. She waved away another glass of wine. Jack splashed liberally into his own glass. After a while, his monologue looped back to his planned voyage.

'So I thought I'd head west along the coast, or maybe south to the Channel Islands. I need to get my head clear.'

Maybe that was what the darkness was all about. If he went now, he'd die out there. George fiddled with her glass, wondering if and how to say *'Don't go'*, or *'I'll miss you'*, but the gentle rub and thump of the workboat against *Draca*'s fenders nudged her to leave. In the sleeping cabin, away from the skylight, it would be dark already.

'You need a crew, Jack.' He looked at her, and for a moment he brightened and his face softened.

'You volunteering?'

George shook her head. She hadn't meant to mislead him, just remind him what a crazy, dangerous idea it was.

'Sorry, I'm swamped at the yard. Chippy Alan hurt his back today.'

'Badly?'

'Slipped disc. He was cranking the hand winch we use to haul boats up the slipway. He'll be off for several weeks.'

'Poor sod. Send him my best, when you speak.'

'Sure. But it's a lousy time for me. Public holiday on Monday, last weekend of the season. Next week, all the clients will go back to the smoke and expect us to do the maintenance on their precious toys.'

'So what will you do?'

'I spoke to the boatyard's owners. Told them I'd have to hire someone to cover. They were more concerned with whether Chippy could sue them under Health and Safety regulations.'

George let her news sink in for a moment, hoping he'd realise where she was leading.

'Jack, I don't suppose you want a job for a few weeks? I need someone I can trust, tomorrow morning.'

Jack stared at her. She reached over and put her hand on his, where his fingers rested on the base of his glass. 'Please?'

He looked down at her hand, but didn't move.

'Let me think about it.'

George sat back, breaking contact. If she and Jack ever got together, she wanted it to be when he wasn't half pissed and hadn't just been dumped.

'Jack, I've got to go soon. I don't want to make my way back in the dark, at low tide.'

'Stay here, if you like.'

George knew he wasn't hitting on her. He just needed company, in the way she'd needed company after her fright in his forward cabin.

'I'd better go.' In full daylight, the saloon had almost felt safe, all polished wood, gleaming brass and sailing books. Now, the memory of something nasty lingered in the corners. Soon, she'd be a frightened little girl and Jack would stop respecting her. When George stood, the light outside had already faded enough for her to see the navigation lights out in the channel.

When she looked back at him, she sensed shadows creeping

out of the corners, stretching across the floor to reclaim him, real enough in her mind for her to climb out of them onto the cockpit ladder. It wasn't the divorce that was dragging Jack down, it was that frigging boat. She turned back to him from the first step.

'See you in the morning?' She could hear the hope in her voice.

'Perhaps. I'll call you later. Make sure you got back safely.'

He'd come. She could see it in his face.

VIII: GEORGE

Some times could be so happy that George would be frightened. She couldn't quite believe that good stuff happened and might keep happening without being taken away from her. The next two weeks were like that. Unreal. Too good to last.

Jack rang her that night, just to make sure she had got back all right, and talking with him was so easy and chilled. They spoke about anything. The yard, and yes, he'd come and help. Boats. People. His parents. George's mother. Happy stuff, too, like they were in their own private world. Maybe it was safer, in a way, being able to chat but not being in the same room, together but not together. The words flowed until his phone battery died, and afterwards George was so happy that she punched the air.

And they made a good team around the yard. Jack didn't have Chippy Alan's shipwright skills, but he knew the basics, so they outsourced the specialist tasks to a boatbuilder. George thought Jack was drinking less, maybe a lot less. He'd also moved back into his cottage to save time rowing ashore in the mornings, now the holiday rental people next door had gone. The darkness around him began to fade, as if the boat had lost its hold on him. He'd arrive on time, bright-eyed, and work hard.

In their breaks, George would sit near Jack, with her eyes closed, just to enjoy the image of him in her mind, and the colours in the image were brighter every day. They told her things that she needed to know, without him saying, things that made her want to run her fingers through his hair and hold him and tell him she felt the same way.

The colours were the colours of love, but Jack's behaviour

was just that of a good friend, like there was some barrier between them, some line he wouldn't cross. At first she thought it showed respect, so for a while it was enough to be together, to laugh and be easy.

One day they sat outside the office, enjoying the sunshine while they ate lunchtime sandwiches. Jack was close enough for George to see the fine, sandy hairs on his wrists as he gripped his sandwich, and far enough away for their lunch wrappers to be on the bench between them. The seagulls wheeled and swooped and made a lot of noise, and from time to time they had to swat them away from the food. *Frigging shitehawks.* They were the only irritation on an end-of-season hot day, a T-shirt day, while they watched a gin palace of a motor launch come alongside one of the floating pontoons. George felt too idle to go and help, too easy with Jack, and besides, there were people on the pontoon ready to take the lines. The skipper of the gin palace was making a hash of his approach and George frowned as he came in too fast. He was probably trying to impress the woman on the foredeck, who held a fender on a rope in one hand and made frantic 'back off' signals with the other. The boat went hard astern, almost jerking the woman into a forward roll overboard, and George winced as the boat's fenders ground against the floating pontoon. Inflated plastic groaned against wood, and the whole structure flexed away from the hull.

Jack swallowed a bite out of a sandwich. 'Is that what they call pier pressure?'

George groaned and punched him lightly on the shoulder. They'd started playing the 'worst pun' game again, now he was more relaxed. The woman on the foredeck threw her line to someone on the pontoon, and shouted back at the man at the controls. She didn't sound happy. George hooked her elbows over the back of the bench, enjoying the show.

'Maybe he'd have been better off picking up a buoy.'

Jack made a deep, rumbling chuckle, and glanced at her. He turned away quickly, but not before she'd seen his look flicker over her figure. George closed her eyes and tilted her head back, enjoying the sun and the warmth of being desired. She had a picture of a flare of red low down, in Jack's core, an instinct that came not from the mind or the heart but somewhere altogether earthier. *Feck, if he felt like that, why not do something about it?*

'We should celebrate.' George broke the silence.

'Celebrate what?'

'Your first week. Will you tikka chance on an Indian takeaway?'

'Naan better.'

Jack fell off the wagon that night. George couldn't afford restaurants, and she didn't like the idea of cycling back from his cottage in the dark, so they ate at her apartment. It wasn't much: one bedroom and an open-plan living area, in a cheap part of town, but it was convenient for the boatyard. Jack brought a couple of bottles of wine.

They were both a bit nervous, which was strange when they were so easy in each other's company at the yard, but having him in her apartment felt as exciting and as awkward as a first date. Jack was restrained with the wine, at first, sipping at a single glass because he had to drive, until she told him he could use her sofa if he wanted. After that he got stuck in. They had the takeaway sitting round the breakfast bar that doubled as a dining table, and by the time they'd finished they'd put a dent in the second bottle and were both a bit mellow. Jack started dreaming about places he'd like to take *Draca*, waving his arms as he spoke.

'Mediterranean. Adriatic. How'd you like to island-hop around Greece?' The way he'd said that made it an idea rather than an invitation, but his eyes were shining and he looked all boyish and hunky so she leaned across the breakfast bar and kissed him on the lips. They were soft and dry, and parted ever so gently. Their faces stayed so close, after, that she breathed spice and wine.

'That's not a yes, by the way.'

Jack was probably too surprised to speak. When George pulled her head back he was staring at her, all wide-eyed and startled.

'I have to earn a living, Jack, see? Besides...'

Jack stopped her with another kiss. This one lasted a bit longer.

'Besides what, George?'

That second kiss had thrown her. She'd lost her train of thought.

'Oh. Besides, your boat freaks me out.'

He leaned back, frowning. Seemed he didn't like that.

'Are you sure it wasn't a bad dream, that night? We'd both been drinking...'

Their beautiful moment began to fade, like a wave on a beach. George didn't want to think about that night. 'It was like being groped, Jack. I was touched. I felt breathing. Even last week, I was frightened on board when it began to get dark.'

'I've slept in that cabin quite a lot, and never sensed anything.'

'Maybe whatever it is doesn't fancy you,' George snapped. They'd just had their first proper kiss and he was getting all defensive about his boat.

'It has good taste then.'

'Or it's got you right where it wants you.'

They stared at each other across the breakfast bar until George sighed and began to clear up. Jack put his hand over hers to stop her.

'Sorry, George. You can sense things I can't. What was it your mum said about you?'

'That I was psychic.'

'And?'

'And a healer.'

'So how do you heal people?' His voice was gentle now.

George shrugged. 'I've only done it a few times. People aren't open to that sort of thing.'

'But how, George?'

'With my hands, like what I tried to do in the boat that night. And you thought that if I touched you we'd end up in bed together.'

'I'm going to feel bad about that army physio for a very long time.'

'I think you should let me try again. Just healing.' It wasn't the army woman who worried her; it was the darkness that gathered around him on his boat, like something was eating him up. 'No promises, no guarantees, but it's worth a try.'

Jack stared at her with eyes that were slightly unfocused. When he didn't speak she took the wine glass out of his hand, and moved to stand behind him.

'This ain't going to work like this.' She had to reach up to his shoulders as he sat on the stool. 'You should be lying down.'

'What do you suggest, George?'

She tugged him to his feet, and led him into the bedroom.

'Just keep your hands to yourself, right?' She wasn't sure if she meant that.

It didn't work out as she'd planned. She made him take his shirt off and lie face down, but she felt him tense at the first touch of her hands. His skin was smooth and soft under her fingers but the knots stayed bunched beneath. The whole scenario felt contrived.

'Relax. Think of something peaceful. Think of Witt Point.' George pushed her thumbs up his spine, strong and deep in the muscles. 'Think of waves on the foreshore.' She let her hands retreat, softly, wave-like, but Jack's back tightened, almost like a jolt of tension.

'Something wrong, Jack?'

He relaxed a little, but still held himself taut, as if ready to jump up and run.

'You called it a 'thin' place, a place where worlds are close,' he mumbled into the pillow.

'It's peaceful.'

'I think I saw a ghost in the trees, near the cottage.'

The healing wasn't happening. To heal, she had to almost empty her mind and unlock something within her.

'You told me.' George knew why she wasn't emptying. Kneeling astride Jack, with her crotch against his bum and her fingers on his back, too much of her mind was occupied by what she wanted him to do to her. 'Charl said Old Eddie did too.'

'What?'

Jack lifted one shoulder, twisting to look at her.

'Charl said she read Eddie's diary...'

Jack sank back onto the bed, but George had sensed the shutting of a mental door as soon as she'd mentioned Charlotte. Soon, he would get up and reach for his shirt. She moved further up his back and began to massage his scalp. Scalp massages are good for stress. She'd been able to send her mum to sleep with one, every time. Maybe that was what Jack needed: sleep.

In time, George felt the tension flow from him, and she softened her touch, letting him go. The more she softened, the further Jack drifted from her, even when she leaned forward and let her chest touch his shoulders. He was so deeply under that he didn't stir when she climbed off and pulled the duvet over him.

There was a little wine left, and she splashed it into a glass and watched Jack from the doorway, sipping, not fully understanding what had just happened. Waves on the shore. Charlotte. And the evening had literally slipped through her fingers. After a while, George took her kit off, found a blanket and curled up on her sofa.

It was still dark when Jack's shouting woke her, and George found him thrashing around on the bed, bellowing something like 'break right, break right'. She tried to hold him and talk to him to bring him out of the nightmare, but his forearm caught her a glancing, painful blow across the chest. She held his arm before he could hit her again, and then lay on top of him, pinning him down while he woke. There was enough light from the street lamps outside to see him staring up at her with eyes that looked big in his face. His chest was clammy with sweat and moved in short, gasping pants like he'd just run a mile, so she let go of his arms and stroked his face, shushing him as if he was a little kid. Jack let out a great, shuddering sigh and wrapped his arms around her, squeezing her tightly to him until the desperation became another kind of need, and George took him into her body.

It must have been a long time since he'd had sex.

George woke at first light to see him standing by the window, looking down at the town through a crack in the curtains, his naked outline perfect until she looked down at the contraption where his foot had been. She went to stand behind him, and wrapped her arms around him.

'Hey.' George inhaled his smell where it concentrated between his shoulders: male sweat and a scent that was uniquely Jack. He reached behind him and touched her side, but lightly, as if he was unsure of his welcome despite the way she pushed herself into his back.

'George, I'm sorry.'

'What for?' It was her turn to mumble. She was savouring the texture of his skin against her face.

'It shouldn't have been like that.'

'How should it have been?' George reached around him and began to explore down his belly. There was a point at the level of his hips where his stomach muscles formed miniature valleys that angled downwards and inwards…

'Gentler. Kinder. More… mutual.'

She turned him, stood on tiptoes to kiss him and once again tugged him towards the bed.

'Show me.'

He did. Which was why George skipped into the boatyard in the morning with this crazy grin all over her face. Perhaps it was a good thing that Chippy wasn't around, because he would have known. Feck, anyone would have known. She was practically shouting it, doing happy dances along the pontoons.

For the next week, they couldn't get enough of each other. Her flat. His cottage. The sail store at the boatyard, anywhere but on board *Draca*. Jack even took her bent over the desk in her office while she was on the phone to a client. That was a seriously weird conversation.

Once he admitted to her that he'd thought she was gay. Charl had even let him think they were lovers. Bloody Charl.

They took a long lunch one day, and Jack drove them to a pub on the downs where Jack drank orange juice and stroked the inside of her legs under the table until they left the food and climbed over a stile to look for a discreet place to get noisy. They were tottering together like a four-legged beast, legs entwined and hands everywhere, so they didn't see the sheep behind the thicket and the sheep didn't see them until George squealed as they scrambled out from under their feet. Jack was so surprised that he fell over, pulling George with him.

'George, I think I've fallen for ewe.'

She could do better than that. 'We've been sheepwrecked.'

'Nah. We're just three sheeps in the wind.'

George was lying on top of him and felt the phone in his pocket vibrate before it rang.

'Ooh, that's exciting. Ask them to ring again.'

Jack fumbled for the phone and George squirmed against his hand, teasing him.

'George, you're baa-rmy.' He looked at the screen and groaned. 'Grandpa's lawyer. Better take it. He might have finally got probate.'

George rolled off him, enough to let him talk, but not so much that she couldn't touch him. Above them, a skylark hovered, twittering, swooped and hovered again as if stitching its song to the heavens, and George had never known such happiness. Between her and the skylark, Jack's lovely face was bathed in sunlight, but the light went out of it as he listened, as if the sun had gone behind a cloud. When he closed the call down his shoulders were high and his face had tightened into hard angles that pulled in all directions and stood out like wires down his neck. George put a hand on his leg, trying to comfort him, and he took three deep breaths before he spoke.

'My father has launched a legal challenge to my grandfather's will. He says Grandpa didn't have the mental capacity to make a decision.'

George swallowed. Part of her reaction was sadness for Jack, but part was selfish, wondering if Jack would move on if he didn't have *Draca* or the cottage.

'He promised.' Jack's voice was dangerously tight, as if he was about to snap. 'He *promised.*'

Then raw anger flared around him like thunderclouds, and for a moment George was frightened because she saw the violence inside.

'The lawyers have called a meeting to see if we can resolve it between us before we burn up the entire estate in fees.'

The thunderclouds boiled and became a lightning bolt as Jack struck the ground with his fist.

'*Bastard.*'

IX: HARRY

Harry was gutted that it had come to lawyers. Five people sat around a table in the offices of the solicitor Old Eddie had appointed to be executor of his will. The executor wasn't up to much: he was just a small-town guy in a suit that was shiny at the elbows and had a collar that was starting to fray. Harry almost felt sorry for him: his man would have him for breakfast. Still, what an obscenity to have lawyers squaring up to each other within the same family. Jack sat with the executor in a scruffy, open-necked shirt and jeans, and glared at him across the table. He smelled of varnish.

Jack looked surprised that Tilly was there, but then it was for her benefit that Harry was doing this. It wouldn't have been fair on her, just to let things run. At least Tilly had spruced up for the occasion, though Harry wished she'd behave a bit more responsibly and less like a kid scoffing the free biscuits. He hadn't asked Mary to come though. She was so keen not to take sides that she'd have said something daft and undermined him. So it was just Harry, Tilly and the best lawyer he could hire.

Harry wished it could have been a discussion, all amiable within the family, but it would have disintegrated into an argument the way it usually did with Jack, so he let his legal eagle do the talking, at first. The trouble was, lawyers don't do discussions, they rehearse arguments, but at least they do it in that calm, superior tone that makes people listen. Harry's guy had put Old Eddie's diary and a copy of the will on the table in front of him, and was going through their case.

'...the will made by Edvard Ahlquist on March 10th this year, in which he left the bulk of his estate to his grandson Jack Ahlquist, effectively disinheriting the rest of his family.'

'There were bequests to Tilly and money left in trust to her children,' Jack interrupted, but Harry's lawyer kept going.

'...disinheriting the rest of the family from an estate which comprised a valuable seaside cottage, a vintage sailing boat and substantial cash assets. We understand that probate has not yet been granted?'

Eddie's lawyer shuffled in his seat. 'These things take time, as you know.'

'Although Mr Jack Ahlquist is enjoying full use of the cottage and boat?' Harry's man sounded smooth. Expensive. Slick.

'That hardly seems unreasonable, given the terms of the will.' Whereas Eddie's lawyer sounded defensive. Good. Jack just glared at Harry, trying to stare him out.

'My client has come into the possession of Edvard Ahlquist's diary for the period from the beginning of this year until he was admitted to a hospice shortly before his death.'

Jack spluttered. 'Come into the possession! For God's sake, my wife gave it to him. Why can't we talk straight? Why can't my father speak for himself?'

The executor put a restraining hand on the boy's arm. 'Let's hear what they have to say.'

Harry's lawyer pushed the diary across the table to the executor. He'd tabbed some pages with yellow sticky notes.

'You may want to read the passages I've marked. Since the handwriting is challenging, we've made a transcript of the key entries.' He slid a small number of printed pages over the table. 'We'll give you a few moments to read them, but the first page alone should be sufficient.'

For about two minutes the only sounds were of pages turning, and of Tilly scraping her coffee cup against the saucer. Harry wished she wouldn't smirk at Jack like that. It was a sad thing they had to do, but there was no point in crowing about it.

Old Eddie's lawyer looked up. 'So?'

'My client,' Harry's lawyer inclined his head towards Harry, 'contends that Edvard Ahlquist was non compos mentis at the time he made the will. If he did not have the mental capacity to make reasonable judgements, it follows that the will must be considered invalid.'

The look on Jack's face was painful to see. There was such fury there. Harry thought in that moment that Jack actually hated him. Maybe when he'd calmed down, Jack would realise that he was only doing what was fair and reasonable.

Old Eddie's lawyer's eyes darted from side to side. The man was out of his depth. 'That is something a court must decide.'

They'd expected that response. Harry's man pulled two copies of a letter out of his briefcase, slid one across the table and held the original ready to read.

'We have shared Edvard Ahlquist's diary and medical records with a highly respected consultant psychiatrist. That copy of his report is yours to keep. Let me read you his conclusions.

"Mr Ahlquist had been diagnosed with cancer of the lung, which by March this year had metastasised, producing secondary cancers in the brain and liver. His condition was inoperable and terminal. While it is not possible to make a definitive psychiatric diagnosis on the basis of a diary alone, some entries show clear signs of mental confusion, including delusions of persecution. Such symptoms are compatible with a condition on the paranoid and/or schizophrenic spectrum..." Need I go on?'

'I will of course study this report and draw my own conclusions.' Eddie's lawyer was stalling. He needed time to think.

'Whether or not Edvard Ahlquist was unduly influenced while he was in this vulnerable state…'

Jack hit the table with the edge of his fist and stood up, sending a wheeled office chair careering over the carpet behind him. He stood by the window, staring out, flexing and un-flexing his fingers.

'…in this vulnerable state, the courts are likely to decide that this will is invalid and that the laws of intestacy should apply. In that case, the entire estate will pass to Edvard Ahlquist's only son, Harald.'

Harry thought Jack was going to try and put his fist through the wall, but at the last moment he opened his hand to turn the punch into a palm-splayed slap against the plaster. Beside him, a picture bounced and slumped sideways, angling off its hook. He turned towards Harry.

'You promised. That day you fixed the engine. You *swore* that you wouldn't challenge the will.'

'That was before we knew he was mad.' Before Harry had evidence, anyway. And before Jack pissed him off with his attitude.

'I hope this is worth it, Dad. You'll rip apart the family to grab money you don't even need. Well, enjoy it. I hope you still think it was worth it in your lonely old age.' He strode towards the door.

'That's not what my client is seeking.' Those words from his dad's lawyer stopped Jack with his hand on the door. 'I suggest you sit down and listen.'

Jack stayed where he was.

'Please, Jack.' Harry had never begged him before. 'Let's compromise.' He waved his hand at Jack's chair. 'Sit down, lad. I'm just trying to be fair, to everyone.'

Jack was still the same kid inside, the one who had to be cajoled a bit and who could look sullen when he was made to do something he didn't want. He slumped into his chair and Harry nodded to his brief to continue.

'My client proposes that the cottage and boat are sold, and that the estate is divided into three equal portions to Mr Jack Ahlquist, Mrs Tilly Smith and Mr Harald Ahlquist. He believes this to be an equitable solution to a situation that would not have arisen if Edvard Ahlquist had remained compos mentis.'

'And if I don't agree?'

'Then we go through the courts and incur significant costs, although the outcome cannot be in doubt. If we have to contest the will, when the court decides in my client's favour he will divide the remaining estate, after costs, equally between himself and his daughter.'

'So I give in or get nothing.'

'I'm sad you put it like that, Jack. I'm giving you an incentive to see sense.' And, privately, Harry was making damn sure he didn't have to see The Slut in his father's house ever again.

Eddie's lawyer cleared his throat. 'I do not act for Jack Ahlquist, I am simply the executor of Edvard Ahlquist's estate. However, I suggest that he and I have a quiet discussion. Will you excuse us for ten minutes?'

They took twenty, during which time Jack's voice could occasionally be heard shouting from down the corridor. When they filed back, he looked and spoke like a killer: crisp and hard.

'I have spent a lot of money restoring *Draca*.' Excellent. He was going to negotiate. The old duffer must have talked some sense into him.

'That's your problem.' Tilly spoke for the first time, before Harry could stop her.

'The bank lent me the money on the basis of the will and the probate valuation of the estate. All of that money has been spent restoring *Draca*.'

274

That didn't take long to think about. 'I'll repay the loan out of the estate.'

'Dad!' Tilly sounded outraged.

'Now the boat's restored, it's more valuable, pet. Besides, we're all trying to be reasonable, aren't we?'

'*Draca*'s now worth about half the cottage.'

Harry could see where this was going.

'If you wanted to take the boat as your share, I'd accept that.'

'But he's already spent all that money on it.'

Both Jack and Harry ignored Tilly.

'And she still needs a new engine.'

'No. No more money. Do we have a deal?' Harry held out his hand across the table, but Jack left it hanging there until Harry let it drop.

'I think I'll go away for a while. Sail south. Get out of your lives.'

That hurt, but Harry kept his tone light. Jack would come round, once he'd thought it through.

'Don't be like that, Jack. In time, you'll see how fair this is. Besides, we said we'd scatter Old Eddie's ashes at sea, didn't we? You and me, together?'

Jack looked at Harry as if he was as mad as Eddie.

'You promised, Dad, and you broke your word.'

Chapter Nine: Djöfulóðr

(Old Norse: possessed by spirits)

From the Saga of King Guthrum

When King Guthrum knew that Jarl Harald was dead, he raged such that none dare come near to him. He landed nearby with many men, at a place beneath a headland where deep water comes close to the shore, and came so swiftly against the Saxons who had slain Harald that few escaped. There also they found the woman Witta, whose blood yet flowed.

There was with the Saxons a priest attending to Witta, and this priest Guthrum crucified. He brought Jarl Harald's dragonhead ship to the beach, then gathered to him all the Saxons who were not immediately slain, and tied them to the ground with stakes, in such a way that they were prostrate before the dragonhead. Now there was among the Saxons one who followed secretly the old gods and who was troll-wise and well practiced in seidr. This man cursed them, saying that if the oath of peace was broken, none would reach the halls of the gods, and that the gates even to Niflheim would be shut.

As Guthrum raised his sword, the man pronounced fǣgþ[1] against them, which in the Saxon tongue is blood-vengeance through all generations.

Then was Guthrum exceeding wroth and slew the one who was all-fjölkunnigr[2] by carving rista örn[3] on his back, in this wise; he stuck his sword into the body by the backbone, cut all the ribs away down to the loins and there drew out the lungs. Then Guthrum commanded his beserks to kill the Saxons, every one. The blood which flowed was held in bowls, and with this they made blood sacrifice. Some they used to stain Harald's dragonhead ship, and some they gave to the dragonhead to drink, that it might taste their vengeance.

Guthrum made the woman Witta watch the killing of the folk, though she died before receiving her own judgement.

As the waters rose over the bodies of the Saxons, King Guthrum prepared to give honour to his son.

1. Anglo-Saxon: vengeance through generations; a blood feud waged against the kin of a murderer.
2. Deeply versed in sorcery.
3. The 'blood eagle' ritual execution.

I: GEORGE

George knew it was bad, even before Jack came back. She'd been thinking about him, trying to hold on to that memory of him up on the downs: clear and pure like sunlight through a stained–glass window, all blues and reds that softened to rose when he looked at her and smiled. But that afternoon his colours could have been those of late evening, with a storm outside, so that the same window was dull and dark, showing the black bones around the glass rather than the light through it. She'd never been so much in tune with someone as she was with Jack. It was frightening.

She tried to hold him when he came back, but he was too tight inside to accept comfort. He just wanted to pace up and down and let off steam, and George pieced together the news out of angry scraps. She left him to rage until he threw himself down on a low wall by the slipway, and swore one more time, crudely. Jack sat there, hunched over his fists, staring across the harbour, and when he hadn't moved for a while she stood behind him, stroking his shoulders.

'He promised,' Jack kept saying. 'He promised he wouldn't challenge it. He broke his word.'

'Look on the bright side,' George worked her thumbs deep into the muscles at the base of his neck, 'if Eddie had just left you the boat and the money to restore it, you'd be well happy.'

Jack grunted. Maybe he wasn't ready for logic, but at least he rolled his head over her thumbs. She slid her hands out to his shoulders and pulled them gently backwards, forcing him to straighten.

'I think I'll move back on board *Draca*. Live afloat for a while.'

George didn't react immediately. Jack wasn't ready for

discussion, especially if he didn't believe what she felt about *Draca*. He'd hardly gone near the boat for the last two weeks, and he'd been bright and laughing and happy, with hardly a trace of shadow. George pulled his shoulders back a little more, until his head was between her breasts, just to remind him that there was more to life than his boat.

'It'll be cold in winter.'

'There's a stove in the saloon.' Jack turned his head to bring his cheek into contact with her chest. 'Come away with me, George.'

'Come away where?' she stalled. The last two weeks had been magic, and she knew she loved him, but she wasn't ready to cut loose from her job.

'Seriously. Let's just sail away, you and me. Go south around Brittany before the weather breaks. Take the canals through France. Spend the winter in the Mediterranean.'

George stepped back to work on his spine while she thought about that.

'There are one or two problems in the way.'

'Such as?'

'I don't even have a passport.'

'Easily fixed.'

'But I do have a job. I've worked frigging hard and I've earned the right to run this yard. I'm not in a rush to throw that away.'

'Then take a holiday. Two weeks around the Channel Islands. Let's find an isolated cove and swim naked. Let me love you senseless on the beach.'

George liked that idea enough to let her hands soften so that they caressed rather than massaged. 'There's one big problem that won't go away.'

'*Draca*.'

'Right on. Like I said, something in your boat freaks me out.'

'Will you try? Come away for a weekend. If it doesn't work,' Jack paused, as if he was reluctant to say the next words, 'if it doesn't work, I'll sell her. Maybe buy another boat.' He twisted to look at her, so George knew that he meant it.

'That's quite an offer.' She swallowed. 'Compromise. Burn that figurehead. It's evil. But do it now.'

'It's ancient. Important. Belongs in a museum.'

'Then for feck's sake put it there, before it takes you over.'

Jack hunched a little, and for a moment he looked like an addict who's been told he can't have any more. When he sighed, George knew he was going to put off the decision.

'Maybe, after we've scattered Grandpa's ashes. That dragon was important to him.'

'I think it'll kill you.'

'George, you have some strange ideas sometimes.'

'I mean it, Jack.'

George worked on his shoulders some more, and felt the strain trickle away. She knew that if they hadn't been out in the open, it would have developed into something else. She sensed he was building up to say something.

'George…'

Jack's phone rang, shattering the moment. He looked at the screen and declined the call.

'My bloody sister.' Jack stood up. He'd been on the verge of some intimacy, but he shed the mood the way he might drop an overcoat on the ground. 'I'm going back to the cottage.'

'It'll be time to close the office in an hour. Want some company?'

'George, I don't think you want to be around me tonight.'

George thought about saying she'd risk it, but she could see that the only companionship Jack Ahlquist wanted that night was with a bottle. That hurt a bit, but she let it go. As he walked over to his car, a shadow followed him the way smoke followed *Draca*'s engine. The darkness was back.

That had her thinking. There's darkness in all of us, some more than others, but it's part of us, inside us. Here, on her territory, she'd seen the real Jack: the man on the hillside, laughing and shining. The man who took himself off to drink alone carried a charcoal smudge with him that was outside of him, creeping inwards, as alien as cancer, and *Draca* was its territory.

She was going to have to fight it for him.

And she had no idea how.

II: JACK

Jack is back in the truck's cab, in the desert, and there's dust all around them. It billows in through the open windows in scorching clouds, and it's smeared in brown half-moons across the cracked windscreen. Chalky White is driving, and this is the moment when Jack knows it's all going tits up. They've slowed to negotiate a chicane of debris in the road, the militia truck ahead of them has disappeared and there's a moment of awful inevitability at the realisation that it's a trap.

Jack screams at White to speed up, break right, get the hell out of there before whatever nasty they've planned goes off. He knows, because he's been here so many times, that the world will disintegrate like the windscreen, and in the midst of the sound they will soar and fall weightless to earth like a shot bird.

This time Jack doesn't get to the explosion. He watches the chicane coming closer in slow motion, and wonders why the hell White has his palm pounding against the horn. Does he really expect a makeshift barricade to get out of the way? But the noise that's coming out isn't a horn sound but the pretty tinkle of a bell, and the bell repeats with each push of White's hand until he holds it there, insistent, constant, until Jack is pulled out of the nightmare into a bedroom that stinks of sweat and stale whisky, and grates with the jangle from Grandpa's front door.

Tilly stood there, stuffed into wide, tight jeans that squeezed her belly into the shape of an over-iced cupcake. The look on her face was somewhere between a grimace of anger and a smirk of triumph.

'You took your time.' She barged past him into the cottage. Her children followed her, pushing excitedly into the hall and squealing loud enough to make Jack's head ache until they saw his prosthetic foot and shut up, staring at it wide-eyed. He'd just wrapped a towel around his middle.

'Tilly, what the hell are you doing?' He looked at his watch. *Shit, he was late for work.* Jack turned to follow her but left the door open. Tilly's husband was still on the drive, hanging back, looking uncomfortable. Jack and Darren never had much to talk about. He was probably a decent enough bloke but, well, he was also the sort of guy who'd marry Tilly. Jack wasn't sure what he did for a living, but it involved driving the van that was now parked outside.

'Wouldn't want you running off with our stuff, would we?'

Her kids lost interest in Jack's foot and ran into the front room.

'*Your* stuff?' The children started poking at Grandpa's model of a Viking longship. 'Please don't play with that, guys.'

'You do what you want, Wayne. Just don't break nuffin.' She turned to Jack. 'I'm entitled, see? You get the boat, we get the house. That's fair, innit?'

'Half the house, I thought? The other half to Dad?'

'We thought we'd live here until it's sold, save on rent, see? But Dad says he's in no rush to sell.'

An echo of the nightmare sounded in Jack's head. Not the fear, not the certainty of pain and death, just the sad weight of betrayal.

'Couldn't you at least have given me the chance to get dressed?'

Tilly sniffed. 'It's plenty late enough for most people. You go ahead, though. We're not going anywhere.'

'For fuck's sake, Tilly.' Jack stopped. Shouting sent stabs of pain through his head and forced him to continue quietly. 'You could have warned me.'

'I called. You didn't pick up. Is your woman upstairs?'

The absence of Charlotte's name or even the word 'wife' was a calculated insult.

'She's not here.'

Tilly's sad little 'oh' of disappointment told Jack all he needed to know. It was a Saturday, Charlotte could be expected to be there and Tilly had wanted the pleasure of throwing her out. Jack was surprised Harry hadn't come along to watch.

Jack was still making himself coffee when the children started screaming upstairs, and they found them fighting in the bathroom. They'd filled the bath with water and tried to play boats with Grandpa's longship model, but it had turned upside down and begun to disintegrate. Tiny, immaculately crafted slivers of wood floated on the surface. The older one, the boy, was trying to push the pieces back together, mashing them in the process. The bow of that pathetic, dripping wreck had started to spring apart like the empty husk of a seed pod. The girl was crying in the corner, saying it was all the boy's fault and she'd told him he shouldn't.

It was time to go.

Outside it was nearly high tide, with enough depth of water to bring *Draca*'s bow into the jetty, so Jack could load directly from the shore. Most of his stuff was still in the suitcases Charlotte had brought, and the rest he packed in half an hour. Darren even helped him push it down the garden in a wheelbarrow and make a pile on the jetty.

There was one awful moment when Jack thought *Draca*'s engine wasn't going to start. It was a calm day, with too little wind to sail out of Freshwater Bay, and he prayed to whatever gods looked after the Ahlquists to spare him the humiliation of pushing his stuff back though the garden to his car. But after much heaving on the starter crank, Scotty the engine stuttered, caught, coughed again and settled into a slightly asthmatic purr. Jack kept her ticking over as they loaded.

There was still a little of the flood tide running, so *Draca* was pointing the right way, and Jack didn't look back after he slipped from the jetty. He wouldn't give Tilly that satisfaction. He just left a cloud of smoke behind him, spreading over the surface like an oily fart.

Jack's head cleared as he wove through the islands across the harbour, inhaling a mouldy, almost-autumn freshness from the shore. Some of the trees had their first touch of yellow. He wanted to be away from there, to be turning for the open sea not the boatyard, to cut the ties as easily as he'd slipped the mooring. All ties except George. A mental picture formed of George braced at the tiller with the wind fluttering that orange-streaked hair around her face, and the wake stretching behind them as the land sank below the horizon. It wouldn't matter where they were going, but sunshine would be good. Sunshine and steady winds and endless chances to see the way her face lightened when she smiled at him, that look that said everything was OK.

George wasn't smiling as she watched Jack bring *Draca* alongside one of the boatyard's pontoons. She stood with her fingers pushed into the pockets of her shorts, thumbs hooked outside, in her slightly slouched, shoulders-back, don't-mess-with-me posture. She took his line and helped him tie up without a word. When he killed the engine she was standing on the deck by the cockpit, frowning down at him.

'I had things I needed you to do this morning.'

'Sorry. Like I said on the phone, I didn't know my sister was coming.' Jack hugged her under her bum and lifted her, holding her with her legs dangling and angling his face up to hers. 'Give me a kiss.'

She allowed a perfunctory touching of lips. 'You need a shave.' She sniffed. 'Heavy night, was it?'

Jack put her down but kept his arms around her body, savouring her presence. 'I vented a few feelings.'

George pushed him away and lifted her chin towards the foredeck, which was piled with suitcases and bags. 'Do you want to put that stuff in the sail loft?'

'Have you thought any more about going away?' Jack tried to hug her again but she broke free. George was in a huff.

'How's your engine working? Looked like you were burning coal on the way in.' The question sounded part serious, part prevarication.

'Hasn't let me down for weeks. Come on, Chippy's back tomorrow, isn't he?'

'Only light work.'

'He could man the office, give you a break.'

George stood braced against the hatch, one hand either side of the companion ladder. Below her, the chart–room and saloon were crammed with more stuff. She shivered for a moment, although it was a warm day. 'This boat gives me the creeps.'

'I think *Draca* has kept me going, these last few months. *Draca* and then you. And she's my home now.'

George turned to face him. 'The last two weeks, you've hardly been near her, and you've been different. Happier. More alive. When you're on board, it's like something's got its claws into you.'

'I'm just pissed off with my father.'

'It's more than that. I'm worried about you.'

'You're my best medicine. Come away with me. Please?' Jack faltered on the edge of an admission, and then said it anyway. 'I love you, George.'

At that, she held him. It was a while before she spoke.

'OK. One night. I'll probably sleep in the saloon. And if it freaks me out, we come straight back, OK?'

Jack tightened his hug, but she pushed him back so she could look into his eyes.

'On one condition, Jack. Dry boat. No booze.'

'I can do that.' Of course he could. For a couple of days, anyway. With the right incentive.

They made an early start on a day of high, dry cloud, and rode the westerly tidal flow into The Race, pushed by a cool south-easterly that was forecast to strengthen through the day. That stretch of water could be exhilarating or seriously nasty, but with the wind on their quarter and the tide behind they had a smooth, fast passage. Once Anfel Head dropped astern and the morning passed without incident, some of the tension in George's shoulders slipped away. She took the helm, cautiously at first, but *Draca* was in a good mood and behaved herself. Jack went forward to enjoy the sensation in the bow, where the boat felt more alive than anywhere. The stern would lift to a wave and the bow dip so that the bobstay, the steel line running down from the bowsprit to the stem, sliced the water. *Draca* would surge forward in a bubbling rush and the dragon would be low enough for its base to touch the water, like wetting its feet, before it rose with its head glaring at the horizon. Jack stood with his legs astride the bowsprit, with the staysail bellied beside him and his hand braced on the forestay, where he could feel the hum of *Draca*'s happiness.

His balance was improving. He could walk back across the deck, with no need to crawl, and George was grinning as he came. Jack's chest filled with contentment, not just with George, but with the knowledge that at last she was experiencing *Draca* at her best, sailing sweetly, proving her pedigree. It was like reconciling two dear friends. When Jack and George sat together in the cockpit, leg to leg, his arm around her, the world was a wonderful place. From time to time one of them would shift to adjust a sail, but then they'd settle back into that companionable huddle with George steering one-handed, her other hand resting inside Jack's thigh. They didn't talk much, but the soft movement of her fingertips spoke volumes. When Jack asked her what she'd like for lunch, she twisted to kiss him, slid her hand a little higher up his leg and answered 'you'.

They found an anchorage where high cliffs dropped to a bare, stony beach. In the far distance, two walkers strode the coastal path but otherwise it was a place of crying seagulls and the faint, gravel sounds of waves breaking on shingle. In the cockpit, she kissed him hard, almost possessively, but squealed when he found the edge of her jumper and slid his hands inside.

'Warm your hands up!'

'I am.'

'Not on me. Let's go below.'

'Are you sure?'

'Well it's too frigging cold up here.' She led the way.

At first Jack didn't understand her mood, that hardness in her eyes as she pulled off her top. This was more assertion than seduction. Then he realised that George was putting her stamp on *Draca*, almost as if she had to prove her right to be there. The way she unclipped her bra, spilling her curves, was downright aggressive. She turned, bare-breasted, reaching for him, in the middle of the saloon.

'Let's not go forward.'

Jack understood. Not in the sleeping cabin. He bent to nuzzle her.

'Jack, can you smell something?'

'You. S'wonderful.' He inhaled her scent: soap and salt, wool, a little perspiration, musk. He wanted her badly.

George gasped and broke away. Jack looked up, alarmed, as

288

she covered her breasts with her arms as if there was someone else in the cabin. She backed against the table, looking around her with eyes that were suddenly wide and frightened.

'Jack, can't you sense it?'

'Sense what?' It was just a cabin. Varnished wood. Racks of sailing books behind brass retaining bars. Leather benches that they'd been about to put to very good use. And Jack had a lovely, half-naked woman in front of him and a painful pressure in his trousers.

'It's here. It knows we're here.'

'I'm not feeling anything.' Jack opened empty hands in a way that showed the double entendre was deliberate. A nervous smile flickered across her face and was gone. Her eyes still darted from side to side. She thumped the table beside her, angrily, but kept the other arm across her breasts.

'George, you're not getting spooked, are you?'

A look crossed her face that was almost a snarl, and which became smouldering defiance as she lifted her arm away from her breasts and braced herself backwards against the table.

'Not a ghost of a chance.'

'That's the spirit.'

George lifted her bottom onto the table and sat there, cross-legged, shoulders back, breathing deeply. 'I'm just going to think nice, calm thoughts.' She turned her hands palms upwards on her thighs, thumbs circled onto middle fingers, imitating the classic yoga pose. Her eyes were now locked on Jack's, and he wished he didn't see the fear there. She was almost shaking.

'George, you sure about this?'

'No frigging spook is going to tell me where I can't have my lover. *Om mani padme hum...*' She waggled her head from side to side, parodying the mannerisms of an Indian guru, until he stepped forward and kissed her, wrapping her in his arms.

As the kiss lengthened she uncrossed her legs and folded them behind his backside, pulling him closer.

'*Om…*'

'George, I love you.' He loved her for her courage. He loved her for her humour. He loved her for the body that was soft and urgent against his, and in that instant *Draca* let out a snarl that reverberated around them as if they were inside the belly of a great, growling beast. Jack could feel it through his foot, and even through his stump. He could feel it through George's body, as if she sat on throbbing machinery rather than a table.

There was a heartbeat of shock before George clung to him and screamed.

III: GEORGE

George couldn't believe that Jack had abandoned her there, in the cabin. She was nearly crapping herself, and gripping him so tight it must have hurt, but Jack broke her hold like she was a child, leaving her breathing the evil. He legged it up the steps so fast there might have been every ghost in hell chasing him. She was on her own as she scrambled off the table, with the boat still snarling around her. George grabbed her top as she ran, holding it across her chest until she reached the cockpit and took in great gulps of air. Jack was already on the foredeck when she turned, looking for him, and that horrible, rattling growl stopped with a final crack that jerked the whole ship.

George almost cried with relief at the sudden quiet. After all that noise there was nothing but sea sounds and the hum of the rigging. There was no smell but sea air. The wind had strengthened, sending whitecaps rolling towards them, and it was cold enough across her back to make her shake. At least, she thought it was the wind.

Jack turned, with his open shirt flapping around him, and made his way back to her, gripping the stays for balance. He was frowning as he climbed down into the cockpit.

'How the hell did that anchor chain slip?'

George started to giggle. Jack must have heard the hysteria because he hugged her, running his hand up and down her back to calm her.

Of course. Heavy iron chain dragged through a metal hawsepipe that was set into the hull. On deck, the sound would have been a natural, end-of-voyage noise. Loud, but normal. Below decks it had been like being trapped inside a drum, and she'd freaked.

But there was more than that. Whatever it was with Jack's

boat, she'd felt it again. Was it really only her who could smell it?

'I mean, it was secure.' Jack's chest resonated against her head as he spoke. 'There's a brake on the windlass, and I know I flipped the ratchet to hold it as well. I don't make that kind of mistake.'

'I felt it, Jack.' George sniffed into his chest. 'There's something nasty in your boat.' She'd been so frigging determined to beat it, and she'd failed.

'It was just the chain, George. It rattled you.'

George pushed away from him. 'Not funny, Jack.' She pulled her top on. She was getting cold, anyway. There had been a presence down there. Not all the time, though. At first it was just like a draught blowing a bad smell out of a corner. She'd remembered that first time she'd been below decks on *Draca*, and felt like a trespasser. Well, this time the owner had been home, and he didn't want her there. For a moment she'd thought *'Sod you, he's mine'*, and when Jack had said *'I love you'* she wanted him so bad that she almost forgot the spook until the roaring started. Then the darkness had been all around them, swamping them, squeezing the life out of Jack, and she screamed.

'I'm serious, Jack. It's there. It's frigging evil. And it doesn't want me around.'

'Sure.' He buttoned his shirt and stuffed it into his trousers.

'Don't patronise me, Jack. I can sense these things.'

'Yeah. Like you said, you're psychic.'

George huddled into the corner of the cockpit, where the cabin gave her some protection from the wind. Jack didn't look at her as he went down the steps, but he hit the hatch in his frustration and George hugged her knees, feeling miserable.

She'd blown it. She'd wanted to show that frigging boat that he was hers. If it had been a bit warmer he could have had her anywhere, anyhow. *Her* man. She'd even had fantasies about him taking her kneeling on the foredeck, with her hands around the neck of that fecking dragon, strangling it. And then when that stinking evil was all around them and the growling started she'd fallen apart. Now Jack was wound up and hitting things and the moment was ruined.

He didn't get it. How could anyone be so blind? It was like he saw green fields without smelling newly spread silage, so he'd calmly inhale something that made her want to gag. And now he obviously thought she was imagining it. Even if he couldn't feel it, at least he might understand that she could.

When he came back he had a sweater on under thick foul-weather gear, and he'd brought her stuff with him.

'So what happens now?' Jack watched her put on her bra. Lust smouldered in his face like embers in a dying fire. George didn't turn away but she was too ticked off with him to make anything of it, and the wind was chill enough across her skin to make her rush.

'I'd like to go back, please. Sorry.' She didn't know whether to be angry or embarrassed or just frightened.

'The wind's against us. It's a long haul.' Jack was probably as irritated with her as she was with him.

'The tide's turning. The easterly flow will help.'

'It'll still be dark by the time we reach Furzey.'

'Jack, I'm not sleeping below, and it's too frigging cold to sleep up here.'

The muscles in Jack's jaw and neck tightened until they stood out like his boat's rigging. He went below and worked whatever ritual he needed to make the motor go. It coughed and fired on about the fourth heave.

'I've a lot of anchor chain to bring in.' He made his way forward and sat by the windlass. It was an old, manual device, with a cog-like pawl that held the links in the anchor chain.

A side lever hand-cranked the chain over the pawl before it dropped through a hole in the deck into the locker below the fo'c's'le. Jack sat with one leg either side of the chain, rocking backwards and forwards as he worked, hauling thirty tons of boat into the wind. Each backward heave brought in about three links, say four inches, and at a rough guess he had about forty fathoms, eighty yards of chain out. Anger crackled across his back with each heave, and each time he bent forward she could see the back of the dragon, its mouth gaping like it was laughing its evil head off.

It took a long while, even with George nudging the boat forwards with the motor to help. When they were under way and Jack came back to the cockpit, he settled into a brooding silence that worried her. It was like he had something festering inside him that was going to explode. When they were hauling up the mainsail, George suggested taking in a reef so she'd be easier to handle in strong winds, but he just glared at her.

'You want to get home, don't you?'

They'd never argued before. Nothing serious, anyway. They were in the dragon's territory and she was losing the fight.

George watched him, once they'd settled onto a course. In the morning, they'd sat together, thighs touching, already making love in their minds. Now they sat diagonally opposite each other: Jack on the windward bench, hand on tiller, staring into the wind, and George on the downwind side, curled in the lee of the cabin. She could read the hunger in him. Hunger for food, hunger still for sex and probably hunger for booze as well. Why couldn't he sense the thing in his boat?

It owns him, her mind replied. It needs him. And it didn't want her to take him away. You threaten it.

Why does it need him?

She closed her eyes to think, and in her mind's eye the darkness came up from the cabin to hang between them, distorting everything so that an ugly version of Jack was at the helm. That frightened her, and after that George kept her eyes open so she could see the real Jack, rugged, still so very fuckable, but dangerous.

That eyes-shut, mental glimpse of another Jack made her think of a time when she was a kid, and her mum had used weedkiller in whatever scrap of garden they had had at the time. For a while the dandelions still grew, but they grew distorted and all misshapen before they shrivelled and died. That had been Jack: dark and twisted like a bad cartoon.

It got worse.

The first tack took them well out to sea until the land was a grey smudge along the horizon and the waves were coming at them in steep, bruising growlers whose tops crumbled white. Jack was in his element, keeping *Draca* close-hauled into the wind so that the boat shoulder-charged the sea. From time to time a wave would thump against the bow hard enough to send drenching sprays of water over them. Jack didn't seem so angry any more, but there was a mood about him that showed in the set of his jaw, and made George stay in her corner.

Jack tacked early, turning back towards the land long before George would have altered course.

'Keeping clear of the sea lanes' was his explanation when she challenged him.

'You'll be heading into The Race.' George knew these waters well enough to know they wouldn't clear Anfel Head on this tack.

'The tide will help us.'

But the wind was against them. To have the tide flowing fast in one direction while the wind tried to push it back the other way would make steep, vicious seas. The closer inshore they came, the lumpier and more unpredictable the waves grew. At the top of a wave, the wind could catch them and blow them almost onto the beam, forcing George out of her corner to stand on the lockers on the downwind side of the cockpit, or to crawl up the sloping deck to hang onto the windward coaming. Soon the seas were breaking over the bow all the time, so the dragon seemed to bite the waves and rise with water streaming from its jaws. Small torrents would come sheeting aft to burst against the skylight and the doghouse hatch over the companion ladder. Sometimes they'd even break over the cockpit coaming in brief waterfalls.

Jack pushed the boat too hard, but George didn't say anything for a while. It was his boat, after all, but it was starting to get dangerous. They should have reefed.

'You know the old saying, Jack?' It was the first time either of them had spoken for some time.

'What?' The word was crisp as a slap.

'Any fool can carry sail, but it takes a true sailor to know when to bring it in.'

That stung him, but he gave in, with little grace. It meant George had to go forward to lower the gaff, the upper spar that braced the sail, then take three rolls of sail around the main boom. It was a rough, dangerous job on an unpredictable deck, and by the time she got back she was cold, wet and miserable.

'You should have done that earlier!' George had to shout to be heard over the wind.

'Nah. She's loving it! Can't you feel it?' There was a hard edge to Jack's question and George didn't answer. The wind wasn't the problem; it was strong, maybe force six, gusting seven, but it was pushing against the tide to build steep, angry seas and the combination was brutal. As they approached Anfel Head, they launched off the crest of one wave, with the hull probably clear of the water for half its length, and crashed down into the face of a huge growler, sending spray and water over them so thickly that George felt the tug of it round her

296

body, pushing her aft. If she hadn't had a grip on one of the rails by the hatch, she might have been swept overboard.

Jack whooped as they broke the surface, still ploughing into the weather. He had a manic grin on his face, water streaming from his hair, and was laughing in a way George didn't like. She'd never punish a boat of hers like that, especially an old lady like *Draca*. Jack deserved to suffer damage.

'How's your 'Man Overboard' drill?' George was half expecting their life jackets to have auto-inflated as the wave broke over them. They should have had safety lines rigged and been wearing clip-on harnesses if he was going to sail her this hard.

'Don't worry. She'll look after us!'

She might look after Jack. George wasn't so sure about herself, but she didn't push the point. She could see the inshore edge of The Race, with the cliffs of Anfel Head looming through the weather. There was deep water quite close into the cliffs, but the wind can do strange things there. It goes upwards, for one thing, or even downwards, and you find weird eddies that can spin a boat or catch you from unexpected directions, so you can lose control while the tide is still pushing you onto rocks. There's sometimes a narrow, calm passage between The Race and the cliffs, but George wouldn't want to risk it. One mistake and even a big, heavy boat like *Draca* would be matchwood before you could shout 'Mayday'.

'Are you going to turn?'

Jack didn't answer. It was George's turn to get angry, and she hit him on the arm hard enough to demand his attention.

'Look, you can play silly buggers with your own life, but don't take me down with you.'

Jack looked a bit grim at that, but said 'ready about' and put the helm down to tack, but he did it with a supercilious air that told George he thought she'd wimped out.

But Jack had a fight on his hands. That ship didn't want to turn. They hung there, caught in stays with their head to the wind and the helm hard over. Once the ship had lost way and lay dead in the water, the tiller was useless anyway. They just lay there, tossed about and waiting for a big wave to roll them over. *Draca* would be unlikely to sink, but it was a shitty place to be out of control. George felt it was almost as if the ship wanted to self-destruct under Anfel Head.

'I'll go forward,' George shouted. 'I'll brace the staysail out.'

She crawled out onto the foredeck, underneath the flogging foresails, and used her body to force the staysail outboard so the wind could push the bows round. She hung there, knees on the deck, arms and body out over heaving grey water, and only saved from falling overboard by her grip on the sail and the pressure of the wind. Slowly, she watched the panorama of cliffs slip past beyond the dragon's jaws as the bow began to turn. It felt like a very personal battle, and as the bowsprit steadied towards the open sea she let the sail fall back into position, and screamed her triumph at the figurehead.

'Not this time, you bastard!'

Jack's nod of respect when she fell back into the cockpit was his first sign of warmth for hours, but they had a major fight on their hands to bring her back through The Race. Nothing would now convince George that *Draca* didn't have a mind of its own, and that the seas under Anfel Head were where it wanted to be.

George was tightening the foresail, heaving at the sheet to bring the sail closer to the centre-line, when she saw the outline on the foredeck. At first it was just a suggestion out of the corner of her eye: a burst of spray that hung in the air, forming a shape in the instant before the wind blew it away, a vague outline that might have been a man. George secured the sheet and gripped the hatch, not believing her own eyes while she waited for another wave to hit.

The next burst was lower, rising only to waist height. Enough to show what might have been legs astride the bowsprit, as real and as insubstantial as if you'd thrown a bucket of water over a glass statue.

'Jack, look! On the foredeck.'

'What?'

Another wave, higher this time, enough to suggest a head, a torso and an arm raised high above the shoulders as the bow soared.

'Don't you see it?'

'See what?'

George looked over her shoulder at him. His face streamed water but he wasn't worried. He hadn't seen. Behind him, Anfel Head was fading into the twilight gloom, a mass of darker grey with a line of paler surf at its base.

'There's something there…'

'What am I looking for?' He wasn't denying it, he just wasn't seeing it.

The next burst scattered, empty. So did the next. Streamers of water ran from the bottom of both the staysail and the jib, and were whipped away on the wind.

'Nothing. S'gone.' Jack's face told George it wasn't worth trying to explain. She huddled into the corner of the cockpit, no longer sure what she'd seen, only sure that it had frightened the hell out of her. And she'd just been down there, on her own, to help them round.

She'd had enough long before they slipped into the calmer waters of the harbour. By then it was dark. She had so much water running down the inside of her foul-weather gear that trickles were changing directions down her back as she moved. Jack had kept hold of the helm, and George wasn't going to go below even to make a cup of tea, so they both stayed hungry. They tied up in silence and George squelched away along the jetty without a word or a backward glance, leaving Jack to stow and tidy up on his own. She was shivering, fed up and didn't want to see Jack-frigging-Ahlquist ever again.

IV: JACK

Jack found George's overnight bag in the saloon. She'd probably known it was still there, but she'd developed this thing about going below, and Jack guessed that by the time they came alongside she was in too much of a huff to ask him to get it. God knows what had got into her. He'd never known a woman change so quickly. One minute she was really up for it, the next she was screaming and wanted to go home. It was only the anchor chain, for God's sake. Loud enough to stop even Jack in his tracks until he had realised what it was. The only weird thing was how the hell it came to disengage from the windlass and run out. He needed to test the mechanism before he sailed again.

Jack took George's bag back to her office the following morning. Chippy Alan sat at George's desk, and climbed to his feet in a way that kept his back vertical, as if someone was pulling a string that ran from the top of his head. He shook hands without bending.

'George around?' Jack asked, once Chippy had debriefed him on the progress of his back and expounded his views of the current state of the Health Service.

'Thought she'd be with you. Took a day off, didn't she? Something go wrong?' Chippy sounded protective.

'We came back early. George doesn't like *Draca*.'

Chippy waited for Jack to say more, but Jack let the silence hang until Chippy lowered himself back into his seat.

'Bit of a blow yesterday.' Chippy was still probing.

'About force 7, but *Draca* was brilliant!'

Jack wasn't explaining this too well. All logic said that it was the kind of experience you didn't want to repeat, but it had been one hell of a buzz.

'And what did George think?'

Jack dumped George's bag. 'I think she was a bit fed up at the end. Thought I'd taken a few risks.' Chippy had managed to get it out of him anyway.

'And did you?'

'Maybe, just a bit. But George always struck me as being a bit more, well, robust.'

'She's a good sailor. Very good.' Chippy wore his disapproving look, rather like a girl's father. 'And where did all this happen?'

'In The Race, off Anfel Head. Wind over tide, but Chippy, you should have seen *Draca*! It was like she was saying "Bring it on"!'

Chippy stared at him. Now the look was blank, disapproving, even calculating. It was time to leave.

'That storm taught me one thing though, Chippy.' Jack paused with his hand on the door. 'I could sail *Draca* single–handed. She'd look after me.'

Chippy sniffed. 'Don't be so sure. And get your engine fixed first.'

But Jack was still on a high. He'd felt balanced, at one with the boat, heart and hand as if they shared one soul, and together they were eating the gale. Why couldn't George see that?

Later that morning, Jack knelt on *Draca*'s foredeck with the windlass's mechanism spread out on an oilskin. It was one of those low-grade tasks that allow a lot of time for thinking. He'd promised George that if she couldn't cope with *Draca*, he'd sell her. But after that sail, would George still want to hold him to that? Would he still have to make the choice between them? OK, so he'd pushed his luck in The Race, but *Draca* had performed so brilliantly that Jack didn't know whether he wanted to make that decision any more. And had they had an argument or a rift? Maybe Jack really could sail her single-handed. Rounding Brittany into Biscay would be a blast.

George. Jack didn't know whether to call her, or let her cool off. For a moment an echo of regret, even guilt, passed through his mind, like a half-remembered melody. Her face as she'd trudged off down the jetty hadn't just been angry, she'd looked almost lost. What had he done? Jack straightened his back, still on his knees. Soft rain moistened his face and coated the figurehead with a sheen of moisture that reflected the grey, oil-filmed water below. Its neck arched away from him and he reached out to touch its scales, drawing a darker line through the wet.

'What do you think, my friend?' *Draca* moved to the wash of a passing boat and the light shifted on the dragon's cheek, emphasising the gaping mouth and giving life to the eye. 'Shall we sail away together, just you and me?'

The slight rocking shifted parts of the windlass mechanism against each other with a faint, metallic clink and Jack dropped his hand. There was nothing wrong with the bloody windlass. Jack swore and began to reassemble it, still thinking about *Draca* and George. George and the dragon. That thought made him laugh, even if the laughter was a bit manic.

'Does Saint George want to kill you, my friend?' Jack was still chuckling as he reached for a spanner and noticed a pair of legs standing on the jetty near him. He looked up.

Jack didn't know how long George had been there, watching him with a sad, wide-eyed look that could have been fear or pity.

V: GEORGE

At first, George had thought she'd let Jack stew. But she'd woken up in the middle of the night, alone in her bed, and sniffled like a teenager at the thought of their plans to curl up together in some anchorage. Then she remembered the times he'd woken up shouting in the night, and she thought maybe she'd cut him some slack.

Chippy called her in the morning, to see if she was OK. Apparently, Jack had been in the office and had admitted that he'd taken risks. *'It's strange,'* Chippy had said, *'that I fell out with his grandfather in the same spot, for the same reason.'*

That started her thinking again. It was like there were two Jacks: the Jack on the hillside, the laughing hero she'd fallen in love with, and the one she'd seen in *Draca*'s cockpit, dark and twisted. Possessed.

Possessed. That was a good description. George knew Jack well enough to be sure that the man she'd seen off Anfel Head was not natural. That boat had a hold over him, and unless she got Jack away it would kill him.

Jack was kneeling on the foredeck and didn't see her coming, but that unguarded moment showed her what she was up against. He had the windlass mechanism spread out in front of him but he was talking to the figurehead, almost like he was praying to it, and the figurehead seemed darker and more solid than ever, an iron-black silhouette that sucked light. George closed her eyes for a moment, and in her mind the darkness reached from the carving to Jack like he was a dog on a leash. When he looked up, his eyes moved from side to side as if his mind was elsewhere and she was intruding on his private world.

'Can we talk?'

'Sure.' Jack waved his arm in invitation. 'Come aboard.'

'Not here.' Nowhere near the dragon. 'Let's go find a coffee.'

There was a cafe near the marina, the kind of place that has chrome tables on the pavement that would be packed with yachties in the season. That day, the rain had pushed everyone inside, where the steamy fug was coffee-scented and full of young mothers shushing screaming kids in buggies. They took their drinks outside and sat under an awning, where they could talk quietly.

'Had any thoughts about yesterday?' George asked him. Neither of them seemed to know where to start, and that seemed as good a place as any. An apology would be good.

'Didn't *Draca* do well?'

George certainly hadn't expected that slow, appreciative smile.

'You nearly killed us.'

'We were so totally in tune, *Draca* and me.' It was as if Jack hadn't heard her.

'Until you asked her to turn out of danger.'

Jack's face fell. He'd heard that.

'You know, Grandpa felt very close out there. He should have been with us. Felt the ship at her best. We'd have laughed at the storm together.'

'Eddie and his friends fell out under Anfel Head. They thought he was going to kill them all. I spoke to Chippy.'

Jack shrugged deeper into his foul-weather jacket. 'I wasn't there. Wouldn't know.'

'It's like you're turning into your grandfather.'

'And the problem is...?'

'Old Eddie? *Mad* Eddie? Eddie no mates?'

They stared across the tables at a matt-grey harbour. Rain dripped from the awning, making tinny noises as it hit the tables.

'Jack, do you believe I'm psychic, that I see things other people don't?'

'I believe you believe it.' Jack took a sip of coffee and slumped back, waiting for her to say more.

'I think your boat took over Eddie in some way, before he got too old and sick to sail. Now it's taking you over. It owns you.'

'I think you'll find it's the other way round.' Jack folded his arms and hunched into his foulies, as if her words were rain to be endured.

'I told you the other day: you're different when you stay away from *Draca*.'

'So?'

'Happy. Lighter. More... yourself.'

'You might have had something to do with that.'

That wasn't much of an olive branch, but it was a start. But 'have had...' Did that mean it was over?

'You've changed since you started living on board.'

'I've had a few setbacks, remember?'

Jack reached for his coffee again and George grabbed his hand, forcing him to look at her.

'Jack, I believe you're in danger. Your boat will kill you. That figurehead is frigging evil.'

His look said it all. Cynical and a bit patronising.

'I thought *Draca* looked after us rather well yesterday.'

George let go of his hand, exasperated.

'Remember you and Old Eddie saw things in your garden that you couldn't explain?'

Jack nodded half-heartedly.

'I bet you haven't seen anything recently.'

'What makes you say that?' He sounded surprised.

'But have you?'

'No. And I'm not sure I ever did. Not really.'

'Perhaps because that frigging carving is back on the water, not in the garden.'

'Then why aren't I seeing things on board?'

'I am. And maybe you're not seeing them because they're becoming part of you.'

Jack laughed in a way that she didn't like.

'Last week you said you'd sell *Draca* if the trip didn't work.'

Jack shuffled on his seat. 'Perhaps we both have things to think about after yesterday.'

George closed her eyes, wondering whether to go on. 'I told you once that I could see things about people.' No good had ever come of talking about colours, but she didn't know how else to explain. 'I can shut my eyes and think about someone, and they'll have colours around them. The colours tell me about them the way a smile says someone's happy.'

'You said.' His tone said 'Get on with it'.

'Colours don't lie. I don't think people can fake them.'

'They wouldn't know about them, anyway.'

'Yeah, whatever. When I was a kid, way back when I first went to school, I thought everyone could see stuff like that. To me it was normal. I learned to shut up about it when all the other kids laughed at me.'

'I'm not laughing.'

'Not out loud. The point is, the colours tell me stuff. I knew your grandpa was going to die.'

'He was nearly eighty and had cancer. Sounds a fairly safe bet to me.'

'I didn't know he had cancer. I did know his colours went black. That's what happens when someone's going to die soon.'

'So how does this explain why you freaked out yesterday?'

'It doesn't. I'm trying to tell you your colours are going black. So black it worries the shit out of me.'

This time, Jack's laugh was more nervous.

'I love you, Jack.'

He still didn't speak, but grimaced as a gust of wind flapped the fringe of the awning and scattered raindrops over them.

'Yesterday, you said you loved me.'

Jack sighed. 'George, yesterday you lost it when the anchor chain slipped. Today you're talking about auras. Don't you think you're giving me a lot to digest?'

'You think I'm neurotic.' She said it as a statement, not a question. Jack didn't reply, just hunched a little deeper.

'Sod you, Jack Ahlquist.' George pushed her chair back, metal scraping over the pavement, and left him sitting there.

George waited until the end of the working day before she called Charlotte's mobile. She picked up within three rings.

'George, darling.' She sounded pleased as well as curious. 'How lovely to hear from you.'

They exchanged pleasantries until there was a what-are-you-ringing-about? pause.

'Charl, I'm worried about Jack.'

'So what's he been up to?' Beyond Charlotte's voice, George could hear another woman. It sounded like she was asking who was calling.

'He's irrational. He's moody. He's taking risks. He's drinking too much. And he's obsessed with that boat.' As George spoke, she realised how lame that sounded.

'That's Jack. What's new?'

'But it's getting worse. He's behaving just like Old Eddie did before he trashed the boat.' George scrambled to find a believable way of explaining. Something that didn't involve colours or ghosts. 'I think he's going to do himself damage.'

'You sound awfully upset. Are you two lovers yet?'

George didn't answer. She didn't want to make things worse for Jack, and she'd always been a bad liar.

'You are! Awesome!'

'Seriously, Charl, I think he could do something really stupid.'

'And you think I can help?'

'I'm looking for advice. You know him better than anyone.'

'Our Jack has been on a downhill slope ever since he was wounded. You know why he drinks so much?'

'Tell me, Charl.'

'I think he's trying to destroy the thing he hates most of all.'

'Which is?'

'Himself.'

George bit her lip. The other woman's voice sounded down the line, quickly muffled as Charlotte put her hand over her phone. The words were indistinct but the tone was petulant.

'So what can we do about it, Charl?'

'We? Haven't you heard? He ain't my problem any more.'

'Me, then.'

'George, darling, if I knew that we might not be divorcing in the first place. Look, I've got to go.'

'Charl, why does he hate himself?'

There was a dry chuckle at the end of the line. 'Ask his father. Keep in touch. Ciao, bella.'

Jack would never have forgiven George if she had gone behind his back and called his father. It was going to be down to her. A battle for Jack between her and *Draca*. A priest might listen, but then she didn't know any priests. So George did the only thing she knew how, and talked Jack into coming back to hers for a takeaway pizza. She had to remind herself he was worth saving. Jack was subdued, but at least he came. He drank wine, a lot of it, until he fell asleep on her bed halfway through the evening. George managed to pull his foot and jeans off, but couldn't do much about the rest.

Jack had another nightmare, and woke up bellowing in the dark. George knew by then that the nightmares were always about the time he was wounded, never about his first trip, when he'd won a medal. He lay there gasping for air, and George cradled him to her, rocked him and stroked his back. His skin was cold and clammy with sweat under his shirt. When he'd been still a while, she asked him if he wanted to talk about it, and he rolled onto his back so that all George could see was a faint profile in the darkness. There was only the hint of a paler grey where his eye caught a little light. He spoke upwards, like to a microphone hanging from the ceiling.

'When that truck was on fire...'

Jack spoke in short phrases, with little gasps in between.

'...Such pain... There was no dignity left, no *humanity*... One part of my mind floated off and watched the rest of me go mad...'

George kept very still. He'd never revealed this much before.

'And do you know the cruellest thing?'

George blinked in the darkness, feeling her own tears welling.

'I can't remember it ending...'

Jack swallowed.

'...The blessed moment of oblivion.'

The hint of grey beside his eye lengthened and glistened, and she leaned over to cradle his face and kiss away his tears.

They found a form of stability for a few days, like the hour around high tide when the sea stretches all the way to the hills on the far shore of the harbour and doesn't seem to rise or fall, and there's only the navigation buoys to tell you about the sandbanks or the currents beneath. They didn't have the passion of the first weeks, but they had companionship, and in a way that seemed deeper because Jack had reached a low place and he knew George was still with him. George made sure he had things to do around the yard, the heavy work that Chippy couldn't manage. Anything to keep him ashore and active and away from that boat. At nights she tried to keep him with her, away from *Draca* and a bottle. Sometimes she succeeded.

They didn't talk about the boat again. If George had forced a decision between *Draca* and her, it might not have gone her way and she didn't dare risk that. Jack didn't talk about going away either. He hadn't found the money to replace his engine, and the long-range weather forecasts showed a storm spinning out of the Gulf of Mexico, wreaking havoc up the eastern seaboard of the USA and heading their way over the Atlantic.

The calm didn't last of course. For a while, Jack was no worse, but he was no better either. It was like George was standing on dry land, trying to hold onto a boat that was being dragged out of her hands by a tidal flow.

All that week the tides grew higher, building towards the highest 'spring' tides of the year. And on a day when they felt the first gusts of the coming storm, and flood warnings were announced for low-lying areas, Jack's father came.

Chapter Ten: Allfeigligr

(Old Norse: having the mark of death plain on one's face)

From the Saga of King Guthrum

Harald was borne to his dragonhead ship, fully armed and with the best of his array. Guthrum placed Harald's sword in his hand that he might be chosen, but all men knew that the manner of Harald's death would condemn him to serve Hel in Niflheim, not Odin in Valhalla. His body was burned with great riches within his boat, and the fire was very glorious, for Guthrum hoped that the higher the reek went up aloft, the higher place his son would receive with the gods.

At the setting of the sun Harald's ship was consumed and sank beneath the waves, but the sea was not deep; when the flames were extinguished, the dragonhead remained above the waters, well bloodied and staring at the shore. At this sight Guthrum swore that it was not yet finished, and Harald was not avenged.

Those that were foremost in the army counselled against war. They spoke of the völva's prophecy, that one woman would cause the deaths of half the army, and that their deaths would be without honour. They feared not death, but desired to die gloriously, sword in hand, and thus join the einherjar. *Many said that the oath on Yngvi's ring had been sacred, and must not be broken. Others counselled that a war would be without profit; they had already done great scathe and there was little more plunder to be had in that region.*

But Guthrum's rage could not be quieted, and with his own hand he slew King Alfred's hostages, that their paths be set. The army divided; half followed King Guthrum towards Exanceaster[1] by land, and half sailed Westwards. In the days that followed Guthrum harried in the lands to the West, pursued by the army of King Alfred. But a mighty storm smote the land and men said that the gods were angry for the breaking of the oath. They watched for their brothers at sea.

1. Exeter.

Draca

Harry was worried about Jack. Him and the wife both were. There'd been no contact, except through solicitors, since they agreed to split Old Eddie's estate.

'Old Eddie'. Didn't seem right to call him 'Mad Eddie' any more, not when they knew he was really mad.

Mary fretted a lot about Jack. She wrote to him at his flat to ask him how he was, and to invite him for a meal, and when the boy didn't reply she called his mobile. Jack said he hadn't had the letter. Seemed he hadn't been to the flat for a while and was living on the boat. She tried to find out if things were going sour with The Slut but he wouldn't say. Mary couldn't pin him down to a date to come over, either. She said he sounded tired.

They didn't feel they knew him any more. They hadn't talked, not really talked, since before his wedding. Back then, they had a son who was tall and proud. Turn around and he's bent over like he's trying to fit under a roof that's too low, and he's lost a foot and won't talk about it. Won't talk about anything. God, that hurt. Something as bad as that and he wouldn't let them help. He was ten miles away and he might as well be a thousand. Mary said they should go and see him, but Harry wasn't sure. He'd tried that, twice: once after Eddie's funeral and once to talk about all the crazy things in Eddie's diary. No one could say he wasn't doing everything in his power to help.

Then go again, Mary said. Let's both go. But Harry put his foot down and said he'd go alone. The block was between him and Jack. God knows why, but they had to sort it out, man to man. Besides, Harry didn't think The Slut would live on a boat, so the boy would probably be there on his own.

Harry didn't ring to say he was coming, just in case Jack made excuses not to see him. Some grey-haired guy in the office gave Harry directions to *Draca* but he sounded suspicious and, within a minute, while Harry was still looking, a young woman caught up with him and asked him how she could help. She made it sound like she'd asked what the hell he was doing. Harry smiled when he recognised the cute little thing that had come to Eddie's funeral, but she seemed sour and worried, as if he'd come at an awkward time. She went ahead of him, showing him where to go, swung herself onto *Draca*'s deck like she knew her way around and shouted down the cabin hatch for Jack.

Harry was still walking down the pontoon when Jack's head appeared in the hatch. He was unshaven and unkempt but he looked at the girl with the kind of smile that told Harry straight off that they were lovers. God, would his family never learn? Jack was just like his grandfather, playing away. That smile only lasted a moment while she whispered to him, before he peered around her and saw Harry, and his face froze. That change, the way he narrowed his eyes and tightened his jaw, hurt more than Harry could say. It was instinctive. Not faked. It told Harry that his own son didn't like him.

The girl straightened and climbed ashore, saying, 'I'll leave you guys to it.' The glare she gave Harry as she passed told him that Jack had shared his opinions. Jack stared at Harry from the hatch without speaking.

'Aren't you going to invite me aboard?'

Jack turned, and let Harry follow him.

'You've done a grand job on this boat!' He had too, and Harry believed in giving praise if it was deserved. Jack was pulling the door to the forward cabin closed as Harry came off the steps. It looked a bit of a mess in there but the main cabin was tidy. Lots of freshly varnished wood and gleaming brass.

Jack leaned his back against the forward door and watched Harry as he looked around.

'Your mum says you're living on board now.'

Jack nodded. He still hadn't spoken.

'And what does Charlotte think about that?' It was an effort to use The Slut's name, but Harry had promised Mary that he'd do his best.

Jack shrugged. 'We've separated.'

It took a moment for that to sink in. Harry supposed he should have felt happy, but then a thought occurred to him and he lifted his chin towards the cockpit.

'Because of that girl a moment ago? George, or whatever her name is?'

That was a mistake. Before, Jack had been hostile but sullen. Now he was angry.

'Why are you here, Dad? Changed your mind?' He waved his hands around the cabin and lifted his eyes to the ceiling. 'You going to take the lot?'

'That was unfair. Unfair and unkind.'

'So why are you here?'

'We're worried about you, your mum and me. I thought we could have a talk?'

'About what?'

It was Harry's turn to get angry. He took a deep breath to make himself stay calm.

'Whatever's making you a stranger to us.'

Jack made a sarcastic little laugh. 'You shun my wedding, ignore my career and take away my inheritance. Now you wonder why we're strangers?'

Harry didn't like the atmosphere in that cabin. The hostility was all around him, not just in Jack, as if the boat itself was angry. 'Look, I know we've had our differences, but can't we try and find a way round them? Just spend some time together?

You and me were going to go sailing together, and scatter Old Eddie's ashes, remember?'

Jack stared at Harry long and hard, and pushed himself upright.

'OK. Let's do it.' His voice had gone sharp, a bit unnatural. 'Let's get it over with.'

'What, today? I'm not dressed for it.'

Jack lifted the seat of one of the benches and began pulling stuff out, flinging it over his shoulder onto the table. 'Spare foul-weather gear. Rubber boots. Life jacket. Everything you need.'

'Yeah, but…'

'Half a day. I know just where Grandpa would want to be.'

'Ain't it a bit windy?'

'You're not going to wimp out, are you? Call Mum. Tell her you'll be home for tea.'

'Well, I suppose…' No way was Jack going to accuse Harry of wimping out.

'Good. His ashes are in the store with the rest of my gear. Change into that stuff while I fetch them.'

The mood didn't lift when Jack left. Harry was so uneasy that he found himself looking over his shoulder as he pulled on the waterproofs, as if there was someone else still with him.

Weird that.

II: GEORGE

George stood at the office window, staring out over the marina to where *Draca* lay alongside a pontoon, and wishing there was some way she could keep Jack and his father apart. She didn't know what it was between them, apart from the will, but she did know that, every time Harry appeared, Jack went darker, like an animal retreating into a cave and glowering at the world.

When Jack came ashore from his boat he was on his own. He strode down the pontoon in a brisk, no-nonsense way that made George imagine him wearing a uniform, leading his men with a gun in his hand. His limp had almost gone, over the summer, so there was just a bit more of a clump as his foot went down, and a slight shifting of his weight. If she didn't know better, he might have had a small stone in his shoe.

And Jack could move fast. He came through the office door hard enough to have knocked anyone flying who was standing behind it.

'Can I have the storeroom key, Chippy?'

'How's it going?' George asked.

'We're going for a sail. Father–son bonding time.' Jack's voice was higher than normal. Like his shoulders.

'Have you seen the forecast? The glass is dropping.' Chippy waved the key at the barometer on the wall before handing it over.

'I know, there's a gale on the way. We'll stay in the bay.'

'And the tide's turned. There'll be a four-knot westerly flow in The Race.'

'Better keep clear then, hadn't I?'

George followed Jack to the store. Like most of the owners, he had a personal locker, and his was jam-packed with stuff.

He rummaged in the pile and pulled out a purple cube, heavy enough to need both hands until he held it against his body. When he tried to close the door it mashed against a pile of clothes and swung open again, releasing a tumble of books, a screwed-up winter jacket and an officer's ceremonial sword.

'Sod it.' He kicked the door and left it swinging.

'Grandpa,' he explained, hefting the cube. 'We're going to scatter his ashes.'

'Don't go, Jack. Not today.' George stood between Jack and the door, and didn't move.

'Why ever not?'

'High 'spring' tides and a storm coming. It's going to be rough.'

'*Draca*'s sound.'

'And your colours are dark.'

'Oh, not that again.'

George tried to hug him, but it was awkward with the box against his body. Jack put one arm around her and squeezed, and with her face buried in his chest George sensed a flare of tenderness, but it was the kind of red you see at the base of burning oil or tyres, half hidden by thick, black smoke.

'I wish you'd believe me. I think you might die today.'

'I'll be fine.' He pushed past her.

'*Please*, Jack.' But he'd gone.

No, he wouldn't be fine. George watched him march back to his boat with that cube under his arm, and the blackness followed him like the shitty exhaust from *Draca*'s engine. As he went below deck it closed around him until that was all there was.

George stood outside the marina office to watch them go, dreaming up bizarre scenarios to stop them. Chain *Draca* to a navigation buoy. Sink a ship across the harbour mouth.

Anything. The sense of disaster was as strong as coming thunder, the way a storm could make her tense up and wait for the first crack. Jack's boat needed at least two people to sail her, and if it was only two, they both needed to know what they were doing. Jack's father didn't. George could tell by the awkward way he moved about the boat, tripping over ropes and getting in the way because he didn't know how to help. One pig-headed fool and a beginner setting off into a storm, like they were perfectly allowed to do.

Jack turned *Draca* into the wind just off the marina to put the mainsail up, and he did that on his own, heaving the halyard with angry great jerks. Feck, but that guy was strong. At least he put in a couple of reefs. Already the wind was moaning through the rigging of the boats alongside, setting their halyards rattling against the masts in a tinny drumroll that said 'Too much to sail'. No one else was setting out, so the marina was crowded with masts. George didn't need an anemometer to know the wind strength: the boats sang it to her, and Jack was setting out into a force 6, rising 7. Later the moan would become a scream and it would be force 8 out in the bay.

But it wasn't the wind that worried George most, or the fact that Jack didn't have a half-competent crew with him. *Draca* was built for rough weather. As Jack let her fall away from the wind, and her sails filled, she looked strong and ready for anything, even beautiful, despite that ugly figurehead snarling at the sea. The thing that really frightened her was the darkness around him, as thick as that frigging carving. It wasn't engine smoke either. That was blowing away on the wind so fast it looked like an oily rag waving from the boat's arse end.

George hadn't been joking with Jack. All the signs were that he was going to die that day.

III: HARRY

At first, Harry thought it was fun. Jack even made a joke about the gods being with them when the engine fired, which was a bit of a cheek after all the work Harry had done on it. Harry stood on the pontoon ready to cast off, and snarled back at the figurehead, happy. Him and Jack again, after all these years.

Jack let Harry steer while he hauled up the mainsail. 'Just keep her into the wind,' he said, and Harry could manage that while this great sheet of canvas went flapping and cracking upwards. It looked like hard work.

'We need to set the sails in the harbour,' Jack explained. 'It'll be rough in the bay.' That should have warned him, but Harry was enjoying himself too much to think. It was special, working together, like they were a team, and Harry didn't mind the boy giving him orders. He knew what he was doing.

Jack didn't speak much, unless it was about sailing the boat, and then he sounded over-bright, as if he was still tense, so Harry shut up for a bit. Let it come, he thought. You don't need to talk when you're sailing. There are things to do.

They shot through the harbour mouth like they had wings, with the boat heeling over and the water bubbling by. The navigation buoys marking the channel were tilted at an angle and trailing their own wake with the rush of the tide.

'Nine knots!' Jack pointed at one of the brassbound instruments by the steps down into the chart-room. It sounded as if that was good. Then a wave lifted the bow and dropped them back in a crash and a spatter of water, making Harry grab onto the edge of the cockpit for support. Another wave hit and it became a pattern: lift–crash–spray, lift–crash–spray. If it had been the same every time, he could have got used to it, but there were swoops or staggers that he wasn't expecting and they caught him off his guard. It was maybe just a bit too exciting, but Jack seemed to be OK with it. He was watching the sails and showing Harry how to tighten them by heaving sideways on the line and pulling a bit more slack around the post as he let it go. Swigging, he called it. Harry got the hang of it quick enough to be pleased with himself.

Jack was in his element. Harry felt quite proud, watching him push against the tiller with the wind in his hair. This was the man Harry used to know: fit and strong and confident. Then a lump of sea burst against the side, showering Harry, and Jack laughed.

'Are you having fun, Dad?' He made it sound like a challenge. Maybe Jack thought Harry was frightened. For a moment, Harry wondered if the boy *wanted* him to be frightened.

'Great!'

'Because it might get a bit rough further out. Let me know if you want to turn back.'

That was definitely a challenge. Harry grabbed the edge of the cockpit and held on.

'Show me what she can do then!' The wind was strong against his cheek, and wet cloud scudded overhead, low enough to touch the top of the headland before it rushed towards them. The motion was still manageable at that point, just enough to make Harry slightly queasy, but then he wasn't going to show Jack he had a problem.

'Shall we scatter the ashes then?'

'They're in the saloon. Port side, forward. In the rack with the books.'

Harry made it down the steps into the chart–room and stopped, gripping the door frame into the saloon. It was a weird feeling, looking at things that didn't seem to be moving while he and they were being thrown about. For one thing, everything was half on its side, with the steps angled over so far that Harry would have slid off them if it weren't for the non-slip treads, and his feet were no longer beneath his chest but way out to one side. Down there, everything looked cosy. The table and benches in front of him were solid enough, bolted to the deck, and even the books were in their proper place behind their retaining bars, but in the little galley area a dishcloth hung at an angle, swaying over the edge of the bowl. Outside, the world had gone mad. A grey and white horizon would appear and disappear in the skylight, and it felt like being trapped inside a child's toy boat that was being kicked down the road. Harry's gut heaved and he knew that, if he tried to cross the saloon to the box of ashes, he'd spew. He made it back to the cockpit, crabbing sideways up the sloping steps, and groped for the seat.

'You OK?' Jack had to shout against the wind.

Harry nodded. It didn't seem so bad when he could look at the water, even if it was dancing around all grey and ugly. Up in the cockpit, he knew it was the boat being thrown around. Down in the cabin, the whole world was moving.

'I'll get them later.'

'We can turn back, if you like?'

Harry shook his head. No way was he going to admit defeat.

'Are you pleased with her?' Harry was making conversation. It took his mind off his guts.

'We understand one another. We both like wind.'

Jack made it sound like the boat was alive.

'This was a good solution. You keeping the boat, I mean.' Harry shut his eyes, swallowing. Bad idea. He needed to look at land. 'I'm glad you saw sense.'

Jack's hands flexed around the tiller. 'You didn't give me any choice.' He sounded angry enough for Harry to look up, and he didn't like what he saw, either in Jack's face or in the scene around them. They were still in the shelter of the land, but beyond Anfel Head, directly ahead of them, the sea was grey–white with breaking waves.

'We're moving at quite a rate.' Harry was starting to get nervous. The cliffs were slipping past rapidly, even though the wind was almost in their faces.

'The tide's pushing us west. We'll have four or five knots behind us once we're round the headland.'

Harry could see a line across the water ahead of them, and coming closer. Even in the bay, where they were, it was choppy enough for the tops of some waves to be blown off in little avalanches of foam. Out there, it was like there was a fight going on just under the surface, turning everything into heaving lumps of grey and white. And the waves weren't moving the way they come into a beach, all in regular lines and going the same way; these waves were big and ugly and chaotic.

'You sure about this?' Harry tried to keep his voice level. To him, it was as if they were about to jump into a raging torrent.

Jack just laughed. It was a weird, high-pitched laugh that made Harry look at him closely and wonder.

A blast of wind threw them so far over that Harry's feet scrabbled for support on the deck and he was only saved from falling by grabbing the edge of the cockpit. There was a moment when they were weightless as the boat fell sideways off a wave, before they hit the trough in a great, shuddering thump and the next wave broke over them. It came sluicing down the deck, spraying upwards as it hit the cabin skylight, and washed over them. This wasn't spray, it was solid water that hit them with so much force it felt like a fire hose had been pushed up Harry's sleeve, and all Jack could do was laugh. He sat there hauling at the tiller with his feet braced against the lockers on the opposite side of the cockpit, and as they went airborne again and crashed back, he let out a 'yee-hah' whoop like a rodeo cowboy.

'OK. You've proved your point,' Harry shouted.

'Come on, Dad.' Jack threw words at Harry in short, disjointed bursts as he wrestled with the tiller. 'What was it. That you used. To tell me. On walks. When I was a kid?'

'Can't remember. "Don't dawdle"?' Another wave broke over them and Harry tried to find shelter in the corner by the chart-room steps.

'Nah. "Man up". I'd be trailing behind. Tired and crying. "Man up", you'd say. "Got to be strong. That's my little soldier."'

'Well it toughened you up, didn't it?'

'Kept my nose out of a book, you mean?'

'So I pushed you a bit hard. Point taken.' Harry decided to humour the boy. This wasn't fun any more. 'Now let's throw Old Eddie overboard and go home.'

'Not yet.' Jack smeared water from his eyes. He was wide-eyed, maybe a bit manic, and staring forward into the storm. 'Let me show you where Vikings go to die.'

'You're mad.' Harry meant that. It dawned on him that Jack wasn't rational any more.

'It runs in the family. Brace yourself.'

He bellowed the last words at Harry in a way that made him twist to look forwards, over his shoulder.

'Oh shit.' Harry rarely swore, but the sight of this wall of water frightened the hell out of him. All around them was chaos, and then there was a wave that didn't seem to move, just sat there in the ocean the way a torrent will flow up and over a boulder. It was high enough for the boat to come more upright when they were underneath it and lost the wind, and then be pushed over as they climbed its side and the sails caught the gale again. By the time they reached its crest they were almost horizontal. Around them the sea stretched out in jagged points. Had they taken a photograph it would have looked like a landscape of the Alps, a horizon that wasn't a horizon but a series of peaks and valleys. The cliffs had become just a menacing smudge in the rain, with a white line of surf at their base. The boat seemed to hang in the air, twisting away from the wind, and Harry could still think enough to realise that so much of the hull and keel were clear of the water that the wind was taking over, spinning them.

They fell into the trough in an explosion of foam so loud that Harry thought the boat was breaking up, and he watched Jack fight to bring her head around, pointing her as close into the wind and the waves as he could before the next wave rolled them over. Maybe even Jack was scared. The scene in the trough was worse than the crest. They were surrounded by moving hillsides of grey water whose tops were whipped away in hissing white.

'Here,' Jack shouted, as they crested the next wave and the wind threw them sideways again. 'Here! This is the oath-breaker's graveyard.'

Oath-breakers. That word made Harry look at Jack, hard, and he was staring at Harry, eyes locked on his face even though he was fighting the boat and the world was moving in every direction. Jack mouthed something at him that might have been *'Remember? Cross me heart and hope to die?'* but some of the words were lost on the wind. For a moment, Harry even wondered if Jack was trying to kill him, but Harry answered as if he hadn't understood, shouting each word to be heard.

'If you. Mean. This is where. We scatter the ashes. Then you f... You get them.' He'd nearly sworn again. Harry had wedged himself in a corner, gripping on to whatever handhold he could find. Even if he'd been prepared to spew all over Jack's cabin, he wasn't going to make it through. He'd be thrown over and break a leg or worse. The bit of Harry's brain that was still able to think had just wondered how he'd steer the boat if Jack went below, when two rifle-shot cracks in quick succession made them both look upwards.

Jack screamed a single, foul expletive as the part of the rigging that held up the mainsail whipped away on the wind, with pieces of rope unravelling through the pulleys and whipping loose from the mast. The sail folded diagonally across its middle as the upper spar swung downwards towards them, pivoting from a point high on the mast. As Harry threw himself into a ball in the bottom of the cockpit, he had a glimpse of the spar arcing downwards at them like the sweep of an axe, with a half-opened parachute of loose sail billowing behind it.

Chapter Eleven: Dauða-dagr

(Old Norse: a day of dying, or the day of one's death)

From the Saga of King Guthrum

The storm drove the Viking fleet back towards the land. So great were the winds that the sails ripped asunder like banners that have been too long exposed, and so high were the waves that the oars swung at air or bit deep enough to break a man's arm. There are in those parts great cliffs, and the sea made war with the land and made the sound of thunder, bursting high as an eagle flies as the gods unleashed their wrath for the breaking of the oath.

All that night the storm raged, and did not lessen until one hundred ships had been dashed against the rocks or had sunk beneath the waves. Not satisfied with the ships alone, the gods broke the bodies of the men into pieces, turning the sea red and the cliffs into the anvil on which Thor's hammer might wreak his fury.

But beneath their foundering ships, the sea goddess Rán spread her net and gathered them to her, every man. Never in one day had her watery realm been so well served.

To this day those cliffs are called in the Saxon tongue Anfilt

Thuna, that is to say the anvil of Thor. It is said that when the wind is strong in the West the lost army, denied both Valhalla and Niflheim, yet call for their sword-brothers.

Draca

I: GEORGE

George had watched *Draca* through her binoculars all the way down the harbour, until they were lost to sight where the channel curved round an island. Already the wind was making it difficult to hold her hands steady, and when she lowered her arms, drops of rain drove into her face hard enough to sting.

To keep herself busy, George tidied up the storeroom. She remembered Jack's locker hanging open and his sword spilling out onto the floor; just the sort of thing that goes missing. Jack had packed his locker so full that as soon as she pushed stuff in, more fell out. Clothes. A photograph of Jack and a bunch of marines in desert combat gear, all cradling rifles. Books. Her phone rang as she was pushing the locker door closed.

'Hey, Charl.' There had been days when George had been excited if Charlotte called. Today wasn't one of them, and her voice must have sounded flat.

'George, darling, something wrong?'

'Jack. He's gone sailing with his father.'

'Isn't it a bit windy? It's blowing a gale here. There's a tree down on the way into town.'

The locker door swung open again. More clothes and a small, flat, leather box fell out.

'Charl, I'm a bit preoccupied at the moment...' George wedged the phone into her shoulder and bent to pick up the box, which had sprung open as it fell. Jack's Military Cross hung half out of it, shiny and smart on its purple and white ribbon.

'Actually, I'm ringing about Jack.'

'Uh-huh?' George was cautious.

'Something you said the other day, about him being obsessed with *Draca* and behaving like Old Eddie before he trashed it.'

'S'right.' George pushed the medal back into its box, where it clicked against a deformed bullet wedged into the lining. She managed to hold the locker door closed with her knee while she snapped the padlock in place.

'Eddie left Jack a strange letter, asking him to sink *Draca* off Anfel Head. "*Draca* will know where", I think it said. "It's where she wants to be." When I read it, I thought what a peculiar notion, as if a boat could think, but I thought you might want to ask Jack… George? George?'

But George was running for the marina office. It all made terrible sense.

Chippy sat at the desk, very upright to protect his back.

'Where's the fire, girl?'

George ignored him. On the wall behind the desk hung a row of boat keys and she looked along the line, mentally discounting each one. Too small. Too big to sail solo. Workboat, useless offshore. Rain spattered against the window behind her, hard enough in the gusts to rattle the glass.

Think again. Workboat. Big, powerful engine. Might catch them up. She reached over Chippy's shoulders and grabbed the keys from the rack.

'I'm going out, Chippy. Watch the fort for me?'

'You're not thinking of taking the workboat out of the harbour, are you?'

'Just down to the harbour mouth. Have a look outside, maybe.'

"Cos she's worse than useless at sea, less'n it's flat calm.'

George knew that. The workboat was flat bottomed, designed with a shallow draught for work in inshore waters.

'I've got a bad feeling about today, Chippy.'

'Jack's old enough to look after himself, and you can't do nothing in the workboat. Any decent sea will turn her over.'

George gripped the keys more tightly, and opened the door. Rain spotted the floor around the mat.

'That boat ain't yours to wreck, girl.'

She pulled the door closed behind her, thinking that this was one of the dumbest things she'd ever done. Out at sea, in any serious weather, the workboat would be as seaworthy as a tea tray.

Of course, the workboat felt rock solid going down the harbour. It's what she was built for: speed in protected waters. There was a deckhouse to keep the rain off, wipers to clear the forward windows and even a chair bolted to the deck behind the controls. If she'd obeyed the harbour speed limit, it would have been as exciting as driving a truck down a motorway.

Except she didn't. Obey the speed limit, that is. All the way out, she braced herself for angry shouts on the VHF, shouts that she'd have to sweet-talk away. But then the harbour master was probably making himself a nice cup of tea and staying out of the wet. Anyway, she'd just take a look outside. If George could see *Draca* in the bay, and all seemed well, she'd go back in again.

VHF. She might be able to talk Jack into coming back.

At first, George thought she could handle it. The sea out in the bay was rough, but she kept the waves fine on the bow, crabbing sideways away from the land in an uncomfortable, corkscrew motion. Speed was impossible. She flew off the top of one wave and smacked the water so hard with the underside of that flat hull that the noise was a thunderclap and the workboat shook to the blow. It wasn't built to take punishment like that and George throttled back so they rolled over the waves rather than jumping off them. If she focused too much on looking for *Draca*, she risked letting a larger wave catch her by surprise. Then the workboat would slew around and roll so that loose gear tumbled over the deck, and her binoculars would swing far enough out from her neck to crack against the deckhouse side window. The little boat had no proper keel, and no ballast, so it would turn over if it was tipped it far enough, and that would be dead easy in waves like these. After a couple of scares, George ignored the binoculars and relied on her eyeballs, searching an empty and wildly gyrating sea, wishing the boat had radar.

Soon the looming bulk of Anfel Head was the only solid feature in view. The lower-lying land behind it faded into the murk of rain and spray. George picked up the VHF microphone.

'Yacht *Draca*, yacht *Draca*, this is Furzey Marina workboat, Furzey Marina workboat. Come in please. Over.'

There was nothing but the crackle of static. The workboat's blunt, almost square bow cut into a wave on one side and spooned enough water inboard for it to come rushing aft as she lifted, breaking into spray against the deckhouse. The seas were getting worse as she neared Anfel Head and began to lose the shelter of the land. This was stupid. Already George could see around the headland to the beginnings of The Race, and she wouldn't stand a chance in that. Wind over tide, the sailor's nightmare. Strong wind from the west pushing against a high 'spring' tide going the other way, and making a nightmare of waves in the middle. George repeated the call, staring at a sea that was more white than grey, until a wave caught the workboat on the beam, tipping her until the propeller thrashed at the surface and the boat hung there on the brink of a capsize, before a trough threw her in the right direction and she fell back upright.

Enough. George could do no more. If she couldn't see them then they were way beyond anywhere she could follow. She waited for her moment to turn for home, watching for a gap in the growlers where she could spin the boat before it was swamped.

II: HARRY

The impact of the spar thumping into the deck was like being next to a field gun going off. Curled on the deck, Harry felt the jolt through his body, as if every timber in the boat had been given an electric shock. He rolled on his back, relieved the spar hadn't hit him, and feeling the soaking cold as seawater slopping over the cockpit's gratings rushed up his backbone, inside his foul-weather jacket. That shocked him into movement and he spun over onto his knees, slumping against the benches as the ship rolled.

The spar had struck between the cockpit and the boat's side, hard enough for a crown of splintered decking to be sticking up around its embedded tip. Part of the sail was still stretched in a triangle between the main boom and the mast, but most of it was flapping furiously over the side, making even more noise than the storm. Lengths of line whipped about, threatening to blind them, and somewhere over their heads a pulley came free and fell, smashing through the skylight and into the cabin. That would have brained anyone underneath it. Jack seemed to be unhurt, but he'd thrown all his weight across the tiller. Another wave lifted them so the angled horizon beyond Jack became all sea and then all sky, and Harry felt the boat slew away from the wind and begin to tip, with the remaining rigging howling louder than the flapping sail.

'Dad, I need you over here.' Jack didn't sound panicked. He was strangely calm, in fact, even though he needed to shout to be heard. Harry had a glimpse of Jack as he might have been in combat, with everything going to shit around him and his troops needing him to show them the way out.

But Harry couldn't move. He stared at Jack, with his guts heaving, and threw up on his deck.

'Dad, you need to help me steer.'

But Harry couldn't give a damn about steering, he was too busy spewing.

'I've got to get that sail down.'

It was a four-foot crawl to the tiller and it took Harry three waves to get there. Plus another puke.

'Keep the wind on her quarter.'

'What the hell does that mean?' Harry hadn't sworn so much since he was a squaddie.

'The wind spun us round. Keep it over your left shoulder while I start the engine.'

Harry felt too bloody weak to do much, but he managed it while Jack went below. There wasn't any subtlety involved, anyway. It was just a matter of pushing his whole body against the tiller. Even to a beginner, she felt sluggish, always wanting to go sideways on to the wind.

Cranking noises came from the chart–room. Harry thought Jack's bellow of *'Please, Scotty'* had an air of desperation about it. Jack kept heaving at the starter lever, which made rhythmic, mechanical noises while the next small mountain came up behind them and they climbed its foothills, all the way to the crest, where the wind caught them and the boat started to turn, rolling sideways. The clanking noises stopped and Jack appeared in the hatch.

'Keep her straight,' he bellowed up at Harry.

'What the hell is "straight" in this mess?'

'Can't you feel the wind on your cheek?'

Yes, Harry could feel the wind on his cheek. Now they'd spun around he could feel it on the back of his neck. He could also feel one half of the English Channel soaking his backbone and the other half running down his legs.

'Sod you, boy.'

Jack went back to try again, a three-wave, useless bloody

rattle. When he climbed up the steps, there was a look on his face that told Harry they were in deep trouble. Jack paused for a moment as if gathering himself, and started hauling ropes out of a locker. He tied one end of each rope to a wooden post by the cockpit and threw them overboard, where they gradually streamed out behind them in the wake.

'What you doing that for?'

'Sea anchor. Stop us broaching.'

Harry had no idea what Jack was shouting about, but after he'd done that Harry didn't have to fight the tiller so much. He looked back, and the ropes were stopping the waves falling over them. They were high and steep, the way a wave gets before it breaks on a beach, and foaming white, but under the dragging ropes they seemed flatter, less angry. Harry grinned for the first time.

'Clever boy.'

Jack shouted into his ear. 'We've got to get that sail down. It's all drag and no push. I'm going forward. Keep her as steady as you can.'

It seemed like madness for Jack to climb out of the cockpit and crawl along the deck, head down. There wasn't even a rail to speak of, just a little shin-high thing that wouldn't have stopped a dog from being swept overboard. Jack worked his way forward on his knees, hand over hand along the ropes that went from the cockpit to the sails at the front end. He stopped where more ropes ran up the mast from a rack of brass pins bolted to the hull. The VHF squawked at them from down in the chart–room, but no way could Harry leave the tiller.

Harry was frightened for the boy. Waves would sometimes break over him, leaving him hanging on with the water streaming past his knees. Worst of all was when he found the rope he wanted and untied it, which took both hands, and a wave came inboard and swept his legs away so that he swung, dangling from the rope and bouncing over the deck. One leg went through the broken skylight, shredding his trousers as he swung back so that his false foot poked out clear and alien on the end of its strut.

Nothing happened, for all his efforts. The mainsail sagged a bit, but the other end of the upper spar was wedged into the deck by the cockpit, so the whole thing was stuck. Jack jerked at the line a few times, and maybe it was a good thing Harry couldn't hear what he was saying.

Jack was still crawling back when Harry lost control. They were pushed to the side by one wave, and then further by another, like a swift left–right double punch in boxing, so that they were broadside on to the sea when a big one rolled over them and the cockpit filled with water. Harry couldn't steer, couldn't see, couldn't do anything but hold on after the water closed over his head. There were heavy thumps and rumbles around him as the sails and spars moved, as if he was locked in a washing machine with a pile of bricks. It was panic rather than sense that made him hang on rather than try to kick free, so that he was still in the cockpit when they broke the surface.

Jack was lying across the hatch, folded around a rope across his middle. He took one great gasp with his mouth wide open and rolled off the hatch into the cockpit. He sat there on the grating, looking up at the wreckage, with a look of agony on his face that Harry knew was for his beloved boat.

'Shouldn't we call for help?'

'What for?' Jack looked numb. 'She's sailing.' He patted the woodwork by the hatch, and hauled himself to his feet. 'That wave freed the mainsail.' The sail lay in a flapping, crumpled mess along the deck. Great, sodden swathes of it were falling into the cockpit by Harry's shoulder. Already the boat's motion was easier.

338

Jack patted the hatch again. 'Good girl! I knew she'd look after us. At least we're pointing the right way.'

'And how do we get home without that,' Harry pushed an edge of the mainsail out of his face, 'or the engine?'

'I'm going to set the square sail. We can make it home on that and the jib.'

Jack tied two ropes to the tiller. 'Lashing it,' he said. 'She'll sail herself now.' How the hell he could be so calm, Harry didn't know. He could feel his fear turning to anger as he realised they probably weren't going to die, so maybe it was a good thing Jack crawled forward again. Down in the chart-room the VHF was shouting again but Harry's guts heaved and he ignored it. By the time Jack came back they had a big, square sail set like the ones Harry had seen in pictures of ships in olden times. The waves were still steep and angry, but they were going with them. Harry felt relieved, but soaked and ticked off, and as Jack dropped back into the cockpit his anger boiled over.

'What the hell did you think you were playing at?' Harry's voice rose until he was almost screaming at him. 'You nearly got us killed!'

Jack ignored him. He just stood by the hatchway wrinkling his nose. Harry was so wound up he could have hit him.

'Petrol.' Jack slid back the hatch and lowered his face to the gap. ' I smell petrol.' He disappeared down into the cabin.

Harry felt suddenly lonely with just the sea and the wind. And it was a slashing wind, the kind that felt like it could strip the flesh from his face. Lonely and frightened. He had absolutely no idea of how to work this boat or how to get home if anything happened to Jack. The motion was easier, but Anfel Head was a menacing slab of grey in the rain and if the wind dropped for a moment he could hear the roar of the surf and its base. They'd lift, stern first, as each wave passed under them, and he could see a desolation of white-streaked grey in every direction.

Harry reached for his phone, only to find his pocket was full of water and the bloody thing was dead. He swore again, staring forwards past the wreckage of the mainsail to where the great square sail bellied, cracked in the wind and lifted. For a moment, Harry could have sworn he saw a pair of legs beneath the sail, standing astride the bowsprit.

'Jack?' Harry put his head into the hatch, and frowned. He had a bizarre idea that Jack had somehow made his way forward, but Jack was below, reaching back into the cramped space aft of the engine. Harry could smell petrol too. Jack squirmed backwards out of the space, sniffing his fingers. The look on his face made Harry forget what he might have seen on the foredeck.

'The gaff hit right on the fuel tank.' Jack looked so forlorn that Harry almost felt sorry for him. 'There's a split that's dripping petrol into the bilges every time we roll.'

Poor kid. His precious boat was being trashed around him. But then Harry remembered that Jack was doing it to himself. And to Harry.

'That'll teach you to take stupid bloody risks.'

Jack's head disappeared as the boat twisted to a wave, although one hand stayed gripping the rail by the steps. A drawer under the chart-table burst open, scattering pencils and compasses. A small, metal rectangle bounced on the deck and slid across towards Jack, who caught it with his spare hand as his head and shoulders swung back into view. Jack stared down at Old Eddie's Zippo lighter as if he was surprised to find he was holding it.

'Don't do anything stupid, boy.'

Jack stroked the Zippo with his thumb. A slow, affectionate smile spread over his face.

'Be a good lad and put it down, now.'

Jack's thumb flipped open the lid.

'No, you stupid boy!'

Jack's head lurched out of sight as another great wave tumbled them over. Harry fell on his back on the grating, watching the hard, wooden horizon of the cockpit coaming rotate against a soft, chaotic horizon of water. He had the bizarre impression that the whole world had tilted, so the boat was flat but the sea stretched upwards, almost vertically. The mighty cliffs of Anfel Head hung at the top of the ocean, and any moment now they would fall across the water to smash into them.

But Anfel Head slid out of sight until all Harry could see was sky that had no form, no shape except swirling stains of greys and wet charcoal. From down in the chart-room came the tinny sound of the VHF radio, and then, even over the noise of the storm, the *thump* of igniting fuel.

III: GEORGE

It was the mast that caught George's eye, over a mile away at the edge of The Race: an eyelash-thin line seen only on the crest of a wave and pushed out of shape by the wet on the workboat's windows. A tricky, one-handed look through the binoculars on the next crest showed *Draca* running with the wind on her quarter and just her storm jib set, an ochre-brown slash more constant than the breaking waves. There was no sign of her mainsail but there was another brown blur along her deck, and in that brief moment *Draca* pitched so that her mast whipped forward like the cast of a fishing rod.

'Yacht *Draca*, Yacht *Draca*, this is Furzey Marina workboat, Furzey Marina workboat. I have you in sight. Do you require assistance, over?'

Again, there was only the crackle of static. *Come on, Jack, pick up the frigging radio. This ain't fun.*

Another line of brown climbed *Draca*'s mast, a narrow triangle that broadened at its point until it bellied out and filled, making a rectangle the colour of dried blood in the lowering light of the storm. If Jack-bloody-Ahlquist was setting his square sail then there couldn't have been much wrong. Already George could see them making headway against the tide. She, on the other hand, was taking a stupid risk. She chose her moment between the waves, and spun the workboat for home. Sod them. *Draca* was built for this madness, the workboat wasn't.

Draca even began to overhaul her with that antique bloody sail set, while George chugged along at her play-it-safe speed, slewing off the tops of waves and hoping she'd make it back into the shelter of Anfel Head's lee before she was swamped.

They'd probably beat her back to the harbour entrance, and she felt a complete frigging idiot for being out there at all.

George kept snatching looks at *Draca*, in between waves. It was weird: a ship with a red square sail set and no main, like a boat from another era. The ugly figurehead at the bow made her look so Viking that George shivered with more than the wet. She remembered that strange conversation with Mad Eddie around Christmas, when he had wanted to rig her out as a longship for one last sail. She was seeing things she didn't understand and it scared the shit out of her.

George didn't understand the smudge that spread along *Draca*'s deck either. For a moment she thought that the evil in the figurehead had taken substance, and spread its darkness around the boat, but this black fog was growing, whipping along the length of the boat and streaming past the figurehead, not flowing from it. A touch of light the colour of sunset appeared around the cockpit, and grew until it was flare-bright. George picked up the microphone.

'Yacht *Draca*, Yacht *Draca*, do you require assistance?'

They were still almost a mile away, too far to see details, but the light spread to *Draca*'s midships, probably coming up through her skylight. George had a strange sense of unreality as she spun back towards them, breasting into angry waves that looked more and more lethal towards *Draca*, where all shelter of the headland was lost. As George keyed the microphone she felt like a bad actor, knowing the lines she had to speak but not knowing how the plot was supposed to unfold.

'MAYDAY, MAYDAY, MAYDAY. This is Furzey Marina workboat calling for yacht *Draca*. Yacht *Draca* is on fire, position one mile south of Anfel Head. Over.'

She didn't even have to repeat the message.

'Furzey Marina workboat, this is Channel Coastguard. What is your position, over?'

'Channel Coastguard, this is Furzey workboat, my position one mile east of Anfel Head. I have yacht *Draca* in sight. Fire is spreading.' George paused, staring at the chaos between her and *Draca* and feeling so bad about what she was going to say that it came out quietly, as if she was guilty. 'Sea state makes it unlikely that I can assist. Over.' Why does VHF language always sound so frigging pompous?

'Furzey workboat, this is Channel Coastguard. Say 'again, over.'

'I CAN'T FUCKING HELP THEM. Over.'

George hadn't realised she was crying. Was that common sense or cowardice?

'Furzey workboat, this is Channel Coastguard. Do you know how many people on board *Draca*, over?'

'Two. Over.' She didn't scream that time.

'Stand by.'

George watched *Draca* while the coastguard put out an 'All Ships' broadcast. When she crested a wave and could see *Draca*, there were two centres of fire on the deck, one just forward of the cockpit, the other aft of the mast, probably the hatch and the skylight. The saloon must have been well alight. Why the feck had Eddie insisted on keeping that ancient frigging petrol engine?

Sod the 'All Ships'. If there was anyone close enough to help, George would be able to see them. Keeping one hand on the wheel, she reached behind her and latched the door of the deckhouse open. The air in the workboat's plastic hull would probably keep her afloat even if she turned turtle, but George didn't want to be trapped underneath.

Very gently, one wave at a time, she edged out to sea. The

344

control seat became useless beyond the lee of the point. Only by planting her legs wide on the deck and riding the boat could she keep any balance.

'Furzey workboat, this is Channel Coastguard, over?'

'YES?' George didn't want to take a hand off the wheel for any longer than she needed, even to hold the mike, and her focus was on *Draca*, where there was a hint of movement in the smoke over her deck that might have been a man.

'This is Channel Coastguard. An air–sea rescue helicopter has launched. ETA ten minutes. Over.'

Thank God for that. 'Tell them to... oh, fuck.'

George was going to ask them to make sure she was still afloat when the helo got there, but a fireball blossomed over *Draca*, sending debris spinning into the air over her deck. It took her a moment to realise that the black, wedge-shaped lump cartwheeling upwards must be her doghouse cabin hatch.

'Furzey workboat, come in. Over.'

George didn't answer. She was still over half a mile from *Draca*, and too busy searching for glimpses of people. Flames now raged the whole length of the boat aft of the mast. *Jack, where are you?*

'Furzey workboat, come in. Over.'

'*Draca* just exploded. Probably fuel tank or gas bottles. Still afloat.'

Fire licked at the bottom of the square sail, raced upwards and the swell of canvas burst into two flaming banners. Of course, fresh from its locker, the old fabric would still have been dry.

The flames silhouetted a figure on the foredeck. It was too far to see if it was Jack or his father, but he was standing with his legs astride the bowsprit, just aft of the dragon, and was taking no notice at all of the fire burning around him.

As George watched, his arm lifted as a great wave rose under *Draca*'s stern and pushed her forwards, but her bow swung away so that she rolled down the wave sideways, broaching, and the figure on the bow was lost behind the burning, tattered remnants of square sail.

Draca went swiftly, long before George could have reached her. George saw her wallowing in the trough, only half righting, still broadside to the waves and with the flames almost extinguished, but she lost sight of her as the workboat dropped between waves. At the next crest, there was nothing there. No wreckage that she could see, no boat, no Jack. There was a strangely calm spot among the waves, a circle fringed with its own ring of foam, that lasted for perhaps half a minute and then that too was gone.

IV: HARRY

When Harry heard the fuel ignite, he'd lain on the floor of the cockpit, his mind rejecting the whole bloody scene. This ain't real. It's all a bad bastard dream. But water slopped over him as they rolled, the way he might once have thrown a bucket over a drunken squaddie to rouse him, and he hauled himself onto his knees. Behind him, the tiller tugged at its lashings. In front of him, the hatchway gaped, the hard edges wavering a little in heat rising from below. Harry didn't want to go near the hatch. Didn't want to see what was down there.

'Jack?'

No reply.

'Come on, Jack, stop messing about.'

Harry began to shake, perhaps with cold, perhaps at the sight of that empty sodding ocean that felt as if it was taking his presence there very personally. The only thing he could see, apart from the cliffs and the surf, was some silly sod of a fisherman bouncing around in a little boat with a square cabin like a brick shithouse, and he was much too far away to be any use. Harry could almost hear Mad Eddie laughing.

'You loved this sort of thing, didn't you, you old sod?'

Harry felt closer to his father there, in that boat, than he ever had when Eddie was alive. Harry began to grope his way towards the hatch.

'This was your idea of fun, Pa, wasn't it?' Talking to himself didn't seem to matter. Harry wouldn't have been surprised if Mad Eddie had replied out loud. Harry knew what Eddie would say.

Get him out, son.

It was surreal, having this made-up conversation in his own head. Harry swore as a trickle of smoke flowed out of the hatch and away on the wind. It made Harry think of the way Mad Eddie used to exhale those stinking cigarettes of his. Harry couldn't see the top of Jack's body from the steps, but his legs stretched into view, lying at an angle across the floor. He wasn't moving.

You always wanted to be a hero, didn't you?

Was that Harry thinking that, or Mad Eddie saying it?

Harry heaved his legs over the coaming and backed down the steps into the chart–room. The heat layer by the hatch rushed him onwards, just to get through it.

It wasn't your fault that you never had the chance, was it?

Jack lay with his body crumpled beneath the chart–table and his head lying in the doorway to the main cabin. He had blood on his forehead and in his hair. Blue-tinged flames were spreading across the carpet beyond. As Harry watched, the flames found Jack's hair, which crisped and frizzled and stank. Harry grabbed the strap of Jack's life jacket and hauled him back, beating at the flames, as something caught light in the cabin and a yellower fireball spread over the ceiling.

Never wanted him to outshine you, did you?

'Shut up, Eddie.'

Harry grabbed the fire extinguisher clipped to the wall above the engine, and doused Jack with powder. He paused in the doorway to the main cabin, crouching against the heat, but the fire in there was already more than a match for any single extinguisher. It looked as if an oil lamp had caught, spilling burning oil onto the sofa beneath. The flames covered the ceiling, funnelling upwards through the skylight.

Get out, son.

Harry managed to get Jack to the base of the steps, but there was no way he could lift him up them, even by hauling on the shoulder straps of his life jacket. Above the chart-table, the

VHF speaker was screaming at them, but Harry ignored it. No time to talk.

You need a rope.

He scrambled back into the cockpit and hauled in one of Jack's trailing ropes. In that short time the flames were coming through the hatch and Harry had to push it wide open and cover his face with a wet handkerchief to get back down there.

Thank God he'd kept himself fit. Harry managed to haul Jack out with that rope through his straps. They got a bit more scorched coming through the hatch, but at least Jack didn't burn in the chart-room. The floor down there was starting to smoke, and Harry guessed that burning fuel was spreading under the deck.

They fell backwards together into the cockpit and Harry stayed there for a moment, too exhausted to move. Jack lay spreadeagled across him, face up and unconscious, with his singed head flopping from side to side on Harry's chest as the boat rolled. He stank of soot and burned hair and a chalky, chemical smell that would be the extinguisher powder. Harry reached up to his neck and found a pulse, thank God, and for a moment it was so tempting to stay there, holding him, feeling Jack's warmth with his fingertips, but above them, near Harry's head, the splintered deck reminded him of the fuel tank beside them.

Time to go, son.

After the haul up the steps to the cockpit, getting him from the cockpit to the deck was easy. Harry was standing with his arms locked across Jack's chest, swaying with the movement of the boat but somehow held there by Jack's weight, when the tank blew and he didn't have to worry about how to get him into the water any more. Harry had a moment when he was flying backwards with a scorching heat on his face and after that he wasn't thinking about anything for a while.

Heat then cold, the sort of cold that makes you gasp, but at least some instinct made Harry keep his mouth and eyes shut. For a while he couldn't tell if his head was under the water or above it. The life jacket had inflated on its own, so he was floating, but there didn't seem to be much boundary between water and air. It was solid, wet sea or stinging, wet spray and Harry couldn't breathe in either of them. And he was being thrown about, violently, the way a dog shakes a rabbit in its teeth. When his back was to the spray, he managed a few gasps of air that came in salty and wet, and at the top of a wave he glimpsed *Draca* sailing away, blazing furiously, but most of the time, if he saw her at all, he could only see the masthead, glowing in the light beneath it.

Harry only saw Jack once, for a moment, just his head and his life jacket, and then an arm which moved in a way that might have been an attempt to swim, so he was probably conscious. In that instant, Jack was jerked backwards, bursting through the top of a wave, and even in Harry's fuddled state he realised that Jack still had the rope through his straps and was being dragged behind the boat. Next time Harry saw anything but water, the big square sail had burst into flame, but there was no sign of Jack. Harry even tried to swim towards the boat, but it was hopeless in all that movement and with the life jacket turning him onto his back. He couldn't get enough breath to shout, let alone swim. At the top of another wave, *Draca* was on her side and the flames were almost out, but after that there was just the wind and an empty ocean. Empty except for one of Jack's legs kicking at air as he was pulled under, head first.

Harry was still staring at the spot when he heard the clatter of a helicopter. By then, he'd nearly drowned in the spray. When he could snatch some air, he'd bellowed, so he was hoarse with salt and shouting, and he still couldn't quite believe that he'd lost him. Harry was swearing as much in his head as in his mouth, angry with Jack for being such a bloody fool, and angry with himself for leaving that rope on him and letting him be dragged down with the boat. God forgive him, Harry thought he even cried. How was he going to tell Mary?

V: JACK

Grandpa rode *Draca*'s final dive with Jack, all the way down.

Jack had come to in the water, concussed, disoriented, not knowing what the hell was going on. One second he was in the cabin, worried about the fuel leak, worried too about how the hell he was going to pay for the damage, but knowing they were running before the wind and not in immediate danger. The next thing he knew, he was in the water and *Draca* was close but sailing away from him, burning like a bonfire.

Jack inhaled enough spray to set him coughing and retching, and the motion in the sea was so brutal that he couldn't think straight. He thought he'd fallen overboard, so Harry must still be there and Jack needed to get back and save him, but somehow one of the lines Jack had streamed over the stern became entangled with his life jacket and he nearly drowned right then as he was dragged after the ship with the water flowing over his head. It stopped when the square sail caught fire and ripped, spilling the wind and the speed as if someone had stepped on a brake.

The flaming sail parted like the curtains on a stage, framing a view of the foredeck as a wave lifted Jack. The figure that stood there astride the bowsprit could not have been Harry, for this figure had long hair streaming past his face in the wind, and perhaps a beard. He seemed quite calm, even though the ship was clearly finished. Amidst the shock and the impossibility of the man's presence, part of Jack's mind wondered where the hell he'd seen him before.

Jack lost sight of the boat as a great wave rose between them and, when it had passed, *Draca* was wallowing on her side with her deck awash and one beam buried so that the sea was already above the deadeyes on the shrouds. The man was still there,

352

beside the dragon, and as the stern lifted and *Draca* started to slide under, he pushed one arm at the sky in a gesture that might have been a balancing movement or a punch of triumph.

Jack didn't have time to grieve. He knew what was coming, and was too busy trying to free the line from his life jacket harness. He was still desperately tugging it through his straps and hyperventilating as he was pulled under.

He'd read that free divers can go down hundreds of feet. Jack had no idea how deep he went, only that the cold rush of water over his face continued until the pressure on his ears was like spikes being driven into his head. He had one hand clamped, vice-like, around the rope, heaving against it to give himself enough slack to drag the loose end clear with the other. He hadn't a chance. The ship was pulling him one way, going down fast, and the buoyancy of the life jacket was pushing him upwards. The pain in his ears became a screaming agony that filled his whole head and above it all was the urge to breathe, even though that would end it all in a paroxysm of choking.

There was a small crumb of comfort in knowing his grandfather was with him, riding *Draca* on her final dive.

Jack, my boy, let us go.

Grandpa's voice in his head was gentle, kindly and unmistakable. Jack's midriff began to heave with the instinct to breathe, like the spasms before vomiting.

Don't worry about me, my boy, I'm in good company. Now let us go.

Jack began to hallucinate. His eyes were shut tight against the rush of water, but he could visualise the dragon ahead of him, now rising high above the deck but plunging ever deeper, while a warrior rode its neck with his hand stretched forward like a charging cavalryman with his sabre. And below them, a vast, sea-grey woman waited, mermaid-naked and terrible in her beauty. She smiled, baring teeth like storm-washed rocks, and swung her arm to cast her net.

Now, Jack.

The net spread high and wide, engulfing the ship as the line slipped through Jack's fingers. Its edge draped over him, jerking him downwards again, pulling against his life jacket. It rasped across his shoulder, became a terrible, back-arching burn, and was gone.

Jack knew he was losing consciousness. The darkness was more than the blackness of deep water. He could feel himself going, with his breath bubbling out, riding upwards with him, but his first, lethal gasp came as he erupted through the surface into a turmoil of salt spray. He hung retching in his harness, drifting in and out of awareness.

He was forced back into consciousness by spatters of stinging sea being driven into his face, and he looked up through narrowed eyes at the red and white underside of a search and rescue helicopter. The sea's surface was beaten almost flat by the downdraught, and a winch line swayed into view with a helmeted crewman and another figure already on it, their feet skimming the water towards Jack. The second man twisted to watch him and Jack closed his eyes with relief on seeing it was his father. He may have fainted again, wondering who could have been on the foredeck if Dad was on the winch line. It was all a bit confused.

Harry gripped Jack's arm as they were hoisted up, shaking him. He was close enough as they dangled in the loops of the harness for Jack to see a small patch of stubble behind Harry's jaw that he'd missed when shaving. The stubble stretched and glistened with wet as his mouth moved, soundless amidst the swamping vibration of the rotors, and Jack tried to smile back at him not because he understood but because the concern on Harry's face was warming. It was like being a kid again.

The concern didn't last of course. There were moments on that wire, and then in the helo, when they came close to showing emotion. But the two aircrew paramedics on board went into emergency mode and pushed Harry aside while they peeled back Jack's trouser leg. His false foot must have been pulled off in the sea and Jack realised they expected to find major trauma. One of them shouted at him but Jack couldn't understand, even with the crewman's face close to his ear. Jack didn't want to try anyway. Too exhausted. The gentle probing for pulse and blood pressure, and the lights in his eyes, were slightly irritating barriers to sleep. After a while they wedged him half upright and pushed a mug into his hands, and Jack was conscious enough to wonder how they had hot soup in a helicopter. The crewman tried to talk again, but although his lips moved, all Jack could hear was the vibration of the aircraft. When Jack handed back the mug they gave him a helmet with earphones and a mike, although only one earphone seemed to be working.

'Helmand?' The crewman nodded at Jack's leg.

Jack shook his head and told him where. His voice sounded strange in his head, as if his ears were full of water. The crewman's eyes narrowed, and he nodded. He knew. He was of the brotherhood.

'I got him out,' Harry shouted, loud enough for Jack to hear. They'd given him a headset too.

The crewman ignored Harry. 'I did two tours in Afghan.' He told Jack his unit.

'And switched to SAR?' Maritime Search and Rescue was a civilian organisation.

'I'd rolled the dice too many times.'

'Rolled the dice'. Jack nodded, understanding. 'It was always good to see you guys.' Throwaway lines by each of them, lightly spoken but heavy with meaning. They were the real heroes, him and his type, the ones who'd fly a lumbering helicopter into the edge of a firefight and sit on the ground, exposed as the biggest target for miles around and sometimes taking fire while the wounded were loaded.

'Hauled him out of a burning boat.'

Harry didn't seem to like being ignored.

'We'll be with you in a moment, sir.'

That ticked Harry off. By the time they had landed at the hospital, he was his old, aggressive self. The questions started as soon as they were clear of the helicopter noise.

'What the hell were you playing at?' Harry shouted over his shoulder. He walked ahead of Jack, trailing wet footprints and holding a shiny space blanket around himself like a Native American squaw. His voice was strangely tinny and Jack could only hear him on one side. They'd put Jack, who was also huddled into a space blanket, in a kind of reclining wheelchair and were pushing him along behind Harry.

'You damn nearly killed us!'

Jack ignored him. He was thinking about *Draca* and didn't want to talk to anyone, let alone try to justify the unjustifiable to Harry.

'Did you mean to do it? Hey?'

They put them in separate bays in Accident and Emergency, with a plastic curtain between them. It didn't stop Harry shouting through it until a nurse asked him to shut up. Jack's mother arrived within an hour and Harry started again, telling and retelling his version of the story, but an injured drunk was raving in a nearby bay, so there was a lot of background noise and Jack could only understand fragments of what he said. One shout ended in the lifting tone of a question, and when Jack didn't answer Harry pulled back the plastic curtain between them and bellowed it again.

Harry stood there barelegged in a knee-length, unisex,

hospital gown with little blue flowers on it, and Jack burst out laughing, almost hysterically. All Harry needed was an outsized nappy on his bottom and a dummy in his mouth, and he'd be a baby having a tantrum. Jack's mum tugged at Harry's hem where little sleeves puffed out from his shoulders, and her mouth formed the words 'put your clothes on, love.' She'd brought a small case.

She came and sat with Jack while Harry changed, her face tight with worry, squeezing her own fingers fretfully in her lap. Her mouth moved again and Jack shook his head, tapping the ear nearest to her.

'Can't hear you, Mum. Burst eardrum.'

She spoke more loudly, and more slowly, so Jack would have understood her even if the drunk hadn't finally shut up.

'How. Did. You. Do. That?' She formed the words with comical, exaggerated movements of her mouth, rolling her eyes as she spoke.

'Dad's shouting?'

The curtain was ripped back again.

'Listen to him!' Harry stuffed a shirt into his trousers. 'I saved the boy's bloody life! Bloody hero, I was. Pulled him out of a burning boat, and listen to the thanks I get.'

At least, Jack thought that was what he said. Once the drunk started shouting at Harry to keep the noise down, Jack lost the thread.

'Mum.' Jack gripped her arm as they were about to leave. 'Call George, will you? At the boatyard? She'll be worried when we don't get back.'

'Of course, love.' She rolled her eyes again and made an outsized nod. 'And Charlotte?'

She looked relieved when Jack shook his head.

After they went there was nothing to keep Jack from his thoughts. 'You can go,' the doctor had said to Harry. 'You'll be right as rain after a hot bath.' But he told Jack he'd be admitted for observation. 'Just a precaution. Concussion, shock, smoke inhalation…' Jack didn't mind. Apart from the suitcases and the stuff in George's store, all he had left was a pile of soaking clothes and his foul-weather gear.

George. God, Jack wished she were there.

It was another two hours before she turned up, looking almost as drowned as Harry had. It must have been raining hard outside. George's hand brushed over Jack's head and he felt it rasp against patchy stubble. Her fingers came away greasy from the ointment they'd put on the burns.

'That's quite a haircut.'

Jack had watched her lips, and understood.

'You're frigging ugly, Jack.'

'I love you too.'

After that she didn't say much, just sat beside the bed, held his hand and left him to talk himself out.

'It was an accident, George.' Having her there was like pulling a cork from a bottle and the words came tumbling out, sounding inside his head as much as in his ears. 'Dad thinks I did it deliberately, but the mainsail came down when, when…'

George squeezed his hand, and waited.

A memory had come back, of picking up Grandpa's old lighter as it fell from the chart-table drawer, and for a moment being mesmerised by it. There'd been a wave afterwards, a tumbling, thrown-across-the-cabin type of wave.

'It was an accident…' Jack repeated himself, as if he needed convincing. George stretched to stroke his face, and her lips formed a 'shush' shape.

'We were bloody lucky, though. Guy on the helicopter told

me. Some fisherman saw us go down and sent out a 'Mayday' call. Stayed nearby and fired flares to guide them in.'

George sat on the bed with her back to the gap in the curtains, still holding his hand.

'I lost her.' George was unlocking the emotion within him. Soon he'd crumble, and he didn't want to crumble there. 'And it was my own stupid fault.' Jack was sinking towards emotional collapse as inevitably as he'd been pulled down by *Draca*.

Another 'shush' face. George looked over her shoulder to make sure she was shielding him, and pushed his fingers inside her jacket, opening layers with her spare hand until he could feel her heat in his palm. The surprise stopped him, as cleanly as if the rope had been cut. George leaned forward, and that ridiculous orange quiff flopped forwards, dropping water onto his face that was as salty as tears. She pushed harder into Jack's palm until their lips were close enough to touch.

Chapter Twelve: *Hēr kemr ā til sævar*

(Old Norse: literally 'here the river reaches the sea', but with
the figurative or poetic meaning 'this is where it ends')

From the Anglo-Saxon Chronicle for AD 876–7

*And this year the [Danish] raiding army stole into… a fort of
the West Saxons. The king [Alfred] afterwards made peace with
them; and they gave him as hostages those who were worthiest in
the army; and swore with oaths on the holy bracelet, which they
would not before to any nation, that they would readily go out of his
kingdom. Then, under colour [sic] of this, their cavalry stole [away]
by night… while the navy sailed west about, until they met with a
great storm at sea, and there perished one hundred and twenty ships.*

I. GEORGE

It was a ritual, on George's day off. She'd make a mug of tea and take the newspaper back to bed. The regional rag, not a national, with stories about real people, not posturing politicians, and news of local events, not gloomy economics.

Jack didn't stir. He'd had a bad night and woken up shouting again. There were still the *'break right'* or *'get me out of here'* nights, but he was getting better. It had been about a week since the last one, and George had learned how to handle them. It was best if she held him, so that he came out of the nightmare with her arms around him. If he was deeply under, it was better to lie on top of him, holding him down and stroking his face until he was calm. What followed after, sometimes, was like their first time: tender, and in a way more loving than any raunchy athletics.

Afterwards he might lie with his head in her lap, spent but still needing her, and George would stroke his head. His hair was growing back: it was no longer scratchy against her palm, but still a crew cut. *'Like a new recruit'*, he said. In the darkness she would imagine she could see his colours again. They'd been thin, after *Draca* sank, like paint dripped into water, but they were stronger now. A little different though. The red was softer and not so primary, except in his belly. She liked that. Jack had a few more things to feel bad about, and they got in the way sometimes, but he was coming back to her. What's more, he was coming back as the Jack she always knew had been in there, the laughing Jack on the hillside. She guessed that she and the dragon had both won. The dragon and his frigging awful, groping friend had got whatever watery grave they wanted off Anfel Head, and she had got Jack back. Result.

Sometimes she felt just a bit pleased with herself for seeing the real Jack through the darkness, and fighting for him.

Western Morning News

30th November

Celebrity Turns On The Lights

Reality TV star Sophie Connerie pressed the button to illuminate the Christmas lights on Thursday night…

Christmas. George and Jack had accepted an invitation to Jack's parents for Christmas day. They were both a bit nervous about that, but it was a start. They'd all met at a pub a few weeks after *Draca* went down, and Jack and Harry had walked off to talk alone. Mary Ahlquist had reached for George's hand as they watched the two men squaring up to each other at the far end of the beer garden, gesticulating. Mary told her that Harry felt unappreciated after pulling Jack out of his burning boat. They both came back to the table more subdued, and it can't have been too bad because the invitation for Christmas followed. At least Tilly and her kids would be with her in-laws. Mary seemed quite pleased at the way things were turning out, and she and George were getting along just fine.

George hadn't told Jack about her role in the rescue, and Chippy was sworn to secrecy. Maybe it would come out one day, but Jack had enough to deal with and she wanted him to stay with her because he loved her, not because he owed her.

George turned the page. Jack lay face down with his cheek on his forearms. The line across his shoulder where the rope had burned through his clothes was a pale, glossy streak that would probably always be there. The duvet lay across the hollow of his waist so that he looked all broad-shouldered and muscly, and George wondered if she should forget the newspaper and slide her hand downwards over his bum...

Nah, let him sleep.

Fisherman Catches Sea Monster

Cornish fisherman Dan Trenowden had a surprise catch when he found a Viking carving floating past his lobster pots. Dan and his son William spotted the strange artefact from their boat the Sweet Susan...

It was on the inside pages, with a photo of a grinning man holding that evil frigging dragon. The sodding thing had floated nearly a hundred miles west.

Jack stirred and turned over. 'Hey.'

'Hey.'

He shuffled his body closer so that his face was against her arm, and began to stroke her thigh with a touch that was hardly there. Jack could be quite gentle, for a big guy. Any other time, George would have been distracted. This time, she pulled the pages closer together before Jack could see inside.

Plymouth City Museum Director Peter Thornbury admits he's baffled. 'It has been professionally preserved but we have no record of any museum losing such an item,' he said. 'Carbon dating would be difficult because of the modern chemicals used in its preservation, but it is almost certainly a longship's figurehead and could be anything from one thousand to fourteen hundred years old.'

'Anything good in the papers?' Jack's hand moved higher, crumpling the bottom of the page.

'Nothing exciting. Usual stuff. Christmas lights. Nativity plays at kids' schools.' She'd take that page out and burn it. No way Jack should see it. George lifted the paper to finish the article, but Jack took her movement as encouragement and slid his hand higher. He knew exactly how to touch her and she began to lose concentration.

'We'll keep it on board while we wait to see if someone claims it,' says Dan. 'If not, it probably belongs in the Maritime Museum.'

How the feck could she warn them without involving Jack?

'Can I offer a little local excitement then?' His fingers teased her. George sighed, pretending to be cross, folded the paper and turned on her side to put it carefully out of sight under the bed. Jack moved in close behind, pushing his urgency against her, spooning her as he ran his hand over her body. Big hands. George made a happy little groan as she squirmed her backside into him.

Dan Trenowden could wait.

Acknowledgements

Several years ago, **Charles Style** invited me to crew for him in his lovely boat *Discovery*. The idea for *Draca* came one evening in *Discovery*'s cockpit, anchored in an isolated inlet on the south coast of England, where we watched the bones of dead ships appear as the tide ebbed. Charles always kept his good humour despite my incompetent sailing, and has been generous with his critiques of *Draca*'s nautical passages. Any remaining errors are wholly mine.

Katharine Kelly, Mats Anderson, Richard Sutton and **Marcus and Susie Bicknell** read and provided invaluable feedback on an early draft.

Editor **Debi Alper** told me some much-needed hard truths.

My agent **Ian Drury** and his team at Sheil Land were as constructive as ever when I thought the book was ready.

'Holistic healer' and friend **Kerry Slade** was the inspiration for George's healing skills.

Andrew Smith, Head of Research & Development at Bainbridge International, offered excellent advice on technical aspects of sails.

Samantha Sinclair and her colleagues at the Maritime &

Coastguard Agency provided swift and enthusiastic validation of the search and rescue helicopter scene.

A Yachtsman's Log by Frank G. G. Carr (Lovat Dickson & Thompson, London, 1935) was a rich source of information about the layout, sail plan and handling characteristics of a 'Bristol Channel pilot cutter'. Frank Carr's boat, *The Cariad*, was built in 1904, and by 1922 was the last sailing pilot cutter in service. She has since been restored and now sails off the southern Brittany coast.

For the vocabulary and style of Nordic Sagas, I drew on the *Heimskringla* by Snorri Sturluson (written ca. 1230), as translated into English by Erling Monsen and A. H. Smith and published as *From the Sagas of the Norse Kings* (Dreyers Forlag, Oslo, 1967).

The fragment of Torbjørn Hornklove's poem 'The Battle of Hafersfjord' is from a translation placed in the public domain by the Department of Humanities at the University of Oslo.

Old Norse words and phrases were verified using *A Concise Dictionary of Old Icelandic* by Geir Tómasson Zoëga (Clarendon Press, Oxford, 1910).

Anglo-Saxon words were provided by *An Anglo-Saxon Dictionary Online* (https://web.archive.org/web/20190717111339/http://bosworthtoller.com).

The short extract from the *Anglo-Saxon Chronicle* for 876–7 is an edited version of the 1914 translation by J. A. Giles, formerly in the *Monumenta Historica Britannica* and now in the public domain (Wikisource).

Finally, huge thanks to Xander Cansell and the team at Unbound for picking *Draca* out of the submissions pile, and for providing the excellent editorial services of Philip Purser-Hallard and Derek Collett.

Unbound is the world's first crowdfunding publisher, established in 2011.

We believe that wonderful things can happen when you clear a path for people who share a passion. That's why we've built a platform that brings together readers and authors to crowdfund books they believe in – and give fresh ideas that don't fit the traditional mould the chance they deserve.

This book is in your hands because readers made it possible. Everyone who pledged their support is listed at the front of the book and below. Join them by visiting unbound.com and supporting a book today.

Jeremy Brooks
John Brown
Jeannette Buckle
Ray & Loraine Butler
David Capes
Richard Carter
Dawn Castle
Jonathan Chapman
Andy Charman
Mario Ciccone
Peter Clarke
Nikki Clube
Chris Conway
Melinda Coss
Stephen Cox
Lana Craker
Anita Cranmer
Pam Crawford
Helen Susan Crawley
Helen Crick
Ian Cundell
Grace Dangerfield
Les Davies
Jackie Dawes
John Deane
Paul Dyer
Michael Elliott
Derek Evans
Colin Ferns
Brian Flanagan
John Flint
Geoff France
Helen and Jeremy Frearson
Rob French
G.E. Gallas
Anne Gardiner
Judith Gault
Monique Goodwin
Josephine Greenland
Helen Greenwood
Sheila Grimshaw
Honeyieh Hamidi
John and Diana Hardacre
Carole Heeley
Liz Henderson
Joan Hutchby

Kathy Hymas
Susan Imgrund
Chris Jagusz
Philip James
Tony Johnstone-Burt
Sylvia Jones
Thomas Keast
Andrew Kelly
Dan Kieran
Fenella Kirkham
Valerie Knowles
Graham Lang
Lucy Lawrie
Lisa Lieberman
Laurel Lindström
Kay Loudon-Bruce
Debbie Marsden
Adrian Marsh
Claire Marshall
Rick Marshall
Lisa Mayhew
Alexander Mayor
Lesley McLaren
John Mitchinson
Jamie Mollart
David and Janice Moreton
Mike Morgan
Roy Morris
Rhel ná DecVandé
Penny Naimski
Carlo Navato
Lorna Nield
Mike O'Donovan
Steve O'Neill
Lisa Pacun
Marjorie Parsons
Gayle Pearce
Kay Phillips
Justin Pollard
Ranulph Poole
Bob Porter
Sarah Potter
Sobia Quazi
John Quirk
Ian Revill
Stuart Robertson

Alicia Rogers
David Rolfe
Bruce and Sheila Ross
Nigel Scarlett
Dorothy Shamah
Phillip Sheahan
Mark Shuttleworth
Sam Sinclair
Romaine Smalley
Kristiina Smith
Dave Snowden
Michael Standen
Nicola Stinchcombe
John Storey
Charles Style
Çetin Suleyman
Sarah Tanburn
Matt Thomas
Sandra Timms
Ben Tompkins

Catriona Troth
LJ Tuttle
Sylvia Valentine
Richard Walmsley
R Janet Walraven
Julia Wassell
Paul Waters
Elizabeth Waugh
Diana Wesseling
Janine West
Maggie West
Denise Williams
Robert (Bob) Williams
Derek Wilson
Graham Wiltshire
Arthur Winning
Sandra Withnall
Jamie and Gabriel Wood
Wooster dry cleaners
Martin Wyatt